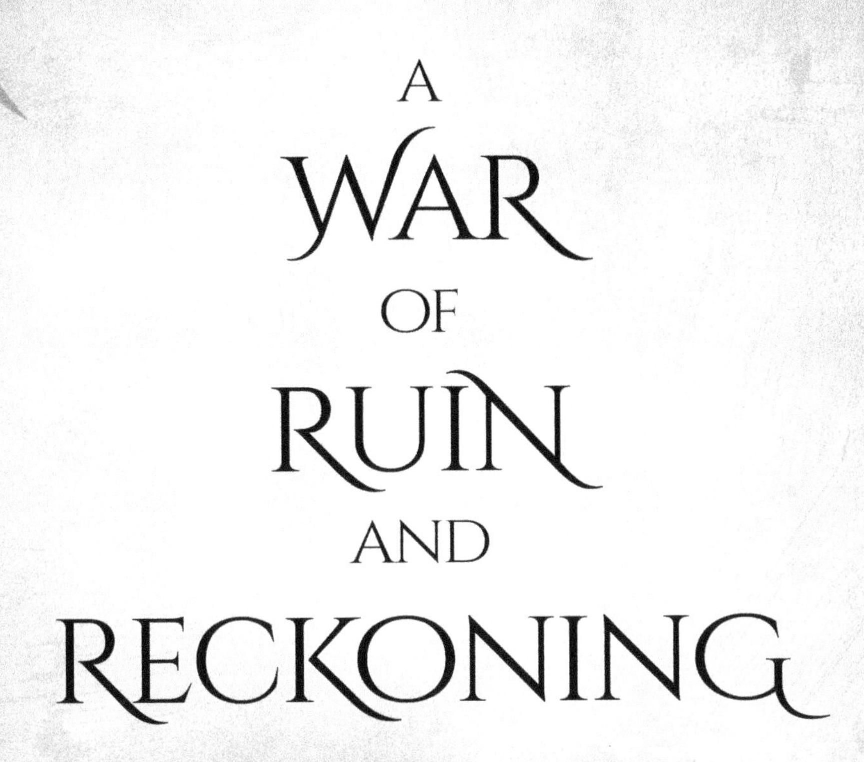
A
WAR
OF
RUIN
AND
RECKONING

A WAR OF RUIN AND RECKONING

LANA PECHERCZYK

A War of Ruin and Reckoning
ASIN: B0C9MQMGK5
ISBN: 978-1-922989-15-4 (TPB)
ISBN: 978-1-922989-16-1 (HB)

www.lanapecherczyk.com

BLURB

A reckoning is coming... but who will it hurt the most?

When environmental activist Nova Morales wakes thousands of years after a nuclear fallout, she is surrounded by magic, monsters, and war. The earth she fought to protect is in pieces, along with her heart. Everyone she loved is dead. All she wants is to find answers, but instead, she finds herself the unwilling prize in an Unseelie mate hunt.

Elf Guardian Leaf has always prioritized duty to the Well. His fate is his own, despite what the Prime and that insufferable psychic Clarke say about him being fated to a human from the old world. He doesn't have time for love when a blight on their magic source has the enemy breathing down their necks. But when avoiding his duty throws him into the path of a beautiful war prize who claims they used to be lovers, he's forced to question everything—even his memory.

The trouble with questions is they lead to answers better left buried. And as more painful secrets come to light, Leaf starts to wonder who the truth will ruin most—the Prime with her machinations, the unhinged Unseelie Queen and her war of vengeance, the crow shifter with a chip on his wings, the lost daughter of an ally... or Nova, the woman he's falling in love with.

ICE WITCH
THE ICE FOREST
ACONITE SEA
HUMAN TERRITORY
UNSEELIE KINGDOM
SEELIE KINGDOM
CRYSTAL CITY
RUSH'S CABIN
WHISPERING WOODS
CRESCENT HOLLOW

NE
OBSIDIAN MINE
SCENDIA
CLAW
BASIN
AUTUMN COURT
RUBRUM CITY
CORNUCOPIA
TRADE CITY
FENRYSFIELD
THE CEREMONIAL
LAKE
THE ORDER
OF THE WELL
DELPHINIUM CITY
SPRING COURT
HELIANTHUS CITY
SUMMER COURT

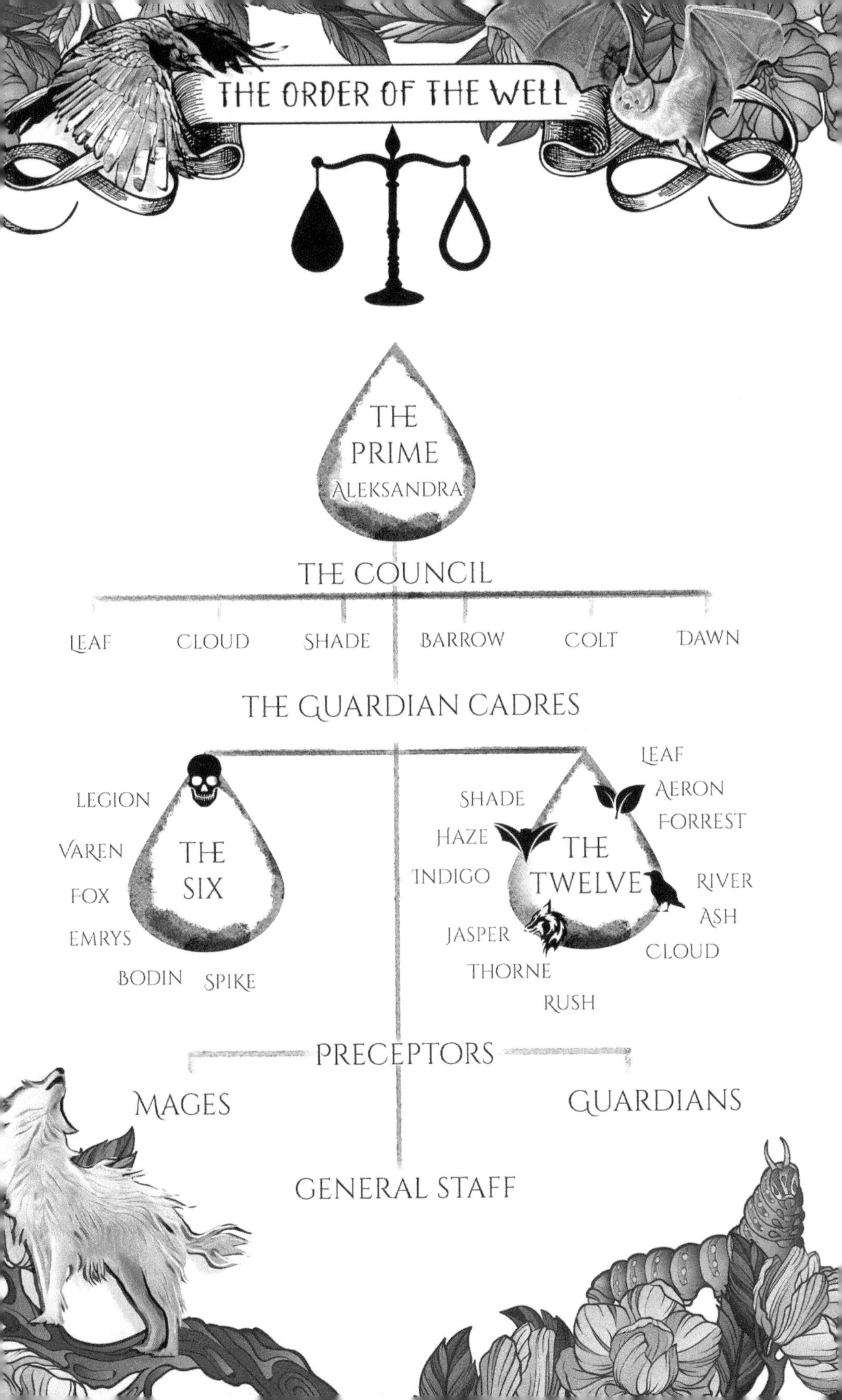
THE ORDER OF THE WELL
THE PRIME
ALEKSANDRA
THE COUNCIL
LEAF
CLOUD
SHADE
BARROW
COLT
DAWN
THE GUARDIAN CADRES
LEGION
VAREN
FOX
EMRYS
BODIN
SPIKE
THE SIX
LEAF
AERON
FORREST
SHADE
HAZE
INDIGO
THE TWELVE
RIVER
ASH
CLOUD
JASPER
THORNE
RUSH
PRECEPTORS
MAGES
GUARDIANS
GENERAL STAFF

J.C. — ENTRY 2047 ANF

As I feared, life on Earth moves in cycles. First, the dinosaurs, then the fae, then humanity, and now the fae again. For those of us who have been alive to see the end of one cycle and the beginning of another, life on this planet seems doomed to repeat until nothing is left.

We are born. Our flaws pass from generation to generation. We ignore warnings from the planet that feeds us. We refuse to change our destructive and selfish ways. We become extinct.

Only this time, I fear the planet will not spare me a second chance, and I am tired of holding onto the hope of reuniting with my Estrella. In her absence, I tried to live as she would have. I fought for her values because I wasn't strong enough to do it back then.

Even now... even thousands of years after our last conversation, I still hear the sound of her voice as crisp as the day she spoke the words, "I refuse to believe this is the end."

Alas, it is.

For me, anyway. Time has a way of catching up with us all. I see the signs in my friends and know that I'm next. I feel it in my bones, in the little obsessions and the bigger lies I tell myself. I told her I would find her, but my time is running out.

I accused the Well of lying and stringing me along with false promises.

I lied first. I couldn't give her up, and that's what I must do to prove my faith.

I must relinquish all I am to become all I can be.

This is my final offer to the Well in exchange for my unending sacrifices to stop our combined doom. This is my last attempt at negotiating for the one thing I've ever asked for in return—a happy ending.

PROLOGUE

Nero pushed a red pin into the map of Elphyne on his desk and then wiped the sweat from his brow. Up here on the top floor of the Sky Tower, the conservatory and humidifiers made the temperature sometimes suffocating. But he needed privacy, and this room was best.

This map was everything. Each red pin symbolized a site where the mad Unseelie Queen had attacked the Seelie, resulting in a loss of life. He had placed orange pins upon intel from his Reapers regarding potential future attacks. Blue pins showed where his soldiers kidnapped Guardians and stole their unique mana. A single green pin sat unused in a bowl on the side of the map. It would signify a successful large-scale mana-harvesting expedition... the Holy Grail.

Ten years was a long time in human years, but according to the tainted fae, it was a blink in time. He'd expected the mad queen to escalate her war against the Seelie because their power source was more unreliable than usual. He'd calculated wrong. He was playing chess with pigeons again.

Unforgivable.

But not unsalvageable.

Ten years ago, there was naught but a handful of red pins on that map. Now, they littered the landscape. Even if Nero had only harvested mana in small chunks, once the Tainted were fewer, he would swoop in and take control. He would finally rule the entire land—under one mind, one set of rules.

"Sir?" Alfred's young voice jolted through Nero.

He had forgotten the new captain was here and inspected the young man's uniform and short ginger hair. Gold epaulets showed his new high rank, which the fool was immensely proud of. That, and the gold buckle on his belt he planned to gift to his betrothed, soon cementing their arranged marriage. The tall, gangly youth had filled out after a few years of service as a Tower Guard. He came to attention through his friendship with Nero's halfling ward, Willow. Alfred was impressionable, amenable, and smitten with the silver-haired wolf-child.

Nero had asked him to monitor the girl as she grew. During the previous captain's unsuccessful coup, they'd almost lost her. Since Nero's plan to control Elphyne relied on the young female's ability to raise an army of the dead, it couldn't happen again.

She was special, that halfling—more than his useless daughter, Aurora. A wave of anger swelled with memories of her insubordination over the decades, but he squashed it with a frown. His daughter had taken too much of his time already. He would not waste another moment on her.

The best quality in subordinates was not experience but obedience; this young man had it in spades. Molding his mind with stolen mana was not even necessary.

"Yes?" Nero raised his brows.

Alfred held out a folded piece of paper. "Sir, I have just returned from overseeing a training session between Rory—ahem—Aurora and Miss Willow in the garden."

"Report." Nero returned to his map, studying the red pins to try to see if he could ascertain a pattern. In his peripheral, Alfred awkwardly dropped his arm.

"Willow's ability to wake the dead is faltering. I think she's succumbing to the same problem the fae are with their magic source."

"Faltering how?"

"Eight out of ten attempts were successful. The other two times were..."

At the silence, Nero faced Alfred. "And?"

The young man frowned. "The bodies vanished."

Nero had seen worse. However, an eighty percent efficacy rate was becoming further from reasonable. The past decade, they'd been fortunate for this halfling to evade the same warped effects the fae suffered. He wished he understood why because, in his opinion, there was no such thing as luck.

"Did the missing undead turn up anywhere else?" he asked.

Alfred hesitantly walked to the map, picked up a red pin, and pierced it into the heart of Elphyne—a neutral city called Cornucopia.

"How many bodies?" Nero frowned.

"Fifty."

Fuck.

"Do the fae suspect us?"

"Not that we've heard. The Unseelie assume it's the Seelie, and vice versa."

Nero had patiently remained in Crystal City for a decade while his halfling protégé matured and trained. Scowling, Nero reached over the large map and gripped the pin Alfred had placed, but he paused at the sight of his hand. Wrinkles and age spots had coalesced on his skin. His ingestion of mana had been reduced due to the poor quality of source material from outside the walls. He was left with only two options inside these walls—his near-empty daughter and Willow.

He pulled the pin out and dropped it back in the red bowl.

"Bring my daughter to the treatment room," he said.

"Yes, sir." The captain gave a salute and turned.

"Captain?"

He faced Nero. "Yes, sir?"

"I haven't dismissed you."

"Apologies, sir." The young man's face paled as he no doubt remembered the consequences from the last time.

"I expect your discretion, as usual."

He gave a curt nod and replied, "Of course."

"Good. Ensure the room is prepared, and the proper precautions are taken, then summon the Scientist. You're dismissed."

CHAPTER ONE

Leaf rolled out the worn map of Elphyne on his desk and studied the marks he'd made over the past decade. He'd traveled from corner to corner, tracing the last known steps of Jackson Crimson. The elf who pioneered their magic system had died centuries ago. Finding accurate information was as impossible as finding a djinn in a storm.

He scrubbed his face and ignored the rough stubble scraping his calloused hands. He ignored the disgrace of his dirty battle leathers. He ignored the inner voice telling him to forget this obsession and return to his duty—to clean the taint on the Well.

Raised voices outside his window made his elf ears twitch. He ignored that, too. With the taint and the war between the Seelie and Unseelie, fae acted like the world was ending. If it wasn't an argument or hot tempers flaring outside on the Cadre's training lawn, it was the libertine sex between Order of the Well Mages and

Guardians. They'd stopped caring about decency years ago. And with the Prime disappearing for months on end, it was almost like she wasn't here.

Maybe he'd care more if Aleksandra was around to lead her people... or, at the very least, reveal how he could relive Crimson's memories about the prophecy. But she was harder than a pixie to pin down.

Maybe he'd care more if he wasn't the next in line to face the Well-blessed and mated firing squad. His lips twisted in disgust. Mating with a human now—even a powerful one—would be a waste of time. Whenever he contemplated the idea, the aversion in his gut made him sick to the bone. He was aware of his hypocrisy, considering his mission to reveal the prophecy also stole time from his immediate duty. But his urges to unlock Jackson Crimson's memories and the whole, unredacted prophecy were harder to resist.

Gritting his teeth, he shut his ears to the argument on the lawn. He smoothed the crumpled map and searched for the location of his latest lead—ruins from the old world. Few monuments still stood after the Nuclear Fallout and the return of the Well shifted the land formations. But with this particular—

"You promised this wouldn't happen!"

Leaf's gaze snapped to the window. That was Clarke's voice. He strode over, pulled the curtains aside, and peeked into the darkness. Like an apparition, she stood on the lawn in a long white nightgown, facing off with three Sluagh Guardians from the Cadre of Six.

Curious.

The Six had an agenda of their own. A decade ago, all stood in the council chambers for the first time. Legion had liaised with Leaf over the prophecy, and he revealed that Maebh had to be unmade to clean the taint. But since then, they'd kept to themselves.

No one was interested in preserving the state of this world. None except Clarke and Rush. Both had been a thorn in Leaf's side, demanding he continue with his duty to find his mate and prepare for the battle Nero would likely send their way.

She'd foretold it would be faekind and humanity's final chance to prove themselves worthy of being custodians of this land.

Intelligence from Crystal City said their military airships were complete and sitting in their harbor, almost as though they waited for something. But that same tension in the air sent Leaf in another direction. He couldn't explain or quantify it but knew he must follow his instincts.

As Clarke's tone and pitch elevated, Leaf rolled up the map and stored it in his leather travel satchel. He spent a few minutes cleaning himself and then donned a less filthy battle uniform. The kingfisher-blue piping represented his team leader status for the Twelve. Shade had always been after his role. Perhaps Leaf should hand it to him.

Just as he slid on his boots, the door swung open, and in stormed Clarke. Bare, dirty feet beneath her gauzy nightgown matched the grubby hem. Leaf's gaze trailed up and took in her messy red hair, the unlaced and gaping collar, and dirty fingernails. Had the woman been gardening in her sleep?

Her blue eyes locked on him with fiery resolution. "Leaving again?"

His brows flicked up. It was humorous how she thought she had a right to know his whereabouts and plans. He bent over and tied his bootstraps. Ignoring her glare, he strolled to the wall by his dresser, collected his baldric, and carefully strapped the belts around his torso. Flexing his back, he ensured he had movement where the scabbard rested between his shoulder blades.

His long hair caught, so he slipped his hand beneath his nape and tugged it free.

Clarke huffed as he sheathed his sword, *Reckoning*. Something about pushing her buttons appealed to him. She was so quick to fire. Almost too easy, really.

When he collected his travel satchel, she lost her battle with sense and yelled, "You're such a stubborn asswipe, you know that?"

"Is that so?"

She counted her reasons on her fingers. "First, you refuse to help with anything about the Elphyne war. Second, you ignore finding your Well-blessed mate. Third, you're not helping Aeron, Violet, or Barrow find anything we can actually use to unmake Maebh."

"Are you done?"

"Not nearly!"

"Will you tell me your argument with the Six?"

Her lips slammed shut, and he resisted rolling his eyes. It was a juvenile, human expression, but the more time he spent with these old-worlders, the more their habits rubbed off on him. He shuddered to think what was next. Practical jokes, one of Laurel's cocktails, spending days locked away in his room—fucking and sleeping. Well-forbid.

"If you're not honest with me," he reminded her, "then I'm not open with you. Simple as that. I refuse to be a pawn in another Seer's game."

"I'm not manipulating you." Shock blanched her pale features. Her next words came out choked and full of emotion. "Believe me, I learned my lesson when we almost lost Willow."

Her child had been taken captive by the human enemy. The girl would likely be on the cusp of adulthood now... if she lived. No one had heard from the child since the taint had worsened, which was odd. Leaf would have assumed humanity's leader, Nero, would take advantage of this weakness amongst the fae. It seemed the perfect opportunity. That they remained in Crystal City likely meant Nero waited for the war in Elphyne to worsen... or perhaps for the taint to annihilate the Well.

He stared impatiently at Clarke. "What do you want?"

Helplessness flittered over her expression. "It's been a decade since I had the vision about your mate. She hasn't turned up, so I'm guessing my psychic abilities were unreliable back then, too. We're on the cusp of an era no Seer has seen. The prophecy—"

"The one the Prime refuses to share completely?"

"Yes." She clenched her jaw. "That one."

He sighed and pinched the bridge between his eyes. "I don't know why you keep trusting the snippets she's revealed. It's not the full picture. And until we get it, we're only following their version. Do you understand?"

"Are you forgetting that I'm also a Seer?" She blinked at him.

"You just admitted your visions are unreliable."

"They are now." She flared her eyes. "But before, I had plenty of reliable visions about the Twelve finding a Well-blessed mate. Each time we add another to our team, we're closer to stopping the horrible Void in our future."

"The taint has changed everything."

"So your answer is to waste years traipsing around Elphyne? However you want to spin it, one truth can be trusted completely—Well-blessed unions. No one can manipulate or fake them. Only the Well has the power to bless a union or a person. As a Guardian, you know this. Maybe they are the solution for the taint, who knows! For someone with such undying duty to the Well, how can you turn your back on what it wants?"

Because the thought of entering a relationship felt wrong, and females beyond sexual dalliances were distractions. Fae politics was a distraction. The integrity of the Well came first. Protecting this earth came first.

Someone had to draw the line. These humans from the old world wanted to change too much. Everything had worked just fine before they'd arrived.

Something in his gaze deflated Clarke's defiance. Her shoulders slumped. She twisted her long russet hair and said, "Willow's life is in danger if she leaves Crystal City before she's reached adulthood."

His eyes narrowed. "Varen told you that?"

Clarke nodded. "The Sluagh are beings born of chaos, which means Varen can navigate the taint and accurately foresee the future through it much better than me. But the problem is..." She frowned, mulling over something before beckoning him. "Come with me."

Her grubby nightgown billowed as she walked out of his room. Leaf stared after her, wondering if this was another manipulation. But Clarke was right—he'd seen no evidence of manipulation from her since her daughter had decided to stay with the humans. Despite her demands that he hunt down his fated mate, she never tricked or forced him into following her guidance.

Eventually, he realized there was nothing for it. He was about to leave again, so what harm did it do to hear Clarke out before he went?

NOVA

CHAPTER TWO

Leaf found Clarke conversing with Violet in the downstairs kitchen. Violet, having a nocturnal mate, was making a sandwich for dinner at dawn. The woman's blue Well-blessed mating mark glowed beneath her battle-stained leathers. While she wasn't an official Guardian—no blue teardrop beneath her left eye—she spent every waking hour with D'arn Indigo, fighting to protect the innocent.

Leaf had tried to stop their involvement with the Elphyne war, but they did it anyway, helping where they could. Leaf had always liked her. Rather, respect was a better descriptor. He didn't like many people at all. But Violet was innovative, practical, and straightforward. How in the Well's name she was fated to that cheeky bloodsucker was beyond him. Then again, it could have been worse. She could have mated with River. That crow shifter was like Indigo on manabeeze—unpredictable, wild, and a little insane.

"Hey," Violet mumbled through a mouthful of food.

He lifted his chin. "Violet."

They watched Clarke open the cupboard doors. Eventually, she found a glass jar and half-filled it with water.

"Clarke..." he sighed. "There better be a point to this."

"Shh." Violet waved him down with a scowl. "She's doing science."

Clarke chuckled. "Who would have imagined little old grifter me experimenting? I'll bet my eighth-grade teacher would be spitting chips right now."

"Intelligible language is more likely to hold my interest," Leaf drawled.

Clarke opened her mouth but shut it and composed herself. "You wanted to know what was said between the Six and me. Well, this is part of it."

Leather creaked as Leaf folded his arms. "I'm listening."

"Here's the thing." She pointed to the water and met Leaf's gaze. "What do you think that represents?"

His patience wore thin. "I'm not a child, Clarke."

"Duh." She gestured down his body. He stood a head taller than her, with shoulders twice as wide and calloused palms the size of her freckled face. "But to be fair, you act like one sometimes. Okay, moving on. So, if you're not going to answer—"

"The Well," he growled out the obvious answer.

Her obnoxious buzzing sound made his ears twitch. "Wrong! Violet, do you want to take a guess?"

Indigo's woman was an expert in science knowledge from the old world. This competition wasn't fair. She finished her mouthful and calmly answered, "He's half right. It's the light side of the Well —the pure, clear, and harmonious side."

"Correct!" Clarke's vigor was far too great for this early hour. She pulled a bottle of cooking oil from beneath the butcher's block and waggled it before Leaf. "And this is the inky side of the Well—chaos." She drizzled the viscous fluid into the clear water. "See how it separates?"

Everyone knew the ink and the clear remained separate. That was how the taint ruined their mana supply. Drawing from the clear often hit a vein of random, floating ink. What was her point?

Violet's brown eyes widened with understanding. Her skin paled. "Oh shit."

Leaf shuffled awkwardly, his gaze darting between the jar to Clarke and Violet.

"Yeah. Exactly!" Clarke pointed at her, victorious.

What was happening? Did the two share an insufferable secret language like Trix and Aeron? He rescinded his earlier comment about respecting Violet. A grumble slipped from his lips. He'd had just about enough of this.

Violet swirled the liquid until the oil and water blended into a new, clouded concoction. She explained, "At the beginning, magic was only tainted when we drew mana and hit a vein of ink. But now, no matter who draws on mana, or from where, we're all affected all of the time."

Dread dawned on Leaf. "The Well is finding a way to balance itself."

"Maybe." Clarke sighed. "All I know is that it's not the same for everyone now."

Violet tapped the jar with her fingernail, watching the liquid separate. Oil floated to the top, but much of the water remained cloudy. "Is this reversible?"

Clarke shrugged. "If we don't fix it soon, the Well will never be the same."

"You think this is why we haven't seen Maebh's demogorgon these past few years?" Violet asked.

Leaf rubbed his jaw. "It needs inky mana to shift and avoid metal. It will likely be weakened if it's also having trouble drawing on a pure source. Maebh's plan to dominate Elphyne is backfiring. Now might be a good time to take her into custody to face her crimes against the Well."

Clarke leaned her hip on the counter and folded her arms, looking at the swirling whirlpool with trepidation. "Varen's psychic visions are no longer reliable. Fae are immortal... but now everything is messed up. Who knows what will happen?"

"I refuse to let this world die because of a mad queen's selfishness." The taint was Maebh's fault. She started it when she created her unnatural pet.

Clarke sucked in a deep breath and then exhaled. "I'm not a book-smart woman like Violet. But I am a survivor, and I agree. We can still save this world." Her gaze slid to Leaf's and held. "Did you ever stop to think this is why the Well paired old-world women with powerful protectors in the new world? Think about it. We know how to live without magic, while you Guardians have no idea what it's like. But you know Elphyne."

"I beg to differ." Cloud strolled in, rubbing weary eyes. Black wavy locks dangled to his shoulders. His hair was longer than usual, knotty, and dull. Mud and monster bile spattered half his leathers and wings, making him stink.

Leaf looked away. This reprobate crow shifter hadn't stopped hunting mana-warped monsters despite his desire to murder a human in Crystal City. Nero's daughter—and likely Maebh's lost granddaughter—had tortured him when he was trapped in the city over a century ago. But Cloud had waited years for his revenge. What was another decade except more time to plot the perfect reckoning?

Leaf's fingers twitched for his sword and patiently watched Cloud slice salted meat with his dirty dagger, slap it between two pieces of bread, and chew loudly, glaring at the women.

"I think what Clarke means," Leaf explained, "is that living without it is different from suffering without it."

Cloud stopped chewing. Lightning flashed across his blue irises and skipped over his black tattoos.

Usually, Leaf wouldn't back down, but he only wanted to escape this damned house. He turned to Clarke. "Anything else to share before I leave?"

She gaped at him and pointed at the murky water. "I just showed you we're all fucked, and you're still skipping out?"

Leaf raised an indignant brow. He leaned over the butcher block counter so she could hear him better. "What I do is of no concern to you."

"Fine," she ground out. "Be a dickhead. If you won't listen to my advice about finding your mate, then..." She shook her head and exhaled. "Then show me where your lead is, and I'll see if I can remember anything from my old visions that might aid your search."

He straightened. Narrowed his eyes. "You'll assist me?"

"I almost killed my daughter from meddling with fate. And before that, I was exploited into handing over codes to nuclear warheads. I'm a fast learner. Manipulation isn't my thing."

"So, what is your thing?" Cloud asked, deadly serious.

Leaf stared expectantly at Clarke.

"Any more testosterone in here, and we'll spontaneously grow facial hair," Violet said, rolling her eyes.

"Right?" Clarke smirked, then leveled her stare at Cloud. "My thing is protecting my family, which includes my daughter and everyone living in this house... that means you, asswipe."

Awkwardness and disgust covered Cloud's expression, and then he walked out. Give him a dagger, and he was your willing opponent. But give him emotion, and he ran away.

Leaf tugged his map from his satchel and flattened it on the countertop. "What can you tell me?"

Clarke scrutinized the map, noting the areas he'd already searched.

He opened his mouth, but she held up her hand. "Give me a minute."

"Stop pouting, elf." Violet swatted him on the ass as she walked out.

He clenched, eyes wide. First, Clarke had called Cloud family. Now, Violet swatted his rear end like one of the lads in the barracks. Everyone in this house was mad.

Wait. Pouting? Leaf did not pout.

"Here." Clarke tapped the pinnacle of the Meandering Woods. "The ruins you're looking for are in there."

"That's a day's ride in the opposite direction of where my intelligence leads me."

"You're looking for a cliff with giant faces carved into it, correct?"

His eyes narrowed. How the fuck did she know? But of course, she'd probably seen many things in her visions and, whether by choice, need, or forgetfulness, had not mentioned it.

She shrugged as if reading his thoughts like a Sluagh and explained, "I don't always know if my dreams are relevant until someone says or does something that triggers a memory. For instance, this conversation right now in this kitchen with Cloud and Violet. I recall a dream with us talking before you head off on a journey. The place you're looking for was once known as Mount Rushmore. It's a cliff with the faces of leaders from my time. If my visions are correct, then it's not situated in the same location now as it was then. I'm guessing your 'intelligence' is from one of Jackson Crimson's journals."

"Perhaps."

She scoffed at his secrecy. "The land has shifted since my time. The shape of this country is different."

Leaf held her confident stare for a long, tension-filled minute before cursing under his breath and retrieving a journal. He unbound the leather tie with rough, impatient motions and flicked through the old pages. Thankfully, the preservation spell on the ancient book had been cast long ago and still held, immune to the taint.

He licked his finger and turned the pages until he found the hastily drawn map and journal entry. Clarke moved to his side of the butcher block to read.

J.C. DATED: 471 ANF

A does more at the Order. It frees me to focus on the still-missing artifact, but I am beginning to doubt its exis-

tence or my ability to find it. The Well whispers some days yet screams on others. Both are as indecipherable as the others. Both are like searching through cloudy water and expecting clarity.

I know what to do, yet I cannot stop searching for my North Star between the gaps of time. If I had the guidance, my faith would remain unwavering. I come here to remember, but the gaps change the shape of memory just as they shape our minds. She would not recognize me even if I found her, for I have changed.

Leaf turned the page.

"Hey!" Clarke snapped. "I was reading that."

"He laments like a love-sick fool for another few paragraphs. You'll be bored shitless. Here is what you might want to read."

Her irritation simmered against his skin, but she read the journal.

... This place holds significance, and I keep returning. Perhaps these crumbling faces will be the last I see one day.

Leaf looked at Clarke. "So?"

"So what?" she tossed back.

"Do you think that's his final place of rest?" Obviously.

"I thought he went into the lake and never came out."

"If Aleksandra is to be believed."

"But she can't lie... right?"

He exhaled. "Correct."

But she could mince words, which worried Leaf the most. The

Prime could have used misleading words all those years ago, and now they were twisted into a bastardized version of the truth. Until he found definitive proof that Crimson was dead or the whole prophecy, Leaf wasn't taking anything as the Well-blessed truth.

"I only know what I've been told and learned at the academy," Clarke said.

Leaf's gaze dropped to the map. He supposed he would have to search the ruins himself. "Are you sure it's there?"

"Look, I'm never sure. As I said, a vision of this conversation in the kitchen triggered the memory of another vision."

"And what was in that vision exactly? No lies."

"I saw you riding a horse in the Meandering Woods. And I saw Mount Rushmore covered in vines and water over mossy rocks. I saw an epiphany on your face. Whether it's what you're looking for is another question. But it's a start."

"The Meandering Woods, you're sure? Not the Whispering Woods?"

"I don't think so. I remember the trees were greener, less snow."

He marked the spot and rolled the map just as Rush strode in naked, yellow wolf-eyes blazing. His silver hair was messy, and his beard was uncut. Since Leaf didn't think the shifters were transforming much these days, Rush's lack of appropriate attire was likely from waking to find his mate missing. His hard eyes landed on Clarke, dropped to take in her nightgown, then he glared at Leaf.

"Step away from my mate," he growled.

"Crimson save me," Leaf mumbled under his breath.

Unbothered, Clarke strolled to Rush's side of the kitchen and tucked herself under his muscular arm. Her gaze softened on Leaf.

"I can't convince you one last time to put this quest aside and hunt for your mate instead?"

"If she's so important, why don't you hunt her down? You've done it for others."

Darkness flittered over her expression. "With them, I knew exactly when and where the old-worlders would wake. But with Silver, Violet, and Peaches, I learned too late. With Melody and Trix, they were locked behind the walls of Crystal City. With the woman I believe is your mate... I have no idea anymore. I thought she would wake years ago, but we've heard not a peep about an old-worlder thawing or waking in this time." She cuddled Rush with melancholy. "I just hope she's not dead."

"Catastrophizing won't change my mind."

Appalled, Rush shook his head. "I always knew you were a stubborn elf, but now I think it's sheer stupidity."

"Babe," Clarke breathed. "I called him stubborn back in his room, and it didn't work."

"In his room? In that nightgown meant for my eyes only?"

She scowled at his nudity. "Seriously?"

Rush's dark brows lowered, and he rubbed his fist in a circle over his chest. "I don't know what's gotten into me. I feel as territorial as I did when we first mated."

"This conversation is positively riveting," Leaf intoned, "but I'll let you have it without me." He almost didn't want to ask this next bit. "And which location did you foresee my... mate"—he almost choked on the word—"waking in?"

She looked at him squarely in the eyes. "Ten years ago, it was in the direction you were already headed."

Snarling in frustration, Leaf stormed out and walked toward the stables. No matter which path he chose, a Seer had meddled in it. He was out of the Order gates and a mile away when something Clarke said halted him.

My thing is protecting my daughter.

She'd argued with the Sluagh outside his window, then immediately came to his room. That wasn't a coincidence. But perhaps Clarke's willingness to help had less to do with Leaf and more with her daughter, Willow. Because up until then, her motives had aligned with the Prime's desire for the Twelve to mate with a human from the old world.

Did Clarke knowingly send him in the opposite direction, or was he overthinking things again?

CHAPTER THREE

Over the past three months, the sounds of war had become white noise to Nova Morales. Screams of pain, angry shouts, and war cries blended until she stopped wondering who they belonged to. But that was just amidst a battle. The worst sounds came at night when she tried to sleep—the cries of pain became more intimate, closer to home. Whether they belonged to prisoners being tortured or those being humiliated, subjugated, or forced, the easiest thing to do was block it out and get on with her job as the camp chef.

So long as she continued to make dwindling supplies last longer, she was safe from harm. For now. A bitter laugh slipped from her parched lips. The one benefit from being an environmental activist most of her life—despite the world having gone to shit anyway—was that she'd learned to make every scrap count.

She flinched at a shout in the night sky. Winged fae were often nocturnal and restless when they made camp. They covered ground faster than those on foot and had spare energy while others rested. Winged soldiers were picking fights or daring each other to leave the camp and hunt the manticore rumored to be prowling the woods.

Focus on the dishes.

Clearing her mind of distracting thoughts, she needed her wits about her, and the sooner she finished, the sooner she was allowed to eat. She plunged raw, chafed hands into the dirty soap water and grappled for a dish.

A low-flying vampire swooped. She ducked, hating how he laughed at her fear.

"*¡Eres un burro!*" she mumbled in Spanish. Jackass!

No matter who they were in this war camp, they could die tomorrow. So forgive her for being jumpy. And she was at the bottom of the food chain—a human in a camp full of vampires and fae caring little for her safety.

They'd discovered her stumbling by the side of the road, disoriented and sick. The sad thing was, she would rather be back there than here. She should have hidden in the forest and not asked for help.

She shook her head and tucked a lock of hair behind her ear. Her fingers brushed the gold hoop earrings, and a pang of longing tugged in her chest. Closing her eyes, she inhaled deeply to stop the tears.

I don't know what's wrong with me tonight.

But she couldn't stop thinking about her old life.

Nova still remembered the day she'd returned home from high school wearing the earrings, and her mother tried to kick her out of the house. Her cheeks heated thinking about it. She'd been so angry at her mother for throwing away all reference to their cultural heritage when her grandparents immigrated years ago from Mexico. She couldn't understand why... until her parents explained they'd had a falling out with family.

Her fingers slipped back into the dishwater. She'd fought so much with her mother about it, but they remained mysterious about their falling out. She wished they'd trusted her enough to tell her. Despite the unrest, they put aside their differences every Sunday, and the family would come together and eat.

She wiped her nose with her sleeve. There wasn't any point in keeping it clean. She'd been wearing the same tattered dress for two weeks, and even then, she'd pulled it from the corpse of a woman who'd been brutally used and murdered by the soldiers in this camp.

Feeling the hairs rise on the back of her neck, she lifted her gaze and scanned her surroundings. Twilight left enough light that she could see beyond her small cooking campsite. Another two women cleaned dishes from the evening's late meal. One had pointed ears. The other was a fae with horns and cloven hooves as feet. Neither spoke to Nova or cared to elaborate on their heritage. Anything Nova gleaned was from snippets of overheard conversation.

This week's camp was stationed between a river and a forest somewhere in a land she'd learned was named Elphyne. Unlike her initial assumption, she hadn't been transported to a new planet. This was Earth... only thousands of years after she was born.

The last thing she remembered was the dire warnings explaining weather disruptions from the nuclear fallout and the dreaded understanding that life as they knew it was about to end. She'd had a horrible argument with her twin brother, Niles, and hated him for it. She'd journeyed inland from the coast, where she'd planned to meet Jace, her childhood friend. With her parents long dead and a falling out with her twin, Jace was the closest to a family she had left.

Jace had been their neighbor in a small, modest suburb in Los Angeles. He was Nile's best friend for years until he hooked up with Nova and claimed her virginity. Nova had always blamed herself for the following fights in their trio. She'd ruined the dynamic by flirting with Jace. Then, he moved across the country with his family.

Niles grew bitter after that.

Wanting to escape, Nova turned to environmental activism. Jace became CEO of his father's petroleum company. The brief romance would never have worked, despite her childhood crush on the hot, easygoing surfer next door. But they'd remained close friends. He sent extravagant gifts on holidays, and she sent him postcards from all the places she visited. She'd not spoken to him for months, but after Niles—she frowned, trying not to think of the horrible argument with her twin—Jace was the first person she'd called when the world was ending.

Now, she was alone again. Humans were banished to a westerly city because they continued to use forbidden substances that stopped the flow of magic.

If not for this war between the fae peoples, humans would be public enemy number one. She probably would have been executed on sight or handed to the Order of the Well for her possession of gold—contraband.

Nova thought about her earrings again, wondering if she should remove them, but as no Guardians from the Order had crossed paths with them, no one wanted to touch the magic-cutting substance. Magic was unpredictable at the moment. Many feared if they lost the connection, even briefly from touching metal, it would be permanent. They'd be mortal... forever.

She wasn't sure if that superstition had any merit, but the earrings had been another layer of protection against these feral monsters. The gold hoops might be tarnished and warped, but they were the last piece of home she had left.

Another swooping vampire flew low enough that his leathery wing clipped her head. She stumbled into the wooden pail, which vomited dishwater and stone crockery onto the dirt.

"*¡Ay, qué menso!*" she blurted. What an idiot, swooping so low as to frighten her. Another string of Spanish curse words erupted from her lips before she could stop them.

The vampire swooped back and landed with a thud, spraying dirt and dust carelessly.

Usually, they ignored her, but her stupid mouth ran away with itself.

He was from the Winter Court. She could tell because his leather battle uniform had an emblem of antlers, roses, and thorns. A scar mutated his long nose. The red-eyed vampire advanced on her with a snarl that flashed sharp incisors. Something dripped from them, almost like drool, but she was sure it had something to do with how easily their prey fell asleep while they fed.

"What did you say to me?" His voice was low and breathy.

Vampires had supernatural hearing... all the better to hear her heartbeat with. And right now, hers continued to rabbit in her chest.

The two females with her were no help. They continued washing dishes with barely a glance tossed in Nova's direction.

She scrambled to her feet, glanced at the mess, and searched for a utensil to protect herself with. But her best weapons were her wit and her tenacity. She lifted her chin and met his bloodshot eyes.

"I said your aerial prowess is wasted in this dirty war camp." Flattery was always a good response. She casually collected her spilled dishes, hoping he couldn't see her fingers tremble. Or hear the fluctuation in her pulse—because if he listened carefully, he'd realize she lied. Sometimes, they forgot she was human and not beholden to the truth by the laws of their mystical Well.

As she gathered dishes, worn boots walked into her periphery and stopped. His heavy breathing was loud despite the other noises in the camp—shouts, conversations, crackling fires, and even someone singing a lewd tale.

"And perhaps your beauty is wasted in this corner of the camp," he purred. "Your hips and breasts are perfect for breeding."

Nova dropped a plate, breaking it.

Ignore. Ignore. Ignore.

She collected the pieces and straightened her spine. The vampire's hungry eyes raked over her scantily clad body. The torn dress hung from Nova's shoulders and gaped to bare her décolletage and the top pillow of her breasts. Nova had never hidden her assets. She loved strutting around the beach in a tiny bikini—especially around Jace. But this attention curdled her stomach.

"I'm here because the captain needs his army fed."

His upper lip curled. Vampires cared little for food. Human blood was extra tasty. Having someone like her in the camp, within smelling distance, and a Don't Touch sign painted on her back was a red flag to a bull.

She was about to turn and reveal that sign when another winged fae swooped in too low, knocking over the bloodshot-eyed soldier. Nova hugged her bucket as two more soldiers ran in on foot, excited at the excuse for a brawl. She inched backward, hoping to become invisible.

What came next wouldn't be pretty, and it was best she stayed as far away as possible. They'd either kill each other or—

"What is the meaning of this!" The booming words shook the ground.

Don't look. Don't look.

Nova's eyes stung as she placed her bucket on the log she'd used as a table. She tried to ignore and clean, but every male grunt behind her pushed fear into her bones.

"C-c-captain." The female elf exclaimed, her eyes wide and focused behind Nova.

Nova didn't want to turn. The first time she glimpsed Captain Grung's green brutish skin, seven-foot stature, and severe underbite, she'd peed her pants like a baby. His enemies' bones dangled from a cord around his neck and clattered like a dreadful wind chime every time he moved. Lice crawled in his matted black hair. Dirt, stink, and poor hygiene worsened his lecherous and lingering stares.

When he'd proclaimed her untouchable, Nova thought perhaps he had a heart under those bulging pectorals. But then she'd learned he just wasn't that clever. He'd decreed her untouchable because the fewer rules to follow, the better.

He'd only painted the warning on her back because, for now,

they needed her to prepare the food. Oh, but he'd groped, fondled, and licked her fingers. One of his soldiers complained each time, saying the same rules applied to everyone.

She was toast as soon as he figured out how to have his cake and eat it. Escape was on her mind daily, but two things had stopped her. Firstly, escapees were killed. The original occupant of her dress was that lesson. And secondly, if she miraculously evaded that fate... where would she go?

Elphyne was at war. Monsters roamed the wilderness. She knew nothing about this place apart from what she'd snatched from overheard conversations.

The female elf hissed and snarled. Glancing up, Nova realized the aggression was aimed at her.

"This is your fault," the fae snapped.

"What?"

Confused, Nova turned to the horned female, and where the elf had grown angry, this one was green with fear. Nova glanced at the soldiers and found their argument with their captain had become contemplative. Grung rubbed his bulbous jaw, casting a thoughtful glance their way.

"What's happening?" she whispered to the elf. "I can't hear from here."

"They're negotiating the evening's entertainment."

"That's not so bad... right?" Games or training battles kept the soldiers occupied. But she supposed even those were running out of steam. They'd been stationed here too long while hunting the manticore. Even the town they'd pillaged was picked bone dry of resources and victims.

The elf flattened her lips. "If you call auctioning us off as brides not bad—"

"Not brides," the horned fae gasped, her wide eyes locked on the soldiers. "Mates. We're to be prizes in a mate hunt."

"What?" Nova's blood ran cold. "But... who will cook?"

"That's why we'll be officially mated. If we belong to an individual and not passed around, we can still cook, but the squabbling over us will cease."

Nova scrambled to assemble pieces of Elphyne culture she'd overheard about mating rituals. It was a little like marriage, only more permanent and revered. Mates were often united for life... only parted by death.

It had taken Grung a few months, but he'd finally found a way to have his cake. And when he was done eating it, she'd be dead.

CHAPTER FOUR

Leaf rode his horse through the small, decimated riverside village. Embers still glowed in the burned and pillaged houses. Corpses smelled like charred meat, making his stomach crawl and yet still clench in hunger.

He'd hoped to rest at the inn before crossing the river in the morning and continuing to the ruins. Ultimately, he'd taken Clarke's new direction over the one he'd sourced himself. Now, he regretted it.

A chill ran down his spine.

His horse's clip-clop echoed in the quiet night. No survivors. No sounds except the sizzle or crack of wood settling. The modest village existed to ferry travelers across the river, but no belongings of value were left behind.

Old, dried blood crusted over the dirty streets. His horse whinnied at a rat scampering past.

"Whoa," he muttered softly, reining it in.

While his steed calmed, he sighed and finally scanned the village. It wasn't a secret that most Well-blessed females disagreed with the Order's policy to avoid fae politics. It couldn't be a coincidence Clarke sent him in this direction. Did she expect him to rummage for survivors? To finally choose a side in the war? Or maybe he was paranoid, looking for a better fate beneath every upturned and incinerated village.

He recalled his last argument with the Prime before she disappeared again. A wild, desperate look had flitted in her ancient eyes.

"You fool." She tossed a book at him. He ducked, and it sailed past his head to crash against the wall. "You were quite happy following the prophecy so long as it didn't apply to you."

"And I'll continue to follow it," he calmly reminded her. "If you reveal the parts you're keeping from us."

"I told you, I don't have it. Jackson Crimson did. If you want to experience his memories, find your mate and return to me."

"Just tell me."

"I just did," she'd snarled, then spread her glorious white wings and took to the sky.

The outburst was the largest display of emotion Leaf had ever seen in Aleksandra's bleak eyes. What the fuck did experience memories mean, anyway? He'd thought if he followed Crimson's steps and read the journals, that was a practical observation of events. But maybe it meant something else. His lips flattened, and he grumbled. He couldn't lose his nerve now. Not when he was so close to finding the truth.

Leaf's thoughts traveled to Jasper—Maebh's enemy and his ex-Cadre of Twelve team member. Jasper had inherited the Glass Crown after killing the old Seelie High King, his father. Before

Mithras had imprisoned him, Jasper often resisted responsibility. But since he mated and spawned, he took to leadership well.

If these villagers had any survival instinct, they would have traveled to Jasper at Helianthus City or Aeron at Delphinium City for refuge.

Honestly, Leaf hadn't expected this war to last so long. He'd assumed most Seelie would jump back into the Unseelie camp and face consequences for their defection. He'd also thought the Order would have learned how to 'unmake' Maebh by now. Or, at the very least, the Prime or Legion would give in and tell Leaf what he needed to know.

His gaze raked over the smoldering village. Maebh's insanity grew after Elphyne split a few centuries ago. And most fae, on both sides of the war, knew Maebh was responsible for the taint on the Well. She was a wanted woman and would stand trial for her crimes.

But the Order's hands were tied as long as her demogorgon protected her, and the taint prevented Guardians from working at their full potential. The Order's power and influence in Elphyne was diminishing, as was everyone else's.

Sighing, Leaf scrubbed his face and veered his horse toward the river. With any luck, a way across would still be viable. Perhaps a boat or a raft... but everything had been destroyed, right down to the jetty.

The river was too wide to cross on horseback and flowed like black tar at night. Riding around the river would add a week to his journey. He might dismount and attempt a portal, but as soon as the thought hit, he remembered Clarke's experiment with the water and hesitated.

A cool breeze brought the sound of male voices. He reached over his shoulder, wrapped his fingers around *Reckoning*'s hilt, and drew. Ringing steel was music to his ears.

He searched for the voices. They could be survivors.

A group of Unseelie soldiers congregated downriver. Leaf squinted into the night and caught movement in the nearby forest, where more soldiers emerged. Possibly bathing in the river. The brazen bastards must have raided the village, then camped here to pick at its bones like carrion. But why did they remain?

He sheathed *Reckoning*. Despite the Order having a warrant for Maebh's arrest, he doubted she would be here. No one had seen her in years. These soldiers were no threat to a Guardian if she wasn't there. This was precisely why ignoring fae politics was a rule for the Order. Leaf could now go about his business without being hindered.

He spurred his horse forward. The group of five or so on the riverbank noticed his approach and moved into formation, ready to attack.

"Put your fangs away," Leaf grumbled, slowing his horse to stop a few yards away.

It took a Well-damned moment for one of them to recognize the glowing blue teardrop beneath Leaf's left eye, his steel sword, and the Kingfisher-blue piping on his battle uniform.

A vampire spat on the floor. "What business do you have here, Guardian?"

Leaf raised an indignant brow at the soldiers still brandishing weapons. Not very clever this lot. He briefly searched for contraband but found none and changed his opinion. They might be a little clever.

"I'm passing through," he answered. "Since you destroyed the village I intended to find food and rest in, I expect you to supply a substitute."

The vampire narrowed bloodshot eyes. There was too much red there for Leaf's liking. Bloodlust turned vampires into insatiable, crazed, unquenchable monsters. Some vampires, D'arn Indigo included, had suffered accidental bloodlust but returned to sanity and control. Others had to be put down.

Leaf tugged the reins and cantered alongside the group, inspecting them further. Half had washed in the river, as he'd suspected. But he also detected a faint atmosphere of anticipation.

"Are you packing up camp?" he queried.

"No."

"Then what is the occasion?"

Unseelie soldiers willingly bathing was a rare sight.

Silence.

Leaf narrowed his eyes.

"Who do I see for food?" he pressed, still pacing the horse. "Who is in charge here?"

"That would be Captain Grung."

Leaf had to stifle an eye roll when no more information came. He smiled tightly. "And where would I find Captain Grung?"

The soldiers conversed in hushed, hasty whispers. Leaf heard every word. Imbeciles. It appeared they would be commencing a hunt soon. It sounded like gratuitous entertainment.

"I don't give a flying kuturi's ass about a hunt," Leaf snapped impatiently. "Just take me to the Captain so I can feed my horse, rest, and then be on my way. I have work to do."

His authoritative tone was enough to spring them into action.

One beckoned for Leaf to follow him into the forest. He urged his steed onward, pleased that the fear of Guardians still garnered him a modicum of respect despite the taint. He supposed even though he couldn't draw on mana without repercussions, he could still use a magic-cutting weapon without losing his access to the Well.

They could not.

So whatever nonsense magic they tossed his way, *Reckoning* could likely weaken it, and then he'd drive the sword into their soft bodies, preventing them from healing.

Tents and campfires sprinkled the clearing beyond the first line of trees. Small gatherings of soldiers stopped their conversations to watch him pass. Another cluster sparred amongst themselves. The odd corpse hung from trees—likely prisoners from the raid—all rotting and a few days old except for a tree with four skinned and gutted animals. They were likely the next meal.

Interestingly, a large empty cage sat off to the side. The wooden bars had been reinforced by elven glyphs, which made them strong enough to hold a mana-warped monster. He wondered which beast they'd hunt.

Food and a few hours of rest would give Leaf's horse enough energy to move onward. Perhaps he would remain awake to avoid any attempts at cutting his throat. A commotion near a large bonfire drew Leaf's gaze to three females jostled into a line. From their reluctance to move, they were likely prisoners... or the hunted.

His hands tightened on the reins. Not his problem. He shifted his attention to the soldier leading him and stopped upon instruction outside an enormous yurt. A giant orc in pants and a bone necklace emerged from a flap in the front.

"Guardian." His voice was deep. "I am Captain Grung."

Grung had recently bathed, which was even more unusual to see than the soldiers. Leaf dismounted but held the reins, keeping his horse close. Orcs were highly territorial. If Leaf remained above Grung's eye level, he'd likely see Leaf as a threat.

"Captain," he greeted. "I'm here for food—for myself and the horse. Perhaps a few hours' rest, and then I'll be out of your hair."

The orc folded his muscled arms and stared down at Leaf. "You are not Unseelie Army. We do not have to give you food, Guardian."

"No, you don't. But if you'd like me to move on swiftly and not inspect the camp, I suggest you take the easiest option."

The orc blinked.

"The food," Leaf prompted. For Crimson's sake. How did this over-muscled creature gain the captaincy?

Grung reluctantly grunted. "You will wait. Cooks are busy."

Leaf's gaze narrowed at the panicked females. Perhaps they were the cooks. "Can I not simply take my own food?"

"Soldiers must not raid food supplies. They must wait for mealtimes," Grung recited.

"I'm not one of your soldiers."

"Same rules for all."

"You're making me wait?" This was preposterous. He didn't have time to wait. Something about Clarke's information made him antsy. "For how long?"

"However long the hunt takes. Then—" Grung stroked his jaw, deep in thought. "Then, depending on who wins, you must wait for them to mate."

"Mate?"

"Yes." Grung pointed at the females. "Is a mate hunt."

Leaf closed his eyes. *Count to three. One. Two. Three.* Then he opened them. "When does this hunt begin?"

"Soon. Hunt will take less than one turn of the hourglass because females are weak. Then the mating. Then food for the next meal will be prepared."

Resting and feeding the horse was a priority. Leaf could leave and take his chances trying to find another village, but if Clarke's information was misleading, and he had to circle back to the site of his original lead, finding food would be difficult. And hunting wild game would take as much time from his schedule as waiting for this idiotic hunt to finish.

Leaf supposed he could rest without safety concerns if this event occupied the soldiers.

Exhaling, he asked, "Where can I take the horse? I assume the feed for beasts is allowed at any time, or are there rules for that too?"

Grung recited, "Beasts must stay harnessed and tethered close by. Beasts must be cared for if beasts are expected to last through battle. Beasts must be fed once daily at dawn and provided fresh water."

The giant made it difficult for Leaf not to regret his decision to stay.

The captain turned to the waiting soldier and said, "Take the horse to the corral."

Leaf stopped him. "I'll keep my bag and weapons."

He didn't want Jackson Crimson's journals getting into the wrong hands. While no specific prophecies were mentioned in the copies he had, information about Aleksandra and Maebh's friendship with Crimson was detailed. This knowledge might help Leaf if the Unseelie thought their queen was a friend of the Prime's, or it would sow distrust. Most of these imbeciles couldn't read, but he didn't want to take his chances. The fewer who knew, the better to retain the impartial reputation the Order had gained.

It was hard enough doing business in Seelie territory with Jasper wearing the Glass Crown.

Leaf slung his satchel over his shoulder and followed the soldier as he led the horse, but Grung barked, "Soldiers stay in camp."

"I'm not your..." For fuck's sake. "Where do I wait?"

"In camp." As if it was obvious.

"Of course."

Grung's feral grin pronounced his underbite. "Now, I must finish washing for my future mate."

What was the point? "You realize the hunt will make you filthy before you bed her."

These mating hunts were common with less civilized fae and often involved competing males fighting and killing each other to get a competitive advantage.

Grung's expression deadpanned as he processed Leaf's comment. But it must have been too hard for his five brain cells to grasp because he ducked back into his tent, whistling a jaunty tune.

Leaf's gaze lifted to the stars. "Blessed Well, give me the patience to last the night."

Make this pause in my journey the right decision.

He exhaled and continued walking toward the large campfire at the center of the camp. He wasn't sure why he expected the Well to answer him. It never did. But he had a habit of speaking or praying to it. Maybe it calmed him. Or helped him make sense of Elphyne's idiotic inhabitants.

At least they hadn't attempted to remove *Reckoning* or recited a rule about weapons being left outside... but a glance showed most kept theirs close. These smaller raiding troops were Maebh's specialty. Her strategy was to spread dissent throughout Elphyne, to harbor hatred for the Seelie, and to nip at their flanks. She liked to extend the pretense of hope—so she could laugh as she crushed it.

Leaf received a few sideways glances as he approached the fire. He should have found a quiet spot away from the commotion. It certainly would have been easier to pass the hours until his horse had rested, but something kept his boots headed in this direction. And the closer he got, the more this something presented as a magnetic pull. Why, he didn't understand. All he found at the fire were three females being inspected like cattle.

He inwardly scoffed at the soldier's desperation.

A growing sense of unease brushed over Leaf's skin. Intuition pestered him. This same feeling had ridden his psyche since he left the Order. The worst part was this feeling made him distrust his own thoughts. His body did one thing. His mind wanted another.

Walking away from these females should have been easy, but his upper lip curled as a wolf shifter sniffed one of their crotches. She yelped and tried to shove him away but failed. Leaf stepped closer. His fists flexed at his side. You wouldn't see elven soldiers lowering themselves to this sort of base, vile—he froze as the female with cascading brown hair turned in his direction.

A tremble ran through his body. His lungs seized. Never had he laid eyes on someone with such a visceral reaction. Something about her arrested every cell in his body, from her warm brown eyes and sun-kissed olive skin to the smattering of freckles on her button nose. Her lips were plump and rosy, and he couldn't remove his eyes from them.

Leaf was not a male who made a fool of himself over beauty, but if he didn't find a reason to turn away soon, a fool was precisely what he'd be.

She was where the magnetism originated. But why was she looking at him like they'd already met?

"Jace?" she exclaimed.

Fuck.

CHAPTER FIVE

Nova's heart soared when she cried out Jace's name.

She waited for him to reply, acknowledge, or say anything, but he stared at her in confusion.

It was Jace. She was sure of it. He wore a strange leather uniform, and a tiny blue glow sparkled beneath his left eye. But everything else was damn near identical to the handsome ex-lover she'd thought she'd lost. Right down to his long, blond hair and surfer-tanned skin. She'd always teased him that the tan was ingrained into his DNA. Even when he moved to the east coast, it never faded.

Wait... that glowing mark beneath his eye. Why was that familiar?

Dread sank in her stomach like a stone.

He was a Guardian. One of those magic police-type warrior fae. The ones everyone hated for... what was it for again? Oh yes, for killing monsters and—her heart stilled—enforcing the forbidden substances rule.

Her earrings.

But it was Jace. He wouldn't execute her. Surely, he would save her.

"Jace!" she cried, trying to step from the log. Soldiers snarled and pushed her back. Panic constricted her chest. Her wild eyes darted to Jace. "Help."

He glanced over his shoulder as if he thought she spoke to someone else.

"Be quiet," the female elf hissed. "You're going to get us killed."

But Nova couldn't stop.

"What's wrong with you?" Her voice croaked. "It's me, Nova Morales. You lived next door until you were seventeen. You shared meals with my family every Sunday. We spent our vacations at your beach house. Come on, Jace. It's me!" Still nothing. Taking a risk, she pointed at her earrings. "You gave me these!"

He bought them when Nova had gushed over them in a store window. Solid gold hoops. These earrings tipped Nova's brother off to their brief, secret relationship.

Irritation swam in his blue eyes. Tendons flashed in his square jaw. He approached, pushing past the soldiers blocking him. They snarled and snapped like animals but, upon seeing his face, backed off with a hasty hand sign of apology.

"Stupid woman," he growled when he arrived at her feet. "You could have saved yourself a world of pain but had to point to your contraband."

Nova's blood ran cold. "Jace?"

It was the same smooth, cultured voice she remembered. It even held the posh note he'd adopted since his Ivy League education. But the anger—the fury in his eyes was so foreign. The last time she'd seen him, those eyes had been full of love and... her throat clogged up.

"My name is D'arn Leaf. I'm—"

"Shut the fuck up," she choked out. This isn't fun anymore. *"Yo no estoy pasándolo bien."*

"Excuse me?" he blinked.

"If this is some kind of *¡estúpido!* prank, I will murder you where you sleep, *mi amigo.*" She searched the crowd over his head. "If my twin is laughing at my humiliation, just tell me. I'm not having fun, so let's be done with this."

"Woman," he growled. "I don't know you. I don't know your twin."

"Sure you do. His name is Niles. We three used to be tight. And then you moved away, and he went back to Mexico and messed with the wrong people and—gah! *¡Nunca escuchas lo que yo dice!* I told you all this!"

Maybe if she'd spent more time with Niles instead of traveling the world, saving a planet that couldn't be saved, her brother wouldn't have said those scary things the last time they spoke.

The world would be better off if it was smaller.

Rallying her composure, Nova looked at her friend. Her heart leaped as his tanned face paled, and understanding dawned in his eyes.

"Finally. You recognize me."

"It doesn't take a genius to recognize you're from the old world."

His gaze darted around, assessing the soldiers as though he

weighed opponents. When he turned, she noticed his pointed elf ears.

She went numb. Sounds warbled. "You're not Jace."

Not Jace.

Not Jace.

He must have died. She was truly alone. Her legs became jelly. Cold, cruel reality sank into her bones. Too often since she'd awoken, her hopes soared, only to be crushed.

She wasn't sure how much longer her sanity would hold. God dangled a cruel, sweet carrot before her eyes. This Guardian was identical to the only man who ever came close to being her everything. The only man she'd ever—her throat closed, and she looked away. She wouldn't give them the satisfaction of seeing her cry.

"Time to begin!" Captain Grung pushed into the crowd.

His eyes smoldered with lust. He'd cleaned and shaved, yet still couldn't erase the monstrous edge to his appearance. Or his foul breath. Nova smelled it when he stopped before her and panted like an aroused dog.

Nova should have panicked. She should have calculated ways to escape. But all she could do was blink. Her mind was shutting down, preparing for the nightmare about to unfold. For disappointment to cycle back, to beat her down, to—

"Wait," the Guardian barked.

Grung snarled, "Guardians do not interfere."

The elf's arrogant, unwavering gaze held the giant orc's almost as if he was bored. "Surely that big, empty skull of yours has some sense knocking around in it."

Gasps and snickers traveled through the spectating soldiers. More arrived at the taste of violence in the air.

"Do not mock me." Grung poked Leaf in the center of his forehead. "You. Do. Not. Interfere."

"Unless, of course, it involves a threat to the integrity of the Well. She wears contraband in her ears. She has broken our laws and must be arrested."

The captain roared in the elf's face, spraying spittle. To his credit, the Guardian barely flinched at the stench-ridden threat. He didn't even reach for the sword at his back. He waited until the orc finished, then pulled the hem of his shirt from beneath his jacket and wiped his face.

Nova forced herself to reassess. Yes, he was the spitting image of her friend. But he did not act like him. Jace ran a Fortune Five Hundred company. But he wasn't rude or cocky. He never laughed at Nova's idealistic views about saving the world. He resented working for his father's company, but a sense of duty had been drilled into him as a child. So he'd dragged himself to that private academy and then moved to college without a complaint. He quit surfing and did what was asked of him so he could be smart enough to inherit a company. He should have been arrogant. But Jace never belittled anyone in his life.

"You cannot take our prize," Grung declared vehemently.

Before Nova noticed the danger, a sharp tug at her ears drew a cry of pain. She slapped her palms over her stinging ears and felt wetness. When someone screamed in agony behind her, she realized what had happened. He'd ripped the earrings out and was cut from the Well.

"She comes with me," the Guardian decreed in a tone so cold she tasted ice.

"No." The captain stomped like a giant, petulant toddler. "We have already decided. The same rules apply to all of us. You included." His voice deepened to a dangerous pitch. "Breaking rules is death."

Grung pointed into the dark forest. Nova refused to look. She knew what was stuck in the ground as a warning. She held her breath as she passed the pikes daily.

Leaf's gaze hardened. Long, torturous seconds passed. Then he straightened. "Understood."

A whimper erupted from Nova's lips. Her brother had been right. This world was past saving.

Nova had always prided herself on her resilience. Even when Jace left them, even when her parents died in their sleep, even when Niles became a cruel, bitter man and Jace had fallen ill... she'd always found a way to look at the world and think, if the magic of life could exist, then surely her problems were minor in comparison.

But now... now despair as she'd never known wrapped around her soul.

"So... you will not arrest her?" It was almost comical how Grung's features contorted into disbelief.

"Oh, you must have misunderstood. I will," he said. "But I'll join the hunt. Same rules apply to everyone, correct?"

The orc blanched. His jaw opened and then clicked shut. The two females next to Nova whimpered as though they were more frightened of this elf than the green-skinned brute.

"Winner must take the prize as a mate," Grung warned.

"Why?"

"Unmated female is a prize for all males. Mated males protect their females. And our cook must be in proper condition. Soldiers must eat." He pounded his chest, rattling his bones. "I must eat. So it is none, or it is a mate."

"Are we doing this?" shouted someone further in the crowd.

Voices raised, impatiently agreeing. Vampires wanted time with their prize before sunrise.

"Don't let me stop you." Leaf displayed his palms. "But I will compete."

"No weapons," the orc declared, eyeing off the Guardian's sword. "No flying. No mana. Same for everyone."

"But your size is your weapon," he pointed out dryly. "And the vampires have fangs. The shifters have claws. The stags have antlers. All can hear, see, and smell better to track the females. I see no other elves competing here tonight. That means I'm the only one at a disadvantage. Taking my weapon would make it worse."

"Fine," he snarled. "One weapon. No metal."

Nova caught the gleam in Leaf's eyes before he scowled. "I suppose you'll choose the weapon?"

With a grunt, Grung stomped into the darkness—toward the severed heads on pikes. Nova thought he might return with one of them, but he continued until he ducked into the supply tent and returned with a flimsy filleting knife made of bone.

"Set the females loose," the captain yelled.

Nova startled. She had no ties binding her wrists. Did he mean now? Her wild eyes darted about, searching for the best place to escape, but seeing in the dark was impossible. Leaf was right. The more animalistic fae would see her coming a mile away. The other females didn't hesitate. They ran—each disappearing into opposite ends of the forest.

"Run," Grung roared, his big voice booming to fill the

surrounding area. His eyes lit up with excitement. "See you soon, my future mate."

As if her heart still hadn't caught the memo, she glanced at Leaf but found him frighteningly unworried. Only someone more lethal than the others would hold that unwavering confidence. How stupid she was to think a fate with him would be better than death.

CHAPTER SIX

Leaf had to be insane. But too many things about this woman didn't add up. She'd mistaken him as someone from her time. Clarke said his future mate would be found on the way to the ruins. Perhaps this was the journey, not the old one he'd been avoiding.

Being the victor in this hunt meant he was doing his duty as a Guardian. He could not, in good faith, leave a woman from the old world here to fend for herself. Despite his belief they were distractions, all who had awoken from that time had contributed to their fight against Nero.

So, using that logic, he would win the hunt and convince the imbecile orc that he had mated with her. If that didn't work, then he'd kill them all.

At least his horse would have rested by then.

Then Leaf would continue to the ruins, find the last journal, and return Nova to the Order, where she could have one of those ridiculous drinks with tiny umbrellas. The last thing he needed was a herd of women harassing him for abandoning this one. That was the only reason he was doing this. Not the pain in Nova's eyes when they'd ripped the rings from her ears. Not the way his pulse seemed to quicken when he looked at her face. And indeed, not the inexplicable notion that her voice shook something loose from the disquiet of his soul.

She was no one to him.

Unstrapping his baldric with short, sharp moves, he glared at his competition as they waited for the signal to give chase. The orc wouldn't be the only threat. Shifters and vampires had the best senses. But vampires preferred to hunt from the sky. Since they were forbidden, they'd have to make do on foot. The shifters, however, were quite adept at running in the forest.

Hadn't there been one that sniffed Nova's crotch?

He located the wolf shifter standing away from the fire, staring in the direction Nova had run. Following the desperado would be Leaf's best chance.

He dropped his satchel next to *Reckoning*. Long before the taint had warped mana, he'd placed protective wards on his belongings. If anyone attempted to steal them, they'd likely find themselves without hands.

Straightening, he put the flimsy filleting knife between his teeth, pulled a leather cord from his pocket, and tied the length of his hair back. It was laughable how easily he'd lulled them into a false sense of security.

If Leaf could rely on his mana, he would have taken Nova through a portal to the Order, Grung's rules be damned.

After securing his hair, he removed the knife from his mouth and spat the bad taste on the ground. Revolting, uncouth, reprobate and—

"HUNT!"

Stampeding feet trembled the trees and ground as soldiers ran past Leaf. For Crimson's sake... almost the entire troop joined the hunt. He stayed back, watching every direction they ran, waiting until the last of them disappeared into the forest's shadows.

Then he reached for *Reckoning*.

Grung's rules were not bound by mana. Fuck him. Nothing would stop Leaf from slicing his way through the competition. Nothing except... his hand paused an inch from *Reckoning*'s hilt as a wild notion entered his mind. He imagined Nova being ripped from his arms because he'd not followed these damn rules. He imagined his magic failing to protect her. He imagined her given to the runner-up. Leaf's fist returned empty to his side.

Playing by their rules ensured Nova was safe until he found the opening to get them out—his horse included. This human was too important to him.

To Clarke, he corrected. Nova was important to Clarke and the other Well-blessed women. And to the Order. Not to him.

Before he set off, he warned a remaining soldier, "Touch my things, and you'll lose your hands. Understood?"

The guard nodded emphatically. Leaf scrubbed his face and jogged into the forest.

It didn't take him long before he found the first corpse. A vampire had been impaled on a branch protruding from a fallen log. From there, Leaf tracked the shifter's path with ease. In their desperation to claim their prize, no one had been stealthy—a fact he had expected. One look at each soldier revealed most had erections. What little sense these males had would be stuck in their cocks.

A woman's blood-curdling scream chilled his blood. He sprinted, pumping his legs and dodging branches. A shadow leaped from the cover of a tree trunk. Leaf blocked a punch, taking it on his shoulder. Snarling, he lashed out to grab the offender by the throat and slid his knife into a palpitating heart. The flimsy blade broke as Leaf registered shock on the shifter's face.

He was the one who'd scented Nova. *Fuck.*

Before the first manabee popped, Leaf was two paces away, searching for signs Nova had come this way. The darkness made it difficult to tell.

The best tracker was gone, and so was Leaf's weapon. He was foolish for believing this would be easy. Wiping his forehead, he continued jogging, hoping he was going in the right direction.

After dispatching two lying in wait and discovering five impaled corpses, he caught up to the captain. The orc's green, sweaty skin glistened in the moonlight as he plowed through the forest. If he still ran, then he hadn't found Nova. That scream belonged to someone else.

Hopefully.

Grung noticed Leaf chasing. He snarled and ripped a tree from its roots, tossing it behind him. Leaf vaulted over it, landing gracefully on the other side. A thud and cry of dismay sounded behind Leaf as the tree hit someone else.

The orc skidded to a halt. Broad, muscled shoulders heaved a lungful of air. They circled each other in the small space between trees. It would be difficult to maneuver. The forest was eerily quiet. No more thudding of footsteps. Only ragged breathing and Leaf's pulse roaring in his ears. And the voice in the back of his mind whispering, *Find her. Find her. Find her.*

"Where is your knife, puny elf?" Grung chuckled.

"Inside your soldier's heart," Leaf drawled.

The orc's humor died. "I let you join the hunt, and you kill my soldier."

"Your rules didn't mention otherwise."

Anger simmered in the orc's gaze, but he knew Leaf was right.

They both looked to where splashing filtered through the trees. That had to be Nova in the river, trying to hide her scent. Clever woman.

The orc bolted, crashing through trees in his way.

Leaf cracked his neck and took a deep breath. Then he gave chase. He spared no energy running after the orc. That voice in his head grew louder, more insistent. Branches whipped his face as he passed. Sharp things scraped at his flesh. But his eyes never lost track of the sweaty green skin. The moment they cleared the forest, Grung ran into the water.

The urge to fling a spell at the brute rose within Leaf like a wave of lava. He barely restrained it from releasing. The backlash inside him caused his head to feel like it was splitting.

He searched the torrential darkness and found no sign of Nova. He jogged into the water, his heart slamming into his ribcage. Grung's enormous body barely fought the currents to remain steady. If he struggled to stay afloat, how could Nova possibly survive?

Leaf's heart squeezed.

She couldn't be dead. Surely she wouldn't drown herself...

Something cracked open in his chest. Despair. Grief. Agony. Why? He barely knew the woman.

But it mattered not. His lungs refused to work. His vision blurred, and he forced his gaze away... only to land on small, petite footprints leading away from the water's edge further down the riverbank.

A flash of white in the forest caught his eye.

Nova.

Her moonlit face peered out from the shadows. Seeing him, she ran from the trees' safety. Grung's roar traveled across the water, almost ashore. Bursting into action, Leaf raced to meet Nova.

"Flee!" he bellowed, gesturing to the forest.

Why on earth did she run toward Leaf? Was she mad? This was her best chance to escape. She'd diluted her scent. Grung had been preoccupied with scouring the water. Many of the best trackers were dead or busy. But the desperation in her eyes told him she wasn't thinking straight. For some stupid reason, she felt safer with him.

Their bodies clashed. Leaf's arms banded around her, trapping her waterlogged and trembling body. Soft, feminine curves pressed against his hard physique. She'd erased her scent with salty water but still smelled inexplicably perfect. His relief triggered tumultuous emotions that warred with his logic. No blue Well-blessed marks sprung from the ground to wrap around their bodies. Nothing passed between them except the pounding of their hearts.

He'd caught her. But she wasn't his fated mate.

A meaty hand landed on Leaf's shoulder and tore him from Nova. He fell, rolled, and clawed the sand to halt his trajectory.

Lifting his head, he targeted the orc. Grung stepped before Nova, blocking her with his big body.

"Mine," he snarled.

"Run," Leaf urged Nova.

But the damned woman refused, so he forced himself to ask the difficult question—was it worth risking his life for a woman who wasn't his mate?

CHAPTER
SEVEN

Nova registered hesitation in Leaf's expression. Her heart lurched. Seconds ago, he embraced her like an old friend... like Jace. That big palm had cupped the back of her head like he used to.

She should have run as he'd urged. Instead, she eyed the dagger in Grung's belt as he stalked toward the Guardian. Bravery—or foolishness—drove her feet forward in the sand. Leaf's eyes widened, but he wasn't fast enough to stop her.

Grung was.

He swung, flinging his giant fist. The blow to her temple sent her reeling. Stars danced. The ground fell away. She landed hard, and river water engulfed her face. She struggled to push herself up, to breathe.

Somewhere on the shore, she vaguely registered Grung's roar of pain through her own. But then strong hands lifted her from the water. The face of comfort was inches from her own, worried and panicked.

"Are you alright?" Leaf rasped.

She tried to nod. Swallowed. He pushed her behind his body and faced the orc.

"I caught her," he growled. "I won."

"No one to witness but me."

The Guardian mumbled "imbecile" under his breath, then roared, "You'll lose control of your troop when they learn their leader doesn't follow the rules."

Leaf's gaze darted down... to the orc's crotch. Nova followed his gaze and almost puked. The captain was ready to lay his claim on Nova on the riverbank if necessary. Right here, the instant the Guardian was no longer an obstacle.

She should have run.

But what was the point if she couldn't be near Jace—Leaf? *Hoja de los Guardianes.* Leaf of the Guardians. Whatever his name was. None of this made sense. All she knew was that she couldn't walk away. And neither could he.

Shouts from the trees drew Grung's attention. Leaf sprung forward. The orc took the punch on his thick forearm.

Nova feared that was the only chance David had against Goliath. But Leaf struck fast, hard, and true. It was like watching a killer cat, twisting and evading capture. He somehow took a hit to his body without flinching, never once removing his laser-sharp focus from his enemy.

The two mismatched opponents sparred along the riverbank. Leaf sent jab after jab to the orc, taking many in return to his body.

He must be made of stone. That's why he felt so solid when she'd embraced him.

Appreciation over the Guardian's physique pushed into her mind. His single-minded tenacity to dominate caused goosebumps to erupt on her flesh. Seeing this warrior elf fight to protect her... and then inevitably claim her was oddly arousing. It shouldn't be.

"Where is she?" A voice to her right.

Soldiers emerged from the forest, and her fear washed back in. They must have failed at claiming the others and came here to try their luck with her.

Leaf stabbed the orc in his eye, staggered back, and straightened his spine. His long blond hair had come loose and dripped down his back. He looked wild, uncivilized, and brutal. A demon shone from his eyes as he shouted loud enough for the soldiers to hear, "She's mine!"

Grung snarled and yanked the dagger from his eye. Thick blood oozed from the socket. He acted like it was nothing as he climbed to his feet.

"I followed your rules," Leaf pointed out, his voice steady. "If you break them, I break them."

To punctuate his warning, blue lightning crackled at his fingertips.

The captain glanced at the witnesses gathering, then bared his teeth.

"You win." He spat blood on the sand, tossed the dagger, and his bloody lips stretched into a terrifying smile. "Now, you must mate with her."

Nova tensed at the implication. Here?

"At the camp," Leaf agreed, backing away from the orc to shield her with his body. "Same as the other victors."

A new kind of panic entered Nova's pulse. What the actual fuck? As if he sensed her spiraling anxiety, Leaf's hand slipped behind his body and squeezed her hip. It wasn't a lecherous grope. It was short and platonic. Businesslike.

He must have a plan.

Did he?

Nova squeaked as he tossed her over his shoulder. It happened so fast. Her arms dangled, and the blood rushed to her head. As her sore temple throbbed, her hair dripped patterns onto the ground while they walked.

But she wasn't looking at that. Not really. Not when she had a face full of flexing, taut buttocks encased in tight leather. Her cheeks heated, more blood rushed to her head, and she promptly passed out.

CHAPTER EIGHT

Nova awoke inside a dark tent with an angry elf pacing by her bedroll. She tried to sit, but dizziness sent her down with a groan.

"Where are we?" she mumbled.

"Where do you think?"

His gruff, irritated tone made Nova's brow scrunch.

Taking a moment to breathe, she let the dizziness abate and took stock of her surroundings. Campfires outside gave enough light for her to register the color and texture of the canvas. It was the same dirty green from the war camp. Her stomach sank. She was still here—still a prisoner.

Her lumpy bedroll smelled musty and was squished against a damp wall. Piles of clothes and hoards of loot lined the length of the opposite wall. With a middle peak high enough to stand beneath, but smaller at two sides, Leaf had worn a path with his restricted pacing in the center of the cluttered space.

This must be one of the soldier's tents.

Carousing and raucous shouts outside ruined her false sense of safety.

The army waited. Celebrating. Did that mean Leaf had already... She patted down her damp dress and pressed hesitantly between her thighs, feeling for bruising.

Leaf stopped pacing. Alarm hit his shadowed eyes, and he hissed, "No, I did not fuck you while you slept. You're the last person I'd—" He quickly shut his mouth and glared at the tent's closed flap.

Voices outside hushed.

"Sounds like she is awake, Guardian!" The mocking voice was unmistakably Grung's. "You best claim your prize, or she is fair game."

Leaf contemplated his palms as if they'd betrayed him. He still wore his battle uniform. The only change was that his long blond hair had been combed. Well, that and his mood.

The voices outside picked up in volume. Leaf resumed pacing. Every time he pivoted, his damp hair flicked. She mustn't have been unconscious for long if they were both still wet from the river.

"You're soaked," she mumbled, which he ignored.

She slid from the bedroll and searched a pile of clothing in the corner. One piece looked like a cloak. That would be fine. When she faced him, two narrow eyes watched her warily. Flattening her lips, cursing in Spanish, she approached him and held out the cloak.

He slapped her offering away. "Don't touch me."

"Enough." Her eyes flashed. *"No puedo creer que los hombres todavía creen que saben todo sobre todo."*

He blinked. "What did you say?"

"I said, I can't believe men still think they know everything about everything." Nova's temper rose like a coiled snake lashing out. She gesticulated in his face. "You are an arrogant fool, acting so much better than me, acting too good to touch me. As if this body is so horrible to look at." She gestured down her soaked dress, knowing the white fabric stuck to her skin and revealing everything beneath. But she was beyond caring. Maybe it was residual bitterness over him not being Jace. Maybe it was her stifled pain and frustration over a life spent trying to save this planet, only to find that two thousand years of evolution changed nothing. Or maybe it was her stupid twin's betrayal or her tiredness of this place. The confusion. The customs. The brutality. Fucking done. She poked Leaf's chest, taunting him. "I'm touching you. I'm fucking touching you, arrogant asshole. *¡Vete al diablo!*"

He trapped her hand against his hard chest. Heat scorched her face as he stared intently. She braved a glance into his eyes and found not amusement but curiosity.

"What did you say?" he murmured.

What did I say?

Then it hit her. "I said go to hell in Spanish."

A snort of amusement left him.

"Spanish." He tested the word on his tongue, mumbled it a few times, then frowned at a leather satchel beside his sword and baldric.

"You recognize the language?" she asked hopefully. Jace had learned to speak it because of her. It was one of the things he'd surprised her with when they'd met up in Vegas that last fateful day.

He let go of her hand and refocused on the exit. The voices had dulled again. The only sound Nova heard was the crackling fire and the unmistakable drag of heavy breathing.

"They're just going to wait out there?" she whispered.

"Yes," he replied. "Because if we don't mate, you will be gifted to the runner-up."

Grung?

"Get on the bed," he demanded quietly. "Take off your dress, and do not speak unless I tell you to."

Her eyes narrowed. She wasn't going to be intimidated by him again. Once she lost her temper, it was like a valve released.

Lifting her chin, she said to his back, "Make me."

He gave a pointed look at the exit. Presumption entered his eyes as he raised his brows in an obvious way. She watched him foolishly try to communicate through expression, gesturing to the bed, hugging his clothes, and then glancing outside and shaking his head.

"*¡Ay, qué menso!* You were never good at charades."

"What are charades?" he grumbled.

She rolled her eyes.

Was he trying to tell her that they should pretend to mate? Play the game, and maybe the soldiers would believe they were fucking? Stupid man. The vampires could hear her heartbeat. The shifters had taken one whiff of her privates and then tracked her across the forest. And his communication method sucked.

With a huff, she lowered onto hands and knees and crawled around the tent, searching through the belongings left behind by the tent's owner. She found soap, useless trinkets, another woolen cape, and moldy food. When she reached for Leaf's leather satchel, he stopped her by waggling his finger.

She mimed the action of writing with a pen. His eyes widened, and he retrieved a leather-bound journal and charcoal stick from the bag. He flicked through the handwritten pages too fast for Nova to read, but slow enough that she noticed the handwriting was in ink and not charcoal.

He found a blank page toward the end and scribbled down the words: *We should pretend.*

Just as she'd guessed.

She shook her head and pointed to her ears. They will hear—duh. From the guilty look on his handsome features, he knew his plan wouldn't work. But he had no alternative.

Perhaps there was nothing for it, and they had to go through with the act. She could lay there and let him—her throat closed up. No. He was a stranger. He wasn't the man who tenderly held her hand while he took her virginity. He wasn't the man who hid love letters in places her twin couldn't find. And he certainly wasn't the man she'd left suffering in Vegas alone during the Fallout.

Her affair with Jace had burned bright, hot, and brief. It left an impression on her heart she still felt when they reunited at the end. One night. That's all they'd had together before the world froze.

This man sitting beside her on a dirty canvas floor didn't like Nova. His opinion was evident through his standoffish body language.

This world was horrible, and she had no more fight left in her soul. Her body was the last part of herself she could control. Giving that up now would cut the rope holding her sanity together.

Breathing through the despair, she took the charcoal and wrote, *Let's do it. Call it an itch scratched. Then we can leave.*

His attention burned the side of her face, but she kept her eyes on her writing. His rough warrior's hand engulfed hers and then tried to pry the charcoal away. She couldn't relax her fingers. They'd seized.

Leaf palmed her spine, angled his body to see the book better, then used her hand to write. The intimate and assuming pose arrowed heat to her lower belly. Her lashes fluttered at the comfort of having a man touch her again. Words formed on the shadowed page, but they blurred and bled into blobs of darkness. All she wanted to do was face him, lean into his body, and pretend he was the man she missed with all her heart.

When he finished writing, he tilted her jaw to guide her attention to his words. She swallowed, blinked the tears away, and focused on his writing.

Or we can fight our way out. I must use mana, and it is unpredictable. It will be bloody, dangerous, and unsafe.

She craned her neck to meet his gaze and searched for signs of confidence. From what she'd witnessed already, he fought with unprecedented skill. But their risk doubled if he used magic, which could just as easily backfire.

He offered her a choice—a way to keep her dignity intact. Feeling a surge of courage, she scrambled across the tent and covered her shoulders with a cape. She found a bag to hold a few other items that might come in handy. She had no shoes, but she could put up with sore feet.

While she prepared, Leaf strapped on his baldric and slipped his satchel over his shoulder. Facing each other, Nova's heart pounded. They were as ready as they would ever be. Voices hushed outside, waiting. She could almost feel their anticipation burning through the thin canvas wall.

Holding her gaze steady, Leaf slowly unsheathed his sword. Blue, glowing marks gleamed on the blade and reflected on the tent's inner walls. He pointed at the rear, just beyond the bedroll. Taking her hand, he hooked her fingers into his belt and gave her a stern look.

Last chance to back out, his gaze seemed to say.

CHAPTER NINE

After Leaf had won the hunt, Grung's eyes flashed with spite. At that moment, Leaf knew he'd have to fight his way out of the camp, no matter what happened inside that tent. He'd managed to collect his bag without a fuss. The sword had been more challenging. He'd scratched transference runes into his palm eight times before the spell activated correctly, and the blade traveled to him.

He'd tried to stall their impending escape. The closer to sunrise, the more passive vampires would be, thus eliminating a good portion of his obstacles. But Nova had been right. The impatient buffoons outside had impeccable hearing. They'd have picked fake mating sounds, and then they'd have retaliated with force.

Leaf preferred to stack the odds in his favor first.

He stared into Nova's glimmering eyes as she bustled about, collecting items he assumed meant she agreed with his proposal. His fate sealed itself in her tears. But the question was... if they survived, would she willingly come with him? Would he have to toss her over his shoulder again?

For their escape to work, there must be no hesitation. There must be trust. He was about to unleash the full force of his power on anything that moved against them. His mana had been building in his veins, pulsating and demanding release. What he carried didn't care if there was a taint. It wanted out of his system. It wanted to be heard.

For him to unleash without worry, Nova had to follow instructions. His doubt ebbed away when her gaze hardened, and she whispered, *"¡Vámonos!"*

Her urgency spurred Leaf into action. He slid the lid on his internal well an inch to the side, allowing a trickle of power to fill his veins and heighten his senses. In this state, he could hear as well as any vampire or wolf shifter. The downside was that it constantly cost mana.

He only entered this state when in dire straits, which before this evening was rare. Pushing aside that uncomfortable thought, he focused on the changes occurring in his body. Goosebumps prickled his skin. Electricity zapped in the air. Sound amplified.

Thud-thud went Nova's heart.

Drip-drip went a nearby leak.

Crackle, pop! went the campfire outside.

Heavy breathing. Someone belched. And someone hushed others in conversation. Another whined about how long they waited before calling it.

Leaf sliced *Reckoning* through the rear canvas wall. Forest scents bustled in with the fresh, predawn air. Feeling Nova's fingers still lodged in his belt, he pushed outside but paused. The slumbering sun had risen enough to paint the sky purple. It wasn't as dark as he'd feared. Nova could likely see well enough to keep up with him and evade attacks as best she could.

He unhooked her fingers and said quietly, "Stay behind me, stay close, and keep up."

When no answer came, he craned his neck to see her, and his heart lurched in his chest. In this hypersensitive state, her beauty arrested him, almost to the point that he forgot what he was supposed to do. Long lashes spiked from moisture. Flecks of gold defined the brown eyes within.

A jolt of adrenaline wrenched his gaze from her face.

He jogged in the direction of his horse, satisfied to hear her footsteps remain close. To her credit, she didn't complain about the sharp sticks and rocks likely cutting her bare soles.

After three more steps, shouts of alarm rang out.

That was three more than he'd planned for. The vamps must already be dozing. *Wonderful.*

An unnatural rustle above. A shadow dropped. Leaf gripped his sword with two hands, stepped, and sliced as he walked past. Elven sharpening glyphs flared on the steel. Blue light arced behind his blade, ensuring it cut like butter. The vampire's body split in two before it hit the ground.

After that, it was chaos. Grung bellowed from the right. Every soldier left awake surged forward in a second wave. But a wave was what Leaf wanted. It felt like home.

Afraid, Nova clutched his sword arm. His other hand released mana like a geyser. It had no form, shape, or intent beyond forging a path forward. Raw power thickened and sizzled in the air, blasting outward in an invisible ring of death. Skin flayed from bodies. Blood sprayed. Muscles, ligaments, and tendons stripped from bone. Skeletons ripped apart as though flimsy sticks in a hurricane.

"*¡Dios mío! ¿Qué pasó aquí?*" Nova's tone of horror wrestled with Leaf's conscience.

But still, his mana surged.

His eyes stung from the force of raw, torrential energy. It was as though he'd tapped into the very Well itself. If it wasn't for Nova's hand squeezing him, he might have succumbed to the addictive pull. Roaring with the effort, he mentally closed the lid on his inner well. Power rebounded inside his body, furious he'd cut it off.

Pain seared his mind. He dropped to a knee, and darkness crowded his vision.

"Leaf!"

She needs me.

He lifted his heavy head and searched for more threats. Instead, he found terror. His jaw dropped at the disaster he'd made of the forest camp. Trunks had ripped from their roots, tents were blown away, and supplies were caught in branches. Anything left standing was painted in bloody innards and bone. There wasn't a soul left alive. His power had blown through everything in a quarter-mile radius.

Shit, the horse.

He tried to rise, but his vision crowded again.

"Horse," he grunted.

Crimson, it hurt to speak. Words were sandpaper on his tongue. His skin ached so profoundly that he feared to look in case he'd flayed himself too. But Nova slipped under his arm, propping him up. It mustn't be too bad.

"I don't see it," she muttered.

"Fuck."

They staggered in the direction the animals had been corralled. They waded through blobs of unidentifiable, biological, and inorganic mess. The further they limped, the more objects and trees remained standing. Eventually, they came across untouched tents.

But no fae. Yet.

Still with *Reckoning* in his hand, Leaf gathered his strength and forced his legs to carry him without Nova's help. If any survivors thought to finish him off, he had to pretend he had the energy to fight. A quick inner assessment told him that thought wasn't entirely false. He did have reserves—plenty, actually.

Odd.

Had this raw power been within him all the time, was it an accident of the taint, or was it... he glanced at the woman beside him, stricken. No. He shook his head. No, he wasn't going there yet.

"Look!" Nova pointed to where the corral stood intact, complete with living animals. And his horse.

"Thank fuck," he rasped, sheathing his sword over his shoulder.

But as they approached the horse, the fae who'd remained behind at the hunt jumped out from behind a feed barrel. "Don't hurt me!"

Leaf's hand splayed on Nova's sternum, holding her back.

The fae flinched, squeezing his eyes shut.

"Let us go, and you have my word I won't hurt you," he said.

The soldier peeled one eye open, then the other. Seeing Leaf hadn't moved, he bolted into the forest.

"Let's go." Leaf walked into the corral, and as he untied his horse's reins from a post, he noted half-eaten bowls of feed. His brows lifted at his luck. It seemed Grung's rules were good for something. Someone had fed the animals as promised at dawn. Someone had also removed the saddle, brushed the flanks, and supplied water.

So even if Leaf was exhausted, his ride wasn't.

Good. He had to get out of there fast. The last thing he needed was to explain to Maebh why he'd slaughtered an entire unit of her soldiers. That female always looked at him strangely. He preferred to limit his time with her.

Leaf saddled his horse, mounted, then offered his hand to Nova. She stared at it and then at the bloody devastation dripping from trees. Something flickered in her eyes he couldn't decipher. He wondered if she'd flee. And then he'd have to begin the tedious task of chasing her down. Although, the thought of tossing her over his shoulder, and gripping that plump ass again, was oddly satisfying.

But she put her hand in his, allowed herself to be pulled onto the horse's back before him, and asked, "Okay, Leaf of the Guardians. What now?"

J.C. — ENTRY 2010 ANF

I wonder sometimes about why we do the things we do.

Since we brought this civilization together under the Well's guidance, I know my reasons. I want to create a better world than the one we left. I want to honor E's life's work, her morals, her values.

A legacy, M says. She thinks if she builds this world to perfection, then A will have no choice but to help her fill it with children, despite the immeasurable pain of their losses.

A just wants answers. Answers, I fear, will never come. Because she has to look inside her heart to find them, but she refuses. And so her heart grows smaller, and there is less room to fill.

CHAPTER TEN

Leaf never answered Nova's question, but without an alternate option and the need to leave, she put her faith in the stranger who'd saved her life.

As they galloped through the camp toward the river, rodents and carrion already picked at the flesh and bones of the army. It happened minutes ago but already seemed like a dream. The shapes and blobs weren't human or fae. Nova had trouble reacting to reality.

Was this her mind disassociating? Was she going into shock?

"Should we... bury them?" Nova asked, trying to turn, but Leaf grumbled and forced her back into position.

"Do you want to be thrown?" he snapped. "Eyes forward."

It wasn't until she did as she was told that he answered her question.

"They're Unseelie. This war with the Seelie is their fault, and consequences come with that."

Nova stared at the horse's cascading mane as they rode. But it seemed to take on a bloodied hue and then she couldn't focus. Each time gravity hit, tears jerked from her eyes. She squeezed them shut and held onto the mane, but closing her eyes was a mistake.

Flesh ripped from muscle. A cacophony of death burst all at once... then a confusing *drip drip drip*. She saw broken, upturned trees and unrecognizable bloody blobs. Then the tiny piece of green skin with black hair.

Time passed in a blur of forest, riverbank, sand, blue sky, and bloody nightmares. She tried hard not to piss off the dangerous elf cradling her with solid thighs and unbending steel arms. She forced herself to embrace the ache growing in her bottom from riding.

The horse labored for breath by the time the sun was high, and she couldn't take the repeating visions of death anymore.

Change the subject. Talk about something. Anything.

She asked, "What is this war about anyway? I overheard a soldier say fighting Seelie is a waste of time when the real threat comes from the west. Did he mean humanity?"

Leaf's chest heaved against her back with a weary sigh. She detected exhaustion in every line of his posture, tone, and sluggish movements as he reined the horse into a canter and checked over his shoulder to see if they were pursued.

"Someone said that?" he mumbled.

"Yes. It wasn't a popular opinion. They beat him up for it." Come to think of it, the soldier might have been one of the heads on pikes.

"Interesting." Leaf clicked his tongue and slowed the horse beside the sparkling river. "But if you're considering seeking refuge in the human city, don't. The soldier was right. The human leader,

Nero, is the true threat—not just against the people of Elphyne but to the integrity of the Well. His people are starved and sick. He steals mana. The damned fool thinks he can break the rules without consequence."

"No one wants to take responsibility for the state of their world. There were people like that in my time. My brother included. There was always someone to blame other than themselves."

Leaf grew silent behind her, which suited her fine, except distracting herself became more arduous by the second. Her stomach quivered and churned. The gallop had jolted all her aches and pains. Her temple still throbbed where Grung hit her. Her ears hurt. Now her ass and thighs hurt, and she'd only been on the horse for a few hours. But she wasn't as exhausted as the elf. His weight against her back grew heavier by the minute.

"Nero hopes we kill each other." Leaf's deep voice was barely audible. "Less resistance when he invades. He's like you, from the old world. Since waking, all he wants is to rule us all."

Leaf's words bounced around in her mind.

Old world.

Rule the lot.

Nero.

She grappled with familiarity. Her soul fought against it. Feeling the bile rise in her throat, she breathed deeply and gulped air.

Look at the beautiful river. Look at it sparkling in the sun.

"What's wrong?" Leaf asked, straightening.

Words wouldn't form on her swollen tongue. Her skin prickled. The horizon of trees and river swayed as those familiar words took shape in her memory.

From the old world.

He's like you.

"Impossible," she gasped, shaking her head. "You're not Jace. So he can't be... no..."

But was he? *She* was here, after all. Could *he* be here too?

"Nova." Leaf's tone turned sharp. "Tell me."

She shook her head, squeezing her eyes shut. But that made it worse. "Gonnabesick."

"Whoa." Leaf reined in the horse, bringing it to a stop. She lurched to the side, intending to fall, escape, or go anywhere he wouldn't see her vomit.

But he slammed his palm on her sternum and pressed hard, pulling her back to him. She gasped. Hiccuped. Looked down at the strong hand splayed over her heart.

Warrior's hands. Dirty nails. Scars.

Not the manicured hands of an Ivy League-educated oil tycoon.

"Breathe." His voice was hot gravel down her spine.

"Can't." She gasped through diaphragm spasms. "Let me off. Let me—"

"No."

"No necesita tu ayuda!" She didn't need his help. She tried to pull his hand away to escape.

The horse snorted and pranced.

"Stay put, Nova," he growled, his hand unyielding. "Breathe in through your nose and out through your mouth."

She whimpered, resisting even though he made perfect sense.

With a grunt of annoyance, he slid his palm up to her throat and then supported her chin. His other hand pressed her forehead, pinning her head back to his chest as he leaned forward at the hips. All she could see was the horse's mane. All she could feel was him.

He breathed deeply behind her, demonstrating how it should be done. His abdomen shifted against her spine with each lungful. Each exhale pushed hot air against her abused ear, tickling the skin of her neck. By his second breath, her lungs mimicked his. On his third, she relaxed so he could be her skeleton. His words became her thoughts. Her pulse was his to control.

"Good." Deep, commanding, calming. "Again. Slower."

Trembles wracked her body, chattering her teeth, but she breathed.

Nausea melted away.

Feeling rushed in.

"I'm okay," she whispered hoarsely.

He eased off. She stroked the horse, then straightened and glanced over her shoulder. His harrowing expression shuttered. He swung his leg behind and dismounted.

He kept doing that—hiding his emotions.

"You saved my life," she said. "And you help me, even though you don't know me. I guess you might be my mate or whatever, but I should thank—"

"Don't," he snapped, irritated. "You're in Elphyne. Surely you understand the rules now."

"I'm so—"

"Let's get this straight," he clipped. "You're *not* my mate. As a Guardian, my duty includes bringing old-world humans to the Order. You owe me nothing. After I take you there, we're done."

His hand enveloped hers, crushed her fingers into a fist, and forced her to hand-sign her apology against her chest. His gaze dipped to her breasts, to where he touched. Then he flung her hand away as if she'd burned him.

Tears stung her eyes, and she glanced at the river. It wasn't even the half of it when she'd called him arrogant in the tent. He was also cruel and mean.

He took the reins. "What made you feel sick?"

"It was the blood."

"Don't lie to me, human. Not after what I risked."

She blinked rapidly. Loneliness squeezed her heart. Despair. The inescapable fear that the cycle kept repeating and she was stuck in a whirlpool. She hunched in on herself.

"Nova," Leaf prompted. "Sit up straight and answer me."

"You said Nero was from the old world. That he was like me. How long... how long has he been in this time?"

"We're unsure. We only learned of his existence when Clarke arrived at the Order about two decades ago. Nero has been using stolen mana to keep himself young."

"What does he look like?" she asked quietly, toying with the horse's mane.

"Tall, dark hair, Roman nose... similar complexion to yours... maybe a touch colder. Why?"

That sick feeling came back.

Her twin's harsh face flashed in her mind. Then, his behavior at the end. After their parents died, he returned to Mexico and reconnected with the family they were told never to speak with—the criminals her parents sacrificed everything to escape.

At first, Niles returned to LA and shared their traditional Sunday meals without their parents. But the meals inevitably turned into arguments whenever conversation touched their opposing values about the state of the world. She had hoped humanity could still change enough to save the environment. He said they would inevitably run it into the ground, and everyone would die.

She always put their unrest down to polarizing political views. Every family had opposing opinions. Why would hers be any different?

"Nova?"

She couldn't answer. Her mind was too far in the past, thinking of the night she told Niles to leave and never return.

"I don't even know who you are anymore!" She threw a plate at his head.

He ducked as the china smashed on the floral wallpaper.

Scowling, he jabbed his finger at her. "This planet is dying anyway."

He always knew how to hurt her the most. Her gaze dropped to the cartel tattoo peeking from his expensive suit sleeve. That was why her mother hated Nova's attempts to reconnect with her culture—she was afraid it would draw attention from people who wanted them dead.

She used to hate how Niles pushed her buttons and backpedaled to make up for it, almost as if he toyed with her emotions to see how far he could take it. At least now he wasn't confusing her with false kindness. He wasn't pretending to care about her feelings.

"Not if I can help it." She lifted her chin. She would never stop fighting for what she believed in. And the world was a worthy cause. Humanity was a worthy cause. "I'm not going to stop trying."

He suddenly calmed, like a shark coasting in water. His following words were devoid of emotion. "Have you ever wondered why fire exists? The First Nations people used to set fires before they moved to another location. First, they pillaged and violated the land for resources. Then they burned it to the ground."

She scoffed. "They did that to avoid wildfires in summer."

"They burned it down so that new life would spring from the ashes." He shook his head. "This practice has been alive since the dawn of our species."

"We're evolved. Fires can now be stopped by"—she pointed to her fingers, counting the ways—"water bombs. Oxygen deprivation. Extinguishers."

"Enough!" His expression turned deadly. "Your ideals will kill you. This world is unsalvageable—kindling. I'd rather control the burn."

"What the fuck are you talking about?"

"Very soon, you'll see that I'm right. But it will be too late. Even if you grovel at my feet, I don't care anymore. You had your chance."

"You think you're right?" she gasped, outraged. "¡Ay, qué menso! You're mad! Insane. How we ever shared a womb is beyond me."

Ice entered his gaze. "I should have eaten you like I did the other one."

There had been triplets growing in their mother.

Maybe something had always been wrong with him, from his dark obsession with cruel historical rulers to his unbending opinions and threats.

A conniving glimmer entered his eyes. She would never have placed it without thinking about how he threatened Jace. Nova remembered walking in on the two arguing, seeing Jace's wounded expression, then Nile's calculated triumph as Jace told her they couldn't be together.

She narrowed her eyes on her twin. "What have you done?"

He tugged his sleeves down and shrugged.

"I did what I always said I would do." His emotionless eyes were at odds with his words. "I beat you. I'll always beat you."

"I didn't realize we were competing."

"We've competed since we were born." His lip curled. "In the womb,

for our parents' love, at school, at friendship. You always seemed to win. But I've been playing the long game, Nova."

Who was this man?

"You know..." He sighed as though this conversation bored him. "I came here to tie up loose ends. You're the only one alive who knows everything. I thought you were my greatest chess opponent, but I see now that I've been playing with a pigeon. In hindsight, I overestimated you. Using you would have been easier than creating another linked energy source, but..." Another sigh. "Let's just say things turned out for the better."

He left the dining room.

"Come back here and explain yourself," she shouted. "Niles!"

But he strolled to the front door, passing the family pictures in the hall without stopping. He opened the front door, stepped into the rain, and looked at the coming storm as though the sun shone on his face.

"I always thought that name sounded weak." Disgust oozed from his tone. "They gave you a beautiful, powerful name. Nova—like a bursting star. I used to obsess over it. Why? Why would they stack the odds against me? Then I realized... the other side of a nova is the black hole it creates in its wake—the Void."

He stared at Nova until she shuddered. The evil wrongness of his soul poured into hers. They'd always had a twin connection and a sense of what the other was feeling or where they were. She often guessed his passwords because of it. But this evil—this was new.

No... not new. Just revealed.

There was no joke in his eyes. No humor. This was the real Niles, and he was right. She was as clueless as a pigeon knocking over chess pieces, not even understanding their game.

She snarled, "Mama and Papa would be ashamed of this man you have become."

"Lucky then, isn't it?" His gaze turned cruel. "Lucky they both died at the same time."

Coming back to herself, Nova frowned. She'd always thought it lucky that her parents died together in their sleep. She told herself it was love. They couldn't bear to be separated, and their broken hearts ended in tandem. But she also thought it was odd that Niles immediately left to reconnect with their criminal relations.

What if he killed their parents to prove his loyalty...

Nova retched, covered her mouth, and then did it again—away from Leaf's side. She fell from the horse and tumbled onto the sandy riverbank. Her hands shot out to break her fall. Her bones jarred as she braced, coughing and choking. Dismay and dread crashed into her, causing her diaphragm to heave, but there was nothing in her stomach.

Empty.

Just like her brother's eyes.

She wilted. Sobbed. A warm hand slipped around her forehead, preventing her face from hitting the ground. Leaf grabbed her chin and forced her to face him. No comfort this time. No concern.

Tired blue eyes flashed with a warning. "Start talking."

"Not you, too," she rasped. "Please don't be cruel. Please don't hurt me. I can't... I can't..."

Leaf's breath hitched. He let go and stood back. "Tell me what the fuck is happening. I'm too tired for this shit."

"You're a bastard."

"Yes."

At least he didn't deny it. She sat back, wiped her nose, and the absurdity of her situation caused hysterical laughter to bubble out.

"How did I get here? With an angry man who looks like someone I loved. With..."

She stopped, about to reveal everything about her brother. Some kind of misplaced loyalty tested her heart. It forced her to consider if Niles was the one she should run to for help. But the instant the idea hit, her heart revolted.

Niles was sick in the head. Always had been, and she'd been too weak to face the truth.

"He always had a morbid fascination with the Roman emperor Nero," she mumbled. "He wrote school papers on him that disturbed the teachers. How did I not see the signs?"

Leaf tensed. "You knew Nero?"

"That wasn't always his name. Looks like he changed it after all." She took a deep breath to steel herself for the rest. "He thought I was his competition. I don't understand. Did I *challenge* him? Did I say something to make him believe that I hated him? I just can't... I can't understand how he thought we were in a *race*. Would he have picked this path of vengeance if it wasn't for my stupid morals?"

"Nova!"

Leaf's harsh tone snapped her back from the edge of hysteria. She faced him, saw the confusion and danger in his eyes, and knew with surety that Jace was nowhere in that mind of his. Even if she could somehow explain the elven ears, the personality was different beneath all that similarity.

He'd have come to the same horrible conclusion if he was.

"I think Nero is my twin." Her voice sounded robotic. "And I think he destroyed my world."

Leaf's expression blanked.

Stupid woman. You just told a deadly warrior that your twin is the man who bombed the world.

But she couldn't run.

Nova had always pushed back against Niles. She took naysayers and used positivity against them. She supposed defiance was something she shared with her brother. Only he created negativity. She challenged it.

"My brother was a calculated man," she explained, feeling her strength seep back into her bones. "He always said the only way this world would prosper was if it was small enough for one person to rule. We argued semantics all the time. I thought he was pushing my buttons, making me furious by challenging my views. But all this time, he was testing... making a plan. I couldn't see it then, but I see it now."

"See what?"

Nova stood and brushed sand from her knees.

She met Leaf's eyes. "He didn't reveal the true depths of his psychopathy until days before the end. But I remember him faking facial expressions in the mirror when we were children. I remember him playing poker, losing money for rounds until he was almost broke—all so he could study his opponents. But he'd win it all back, and then some. Niles *always* had an ace up his sleeve." Her voice quietened. "And I somehow guessed every time."

"I don't know what you're talking about." Confusion hit the Guardian's achingly familiar blue eyes.

"The day before the first bomb dropped, my brother visited me. We had dinner. We argued. And then he boasted about winning a race I didn't know we were in." She grabbed Leaf's collar and tried to shake him. "He was so smug, so sure that I would come running to him, begging for forgiveness. But all I wanted to do was find you —I mean, find Jace. He was the only person I thought of when the world ended." Tears glimmered in her eyes as she studied the face of her friend. She punched him on the chest. "Why can't you be him?"

Leaf stepped back. "Because I was born... not thousands of years ago."

"You don't know when you were born?"

"The point is, I can't be him. The sooner you stop hoping I am, the better." Leaf's cold calculation returned. He continued as though he hadn't just crushed her heart. "So you believe Nero destroyed the world because of a vendetta against you? Because he couldn't beat you in games?"

"I might enjoy strutting around in a bikini, but I'm not that conceited. It might have started that way, but he soon realized that if he could manipulate me in other ways, my family, friends, and Jace... Eventually, he manipulated the world. Even though it feels like months to me, I've probably been gone from Nile's life for decades from the sounds of how long 'Nero' has been here. He's moved onto the next obstacle."

"Ruling everyone."

A sad smile stretched her lips. "It's ironic that he thinks winning these so-called races will fill the gaping void in his soul. But he's a psychopath. He doesn't have that emotional capacity." Her eyes lost focus as the stark reality of their future hit. "You think he's dangerous now, but he was broken from his conception. Just wait until he realizes nothing fills that void. Not even ruling the world."

CHAPTER ELEVEN

Stationed at the door of Queen Maebh's private chambers, Pollock tried not to stare as she paced her library like a dark, veiled wraith. *Sweet-Mighty Moon Goddess*, yes, he tried very hard. He tried even harder not to notice the drool dangling from the demogorgon's split mandibles as he watched the guards.

Patting his sweating jowls, Pollock wondered how he'd lasted three years. He and his co-guard had not seen their queen's face beyond portraits gracing the palace's obsidian hallways. They'd witnessed everything from bloody murder to emotional wailing and cold despair.

Well-damned cousin Dingus. If Pollock ever found his good-for-nothing half-goblin cousin, he'd give him a *what for.* The floater had recommended this job—put in a good word for Pollock. Didn't mention that he would be stuck at this door every waking minute, fearing for his life.

Today, the queen wore black lace from head to toe, including gloves. Sometimes, her pacing stopped, and she would stare at the crackling fireplace for hours. Sometimes, he thought Her Majesty was dead—a petrified statue beneath those veils—but then lace rippled at her mouth, and she continued pacing.

Then there were the books. *Sweet-Mighty Moon Goddess*, don't get him started about the books. Since Pollock commenced his shift this evening, she'd pulled no less than twenty ancient tomes from the shelves.

It was sad if you asked him. Sad because she did something that broke the preservation spells as she flipped through the pages. She would tear them out sometimes, stare at them against the flames, then drop the book, utterly ignorant of all the others decaying on the floor.

Pollock might not be a fan of humanity, but he liked books. Watching historical artifacts wither away made him highly irritated. His queen didn't even see the rotting pages. She kicked the dust left behind as she paced about.

He'd once offered to tidy, to see if he could salvage the knowledge, but she'd hissed at him loudly behind her veil.

He wasn't stupid like his cousin, Dingus. He never asked again.

But today, the frigid air was fraught with tension. It felt like something was about to snap. Or, if he let his mind run off with itself—and he did sometimes because he fancied a tale or two before going to bed—a tear in the world might open beneath them.

Her Majesty was particularly obsessed tonight with locating something. She strode to her war table at the center of her library and stared at the map of Elphyne. One of her generals came once a week, apprised her of progress, and marked out territories he'd claimed or razed in her name. Then he left.

She used to care.

She used to tell him what land or city to destroy next.

But that was before she started searching her library.

A low, guttural growl slipped out of the basking demogorgon. *Oh, sweet Goddess.* It growled at Pollock. He must have scowled or something.

He gripped his spear to stop his fingers from trembling and made his expression clear. When the demogorgon relaxed and blinked at his queen, she pulled another book from the shelf, searched through the pages, snarled, and tossed it—already forgotten as she pulled another. Pollock's colleague held his vacant stare at the air and shrugged.

"Not our place."

The queen gasped. Pollock's gaze shot to her in time to glimpse folded paper tumbling from the pages of a book. She picked it up, unfolded it, and stilled as she read.

"Aleksandra." Her hissed breath puffed the veil.

The Prime of the Order of the Well?

They couldn't see her eyes. Couldn't see her face. But they understood the queen's intent when she strode to the war table, swiped everything from the map, and placed that paper in the center.

She beckoned her pet. Stench bloomed as the nightmarish creature unfolded and slinked to her side. It crept on four legs, trailing tentacled wings through the dusty floor, then sat on its haunches so the queen could scratch beneath its chin.

"I haven't lost everything yet, have I pet?" Her voice was shaky and weak.

The demogorgon clicked in the back of its throat, replying to the queen in that strange language only she understood.

"That's right," she rasped. "She thought to steal my Sluagh. She thought the Well would keep them from me, but I can still command the Wild Hunt. All I must do is lure them to me."

The demogorgon preened and cooed.

She nodded in answer to whatever it had said, then stared at the piece of fallen paper on the table. Her voice grew distant... distracted. "Yes, precious. Go. Hunt. But I am the one who will breathe the last from her body. I will drink the blood from her veins." She tapped her finger on the map. "And I'll do it where it all began."

CHAPTER TWELVE

Nova's confession changed everything. Leaf contemplated his next move while she petted the horse. They were all exhausted, hungry, and thirsty. He wanted to sleep on it, but deciding what to do with her couldn't wait.

From how she violently reacted to her twin being the evil man destroying this world, he believed she was on Elphyne's side, which made things worse. He could have killed her right here and now if she was bad. He already found it hard to walk away from her, but now he'd be stuck with her for some time... at least until he delivered her to the Prime or the Order.

A distraction.

And she wasn't even his mate. No blessing from the Well had sprung between them. Perhaps it was too late for such things now that the taint had warped mana into something that blasted entire troops from existence. Remnants of his release simmered inside his soul, making him hot. He removed his jacket, hoping the cool air helped, but his linen shirt was heavy and scratched at his skin.

Irritation growing, he strode to the horse and pushed past Nova to check the saddle. She took a meek step back but didn't complain. Her very smell sent him to the point of impatience. She needed a bath. So did he. They needed food and water, and... he shut his thoughts down and let go of the saddle.

Usually, he'd stop in and talk with the Prime about this sort of thing. But she was part of the problem. She likely hid in the owl shifter habitat close to the icy wastelands. He'd always known Aleksandra escaped there to avoid conflict. For years, he'd portal about Elphyne, hunting her down when she fled responsibility. She was unaware that he'd discovered her secret hideaway. There was no point ambushing her unless he could fulfill her ultimatum.

Leaf straightened, wide-eyed, as an idea popped into his head. Aleksandra didn't know Nova and he weren't mated. What if...

"What?" Nova asked, noticing he stared at her.

"Earlier, you wanted to thank me for saving your life, but I stopped you."

"I know."

"But there is something you can do to repay me."

"I have nothing to offer. I don't have mana. I don't even have shoes."

"The Prime is the best person to reveal your wealth of knowledge to about your brother." He paused. "I'm assuming you want to stop him from further destroying this world?"

"Of course I do," she exclaimed. "I don't condone *anything* he does. And I know things. I'm sure if I—"

He gestured for her to stop. "No need to go into details now. But if I take you to her, I may as well gain something from this setback."

Her brows lifted at his insinuation, but he was too weary to pretend civility.

"Okay," she said slowly. "And what do you get out of it?"

"The Prime won't reveal important knowledge about my fate until I succumb to her machinations and claim a Well-blessed mate." Irritation clipped his words. "Naturally, it's ridiculous that I should be forced into mating, regardless of what a supposed prophecy says. So I'd like you to continue the ruse of being my mate."

Her jaw clicked shut. She seemed like a clever woman. This shouldn't be a problem. But suspicion and a touch of disgust flickered in her gaze.

"In my time, some people did nice things like rescue innocent women from bad people just because it was right."

"But you wanted to thank me." He frowned, increasingly annoyed. "I stopped you from owing me a favor. Ergo, I did a nice thing without expectations."

"Oh my God," she mumbled, suggesting he was too stubborn to understand the point. "Fine. What will this *ruse* entail?"

"Exactly what it sounds like." Was she making him spell it out?

"No need to get prickly, Mister."

"My name is D'arn Leaf," he corrected.

"I'm simply understanding expectations. For example, how far does this ruse need to go? Who are we fooling—just your Prime or others? Will we need to be physically intimate to convince other fae that I smell like you? Is it just hugging? Do I sit on your lap while you pet me? Am I chained to you while dressed in a bikini? Do we kiss? In case you missed it, I am not fae. I do not understand your customs. So please, *Hoja de los Guardianes,* break it down for me."

Such fire in her eyes... such spark. Leaf's blood heated inexplicably, and he couldn't tell if it was from anger or arousal. They were clearly from different worlds, but the more time he spent with her, the more she challenged him and the more he felt drawn to her. He leaned into her space, enjoying her flinch at his proximity. It wasn't from fear. Well, perhaps a little when she was reminded of his size and strength. But the flinch was quickly followed by a dilation of pupils, a caught breath, and a pleasant flush to her grubby cheeks.

Her attraction to him was wholly refreshing. Most females wilted under his domineering energy. But not her. Perhaps that's why his mouth continued to say stupid things. "Publicly, I expect you to act like you are in love with me—as mates are known to do. I expect you to lie with your wicked human tongue when I cannot. And I expect you to be a good little mate and do as you are told."

"Do as I am told?"

"Obviously, in return, I will continue to protect you. I'll even feed and clothe you." He plucked her dirty, torn dress. "If that includes a Well-damned bikini, I will find it for you. You'll have to look the part if we're to convince the Prime you're my mate."

"Do you even know what a bikini is?"

"You've mentioned it before. It must be your outfit of choice."

Her eye twitched. She stepped forward until her soft breasts clashed with his torso, and it was his turn to catch his breath. From the way his skin tingled, his linen shirt may as well be missing.

Looking up fearlessly, she asked coyly, "And exactly what *acts* do you expect of me, *Papi*?"

His nostrils flared. She kept using her secret language on him, which infuriated him, especially when she annunciated the *P* sarcastically, as though that last word was an insult. *Papi*, as in a pup? Like an infant vampire or wolf? He despised not knowing and refused to lower himself and ask for a translation. Their relationship would end once he delivered her to the Prime and got what he needed. The less he knew about her personally, the better.

"Touch me," he explained dryly. "Smile, kiss, gaze lovingly into my eyes. What the fuck did couples do in your time publicly? Do you require a written list of acceptable behaviors?"

Outrage flushed her complexion. It made her eyes sparkle, her skin luminous, and her lips—his gaze flicked down to them. They were rosy, plump, and extremely biteable. He wondered what she would do if he did that very thing. Indignation became her, and it aroused him.

"Yes," he murmured, imagining how nicely she would clean up. He wiped dirt from her cheek with his thumb. There was a striking face beneath all that mess. "Once you bathe, wipe that sullen look from your face, and dress into something more fitting, I imagine it won't be hard for me to pretend. I might even enjoy kissing you."

In fact... he lowered his lips to hers.

His face jerked to the side. His cheek stung. It took him a moment to understand that she'd slapped him.

"¿Sabes qué, Papi?" She shoved him hard, causing him to stumble. The whites of her eyes made her appear a little unhinged, but again, he desired her even more. She tossed her hands in the air and shouted, *"Quédate ahí con tu 'pretend mating' y déjame en paz."*

"You seem... disturbed."

"No shit. I'm still coming to terms with the fact my world is gone. My brother is an evil tyrant. I almost died. And you look like my friend, but you're a *hijo de puta*—gah!"

She stormed down the riverbank. She had no horse, no food, no weapon, no shoes.

His lips twitched. "Where are you going?"

"¡Vete al diablo!"

"I can't understand you." He rolled his eyes.

"Understand this!" She faced him, flipped up her middle finger, and continued walking.

Laughter burst from his lips. He laughed so hard he spooked the horse. Even when she stomped back as though she was about to chop him into little pieces with that razor-blade glare, he couldn't stop.

He laughed through her absurd attempts at hitting him with her dainty fists, more of her indecipherable Spanish, and the power of a thousand fiery arrows shot from her eyes. All he felt was humor and the underlying desire to throw her over the horse, lift her skirt, and... *It must be the exhaustion.*

"You laugh at my misfortune? *Hijo. De. Puta.*" Nova slapped him on the biceps. "Son. Of. A. Bitch."

She pointed at his face and said... nothing. Her lips flattened. Her complexion went red. Then she pulled her hair and screamed in frustration. Her cape flung from her shoulders when she pivoted away. She tried to straighten it, gave up, and continued walking off in a huff.

A jolt of panic hit Leaf's chest.

"Nova." He jogged after her and spun her to meet his eyes.

Anger often masked vulnerability. She was so alive and confident, yet sad and lonely. He felt it in his bones. He was wrong to laugh at a time like this.

"Kiss me without permission again," she warned, "and I will bite off your tongue. Understood?"

He wanted to say something charming, to erase his earlier assumption. His words never formed. Nothing seemed right. What came out was wholly unexpected.

His gaze dipped to her lips again. "And if I ask permission?"

"To kiss me?" She blinked.

Leaf cleared his throat. "For the ruse."

"The ruse."

His hand burned where it still held her bare arm. His thumb brushed her velvety skin, addicted to how he uncovered something pure under the filth, how he wanted to see more. He let go and clenched his fists, willing them to be civil. It was bad enough that his tongue alienated everyone around him, but he wasn't sure he could live with himself if his actions did the same.

She folded her arms. "So you want to kiss me to test my acting skills?"

His lips parted, surprised. That wasn't exactly what he'd meant. *Well-dammit,* he was a louse at this nonsense. Probably because he was tired, his body gave him mixed signals about this woman, and he needed something from her. None of it made for an appropriate relationship.

"Forget it," he mumbled and gestured at the horse. "I'll—"

She lurched upward, lifting her lips as though coming in for a kiss.

He froze.

But she didn't kiss—not yet. Her velvety lips swiped his, triggering a seismic reaction in his body. He wanted to both close the gap and run away. She licked along the seam of his lips, and a bolt of heat shot straight down to his groin.

He stood stock still as his body made a fool of him. She exhaled, and he shuddered. She touched his jaw, and his lashes fluttered. Small, dainty fingers scraped down his chest and hooked in the waistband of his leather breeches. And he didn't stop her. He allowed her to tug his hips against hers, felt the surprising ache of an erection, and released a guttural moan.

That needy sound was *not* something an elf like him made, especially not with a woman he wanted little to do with. She'd barely touched him, yet his blood was on fire. This was how he'd reacted when he first saw her standing on that log, being pawed at by a shifter.

She'd run from them but had run toward him, right into his arms. And this... this magnetism was hard to deny.

Perhaps this arrangement was a bad idea—the kind of distraction that messed everything up. Breathing hard through his nose, he composed himself. Clearing his throat, he prepared to tell her the new plan—that he'd take her to the Order and continue his mission. But mischief flashed in her eyes, and she suddenly became more feminine. How that was possible, he had no clue. Something about her awareness of her beauty, perhaps. Confidence. Knowing.

She crushed her lips against his.

Fuck.

Fireworks went off in his blood. He cupped her jaw, plunged his tongue between those sweet, juicy lips, and sought hers out. With wet slides and plundering sweeps, he claimed her mouth. Her responding whimper encouraged him to kiss her harder, holding her still to take her mouth as he wanted—with complete and utter possession.

Nova broke away, panting, eyes unfocused and wild. She looked at him with a mix of confusion and... victory.

"I'm not done." He chased her mouth with his own.

She averted her face, taking his kiss on her cheek. He stilled, expecting more dainty fists to flail at him, but she took a step back.

Frowning, he straightened. Had he offended her again? But she'd kissed him first. He hadn't misled her, had he?

Nova stroked the horse's neck, smiling to herself.

"What was that?" he demanded.

"You enjoyed kissing me, even in these *dirty* clothes."

Never had a female schooled him with his own words.

"Fine." His fists flexed. "You made your point. If you agree to this fake relationship, you won't need to dress or do anything differently. You may remain in those tattered clothes forever."

Her gaze snapped to his. "I didn't say that."

"Will you agree to the exchange?" he asked, folding his arms. "If I take you to the Prime, will you pretend to be my mate?"

"Yes."

"Good." He rubbed his eyes. "Good. We should probably find food and make camp... or..."

"I have a demand of my own."

He sighed. "What is it?"

"When I think of it, I'll let you know," she replied with a haughty expression.

How bad could it be? "Agreed. We have a bargain."

He touched her on the arm, but no snap of magic solidified their pact.

"*Papi*, what are you doing?"

"Waiting for our bargain to be enforced by the Well."

"Okay. How long must we wait?"

A grim frown tugged at his brows. He let go and replied, "Perhaps forever."

CHAPTER THIRTEEN

Nova woke at dawn, surrounded by whispering trees and chirping birds. Her body ached from sleeping on the ground. Her stomach felt terrible from all the nuts and wild game eaten over the past four days. And she really, *really* needed a wash. Dirty skin and unwashed clothing made her itch.

Mister Arrogant Leaf of the Guardians refused to stop moving unless they hunted, ate, or slept. He was a machine, never letting go of his goal to ride to this frozen land where his owl-shifter leader concealed herself. She might have pushed his buttons a little too much before agreeing to help him, but she couldn't help it.

He was Jace, but he wasn't. He was pleasant, then he was rude. He couldn't care less, and then he did things like helping her breathe when she felt like vomiting or fixing her oversized cape when she couldn't work out the laces.

It wasn't like he'd forced her to go with him. When she'd called him on it, shame had colored his pointed ears, and they twitched awkwardly. She had the sense not many people called him on his abrupt behavior, or if they had, he didn't care. But something about her made him think twice. It was enough to convince her that she should stay with him, at least until he delivered her to his boss.

Already awake, Leaf was somewhere down by the water, flinging his hand about, trying to make magic circles in the air. He didn't think she knew he was on the riverbank practicing, but she woke every time he left her side. It was a sixth sense. He moved, she knew.

Dusting herself off, she found a quiet place in the trees to relieve herself and heard the distinct sound of a waterfall in the distance. She cocked her head and strained her ears. Yes, cascading water. It was in the opposite direction to the riverbank. That sounded like the perfect place to bathe.

Maybe he wouldn't complain about wasting time if she went now while he practiced.

She had a quick nibble of the foraged nuts, a drink from the waterskin, and collected the soap she'd stolen from the war camp. Leaf's leather satchel lay conspicuously on the ground. He often flipped through that journal but refused to tell her what was inside. He also warned that her hands would blow off if she opened the bag without his permission. So... yeah. She left it alone.

She waved at the trees. "Time to bathe."

They answered by rustling their leaves, and she smiled. Even though she was filthy and stank, being outdoors without anyone harassing her had been nice. It reminded her of home when she'd gone camping or lived out in nature while volunteering with environmentalists. She'd come across so many characters. Some were pompous and rigid in their views, like Leaf. Some were easygoing and so chilled out that she got bored. Having a little fun to brighten the day after strenuous work didn't always go so well. Sometimes, she just wanted to play beach football, build sandcastles, or throw mud pies in someone's face. Jace would always entertain her annoying urges. Niles hated it and said he was encouraging her.

She forced the past out of her mind, but it roared back when she emerged from the forest. She gasped at the picturesque waterfall spilling from the crumbling ruins of Mount Rushmore. The carved face of Abraham Lincoln was overgrown with vines, ferns, and moss. It broke her heart to see time ravage such memories, but it made her feel nostalgic and at peace. A small smile tipped her lips.

Even more interesting was that Leaf worked tirelessly at his magic portals from a flat rock at the base. Maybe he had the same idea as her—but his Guardian uniform was dirty, and he still had a sheen of dust on his face that had started to streak from the water spray running tracks down his angular cheekbones and jaw.

Each time he failed at the portal, his frown deepened. He scratched his thickening jaw scruff and then shook his limbs out with irritation. The familiar mannerism washed melancholy over her soul.

She'd caught Jace once in his beach house's kitchen attempting to work the fancy blender his mother had bought. Having just arrived from a surf, his wetsuit was peeled halfway to the waist. Wet hair fell over his handsome, brooding face and dripped all over the floor. Nostrils flared with determination, he'd put the blender down and shook his limbs as if shaking off the failure. But it never worked. His shoulders would droop and hunch inward. When Jace thought no one watched, his vulnerability was there for all to see.

Nova watched Leaf as the memory took hold.

"What did the blender do?" she teased, pushing off the doorframe and walking into the kitchen.

Jace glanced at her, surprised. "Nova."

She leaned on the counter separating them and rested her chin in her hand. "Hello, Jace."

He hid the blender behind his back. The action pulled his abdomen taut. Every muscle in his God-given body flexed. He'd grown so much since they'd last seen each other. It would be torture waking up to this every day while on vacation. But Niles would be the third wheel if she acted on her feelings for Jace. And he was a miserable son-of-a-bitch when he felt left out.

But Nova could look. And she could admire.

"I didn't realize you were already here," he mumbled sheepishly. "Thought you and Niles weren't arriving until next week."

"I finished exams early." She'd actually failed and left early, but Jace didn't need to know that. Her parents had given her enough grief over it. Anyway, Nova planned to spend her life helping third-world countries clean up their poor waste systems. What use was an education?

"Oh." His ears turned pink.

"Niles has a few more exams, then he'll be here."

"That's good."

They stared at each other. It had been nine months since Jace transferred to a fancy school, and his smile was still as heartbreaking as the day he became her neighbor ten years ago. She'd watched him pull up in his family station wagon and had waved through the attic window. He'd caught her movement, and those sad, baby-blue eyes burned bright. He'd grinned.

"I mean... it's good that he's almost done." He gave a self-deprecating laugh, shaking his wet hair.

She was surprised the school hadn't forced him to cut the long sun-bleached locks. But, she guessed having a father who donated enough to build a new gymnasium helped.

Nova allowed herself an indulgent moment to admire his changes. He'd gained another inch in height. Despite his lack of surfing opportunities on the east coast, his shoulders seemed broader and more muscular. He must have picked up another sport. Maybe swimming.

"You look good," she said. What she wanted to say was, I missed you.

His eyes softened. He placed the blender on the counter and walked around to her side. Probably to swoop her into an enormous, brotherly hug. She considered remaining on her elbow, her spine curved, her shapely bottom on display. But she straightened and propped her hip on the counter. That softness in his eyes smoldered when he noticed she wore a tiny bikini beneath her sheer kaftan.

Yeah. She'd changed, too.

She bought the bikini for this moment—for the longing in his eyes. For the way he swallowed and drank in every inch of her body. The way he held his breath when she slipped past him, brushing her breasts against his bare chest.

"I can help with the blender," she said quickly, suddenly feeling awkward.

He latched onto her hip, stopping her.

Their faces angled to each other, cheek to cheek. His fingers branded her skin with his name. Without looking up, she could tell he was a mess... just like her. His breathing was shallow, haggard. Goosebumps broke out across his golden skin. And then he lowered his lips to her ear and whispered in a deep, husky voice, "I missed you, Estrella."

Every cell in her body begged him to say something else, to rip her top down and lick around her nipple or push his hand down between her legs. But he'd never be so demanding.

"Why do you always call me a star?" She licked her lips. "Because of my name—Nova?"

He hooked a finger beneath her jaw and lifted her gaze to his. Within the fathomless depths of his blue eyes, she found affection... and something deeper.

"No," he'd murmured. "It's because you guide me home."

Nova shook off the memory. It was pointless to think about now. That moment led to their first time together. She'd made the first move, the next, and the next. Eventually, he grew confident and made a few moves, too. His letters were her favorite. They weren't fancy, but heartfelt.

They were two teenagers desperately in love. He was sad and aching under the expectations of his parents. She didn't know it then, but she was also sad. Her brother was already changing. She'd buckled under the pressure of competing with him at school. Arguments in their household were a nightly occurrence. Niles was on his destructive path. Nova and Jace were his first victims.

She blamed Jace for leaving their relationship, but she never fought for him. And when the world ended, and they dared to find each other, it had been too late.

A bird called in the trees, and another answered on the other side of the waterfall. This was a beautiful location. She shouldn't feel so sorry for herself. Not when the world had survived. Tilting her face to the sun, she basked in the warmth. Niles was wrong. The world was not dead. It was here. The sand and river stones beneath her toes were real. *I am alive.*

CHAPTER FOURTEEN

Since they'd begun traveling together, Leaf struggled to sleep with Nova next to him every night. He told her it was better that he remained awake more often to keep watch. Without proximity stones keeping vicious fae from wandering into their camp, one of them had to remain alert. But that was only partly true. The rest was about his inability to relax when she smelled so enticing—he'd even refused to let her bathe in the hope that grime would hide her feminine appeal.

It didn't work.

He'd awoken with a hard cock and remnants of dreams where she took center stage. Then he'd realize what was happening, grow infuriated, and storm off to attempt to make a portal. Stupidly, he kept thinking the exercise would help alleviate his frustration, but failure to use his Well-given gift only made him feel worse.

Each Guardian in the Cadre of Twelve had different magical advantages. The crows and vampires could fly. The wolves had preternatural hearing and smell. But Leaf's value came solely from his deep inner well and ability to cast spells. He'd drawn on more mana than he'd known possible at the war camp. Now, he could barely muster a portal. The uneasy feeling that Clarke was right about finding his mate kept circling, along with the notion that perhaps he'd missed his chance.

Feeling impotent while his cock throbbed from arousal was infuriating. It was worse than finally finding these ruins, searching beneath every rock, and coming up short of Crimson's last journal. Leaf had spent the morning scouring every cave and hidden alcove. Nothing.

Another failure.

These past few days felt like he was running headlong into a nest of vipers while doing nothing but watching his ruin from afar. To be honest, he hadn't felt like himself for years. All this wandering around Elphyne, hunting for something that probably never existed, seemed like his wits had been enchanted. It wasn't him. He'd wasted time, and it was unforgivable.

For fuck's sake. Now, he was being as dramatic as the other Guardians. No, his recent failure wasn't unforgivable. He still believed the solution for the taint was not with the humans who destroyed everything to begin with. He should continue to understand the first fae. Somehow. Clenching his jaw, he ignored the mist itching his face, shook his limbs, and drew mana from his personal well. Energy zipped into his arm, flowed through his veins, and spilled from his fingertips. He weaved the invisible force into a portal.

He envisioned the snowy landscape before Frostwing Village and the boughs of the great icy tree of wisdom peeking over its boundary walls. Ozone and crackling energy filled the air, and a portal opened to a place filled with lush green trees dripping with rain. Shutting his fist, he pinched off his flow of mana. The air turned bitter and then sweet with moss and mist.

Each failure was worse than the last.

The taint was a constant heckler. It slugged around his veins, spitting out wrongness with every drop of mana spilled.

Snarling, he flung his hand and released one last blast, but the energy fizzled and crackled, not even forming the portal despite having plentiful mana to throw at it. An uncouth curse slipped past his lips.

"Can't get it up?"

He jolted at Nova's voice. Turning, he found her standing on the rocks a few feet below him. Her pale, sullied dress hung from her form, a shameful reminder that he'd also failed to procure her better clothes.

He scowled. "If that was your attempt at humor, it failed."

No hate or ill intentions existed in her large, expressive eyes. He exhaled. He shouldn't take out his frustration on her.

"Can I help?" she offered hopefully.

"No."

"You seem tense." She flicked her long hair over her shoulder. "Why don't you join me in the lagoon? It's perfect for bathing. Lord knows you need a break before we head out again."

Soon, they would be on their way. They would stop to hunt or forage in the afternoon, then ride again before finding a camp for the night and eating leftovers. He reluctantly admitted Nova had a knack for making a bland meal delicious. Usually, by now, he'd be itching to visit a local tavern for a good hearty stew. But they saved time with her culinary skills, keeping them on track.

"Perhaps," he admitted.

"Now, who's the sullen one?"

Still grumbling, he stalked back through the woods to their camp and collected their belongings. He checked to see if his satchel had been touched, but it was intact—as were her hands, which meant she continued to heed his warning about the protection spell.

Leading the horse, he returned to collect Nova. A flash of skin in his periphery stopped him dead in his tracks. The horse bumped into him with a snort of annoyance. But Leaf was rooted to the spot, watching Nova's naked, curved bottom flex as she walked toward the water. How was it possible something so natural could be so enthralling?

Logically, two muscles were pulling to move legs, but his eyes weren't just seeing muscle. He saw the dimples winking, the softness of shape, the way her flesh bounced as though each step was a dance.

It wasn't until she was half submerged and wading toward the waterfall that he caught himself ogling.

Slamming his brows down, he turned his back and faced the forest. He couldn't afford this *thing* happening to his body. That kiss a few days ago was bad enough. This should be a partnership of convenience. Feelings made things messy. They caused duty to take a back seat. Look what happened with the mated guardians!

Not that he had feelings.

He had a cock. That's all. He wasn't immune to a beautiful,

naked woman walking before him. That was the only reason he'd forgotten what he was doing. What had he been doing?

Tying the horse. Collecting her for the journey.

Fuck.

Grumbling to himself, Leaf traveled farther down the riverbank, away from the waterfall, and looped the reins around a tree. But not too far. He needed to hear if anything went wrong. Or if prying eyes stumbled across them. The intrusive thought prompted him to scour their surroundings for intruders.

"Are you not coming in, *Hoja de los Guardianes*?" Her voice held a hint of tease, as though she knew she affected him.

"I'll wait until you're done," he shouted back.

"I didn't think you were a prude."

She splashed around as though having the time of her life.

A prude?

His brows lifted, rising to the challenge. His lips curved as he removed his jacket, then reached over his neck and tugged his undershirt clean off his body. But he stopped short of giving her the satisfaction of seeing him hurry. He folded his clothes neatly, put them next to his bag, then did the same for his breeches.

He strode into the water, ignored the cold temperature, and dove. When he broke for air, a tiny projectile flew at his head. He caught it and opened his palm—soap.

"You smell!" she called, grinning from ear to ear.

He lathered his torso and raised his brows. "You have no problem with invading privacy, do you?"

She shrugged, quite happily watching him scrub. "I figured we should probably start practicing these mately rituals."

His skin buzzed under her attention, and his blood heated as their gazes clashed.

"Mately is not a word." He turned his back on her.

"My God, are all fae such killjoys? In my time, women would parade around the beach wearing nothing but a string covering their tits and ass. It was too hot to be shy." He glanced over his shoulder to find her smiling wistfully at the sky. "I had the tiniest little two-piece. It was so revealing. It made all the boys wild. My biggest worry then was what to tell my mother about my failed exams. Such simple times, no?"

Leaf pictured Nova wearing such an outfit as she described. Then he imagined her walking out of the sparkling ocean, water sluicing down her sun-kissed skin, forging paths around all her curves, especially in the crack between her mesmerizing bottom cheeks.

He attacked his hair with soap and vigor, scrubbing hard. Feminine hands landed on his shoulders and tugged him backward.

He resisted, tensing. "What are you doing?"

"Relax, grumpy. I'm taking you to your shower."

Another moment of hesitation hit him, then he relaxed. With soap falling in his eyes, he had to trust her. The roaring waterfall grew louder. Nova squealed as the cascade hit them, laughed, and left. A deluge pelted his head and shoulders. He wasn't sure what she tried to accomplish, but he felt at home. He tilted his face, washed the soap, and enjoyed the therapeutic massage of water hammering knots in his shoulders.

He much preferred the muffled solace here to his responsibilities and failures. His mind returned to the image of Nova walking out of the ocean in his dreams. Then he had the odd sensation of floating, drifting on lazy waves, staring at a clear blue sky. With regret, he stepped out of the cascade and was surprised to see Nova waiting with her brows knitted together.

She blurted, "You were there for a while."

"Worried?"

"No." Her brows lowered. "I mean, you're my ride to the Prime. Of course, I was worried. Plus... who else will have a water fight with me?"

Her fingers flicked and splashed him.

"Playing is for children."

"Ugh. You're such a party pooper, *Papi*." She flopped back, submerged until just her face showed, and rolled her eyes at the sky. The angle raised her breasts to the light. The dark shadow of her nipples teased him just beneath the surface. "Just have fun already."

If he didn't leave now, he'd do something he'd regret. Something in the vicinity of those perky, erect nipples and his mouth.

"Fun is a luxury." He swam to shore and strode to the horse. His movements weren't so stiff this time around. The massage had eased the tension from his shoulders. Pity about the stiffness remaining in his cock. But that was why he left the water first.

He was fully clothed and strapping on his baldric as she joined him, also clothed and squeezing out her hair.

"Better?" she asked.

"The water calmed me," he admitted.

She fiddled with the horse's unbuckled saddle. "Jace was like that, too. There was a time when he practically lived in the ocean. I'd hear him drag his surfboard down the path between our houses even before the sun was up. I remember admiring his tenacity to wake up every morning and forgo sleep, but I think he needed to let off steam. His parents put a lot of pressure on him."

And just like that, Leaf's peace evaporated. With a huff, he faced the water. Shaking his head, he forced himself to concentrate on Frostwing, not how she compared him to a dead man. It wasn't her fault. She was still adjusting to Elphyne. It was unfair of him to make her feel uncomfortable. And it was another reminder that he had to keep this relationship professional.

The water had been comforting—the way the Well used to feel. She'd given him that.

She made a sound too much like a sob, and his ribs squeezed. *Well-dammit*, he could not figure out females for the life of him. And it was entirely his fault, not theirs. Feeling foolish for his outburst, he decided he should give her something back. He removed the unbuckled saddle from the horse and softened his voice to say, "Give me your hand."

"Why?" Her eyes were wary, but she offered her palm.

He placed it beneath the horse's throat, then guided her other hand to its back so it faced her toward the beast. He guided her ear to its heart. The horse snuffled.

"There you go," Leaf crooned. "Embrace the horse. Listen to her heart, that's where the truth lies. Let her soothe you."

She flicked him a bashful pout, but he encouraged her to keep at it. A small smile touched her lips after a few minutes of listening to a heartbeat.

Letting his mood sink back to that place of solitude, Leaf instinctively drew from his inner well. He stepped away and thought of Frostwing, of that peace she'd gifted him. Just before he started a portal, Nova's gentle touch landed on his hand. He didn't tell her to leave this time. Instead, he continued to draw on mana and marveled as it flowed out. He knew before the portal opened that it had worked. This time, his expenditure felt different. Clean. Bright. Balanced.

Blue light and sizzling energy crackled and buzzed in a widening circular formation, opening in the middle to display a snowy landscape. A single snowflake drifted in from the other side.

"Well done, *Papi.*" Nova patted his hand.

"If that word means what I think it means—"

She smirked. "It means daddy."

His jaw clicked shut. He was about to say pup, but this was worse.

"You're so bossy," she smirked at his furrowed brow. "It's a good fit."

"Absolutely not." His teeth ground, and he collected the horse. "Let's go. Put on your cloak."

"Yes, *Papi.*"

"Nova," he warned. "I mean it."

"Fine. *Hoja de los Guardianes.* Always with the official names. Sheesh." She tossed her cloak around her shoulders and jogged after him. "But for the record, a term of endearment would make this fake mating thing more believable."

Leaf mounted the horse and offered his hand as he considered her words. Haze called Peaches sweetness. Shade called his mate darling. Even Rush, the brooding shifter, called Clarke princess.

"Not me." He lifted Nova onto the horse.

She settled snuggly between his thighs. "I called my ex Jace, and he called me Estrella—a star. Nova is also a star, but nicknames are far more romantic. Don't you think?"

"Names other than official titles are ridiculous and confusing." He splayed his hand over her stomach and tugged her hard against him. Her squeak of surprise was utterly satisfying. "Any mate of mine would know that."

"What's this for?" She pointed to his hand on her stomach. He usually avoided touching her while they rode.

"We must be physically connected when we enter the portal," he explained, voice deeper than intended. "There's a chance we end up in different locations. And there's a chance you'll fall off vomiting again. Would you prefer I touch you elsewhere?"

She covered his hand. "It's fine."

Nova's hand still covered his as they crossed, and as they rode over a snowy field. The ruse, he reminded himself. That's why he didn't shake her free. The ruse had to look convincing.

CHAPTER
FIFTEEN

Nova shivered beneath her stolen cape and wet hair. She'd have waited to bathe if she knew they were about to enter a cold climate. But Leaf didn't wait for permission, nor did he ask her opinion about his plans.

Thankfully, the moment they passed the portal's electrical field, she saw the habitat less than a mile away. Unfortunately, the crossing made her nauseous. Coupled with the sudden violent shivering, she almost toppled from the horse. Strong arms banded around her, squeezing her tight.

"Won't be long." Leaf's warm breath tickled her cheek.

She tried to nod but shivered instead.

"Tense your muscles."

"What?"

"Do it."

Nova focused on the carved wooden gate a mile away. Clumps

of snow covered the tops of the walls. With her shuddering, everything blurred.

"Tense," Leaf said.

She tightened every muscle.

"Hold." He squeezed his arms around her. "Hold until the trembling calms. Release."

She exhaled and relaxed. She still shivered. And now her nose started to run.

"And again."

Arctic, bone-numbing wind bit into her skin like razors. Nova tensed, holding her breath.

"Spare a thought for the horse," Leaf said dryly. "You'll be fine."

"Worried?" she teased after relaxing again.

He grunted. "It's what a mate would do."

Powdery snow exploded as angels with white feathered wings surrounded them. Nova gasped, bringing in a bolt of icy air at the miraculous sight. Her mother would have dropped to her knees and prayed.

Dressed in pale leather armor burned with intricate patterns, the four soldiers—each with bone-white hair and eyelashes—bared talons and teeth.

"Halt!" barked a male with mahogany skin and pale freckles. Nova's heart pitter-pattered as she took in his strikingly handsome face. His cropped silver hair accentuated gray eyes that reflected the icy landscape. These owl shifters had curved round ears like the crow shifters in Grung's army.

The other guards were two females—one with white afro hair but brown skin and the other as pale as a person with albinism. She might have entirely camouflaged against the snow if it wasn't for the burned patterns on her leather.

The fourth guard stood back with his arms folded and an unimpressed expression. He gestured at Leaf's face and said, "He's a Guardian, Storm."

"I have eyes, Alaric," replied the first male guard—Storm.

Cool name, Nova thought. But then panic filled her when the owl-shifter's lip curled in disgust as he glared at Leaf. The last thing she wanted was to be caught in another fight.

"State your business at Frostwing." Storm took a threatening step forward.

Nova was sure Leaf mumbled the word *imbecile* when he exhaled. But he slid his forearm up from her waist and banded it around her breasts. Was he groping her... now?

"We are cold and seek refuge," Leaf grumbled.

Storm's gaze dipped to the placement of Leaf's hand, then up to Nova's face, where he stared longer than appropriate. Leaf thought so, too, because he emitted a low, breathy growl.

"You're mated?" Storm asked gruffly, his brow rising in disbelief. "A Guardian?"

It finally clicked why Leaf had groped her. He couldn't lie and call them mated, but she could. The ruse began now.

"He's my mate," she confirmed, her teeth chattering uncontrollably.

"And she is freezing," Leaf snapped. "Do not let us remain in the cold longer than necessary."

Storm's gaze narrowed. "Or what?"

"Or I tell the rest of the Order where their leader hides away from responsibility. It won't be long before every Mage and Guardian turns up at your gates needing decisions and guidance."

Each owl shifter stilled. Storm scoffed, unperturbed by the threat.

"Don't deny it," Leaf said. "I know she's here. Tell her D'arn Leaf is here, and he means to talk. Mention my companion if she attempts to leave."

"She's indisposed."

"I don't give a fuck," Leaf muttered. He kicked the horse's flanks and spurred them onward.

White feathered wings beat hard, stirring up wind and snow as the guards gave chase. Storm flew above them so close that Nova could reach up and touch his armored abdomen.

"Do not think to burst in uninvited," Storm shouted down at them.

Leaf remained silent.

The owl shifter sped up and landed, bravely blocking their path.

"I won't repeat it," Storm growled. "She is indisposed."

"Doing what?" Leaf yanked on the reins, pulling them to a stop. "Hiding under her blanket?"

"She's in the middle of the Songs of Remembrance."

"The what?"

"A wake," interjected the pale female as she swooped overhead. "To interrupt now would be disrespectful."

Leaf said, more respectfully this time, "I was not aware someone had died."

"Why would you?" Storm looked down his nose at them. "In Frostwing, we celebrate life *before* death."

"How long will this wake go for?" Leaf asked.

"You have arrived on day three of an eight-day ritual."

"I must wait five more days?"

The owl shifters whispered amongst themselves, which irritated the stalwart Guardian growing impatient behind her. Nova felt his lungs heave with a breath, preparing to release a demand, but Storm stepped forward with an offer.

"You may stay at The Lodge. You may respectfully attend The Offering of Light, The Dance of Silent Flight, The Feast of Nourishment, and the Final Farewell, but you may not attend the Sharing of Wisdom. That is for the owl-shifter community only."

"Trust me, I won't stay longer than I need to," Leaf answered.

"Very well. Follow us."

The guards shadowed them the rest of the way. Nova wanted to be awed by the village's incredible wooden architecture and the glimpse of an enormous luminous tree over the gates, but her inner ears stabbed with pain. Her eyes and nose watered. The cold was too much for her damp body to take.

Once inside the gates, they dismounted, and a guard took the horse. Storm watched closely as Leaf gathered his bag and sword. Leaf put his arm around Nova's shoulders, pulling her in, continuing their pretense. But it wasn't hard for her to act all cuddly. His body was warm and inviting.

How he remained unaffected by this cold shocked her. But she supposed she was used to a warm Californian climate. All the places she'd volunteered at were oceanside. She'd never seen snow before the Fallout.

Nova couldn't stop shivering. It took a further hour of standing in the cold for Leaf to arrange for food and accommodation. By the time they walked over to the wooden Lodge, Nova was well and truly in the throes of the flu. She barely registered Leaf's rumble and payment to someone at their door. She only wanted to remove her freezing clothes and climb beneath the fluffy blankets on the bed in the corner of the quaint bedroom.

Scratch that—she crawled down on the plush rug before the crackling fireplace. *Mmm.* The heat was so good on her skin. Footsteps approached, but her eyes were too heavy to open.

"The bed is large enough for both of us," Leaf grumbled. "No need to make this awkward."

She couldn't stop shivering.

"Nova?"

"Go away. Can't you see I'm coming down with something?"

His knees creaked as he crouched beside her. "Coming down with what?"

"Qué menso." She pouted. "I am sick—unwell. Sore ears. Maybe a cold. Maybe the flu."

Silence stretched. The fire crackled. Nova's pout deepened. She just wanted to sleep and forget about everything.

"You are unwell," he repeated. "As in... a disease of the body? Is this a human affliction?"

"You make it sound so delightful."

More silence.

"I feel your eyes on my face, *Hoja*. Why are you staring? Have you not seen someone get sick before?"

"No."

She opened her heavy eyes, wasn't prepared for the bright firelight, and sneezed. Pain burst in her ears, and she groaned, clutching them.

"Are your wounds not healed?" he asked.

“It’s the insides,” she moaned. “Earache.”

“Inside.”

“Yes!”

“Is it fatal?”

“God, I hope not.”

“How long will it last?”

“Always with the questions.” She shooed him. “Just leave me to die in peace.”

“You said it wasn’t fatal.”

“It’s not. It’s just an expression of… *¿Sabes qué, Papi?* Never mind.”

Leaf hated being unable to use his mana to fix what ailed her. “I will send for a healer.”

“I just need to sleep it off,” she mumbled. “But I wouldn’t say no to lemon-garlic tea.”

“Gahr-lick.” He snorted softly. “Sounds like something a Fee-Lion would do.”

Whatever that was. She snorted but lost the energy to talk. Eventually, Leaf’s footsteps receded, and she fell into a delirium-induced dream stuck somewhere in her memories. Her mother touched her burning forehead and then made her drink a tea her father had prepared. It tasted disgusting, nothing like she used to make. But she gulped it down like a good little girl and slept.

CHAPTER SIXTEEN

After feeding Nova the healer's tea, Leaf redressed her in comfortable cotton nightclothes provided by the Lodge's steward. Despite her groans about remaining close to the fireplace, he carried her to bed. The resident fire sprites watched her warily. He wouldn't be surprised if they hurled embers as a deterrent. He certainly couldn't leave her unattended.

Once settled on the bed, she hugged a pillow and mumbled something.

"What was that?" He kneeled and leaned closer.

She whimpered, then pouted in a way he was becoming accustomed to... but not opposed to. It had never been obnoxious, selfish, or childish. Usually, it preceded a display of her strong spirit.

Leaf studied her face while waiting for an answer. Dark, long lashes left shadows on her cheekbones. He never noticed, but the freckles there reminded him of a constellation, perhaps even a map, like sailors once used to guide their way home. No one sailed much these days. The oceans were fraught with mana-warped monsters from the deep... and uncivilized water fae. He shuddered, grateful that being a Guardian took him nowhere near those uncharted places.

Nova's sigh dislodged a lock of damp hair stuck to her forehead, ruining his view. He traced it with a fingertip and slid it from her face. Then he traced down her soft jawline. Every inch of her skin was like velvet.

She rolled into his touch, mumbling, "Never works, Ma."

"What doesn't?"

"Checking forehead for fever. Stupid old wive's tale."

"Is it?" He pressed the back of his hand to her brow. It burned hot beneath his touch.

Perhaps Nova's mother had been right about something because that certainly didn't feel good.

Fever.

He scratched his scruff-covered jaw. Most humans he'd spent time with in Elphyne were Well-blessed and immune to illness or disease, much like all fae. This immunity was a gift from the Well in return for being good custodians. The only other instance he saw of a human falling indisposed was after a mana drain.

The owl-shifter healer hadn't known much about this affliction but left a tea and went to consult the ancient wisdom stored in their sacred tree. Over the past few years, like most healers in Elphyne, she'd reverted to old-world herbal lore to heal the body without magic. Usually, it revolved around wounds, not illnesses. She had no idea about gahr-lick.

Fluids and rest was her official prescription.

Leaf briefly considered sending a message to Forrest's mate,

Melody. She'd recently relocated human friends from Crystal City to Elphyne. Come to think of it, any Well-blessed woman might know what to do about this fever disease. The Seelie High Queen, Ada, had trained as a fae healer, but she would surely know about old-world ailments.

At any rate, seeking their opinion was impossible from here. He doubted an owl shifter would volunteer to fly across the continent for him.

And Aleksandra was indisposed. He'd asked around. There was, indeed, a living wake in progress. If he interrupted, he risked offending the entire shifter population. Remote communities like this were tight-knit and stalwart in their ways. But he needed Nova in her best condition to fool the Prime with their ruse.

Deciding the rest prescription was good enough, he called for the steward and ordered more food, spiced wine, and dry clothes for himself. His Guardian uniform smelled, but he'd have to wash it himself. Sending it out for laundering was forbidden. Anyone could steal it and use it to impersonate a Guardian. The glowing teardrop mark was impossible to fake, but some imbeciles didn't look that hard.

A sliding wooden door separated a small bathroom from the bed chamber. He washed in the bathtub, shaved, and dressed. Then, he frowned at how snugly the woolen breeches fit his thighs. These owl shifters were lithe creatures. The open tunic provided extra warmth and covered the obscenely fitted shirt.

After washing his uniform in the tub, he hung it to dry near the fire and settled on the upholstered chair to read another entry in Jackson Crimson's journal. Taking a sip of spiced wine, he flipped the pages to find his bookmarked spot. Inadvertently, he flipped too far to the page he and Nova conversed on at the Unseelie war camp.

Already, it seemed like a distant memory.

He read Nova's feminine scrawl: *Let's just do it. Call it an itch scratched. Then we can leave.*

She'd been willing to fuck him in that tent... in front of lecherous ears and prying soldiers. Instead of asking her if she was okay, he'd been too occupied with—*Crimson*. He didn't even check to see if the soldiers had taken liberties with her. His stomach churned at his obvious neglect. Frustrated at himself, he flipped to an entry dated *Eve of Samhain, Year Fourteen-Twelve ANF.*

This time of year is always the hardest. While we no longer call it Halloween, and pumpkins don't exist anymore, I see reminders of Estrella everywhere—from the orange wreaths on doors to the bountiful meals shared at family hearths. When we were younger, she would drag me around the neighborhood to go trick-or-treating. She always dressed as a witch. Every damn time. Her brother liked to be the scariest serial killer around. I wasn't supposed to go. "It lowered the tone," my parents used to say. But I snuck out, and she had something for me to wear, even if it was a simple painted skull on my face.

Leaf glanced up. Frost left crystalline lace on the window glass. Sunset wasn't due for a few more turns of the hourglass, and it snowed outside.

Usually, he skipped reading the parts of Crimson's journal about this woman he'd lost, but something drew Leaf's gaze back to the words. He sipped his wine and continued to read.

Aleksandra already forgets these little details. Maebh is too invested in old Celtic folklore from her found books. This is why we have to call it Samhain now. We humored her desire to rename this world, but I worry it's now an obsession. Everything needs new, ancient names. And I get it. Pain—great pain—comes from great losses. They hurt deeply for who they lost. Whoever said it gets easier over time lied. I also lost. I also hurt. Just because mine is...

The point is that erasing history isn't the answer. We should remember our mistakes. We should honor those we lost by building a better world.

Sometimes at night, when I stare at the unchanged stars, I think of her and fantasize about what she would say if she learned I continued her crusade... even though I wasn't strong enough to fight for her back then.

She'd been right.

I should have listened to her. We should have all listened to her.

Leaf woke with a stiff back from dozing on the armchair by the fire. *Too much wine.*

The fire sprites snoozed too.

"Hey," he grumbled and dropped some kindling on the smoldering embers. The tiny elemental beings squeaked in fright, jumped up, and hopped about looking for danger. Upon seeing it was him, one shook its tiny flame fist. He put another log on. Sparks flew through the stone chimney. "Do your Well-damned job and I wouldn't have to now, would I."

Realizing they couldn't add the wood themselves, he gave a self-disparaging shake of his head. He ignored the squeaking tirade and settled back for another nap. Sleep was good. He detested being on the road for so long. It was just another reason he needed to find the full prophecy. Fixing the taint was surely rooted in Crimson's history.

More entries in his journal pointed to Maebh's obsession with old-world folklore. And if she'd found the way to summon the Sluagh from one of these books, perhaps the secret of unmaking her was also in one. It was unlikely she'd simply let him walk into her private chambers to scour her collection.

Nova's moan jackknifed him up. Adrenaline shot into his system. Wiping his face, he crossed the small suite. A moonbeam filtered through the window, landing on her sweaty face. Her bedding and clothes were drenched as though she'd slept in the rain. He tested the temperature of her forehead and found it burning.

"Jace?" she mumbled.

He opened his mouth to deny it but didn't want to add to the agony crumpling her face.

"Yes," he whispered, lowering to her level. "I'm here."

A sob tore out of her lips. Leaf flinched as fluid leaked from her eyes and nose. He should probably get her something to wipe it. Humans leaked a lot more than fae.

But when he moved, Nova clutched his hand, holding it to her heart. "Thank God it's you," she croaked. "I had the worst dream. Niles ruined *everything*. The world was dead. And you were mean—*so* mean to me."

Her eyes squeezed shut, and more fluids leaked. Leaf didn't know what to do. He was at a loss for words. But the time for respecting Aleksandra's ceremony was long past. Surely she would understand if he interrupted her for this.

He pulled away, but Nova refused to let go. "Don't leave me again."

Again? His brows lowered.

"I won't." He held the tea to her lips. "Drink."

"Don't want to." She averted her face.

Leaf's lips flattened. He tugged free from her hold, found a towel, and wiped her face, then held her jaw and pressed the cup to her lips. "You must drink. It will help you heal."

Her face went slack, and panic sliced through him. He shook her awake, but she struggled to rouse. His mind raced, trying to think of a way to capture her attention. What was that term her friend had called her?

"*Estrella*, drink for me."

That's the word, wasn't it? He suddenly straightened and glanced at the open journal. Shit. Fuck. Didn't he just read that word there too?

Nova groaned, albeit ungratefully, and parted her cracked lips. After a few gulps, she'd had enough and fell back into delirium. But not before she took his hand and begged him not to leave again.

"I won't," he replied, unease churning in his stomach.

"Good." She sighed, drifting off. "Last time it broke my heart."

LEAF POUNDED his fist on the Prime's door. The porcelain number eight rattled against the wood, but he cared little about waking the Lodge's other guests. Owls were often nocturnal. They would survive.

"I know you're in there, Prime!" he bellowed. "Open the door, or I'll—"

The door opened to Aleksandra bathed in shadow. Her white hair and feathered wings appeared gray. The pale woolen robe looked ceremonial, but she didn't mention it.

"D'arn Leaf." Annoyance flashed in her eyes. "I was wondering when you'd turn up. I'm surprised it took you so long."

"I need your help." He also needed answers about Crimson, but Nova came first.

"What's new?" She rolled her eyes in a very un-Prime-like way.

Leaf's eyes narrowed, and he forced himself to reassess her. Outwardly, she appeared the same. Her ageless brown skin was smooth. White lashes surrounded her wide, dark eyes. And that haughty chin never failed to jut out. But something in those eyes stopped him. Usually, they were cold and empty. Tonight, they were full of sadness.

Questions later.

"Nova is unwell," he barked.

"Your mate?"

"Why else would I be here? She suffers from a human affliction of something called fever." Aleksandra's gaze softened at his words. He forced himself to relax. "Perhaps you know what to do since it's an old-world disease."

"Oh, D'arn. If she's ill, you've waited too long, and the Well no longer blesses her."

"Don't blame this on me." His ire rose swiftly in his defense.

"Take me to her."

Leaf strode through the Lodge hallways, heedless of eyes peeking through door cracks. He did not stop until he barged into his room. Aleksandra followed and immediately gasped.

"Why is it so hot in here?" White feathers rustled as she rushed to the window and opened it.

A blast of icy air bounced her ringlets.

"It's freezing out there." Leaf gestured brashly. "She is not like us."

"Fool." The word was for him, but her eyes were on the woman in the bed. "She has a fever. Heat will make it worse."

"The cold has done this to her. It's preposterous to think that it can fix her."

"Stubborn mule, isn't he?" Aleksandra spoke to Nova as though Leaf wasn't standing there, looming over them.

Nova roused briefly and chuckled. "Jace is a typical man."

Aleksandra's eyes slid to Leaf. She raised her white eyebrows.

"She thinks I look like someone she knew," he mumbled quickly, then shook his head. "And I want to speak to you about that. But first, she needs attention. Cold won't be the solution if it is the cause."

The Prime pressed her palm to Nova's forehead, much like Leaf had done. Keen to prove he knew *something*, he said, "I already know she is hot to the touch. It's how they tell if someone has a fever."

"You knew to check for her temperature, yet kept the room like an oven?"

Her words squashed his pride. No one in the world could do that except her, and he couldn't understand why she had this power over him. For all the expectations Aleksandra tossed at Leaf, she also gave him more wiggle room to do as he pleased. It stood to reason that he shouldn't always feel so... inadequate around her.

But since Nova's arrival, he had done that all on his own.

"A fever," she explained, "is when the body's inner temperature increases from an infection. If it gets too hot, she will die. Helping her body cool down will aid temperature regulation. Hopefully."

Leaf folded his arms. "What would you have me do?"

"Run a cold bath." Aleksandra's brows puckered as she felt the damp night clothes. "And get her out of these wet clothes."

"That's it?"

"It will help. Administer more fluids and rest. Ah. The poor thing." She maternally caressed Nova's face. Leaf had never seen the Prime like this. Not only was she recalling ancient memories, but she was full of compassion. "If aspirin were a thing in this time, I'd find her some. The drug was derived from an herb, but I don't recall which. Not many people knew. The local healer does have a vast library. She might be able to help."

"She's already provided tea. So... Nova will live?"

The stoic owl shifter tucked in her wings before meeting his eyes. "Almost certainly. A young, healthy woman usually outlasts the flu. Although... the germs in this time could be vastly different. And unforeseen complications are always a possibility. Without pure mana to harness—" She shot Leaf a reprehensible look. "We will have to wait and see. If you cool her temperature and her fever doesn't break by morning, I'm unsure what else to do. Can you feel if she's distressed through your mating bond?"

Leaf tensed. "I can't tell anything in this state."

"Hmm."

"How cold should I run the bath?" He pushed past her to access the bathroom.

At least these shifters had plumbed water, and most establishments in cold Elphyne climates had the pipes spelled to withstand freezing temperatures. The spell would hold for years like his satchel if it weren't broken.

Heating was another convenience of mana that would disappear if the taint wasn't cleansed. Heat-filled mana stones were already few and far between. Grumbling to himself, he turned on the faucet.

"How cold?" he repeated.

"*Cold.*"

Right. Because that's a good explanation. From the rustling coming through the bathroom doorway, it sounded like she moved about. *Better not be spying on my belongings.* But if she lost her hands, he'd soon find out.

"And the temperature of the room?" He held his hand in the running water. It was as cold as it would get.

"You can close the window after her bath. Instruct the sprites to keep the blaze to a minimum."

He searched the bathroom cupboards for salts to put in the water. Perhaps... he opened the cupboards and found fresh towels and paper for the flushing latrine. Maybe adding anything to the water was a bad idea. He should ask the Prime. He'd been wrong about everything else, after all.

Watching the water fill, he suddenly felt an acute kinship with Crimson, lamenting his failures. It seemed the harder Leaf tried, the bigger the mess he made. But he wasn't the type to give up. Unlike Crimson, the thought of entering the ceremonial lake a second time made his skin crawl.

Unease prickled his skin again, almost like déjà vu. The tub was nearly full, so he turned off the faucet, rolled up his sleeves, and returned to the bedroom—time to ask some questions.

The Prime had left. But she'd stripped the sheets from the bed and replaced them with dry ones. Leaf scowled at the closed door. A steward or a guard must have been outside, waiting for direction from the influential Prime of the Order of the Well. She was likely a guest of honor in these ceremonies, hence the robe. Before he could ponder more, Nova whimpered and shivered. Her clothes were still damp, and with the frigid air blowing in, likely freezing against her skin.

But wasn't that needed?

"Aleksandra better be right about this," he grumbled, scooping her into his arms. Shockingly, she was still hot to the touch. He submerged them both in the tub water, fully clothed.

"Jace!" she exclaimed and tried to scramble out.

"Shh." He tightened his embrace. "You must cool down, Estrella."

It was shocking how easy it was for him to use that name. And every time he noticed it, that unease grew in his gut. He knew what it was but refused to admit it.

She groaned and rolled into him, pressing her cheek against his chest, panting with the effort to breathe. He detected a slight rattle in her chest, and the crease between her brows hadn't left.

"I don't like being sick," she mumbled.

That familiar sense of unease swirled in his gut.

Should he have searched for Nova when Clarke first told him where to look? But she had only thawed a few months ago. Surely, that meant fate waited for him regardless. Or maybe he'd have found her encased in ice. Maybe he'd have melted the prison with mana because... because there was little taint to worry about back then.

Maybe she'd have helped avoid this entire war.

After the bath, he slipped a dry nightgown over her head, closed the window, and settled beneath the blankets beside her. He wanted to monitor her breathing—to ensure it stayed regular. The rattle was still there, but the crease between her brows was almost gone, and her skin no longer burned as though a fire pumped through her veins.

He'd ask the Prime tomorrow about his suspicions. Tonight, he'd ignore them. They were likely him overthinking things. Besides, once one answer was revealed, he sensed the rest would unravel like wool on a spool, making a further mess of his life. But—he yawned—he'd figure it out tomorrow.

CHAPTER SEVENTEEN

Nova opened her eyes and blinked at the ornately carved wooden door across the room. Where was she? What happened? Was this a hotel room? It certainly wasn't a forest floor.

An empty earthenware mug was beside her on a table. It smelled bitter. She licked her lips, almost tasting the scent, and scrunched her nose with a shudder.

The last thing she remembered was the waterfall... then the portal and riding into the snow. Oh yes, then there was the freezing temperature on her wet hair and ears—she touched her ears. They'd hurt and... and she caught a cold... or a flu.

It all came back to her. This was the Lodge where that hot guard had taken them. What was his name? Storm. She gathered the warm blanket to her chest and sat up to see the room better.

Wooden beams crisscrossed over the ceiling, a small fire crackled in the fireplace, and a nude Guardian elf slept beside her.

Leaf snoozed with one hand behind his head and the other... her gaze swept slowly down his sculpted body, landing on all the mouthwatering places she shouldn't be staring at. His stretched pose pulled the skin taut over muscle, reminding her in great detail of the strength he possessed. Her pulse quickened as she followed the path of his arm lower... down past his abdomen, all the way to a suggestive long bulge beneath the blanket.

She sat up suddenly, intending to give him privacy, but accidentally pulled the blanket from his hips.

"*¡Ay Dios!*" she mumbled. Blood rushed to her cheeks when she saw the long, thick, hard appendage he gripped in his fist.

She turned away so fast that she accidentally pulled more of the blanket from his body. Oh no. *¡Estúpido!* She tried to put it back, but his blue eyes popped open and speared her to the spot.

"Nova?" His voice was rough with sleep.

She covered her eyes and cringed. "Yes?"

A few more excruciating heartbeats passed before he jackknifed up and pulled her hands from her face.

"Are you still afflicted with the fever disease?" He pressed his hand to her forehead and frowned in concentration. "Seems cooler." He pressed his elven ear to her chest and demanded, "Breathe."

"Um. Okay." She inhaled, felt a slight rattle, and covered her mouth to cough. Memories of the night hit her hard and fast. Leaf had cared for her. He'd fed her tea and watched over her... Her brows puckered. Did he put her in a cold bath?

Leaf straightened. "Not nearly as bad. The tea likely helped, or perhaps you're finally transitioning to Well-blessed. I must remember to ask the healer. How do you feel?"

"Tired. Thirsty. A little embarrassed. Probably could do with blowing my nose."

He grunted in approval and slid off the bed to stand. "You had many fluids leaking from your face. I will find you something."

Nova suddenly had a face full of golden glutes. His yawn and stretch popped muscles in his back. Then he stumbled toward the bathroom.

"You slept naked?" she exclaimed, her voice pitched high. "Next to me?"

Holding his...

He shot her an amused look over his shoulder. "You were naked at one point, too."

"What?" she squeaked.

"Why are you upset? I saw it all at the river, anyway."

Her brows slammed down. "So that permits you to sleep beside me with your hand on your junk? While you're naked, and I'm sick. And... and..."

He flashed her an incorrigible grin as he reached the bathroom door. "Even though I went above and beyond the expected duties of a fake mate, the terms of our bargain have not changed."

Her gaze dropped to the still-hard appendage jutting from his groin. He made no attempts at hiding it. Seemed quite proud of it, actually.

"And don't worry." His voice lowered. "I won't ask you to—how did you write it? Ah yes. I won't ask you to scratch my itch. I'm sure I can handle that myself."

He closed the door. Opened and tossed a cloth for her nose, then closed it again. It took her far too long to think of a witty comeback. It had to do with needing cream for his itch, but she wasn't even sure he'd understand the joke. Ultimately, she shouted at the door, "Why are you in such a good mood?"

"I am?" he yelled back.

"Clearly!"

Two seconds later, the door opened, and he wore tight breeches undone at the laces. A smile still twinkled in his eyes, and he shrugged.

"Perhaps it is because you are not dying and can still fulfill your end of our bargain. We will see the Prime tonight, and then I will be on my way and you on yours."

Her mood soured. Of course that's why he'd be in a good mood.

"I need to pee," she grumbled and shoved past him, slamming the door behind her.

"You are much better." His voice carried through the wood. She covered her mortified face as he continued. "For a moment, I thought your fever delirium would overcome you."

Oh, God. What did she say? But for once, Leaf had the decency not to elaborate. She went about her business, washed her face, and looked at herself in the black glass hanging over the sink. It wasn't quite a mirror, but she could see her reflection well enough. She pulled the skin beside her tired eyes, giving herself a facelift before sighing and letting go.

Outside, Leaf handed her a fresh cup of water from a pitcher and made her drink the entire thing.

"I have sent for more tea and a meal to break your fast."

"Just say breakfast."

"Then I will locate the Prime and solidify our plan to speak with her."

"Understood." She sat on the bed.

"You should rest for as long as needed." He clicked his fingers and pointed at the pitcher. "And more fluid."

His good mood remained as he put on a tunic. But her mood was well and truly curdled. This could all be over by the end of the night. Then she'd likely go to the Order of the Well. Without him.

At least other women were there like her. That had to be a good thing. But the more she thought about it, the less positive she felt, and it had nothing to do with meeting other people or helping them understand her brother's motives.

Leaf had made a point of mentioning their bargain would soon end. He'd also made a point that even if aroused, he'd scratch his own itch. But did that mean he was doing it himself? Or did it suggest he intended to seek relief from another source? As in, another woman?

Why was she getting anxious about this?

Their dealings weren't romantic. He made a point to remind her of that time and time again.

"Out of curiosity," she asked Leaf as he strode to the door. "If scratching each other's itches isn't part of the deal, I'm assuming we are free to seek relief from other sources."

Leaf stopped dead in his tracks. He stared at the door for a long, hard minute. Finally, he turned to her with narrowed eyes. "I'm not sure I understand."

"You know," she mumbled, playing with the bedsheet. "I'm saying that I won't keep you from seeking physical companionship with other people. We only need to fake it for the Prime's benefit, right?"

"Yes," he clipped. "Which means in public, as far as anyone knows, we're mated."

"But privately," she stressed. "You should seek out physical companionship if you need it. And the same standard applies to me. We're both adults with needs a fake romance won't meet."

He stared at her, fingers twitching at his side. "I see."

"I mean, we're not *actually* mates. You made it abundantly clear that you're not interested in one."

"I did."

"And you look like someone I used to know, which is very confusing, so—"

"Yes, Nova," he snapped. "No need to harp on about it. If this arrangement is so confusing, let me make something else abundantly clear: Who you fuck in private is your own concern, so long as it does not hinder the success of the ruse."

He slammed the door on his way out.

CHAPTER EIGHTEEN

Nova waited all day for Leaf to return, but he never came. She slept, rested, and ate the food the steward delivered. She bathed, dressed, and tried to communicate with the fire sprites. The grumpy couple ignored her until she fed them kindling and a handful of chestnuts left from her meal. They'd never burned nuts before and had a great old time.

But when that was done, she returned to the bed, staring at the sun setting over the snowy field, wondering if Leaf was getting busy with another woman in private. It would make sense why he was gone so long. She should stop stewing over it because it was none of her business.

Perhaps she should take a page from his book and consider moving on. She felt remarkably better since coming down with the flu. Never in her life had she recovered so quickly.

Leaf had mentioned something about her being Well-blessed,

and perhaps that was why she'd recovered. He'd talked about the other women from her time. She'd never felt connected to the Well, so she had always assumed she was as human as the day she was born. But she'd also worn gold earrings for most of the time since she'd awoken. Could she dare to hope she'd receive the gift of immortality like the others?

Even though her twin was someone so vile?

Part of her was excited to meet these other women. But a part of her wondered, what if she had nothing to offer apart from her history with her brother? What if she imparted all that knowledge, and without any other value, she would become a burden? Wouldn't it be better for everyone if she found somewhere else to live?

Whatever the case, if she sat around and waited for Leaf, she would get nowhere. And she wanted to be armed with as much knowledge as possible before deciding what to do after this deal. Movement outside caught her attention. She tossed the blankets off and ran to the window with delight.

A single, tiny lantern lazily drifted upward. It seemed to come from over the Lodge's roof. Perhaps tonight's ceremony for the wake was in that direction. Didn't Storm say they could attend some of the rituals?

Making a split decision, Nova found a woolen cape and tossed it around her shoulders. Her clothing was more for indoors, and the booties she'd been wearing around the room were simple and unsuitable for snow, but the thought of staying locked in this room while Leaf was out there, potentially scratching his itches, made her feel ill.

"Don't wait up," she said to the sprites.

As Nova walked through the wide hallways of the Lodge, she noticed small architectural details that accommodated creatures with wings. Things like wide doors, and windows that led to balconies from which one could take flight. The seats rarely had high backrests. She supposed they would constrict.

Outside the Lodge, an enormous, pale, glowing tree dwarfed the circular wood-and-stone village at its epicenter. By enormous, she meant skyscraper height. Wow. Her jaw dropped. She almost got a crick in her neck from craning to look up. Maybe it was even the height of the Empire State Building. Okay, maybe not that high, but it felt like it from where she stood. The bark was pale, almost white, and branches supported drooping foliage that belonged on a Weeping Willow, except for the part where tiny turquoise leaves glowed and lazily drifted like anemones in water. The thick boughs provided a canopy over much of the ground buildings, and when she squinted, she noticed the limbs also functioned as rooms. The tree was a village in its own right—or a bustling community center.

Many owl shifters and other fae traveled between the tree by wing or via walkways radiating from the trunk like spokes on a wheel. Situated at three levels up, these platforms led to another walkway surrounding the circular village's boundary. Guards patrolled that one like a battlement, but Nova wasn't sure what they were watching for. As far as Leaf had suggested, this place was remote and rarely visited by outsiders.

Some pale branches were so thick she thought you could easily drive two vehicles across them. Beneath the tree, the market was closed. Most tents, huts, and carts had been cleared. A few straggling merchants tidied up the last of their wares.

Her eyes widened at the thought of a little exploration. This was the perfect—

A wing bumped her as a shifter hurried past and flew up to where more gathered on a bough. Soon, her path forward was filled with fae, and she became caught in the wave as they traveled. It took a concerted effort to extricate herself from the flow and stand back to watch them all wait for an opening to fly up into the tree where more lanterns were lit.

"The view is better from up there," a deep voice said beside her.

Nova glanced to her right, surprised to see Storm. This evening, he wasn't dressed in the white leather battle uniform. His fitted cream shirt was unlaced at the collar, revealing a smooth, muscular chest. His gray trousers were also fitted. She had to admire the fashion, as it accentuated his lithe, athletic body. His feet were bare. Interesting.

Her wide eyes darted back up to his amused gray gaze. Those long white lashes were so striking against his dusky skin.

"We don't feel the cold as other fae do," he explained.

"I didn't mean to stare."

His eyes crinkled. "Your curiosity is understandable. Outsiders are uncommon here, so I'm sure you have questions. Nova, is it?"

She smiled and nodded. "And your name is Storm, right?"

"Yes. It is good to see you looking well."

"It's good to see you out of uniform." At his flirtatious smirk, a wave of embarrassment washed over her. "I mean... not working. Relaxing. It's good to see you're not always working."

He glanced about. "Where is your mate?"

"He's... running an errand."

His brows flicked up. "He left you alone on this glorious night to fumble through foreign customs? Please, if you have questions, it's my pleasure to answer."

"Forgive me if this is rude, but are the lanterns part of the wake?"

"Yes. It's called The Offering of Light. The ritual signifies the beginning of the soul's journey back to the eternal Well."

"Like manabeeze." She smiled, remembering how little balls of energy popped at the time of death and floated into the sky.

"Precisely."

Nova watched avidly, loving how this community smiled as they worked. It was nice to see them coming together to celebrate life, and in a way that respected nature... or did it? What went up must come down. "What happens to the lanterns afterward? Does someone clean them up?"

She certainly hoped so. Balloons and other waste from human recreational activities were a huge problem in the ocean. Storm gave her a quizzical look and said, "I don't think anyone has ever asked me that."

A blush heated her cheeks. That was a stupid thing to say, but she guessed old habits died hard.

"My job used to revolve around the environment," she explained.

"Right. Well, the paper lanterns disintegrate at a certain height. No waste. I could take you up to watch the release?"

"Really?"

"Yes."

But if she was seen with another male, would that hurt their ruse? Probably. She glanced at the handsome shifter and studied him. The contrast of pale freckles against mahogany skin was so striking that she had trouble pulling her gaze away. She'd bet he was never lacking for someone to scratch his itch.

"I'd love that," she replied, "but perhaps another time."

His dark eyes sparkled. "Then I will ask again... another time."

A chorus of eerie hooting rose over the marketplace. Nova glanced up as the lanterns released. Orange glowing lights lazily lifted against the backdrop of turquoise foliage and twilight sky.

"Beautiful," she breathed, awed.

"Yes," he agreed—looking at her. "Like nothing I've seen."

A blush warmed her cheeks. He was obviously into her, and she found him attractive. Storm was the perfect candidate to help her move on with life here in Elphyne. Even if he were a distraction... she wouldn't think about Jace or Leaf for a while. It might give her a clean break—a way to distance her heart.

"I should go," she mumbled, turning toward the Lodge.

"Will I see you tomorrow night?"

She frowned. "I'm not sure. What's tomorrow night?"

Concern flittered over his expression. "Unforeseen circumstances have caused us to shorten the wake's events. The Dance of Silent Flight, the Feast of Nourishment, and the Final Farewell will merge into one spectacular evening."

"If Leaf will be there, so will I."

Storm's concern brewed into something darker. "Your mate will be there, sitting beside the Prime. He didn't mention it to you?"

Dejection swarmed in her blood. She stopped short of saying something she shouldn't. "I look forward to seeing you again."

Leaf might be gone by the end of tomorrow night. Nova had to stop living in the past. She said goodbye to Storm, returned to the Lodge, and headed straight for her room. When she opened the door, her gaze clashed with an angry warrior elf sitting on the bed, waiting with a scowl.

"Where have you been?" he growled.

CHAPTER NINETEEN

When Leaf returned to the room and found it empty, panic had set in. Nova was gone. He'd been short with her this morning and then stormed out. Then she'd left. He'd paced the room for a few minutes, feeling irritated and unable to focus. During the day, he'd tried to locate the Prime multiple times, but all he'd learned were secondhand messages and rumors that she'd be at tomorrow night's sudden change of events.

So he'd spent the day collecting supplies, fulfilling his end of the bargain for Nova, and training with the guards down at their small barracks by their gates. The distraction had been just what he'd needed to cool down, to release the pent-up sexual frustration he'd woken up with. But he'd lost track of time. He realized it was late when the lanterns floated in the sky.

"Where were you?" he asked again.

Her expression dropped. She stared at him from top to toe, no doubt seeing that he'd been training and neglecting his duty here. More guilt bubbled inside him, and he couldn't look her in the eyes.

She shut the door and answered, "I was just outside the Lodge."

"I went out there looking for you."

She scowled, removed her cape, and hung it on the hook behind the door. "I was under the tree, watching the lanterns. Why do you care? You weren't here all day."

Why should he care? Anger tightened his chest. Why *should* he care? The question repeated itself in his head, but he refused to answer, afraid he'd known all along and...

Cutting his thoughts off, he grunted and nodded at the bed. "You should be resting."

"I feel better." She frowned. "Anyway, it was only a few minutes, and I was tired of being stuck here all day."

He shouldn't feel good about that. But knowing she hadn't, in fact, been out there gallivanting around with her curvy body, leaving a trail of drooling males was a relief.

"Well, you'll be happy to know," he said, straightening, "that you won't be stuck with me for much longer. Tomorrow night, we dine with the Prime."

That was why he was in this Well-forsaken place.

Nova strode to the pitcher by the bed and poured herself a glass. Her voice raised as though she forced herself to sound cheerful. "Oh yes, I heard about the changes to the schedule. Something about a flight, a dinner, and the last goodbye. Won't that be awkward? I mean, we don't even know the person dying."

"Who told you that?" His brows lowered. Who had she been speaking with? His mind went to what had occupied hers before he'd left, and his anger surged. "You were careful not to ruin our ruse?"

The cup paused on the way to her lips. She lowered it without taking a sip. "If you're asking if I ran naked and threw myself at the eligible males, I did not. I barely had time to breathe out there. But I did bump into one of the guards. He offered to fly me up to watch the lanterns release from the tree. I politely declined. Is that suitable behavior for a mate?"

He stared at her for a moment longer, knowing he had no reason to be rude, but couldn't help it. "Have something to eat," he said. "Then get some rest. We'll need to be at the top of our game tomorrow night."

Without waiting for another word, he parked himself in the armchair by the fire and pulled Jackson Crimson's journal from his bag.

J.C. — ENTRY 2046 ANF

The Well has always been my companion. She talks to me in sweet whispers, telling me about all the good we can do to rebuild this world, telling me how each soul is a seed with the potential to grow into something magnificent or to wither and rot. But that first kernel of life is always the same. Always fresh and new with a clean slate. Always filled with the possibility of reaching for the stars... or digging down into the ink and spreading darkness.

She sounds like my Estrella. Sometimes I dream it is her whispering sweet promises in my ears, encouraging me to be a better person. Sometimes I dream we're back in that room, locked away in a world where no one could touch us but each other.

But one lesson I've learned in my millennia alive on this planet, from all the people I've seen and the places I've been, to all the souls I've lost who have stolen my heart, and all the enemies who've broken it, is this: Unfulfilled promises are just lies.

Centuries ago, I made her a promise. But I still haven't found her. Does that make me a liar?

CHAPTER TWENTY

Nova let the warm tub water do its thing and relax her. Since she'd argued with Leaf the previous night, she'd remained sullen, and so had he. They'd barely spoken a word. Not wanting to rock the boat, she left him to read the journals he kept obsessing over.

With nothing else to do, she'd fallen into a self-indulgent pattern of dreaming about everything she'd lost and missed. Her hope had been inside one of the lanterns as it drifted into the sky. As the evening approached, she realized she'd been holding it together since she'd awoken. She was about to either lose her mind in grief or enter a manic state of denial.

She was alive, yes.

But she was alone.

The mind often refuses to process grief. When her parents died, she didn't go through their belongings. Their bedroom was exactly how they'd left it when the bombs dropped worldwide. She'd denied her brother's view of the world. Her fight to clean it up had kept her mind busy with purpose... but like everything back then, it had been a lie.

In the bath, enveloped in warmth, she finally let herself think about all that had transpired in the past few months of her life. She'd learned her twin had used his immediate family circle as his training ground, the same way a serial killer might start with a puppy before moving on to people. Niles played with her emotions, killed their parents, and broke up Jace and her. They found their way back to each other, but then the Fallout changed the world. And now, the nail in the coffin was that she was forced to spend time with someone who looked like that missing lover but was the furthest from his personality.

She wondered if Niles was still manipulating events, somehow laughing at fate playing with her heart.

Outside, strong winds buffeted the Lodge walls and shuddered the foundations. Air howled through vents in the ceiling. It sounded so familiar. She tried to dunk beneath the hot water to hide from a memory forced into her mind. But goosebumps broke out on her skin even in the cocoon of warmth.

Nova's pulse quickened. She rose up from the water, gasping for air, but she was not in a warm bathroom. The air was not humid from the steam. Air inexplicably froze, and it hurt to breathe. Panicked shouts pushed into her thoughts. She slammed her palms over her ears, but the sounds came inside her head. Groans of pain. Rattled coughs. Distant sirens.

Cold. So cold. Nova shivered no matter how many layers of clothing she'd put on. The Bellagio Hotel's central heating had stopped days ago. The staff abandoned ship yesterday, moments after she'd checked in.

Outside, the fountains stopped spurting, and police patrolled nightly. But they couldn't catch every panicking citizen from doing stupid, crazy things. Sirens, blood-curdling shouts, and screams had become the soundtrack. The downfall of society was a train wreck... but she didn't care because she'd made it here—to Vegas, where Jace waited for her in this penthouse with a bouquet of roses and eyes full of emotion. The years and distance between them evaporated from the moment they'd clashed.

They fell into bed, making love passionately, desperately, and voraciously. They'd clung to each other as the sirens wailed outside. They refused to talk about anything except how much they needed each other.

Tomorrow—she had told herself. Tomorrow, she would tell Jace everything about Niles. And she sensed he had things to tell her, too. He would have held onto whatever Niles said to keep them apart. But they both agreed that son-of-a-bitch had no place in their happy reunion. At least not for that night. Despite a world falling apart, they'd found a miracle in each other.

But when Nova woke in the morning, cold and shivering beneath blankets, Jace was ill.

On her journey over, she'd glimpsed television reports about strange illnesses. Some blamed radiation. Others refuted it, saying not enough had arrived here in the States. The government denied anything was wrong. Some blamed the changes because the nuclear bombs had changed weather patterns. The Continental Drift melted icecaps too fast, releasing ancient pathogens that had lain dormant since Pangea.

None of it mattered. All Nova cared about was Jace.

Only an hour had passed since she'd awoken, and he was already unrecognizable in his illness. His eyes and ears were so puffy they'd swollen to twice their size. He wheezed with rattling breaths. Surely, this was an infection. It was some bacteria that had affected his eyes and ears.

Even though the hotel's staff had left during the night, and the sirens today were becoming few and far between, she hoped the pharmacy down the road would still be open. If not, then she'd break in and steal the medication. Jace's life depended on it.

"Mi amor," she whispered, touching his hot, sweaty forehead. "I'm going to find medication."

"No," he rasped, hand grasping hers.

It was so clammy and weak. It took every ounce of control to keep her voice from trembling.

"I must, my love. You need help. If I wait another day, who knows what it will be like out there."

Who knows if he will be alive or dead?

"Don't go," he begged.

"I'll be back. I promise."

He tried to stop her, but a convulsion wracked his body, bowing his spine from the bed. His agony brought tears to her eyes. After everything that had kept them apart, they'd found their way back to each other. He had to see that nothing in this life had the power to break their bond.

"Jace." She gripped his hand tightly. "We found our way back once. We'll do it again."

"I hear their screams," he murmured, tilting his face to the window as though he could see through his swollen eyes. "It's too dangerous. I'll lose you."

"You won't, and you know why?" she asked. "What did you say to me last night?

He licked his dry lips. "You're my North Star. Mi estrella brillante."

"That's right. And why do I call you Jace?"

His chuckle caused a coughing fit so violent that Nova held a cloth to his mouth. When she pulled it away, red spotted the white. He wheezed, "Because I'm too handsome."

She forced herself to smile through her tears and squeezed his hand. "So handsome that I misheard you introduce yourself. So you see, I have loved you since I saw you. And no good-for-nothing brother of mine will keep us apart."

A tear spilled from his left eye. "I should have fought harder for you."

"Me too. But we were both pawns in his game." She held her breath, trying to stop the fury she had for herself, for failing to see the true depths of Nile's villainy. She refused to make her parting words about that.

Jace whispered, "He's done far worse than you'll ever know."

"Tomorrow. We will talk about that tomorrow. For now, we focus on you getting better. The pharmacy is only a five-minute walk. I'll return to you soon, I promise."

Their fingers dragged over each other's as she pulled away. She kissed her fingers and pressed them to his lips. As she walked away, he called her name, "Estrella?"

"Yes, mi alma?"

"If you don't... I'll find you."

Nova wiped silent tears from her eyes. Some part of her heart had held onto the hope that this Guardian who looked like her love was somehow a miracle in disguise. But now that she'd forced herself to remember those final moments, she knew in her heart Jace was dead.

She never made it to the pharmacy. The moment she'd stepped outside the Bellagio, it started snowing. People rioted. Someone pushed her clear over the balustrade into the fountain's freezing water.

Thud thud thud.

A knock at the bathroom door startled Nova.

"Yes?" she croaked, hastily wiping her eyes.

"Are you well?" Leaf called through the door.

"I'm fine."

A pause, as if he listened for her lies.

"I just," he started, then paused again. "I felt like you were..."

She forced happiness into her voice. "Never fear, *Hoja de los Guardianes.* I will be out, dressed in the outfit you provided, and the very picture of health for our final evening together."

His shadow beneath the door remained. Finally, Leaf's soft grunt filtered through, and then he left.

CHAPTER TWENTY-ONE

While Nova was in the bathroom, Leaf sat on the edge of the bed, staring at his hands and mulling over Crimson's journals.

Throughout the entire collection, one theme had never faded. Crimson was obsessed with finding his lost love. He searched for thousands of years. The earliest entries had been full of grief, guilt, and hope that the Well would lead him to her again if he continued to protect it. He talked about unfulfilled promises, which led Leaf to believe he had bargained with the Well for her return. His final days were full of despair, exhaustion, and fixation.

Puzzle pieces started fitting together. Pieces like the word *Estrella* in Crimson's journal, the similarities between Jace and his initials J.C., the Spanish terms, and the stories about him being manipulated by his parents and betrayed by a close friend. That friend had to be Nero.

There was no doubt in Leaf's mind that Crimson was Nova's lost love. And she was his.

But Leaf couldn't be the same man—even if he looked similar and felt a connection with Nova that was beyond logical. Fae could not lie, which meant the Prime told the truth when she said Jackson Crimson never walked out of that lake again.

If Nova knew her lover grieved and searched for her for thousands of years, then ended his suffering because he thought he'd failed... her heart would break. To her, she saw him only months ago. That pain would cut deep.

Immortality wasn't a gift. It was punishment without happiness. No wonder Aleksandra was so emotionless, and Maebh was mad. No wonder Crimson gave up.

The last thing Leaf wanted was to cause Nova more pain. And what point was there for him to get involved with her when so many who'd come before him had suffered because of love?

Spending time with her already muddied his motives. She slid beneath his skin like no one else. He'd put her safety and happiness ahead of duty. But the Well had not blessed their union. They were not mates. Falling for her now would complicate things, and he must not be distracted like Crimson was. The integrity of the Well counted on Leaf's dedication to cleaning the taint.

He'd read enough journal entries to feel like he relived the man's life. Yet he was no closer to understanding the whole picture, particularly what the Prime seemed to know. Part of him questioned the validity of such a prophecy, considering Clarke's more recent visions were often inaccurate. But he wouldn't be able to function if he didn't see this through. So the goal had to remain the same—continue their ruse and convince the Prime to tell him everything. Then he could work out what to do next.

The bathroom door opened. His gaze snapped up, and his breath caught. Nova wore the red dress he'd purchased from the market yesterday... and it fit her better than expected. A little too well.

"I'm ready," she said quietly.

Forcing himself to breathe, he slowly stood and gazed at her—taking in every detail, like water to a parched man. The long-sleeved red knit dress hugged her upper body and hips, but a high split up to her thigh gave her room to move. The low, V-shaped neckline gave him a delectable sample of plump cleavage, and with her lustrous waves tousled into a high knot, her graceful neck was on full display.

"Turn," he murmured. "Show me everything."

Nova's slow pirouette gave him sweaty palms. Her thigh flashed through a split as she pivoted. Lust speared through him when more bare skin was revealed. The back of the dress was even lower cut than the front to accommodate wings. The feminine line of her spine drew his eye downward to the shapely curve of her bottom. The red knit clung to her cheeks like a loving embrace. He wanted to be that fabric—to be the one embracing her. Heat unfurled in his body, pumping his heart faster and engraving his veins with need. When she completed her pirouette, his gaze lifted to the polished wooden hoop earrings he'd bought with the dress.

After catching her touching her ears in a melancholy way during their journey, he'd guessed that she missed her old ear adornments.

"You look..." His voice sounded far too husky. "I'm speechless."

The sadness in her eyes melted. "Not so bad when the dirt is gone, huh?"

His lips parted, and he closed them again. "I'm never going to live that down, am I?"

Her red lips curved, and she shook her head. Then she touched her fingers to her mouth and pushed them down and out toward him, signing her gratitude.

"It is a beautiful dress," she said, "and exactly what a mate would buy his female. I'm sure it will go a long way in convincing the Prime of our ruse. I hope you get your answers tonight."

The Prime's name broke the spell and reminded Leaf of everything he'd been thinking of while she was in the bathroom. He glanced at a closed journal by the bed and felt sick. He hated not knowing secrets about him. Why would Nova be any different? Maybe he should tell her.

After tonight. Giving bad news before an event would make her miserable. She should enjoy herself one last night.

Leaf exhaled, draped a new cape over her shoulders, and tied the ribbon at the front. He might have lingered longer than necessary to graze her neck with his fingers. It was like they had a mind of their own, and if he had any less self-control, they might not have made it out of that room at all. Her sweet floral perfume curled through his body, testing that theory.

He stepped back before his arousal became obvious.

Nova touched the hoop earrings. "And you bought these?"

"Yes," he clipped. "Shall we go?"

At his dismissive tone, Nova's good mood evaporated. She shoved him aside. "Let's get this over with."

Leaf closed his eyes and sighed. When would he stop saying the wrong things? His self-disparaging scowl remained when they walked across the frosty grass path toward the sacred tree. Owl shifters preferred to fly up to the sky walkway to enter the tree, so the path lit by bonfires was relatively empty.

That didn't mean they were immune from Nova turning heads. Winged fae craned their necks as they flew. A group of males a few yards away hesitated as they were about to take flight and decided to walk instead.

Nova took his hand in hers. "We should be a bit more obvious."

"Good idea," he mumbled. He glanced at her just as her cape billowed open, giving him a glimpse of her cleavage, and he stumbled.

Nova's hand slid up to his elbow. "Are you okay?"

They stopped in the middle of the path. Heat crept up his neck. What the fuck was he thinking buying her that dress? He couldn't keep his eyes off her. Naturally, every male in this place would be doing the same. He should have worn his baldric and *Reckoning* over his dress shirt. Fuck the wake and propriety. Fuck that market stall attendant who said this dress was the perfect gift. At least if they were still, the cape fell and appropriately covered her. Maybe he'd ask her to keep it on while inside the tree. Surely, it was cold up there. Tugging his collar, he cleared his throat and searched for words. But every time his eyes landed on her, he forgot everything.

"Leaf?" she pressed, her frown deepening.

He didn't deserve her concern, especially not after what he knew.

"I need to tell you something," he confessed.

"Okay." Her concern morphed into anger when she glanced over his shoulder and shouted, *"¿Qué estás mirando?"*

She continued to lecture someone in Spanish. Leaf slid his gaze to her target and found a group of male shifters scurrying away. It wasn't until he heard Nova say *Guardianes* that he realized she spoke about him.

"What's happened?" he asked, tensing and narrowing his eyes at their spectators.

"They're looking at you," she huffed. "They see your Guardian mark, and they *look*. I'm not blind—that's right, *puta, I see you staring!*" She explained quietly to him, "First, it was the snide comments the soldiers sent your way at the war camp, then here before we entered the gates, and now this. I know I've not seen a fraction of what Guardians do for the fae people, but you don't deserve to be stared at."

Warmth bloomed in his chest.

"Nova," he murmured, putting a finger to her chin and guiding her fiery gaze back to his. "They're not looking at me."

"Of course they are. What else would they be staring at?"

"They don't get outsiders. You're the most beautiful thing they've seen in decades."

Before she could deny it, he gripped her hand, ignored the riot in his blood traveling south again, and tugged her toward the hollow at the base of the sacred tree. The spiral staircase inside was blessedly empty—no gawping shifters.

"What is this magic?" Nova gushed as he pulled her up the spiral staircase. The tree's inner veins pulsed as though alive and flush with pale, glowing blood.

"Mana," he explained. "But don't touch it. Who knows what transient effect the taint has."

At the first-level landing, they walked through a curtain of foliage into a hallway enshrouded by branches and bioluminescent leaves. Leaf's eyes crinkled as Nova's steps kept slowing while she tried to study the beautiful sights. Tiny glowing sprites flittered and buzzed through the darker recesses and hidden hollows.

"If you want, we can explore the tree after we speak with the Prime," he offered.

"Really?" Her face lit up as she turned to him.

Butterflies swarmed in his stomach. He shouldn't promise things like this, but the joy on her face was so much better than the thought of her impending sadness at the news.

Clearing his throat, he said, "I think it's this way."

He tugged her along another enshrouded hallway. They walked up another staircase.

"This tree is a maze," she mumbled, ducking beneath a low-hanging vine.

"Hmm," he agreed. "It's much easier for the shifters to fly to the level they need."

They finally emerged onto a long bough wider than his house at the Order. Rows of tables with stools accommodated attendees and their wings as they enjoyed small bites. A curtain of draping branches made a wall on one side of the bough. All tables faced the side open to the starry sky, so it was likely a stage for an aerial performance.

A steward walked up to Leaf and Nova with a tray of bubbling drinks.

"Where is the Prime's table?" Leaf asked.

"She hasn't arrived, but Raven will show you to your seat, D'arn."

Another steward with dark hair and wings appeared and held out her hand to Nova. "May I take your cape?"

"She will get cold," Leaf grumbled.

"Honey," Nova replied, smiling tightly at Leaf. "I'm feeling quite warm tonight, so yes, Raven—take my cape."

Honey?

His brow raised, but Nova ignored him. She unlaced her cape and peeled it from her shoulders. The gaze of every male in their proximity landed on her seductive form. He glared at them until they looked away.

"Follow me," Raven said, taking the cape.

CHAPTER TWENTY-TWO

With tension tightening his shoulders, Leaf placed a palm on Nova's lower back and held that glare as they walked through the collection of tables. Halfway across the bough, they crossed smooth parquetry that would likely become a dance floor. More tables were set on the other side.

"Nova," a male voice called out.

Leaf stilled as Storm rose from his seat, staring at Nova with obvious delight. Nova grinned and waved in return. Something insidious crawled through Leaf's heart at the exchange.

"No time to dawdle," he growled low, pushing Nova onward. He didn't stop until they arrived at an empty table toward the tip of the bough.

Raven gestured for them to sit.

"Where is the Prime," Leaf snapped.

"I'm not privy to the Prime's personal—"

"This is unacceptable."

"Honey," Nova hushed.

His voice had risen above the conversation, and a few hard stares had been tossed his way. Raven hand-signed her apology, muttered about finding out, and rushed to the edge of the bough to fly out.

Leaf shook his head. "If she's trying to evade us again, I swear to the Well..."

"Oh, pipe down." Nova scowled at him. "It's bad enough they stare at you because of a reputation, and then you give them something to stare about. You didn't even let me say hello."

A heat wave rose up Leaf's neck, hitting his ears and making them twitch. It felt suspiciously like shame. Frowning at himself, he pulled out Nova's stool and made sure she was on the furthest side from the main group of attendees—the side where not much else existed but a curtain of foliage.

As she sat, he grumpily tested the curtain wall behind them. The foliage connected with the bough, securing the backdrop. At least they wouldn't fall through to their deaths. Forcing himself to exhale, he sat beside Nova and glared at the main crowd.

In the silence that followed, Nova polished off her wine and looked for more. When no steward noticed her gesturing for more, she sighed.

"I will find you another glass," Leaf offered, partly rising from his chair.

"It's fine," she clipped.

"You are mad." He sat back down.

"We are meant to be in love. Stop scowling at me."

He'd been scowling at himself, but before he could correct her assumption, the Prime's glorious white wings flashed before them in the open night. She landed on the bough with expert prowess and a flurry of robes. She wore the same boring ceremonial garb as before, which struck Leaf as odd because she usually favored beautiful blue dresses.

The Prime's eyes had returned to her usual emotionless, dry state. Her aura of power pulsed in the atmosphere as she approached. He tensed, preparing himself for a battle of the wills that would surely come.

"It is good to see you've made a full and speedy recovery, Nova," she intoned as she adjusted her wings to fit behind the stool beside Leaf. Her white ringlets bounced as she sat. "D'arn."

"Prime," he grunted, tapping his finger on the table.

"I feel much better." Nova's brows knit together, and she leaned forward to see past Leaf. "I'm sorry, have we met?"

Aleksandra glanced at Leaf. "Your overprotective mate dragged me from my room in the middle of the night to consult on your health."

"What?" Nova squeaked, her eyes wide at Leaf. "You let her see me like that?"

He shrugged. "You needed help."

"Don't worry," the Prime said, a small smile touching her lips. "It was oddly nostalgic to see someone afflicted with such an illness." She sighed. "And you reminded me of someone. I was happy to help."

Nova stared at Leaf, then back at Aleksandra for longer than appropriate. When he didn't pick up the hint, she pinched him beneath the ribs and raised her brows.

What? He returned Nova's questioning look.

"Honey," she mumbled. "You haven't officially introduced us."

"Nova, this is the Prime of the Order of the Well." He gestured between them. "Aleksandra, this is Nova Morales."

"I'm his mate, as you mentioned. Just confirming that." Nova reached around Leaf's chest toward the Prime. Her white-lashed eyes narrowed on the outstretched hand.

"This is a human custom," Leaf explained to Aleksandra, in case she'd forgotten. "Do you recall the shaking-of-hands ritual?"

They briefly clasped hands before Leaf, then just as the Prime pulled away, Nova gripped harder and said thoughtfully, "I feel like we've met before."

Aleksandra tugged her hand from Nova and turned emotionless eyes to the airy night stage. "You must tell me, D'arn Leaf. How did you meet your mate?"

"He won me in a mate hunt," Nova said, elbowing Leaf in the ribs. "Isn't that right, *mi amor?*"

"Yes."

"Hmm." The Prime's lips pursed. "So it's true then. You were responsible for the obliteration of one of Maebh's troops."

"It was an accident," he admitted. "And necessary to rescue Nova."

His boss gave another unimpressed sound. As a steward deposited three glasses of wine and bite-sized appetizers, Leaf realized her hum was suspicious, so he added, "She is from the old world."

"You mentioned that already."

"But I didn't tell you that Nero is her twin."

The Prime blinked. For a moment, Leaf thought she'd entered a trance. She'd gone so still. Then she shook her head briefly and gazed at Nova, this time with more shrewd cunning and dangerous attention.

"Is this true?" she asked.

"I heavily suspect," Nova answered, staring quizzically at the Prime. "I haven't seen him face to face yet, but from what I understand, not many of you have." She leaned forward to see better around Leaf. "Are you sure we haven't met? I feel like maybe with darker hair, I've met you before."

The Prime suddenly faced the front. "We will speak about this later."

"When?" Leaf argued. "You're never at the Order. If Nova has information we can use, shouldn't we call a Council meeting?"

"The taint remains an immediate priority."

"Speaking of that," Leaf grumbled. "It's time for you to reveal the full prophecy."

White feathers ruffled. Aleksandra hissed low, sideways through clenched teeth, "Do you think I'm a fool to believe you are mated?"

"I have done what you asked." Leaf's brows lowered. "You must honor your promise."

Lyrical flute music started playing down by the dance floor. Fae made their way there, laughing and tucking their wings out of courtesy. A few came to their table to pay respects to the Prime before returning to dance. She smiled tightly and nodded, giving polite responses. When they were gone, Leaf continued to press his point.

"Clarke has discovered the chaos in the Well is almost at a point of no return," he said. "Tell me the full prophecy so I can find a way forward for us. We cannot afford any more delays."

"No, we cannot."

"So you agree."

Nova said something, but Leaf's ears were full of rage. He barely darted a glance her way before returning to the Prime. He'd had just about enough. No more evasion. No more lies. Pretending to be mated hadn't worked and caused more delays than Leaf was willing to accept. He was foolish to believe the Prime would go for this.

"Aleksandra?" he warned. "Answer me."

"Your *mate* is asking you something."

"She's not my mate," he barked. And then, because he'd abruptly revealed the only card up his sleeve, he added with indignation, "Despite your best efforts, I remain my own person. I am *not* a pawn in your game. Unlike Crimson, who spent thousands of years under the Well's thumb, I will not now, nor ever, accept a mate—especially not Nova Morales."

A gasp to his right burned his face, but he refused to look at her. Once he explained, she would understand. But she abruptly mumbled something in Spanish and walked toward the exit. *Fuck.* He watched her until she melted into the crowd on the dance floor, and then he glared at the Prime—ready to unleash the full force of his fury.

She was already staring, twirling her wine glass absently. Before he could respond, she put the glass down with a weary sigh.

"D'arn Leaf," she said, voice gentle and disarming.

She looked at him like when he'd burst into her room that first night. Her brown, white-lashed eyes were full of emotion, recognition, and affection. It wasn't romantic, he was sure of it. While she struggled to find words for her churning thoughts, he tried to place that look in her eyes. It was the look she gave Nova in her sickbed—the affection one had for family.

Aleksandra had said Nova reminded her of someone... and Nova said the same.

Finally, she placed her palm over his and looked him in the eyes. "For those lucky to live as long as us, there are three possible fates. Maebh suffers the first—obsession and eventual madness. I am in the throes of the second—soullessness. My dear friend, you are lucky to be within reach of the third fate. I wish I still cared enough to want. Whenever you speak about her, I see this desire in your eyes. Your wounded pride makes you blind."

"Stop deflecting. Tell me what I need to know—why is it so important for us Twelve to be mated and Well-blessed? It's a ridiculous caveat on the truth."

She pinned him with an unnervingly agonized stare. "Know this, D'arn. No matter which fate is yours, one constant remains. Memories fade, they warp, but the heart never forgets."

She glanced at the dance floor, where Nova smiled up at Storm. As though sensing Leaf's attention, his graceful wing stretched to block their faces from view. But not before Storm touched Nova's shoulder, his thumb idly tracing a path past her neckline to bare skin.

Violence slammed into Leaf's body. He trembled from the force of containing it. Not just rage, but jealousy, longing, regret, and denial. He reeled from the potency of it all as his eyes were stuck on that single point of contact, still somehow visible through a gap in Storm's wings. As though the shifter did it on purpose, teasing Leaf with his inappropriate touch.

"She's just saying hello," he gritted out, a vein in his temple throbbing. "That's all she said she wanted to do."

"You must have misheard." The Prime smirked, then calmly sipped her wine. "She said something about scratching an itch."

Leaf was two steps toward the dance floor before his stool hit the ground.

"D'arn!"

The authoritative tone in the Prime's voice was too ingrained to ignore. He halted, clenched his jaw, and glanced back at her. Desperation poured from her eyes. A bolt of alarm sliced through him at the raw, foreign emotion.

"If you have more questions," she warned low, "ask them now. You might not get another chance."

More alarm bells went off. The ringing in Leaf's ears increased as all the clues came together. Her ultimatum, talk of love and regrets, her robe, and rare flashes of emotion.

This wake was for her.

CHAPTER
TWENTY-THREE

A shadow flew over Nero's war maps on his conservatory desk. He reached for his pistol and aimed at the conservatory's glass dome ceiling. Narrowing his gaze, he tried to see through the condensation to the gray sky above. He waited, heart pounding as something fell behind him with a clang. Jolting, he pivoted and shifted his aim, but he saw nothing beyond the ferns and plants. The copper humidifier released bouts of steam —*pip, pip, pip.*

Embarrassed at his jumpiness, he shook his head. The ventilation gaps in the glass were too thin for any creature to drop through. He'd ensured his safety decades ago after an unwanted visitor stole something important.

Tick-tick-tick-ticking on the glass dome lifted his head as something white fell through the slot. It landed on his map and rolled. Nero cocked and aimed his pistol at the dome, but no one was there.

Another full minute passed before he was satisfied he was alone and put the gun away.

He used a pin to test the white roll of paper. Nothing happened. So he unrolled it and read the message.

A battle to decide the fate of Elphyne will be on Samhain.

Nero frowned and glanced up again, narrowing his eyes in suspicion. Bones had set up a network of spies in Elphyne decades ago. It appeared some were still loyal. He turned the paper over and found the name of a city. A slow smile curved his lips. He pushed a green pin into the map—on the city called *Cornucopia.*

CHAPTER TWENTY-FOUR

Storm's voice warbled from far away as he spoke to Nova. Instead, all she could hear was Leaf's declaration to his Prime: *I will not now, nor ever, accept a mate—especially not Nova Morales.*

It shouldn't hurt so much. He'd made that clear from the start time and time again. But it was the tone he'd used, the vehemence and disgust. Then he'd treated her like she wasn't there.

All she could think was there was no reason for her to stay. No reason to submit herself to that treatment. And then she'd caught Storm's eye from across the room and knew what to do. She had to distance herself from the elf that looked like her lost lover. She had to forget about her guilt over leaving Jace behind. And she wasn't talking about the end... She knew Niles said something to push Jace away. But she let him go.

Forcing air into her lungs, she focused on Storm's lips.

"So it was a ruse?" he asked, brows lifting.

"Yes," she confirmed, her lips stretching into what she hoped was a smile. "He saved my life, so I helped him in return. But that's all over now. As you can see, he's—" She gestured in Leaf's direction, but he wasn't at the table. Neither was the Prime. "He's not even there."

"Good," Storm declared, his gray eyes turning dark. "Then I hope you'll do me the honor of dancing with me."

Nova stepped into his awaiting arms, felt the hardness of his body against hers, and couldn't help wishing it was someone else. God, she was hopeless. No wonder Niles had been able to pull the wool over her eyes. He was bereft of emotion, and she had too much. Unable to meet Storm's attentive gaze, she locked her vision firmly on his chest. A pretty flute melody gave them the rhythm. She tried to be graceful like the angelic warrior sweeping her around but stepped on his feet too many times.

"Perhaps we should sit until the performance," Storm said, as he adjusted their steps. "The dancers have worked hard to re-enact Aleksandra's life."

"Aleksandra's life?" She sounded robotic.

"I've heard it's an evocative show."

Nova detected a husky note in his tone. His eyes were full of dark lust and hope when she met his gaze. She should leave. Leading him on wasn't fair if her heart wasn't in it. But somehow, when his gaze darted to her lips and he lowered his mouth, she did nothing. She *felt* nothing.

Storm abruptly halted and frowned, his lips an inch from hers.

"Remove your hands from my mate." Leaf's deep and unnerving tone sent a shiver down her spine. Over Storm's shoulder, she locked with a set of blue, thunderous eyes.

Leaf hadn't left.

And... and... he'd just called her his mate. But how? She thought he couldn't lie. Hadn't he just declared that he wanted nothing to do with her?

What was wrong with him? As if she wasn't confused enough as it was.

How dare he?

She stepped away from Storm to confront Leaf, but Storm's grip tightened protectively. He tugged her closer to him. Panic quickened her pulse, and a sickening sense of déjà vu rocked through her. She smelled Grung's sour breath and felt the bile rising in her throat.

"I won't warn you again." Leaf's tone was low and lethal. "Remove your filthy talons from my mate."

"You had your chance."

Leaf's fist met Storm's jaw. The impact sent him sprawling backward, wings fluttering and knocking into people. Nova gasped as Leaf held nothing back, unleashing his rage on the owl shifter, climbing over him and pummeling his face with untapped fury.

"I can't believe this," Nova gasped, vision blurring. "What did I do to deserve this fate?"

An overwhelming sense of despair weighed her down. She kicked off her shoes and ran. She pushed past judgmental eyes, feeling like her sanity was slipping away. Niles had won—well and truly. There was nothing left in her life but pain. He wasn't even here, and he'd won.

"Nova!" Leaf bellowed behind her, but she blindly ran, ducking through the exit and into a hallway of glowing branches she once thought were magical. Now, she only noticed sharp twigs and crushed leaves that smelled moldy. She reached a curtain leading to one of the spiral staircases when he caught up to her. His big hand landed on her shoulder and spun her around. "Nova, stop. It's not safe for you to be on your own. Let me—"

She slapped his face.

"Safe?" She shoved him hard. "With you when you act like an angry ape?"

His expression darkened, and he pointed in the direction he'd come from. "He had no right to steal your kisses when they belong to me."

"¡Ay, pobrecito! ¿Piensas que eres tan poderoso? ¡Hoja de los Guardianes, lo que puede hacer todo! Pues escúchame bien. No quiero ir contigo. No quiero tu ayuda. No quiero tus besos. Solo quiero que me dejes en paz."

He looked at her in abject horror, helpless to understand her rage.

"Please," he begged, eyes wide. "I don't understand."

"Then allow me to translate so it's crystal clear." All emotion leaked from her tone. What came out was cold, heartless, and bitter. "You poor baby. You think you're so powerful? Leaf of the Guardians, who can do anything. Well, listen to me good. I don't want to go with you. I don't want your help. I don't want your kisses. I only want you to leave me alone."

Hurt flashed in his eyes. "Don't leave."

He looked so much like Jace at that moment. A sob tore from the tight center of her chest. She covered her mouth, but her shoulders convulsed as her pain demanded release.

"You have every right to be furious at me." His deep voice

pitched low. "I have used you. I have been rude to you. And I have kept the truth from you."

She walked toward the glowing vines hiding the staircase.

"For Crimson's sake, Nova. Let me explain."

Time stopped. That word became the beating of her heart.

Crimson.

Crimson.

Crimson.

"What did you say?" She whirled to face him. Guilt flashed in his eyes, and she couldn't comprehend. Couldn't attempt to revive that hope because she'd been crushed so many times.

I have kept the truth from you.

He stepped forward, reaching out. She stepped away, her back brushing the curtain.

"Don't," she sobbed. "Don't play with my heart. It won't survive."

His brows lifted in the middle, and he swallowed. "You said he called you Estrella. Last night, while reading Crimson's journals, I found your name."

"Crimson?" she rasped, confused. "As in... Jackson Crimson? *My* Jackson Crimson. My Jace?"

Leaf nodded cautiously, taking another step closer. "I've been reading his journals."

"But... how? Jace never kept journals."

"Have you not heard of the Order's founder?" Another step closer.

She should leave now. She should duck through the curtain and never speak to this manipulating, warped copy of the man she once knew. Except too many things weren't adding up. Leaf appeared as lost and forlorn as she was. Was he a liar, a cruel trickster like her brother, or was this something else?

"Founder of what?" she gasped.

"Shit," he muttered, shaking his head. "You've never heard fae cursing his name?"

"You curse his name? Like... like some kind of god?"

"Jackson Crimson discovered the Well. He was from your time and could hear the whispers of the Well itself. He founded the Order and set the rules about forbidden substances. He did it hoping the Well would bring his Estrella back to him, but also knowing if he protected the environment, he'd honor her values."

"You keep saying he. He! But is it you? Is that what you're telling me?"

"I'm not him." He honestly looked disappointed.

"Why would you lie to me?" she sobbed, gesturing at his face.

His hands enveloped hers. They were bruised warrior's hands—bloody from jealousy and possessive rage. They were the furthest from what a corporate businessman would have, as were the ropes of muscle and coiled strength in his imposing frame.

"When you left the table," he said, "Aleksandra said something that made me think. Memories fade, but the heart never forgets."

She searched his eyes and believed he was as confused as her. She could almost feel his heartache, his longing and fear. "What are you saying?"

"Something isn't right about the truth." He dropped his forehead to hers. "I've run from relationships because giving my heart away felt wrong. It felt like a betrayal, and it made no sense. When they told me I was next to find my mate, I couldn't do it. I convinced myself I had to search for other answers and ran. But when I first saw you..." He pulled back and looked deeply into her eyes. "For the first time, my heart wasn't telling me to run."

"The heart never forgets." A silent tear trickled down her cheek. "So you are my Jace?"

"I came to the Order hundreds of years after he went missing. The Prime says he's gone. Maebh says he's gone. Fae can't lie."

Nova's heart broke into a million pieces. She tried to pull away, but he tugged her back so hard she slammed against his chest.

"He's gone, but I'm here."

"I can't."

"For the past decade, I've been searching." His chest heaved against hers as he took a ragged breath. "Aleksandra will die soon. This wake is for her. She offered me the chance to have my questions answered, but when I saw you with Storm, all I could think was that I couldn't lose you. I've been so..."

"Stubborn," she offered, raising her brows.

"Yes, and—"

"Arrogant."

"Yes, and—"

"Cruel. And worse than a liar. And..." She thought about things, and her heart softened. He had shown her kindness in moments. Like with the horse hugging, or tending to her when sick, or buying her things and rescuing her from a horrible fate. "And I suppose you've also been caring, generous, and honest."

"Honest?"

"You said from the start you didn't want a mate."

"I was lying to myself. This is what I'm trying to explain. I ignored what my heart was trying to tell me. No answers from a dying woman are worth that."

This was all too much. "How can I trust anyone?"

"Trust this." He rubbed her hand over his rabbiting heart. "I was against being mated because it felt like I betrayed someone for wanting you... but feel it. Feel it beat for you. Nova, you were the answer all along. When I'm with you, I'm no longer searching."

CHAPTER TWENTY-FIVE

Nova's eyes closed. She had nothing left in the tank but exhaustion and raw emotions. She could see he was trying to do something right, but all it did was confuse her more. She shoved the big Guardian away and jogged down the spiral staircase.

"Nova?" Thudding footsteps behind her.

"Go away."

"No."

"Please."

He leaped down three steps and blocked her with his hand against the wall. "Tell me what I said."

"I never thought I was in a race with my brother. Never cared." Rage filled her. It bubbled and simmered and burned. "He was an idiot. A nut job. But he still has a heart in one piece while mine is shattered. You're him, then you're not him. I'm done. I want none of it."

Leaf's brows joined in the middle. "Estrella—"

"Don't you dare call me that! Jace earned that name, and he is dead. You? I hate you."

Agony contorted his face as he inhaled, but his expression changed on the exhale. His crystalline eyes became hard. His jaw set. He stepped up until they were eye to eye.

She spat to the side, showing her disgust. When he failed to budge, she snarled, "Move."

"No."

"Move!"

He leaned closer until their faces were inches apart and repeated, "No."

"You don't intimidate me, *Hoja de los Guardianes.*" She intended her voice to sound strong and impenetrable, but what came out was husky and weak.

Bioluminescence glanced off his skin. She was so close that she could count every pore on his face, every whisker on his jaw, and every dark lash around those smoldering eyes. Her body reacted to his proximity, arousing at the power vibrating from his skin. Damn her. Damn her for knowing the weakness in Jace was now Leaf's strength. It was as though the Well reached inside her mind while she slept encased in ice, and it stole her dreams and desires. It sculpted her love into something merciless, someone who was powerful and unbreakable in mind and spirit. Someone who would fight to the death to keep her safe. But who wasn't him?

Suddenly, the air was too thick. Her skin was too tight, and her blood too hot.

Her breathing quickened. Leaf's gaze dipped to the swell of her breasts heaving, then to the hardness of her nipples pushing through the fine red knit. When his gaze returned to hers, that arrogance was back. His lips tugged into a self-satisfied smile, and he murmured, "You don't hate me."

He advanced, prowling up like a panther, eyes growing darker as she stumbled backward—up the staircase. When her ass hit the wall, he slammed his palms beside her head, caging her against the hollow.

Biceps bulged beside her face. Muscular pectorals twitched beneath his tight, creamy shirt. His neck was so tense the veins bulged. She couldn't take her eyes from that smooth, velvety skin encasing the hard column. God, he smelled divine.

"He never fought for you, but I will."

Her lips parted as he leaned in. Energy skipped over his skin. Danger flared in his eyes.

"He didn't think he was good enough for you, so... so..." His eyes darted back and forth, understanding dawning on his expression. "So maybe he became me."

She'd just thought something similar. Goosebumps erupted over her skin, and she couldn't deny there was some kind of supernatural force at play here. But instead of making her feel safe, she felt small. Powerless.

Need, pain, and defiance warred over Leaf's expression, hardening every handsome line of his face. He hungered for her so badly that he had to restrain himself. He trembled from the force. The very thought caused a flood of heat in her lower abdomen.

"It's all becoming clear now," he said. "It feels right thinking it. Crimson knew he would go mad from his obsession to find you, so he sacrificed his memories. The Well held onto him, cocooning him in its watery embrace while you were frozen all these years. When your twin turned up in this time, so did I... with no memories. But I'm not him. I'm a better version of him."

"I hate you," she repeated weakly. "Fucking arrogant pig, to say mean things about someone you never knew."

"Am I wrong? Was your love perfect?"

Her throat closed up. "Is any love perfect?"

But he wasn't listening. He was too busy watching his finger trail down her jaw, neck, and across to the pillow of her breasts. She shivered as he tugged her neckline down, and her aching breast popped free. Every ounce of her awareness shot to that tingling point as the cool air hit her sensitive nipple. She hated how much this turned her on. Hated that he knew it would, almost like he knew her heart.

"I'm not your prize," she tossed at him.

"But you kind of were." His humor died as he twirled his finger around her nipple, watching avidly when she moaned and pushed into his touch. She slid her palms down his hard stomach and gripped his erection. He groaned as though he was falling under her spell.

"Don't you see?" he muttered. "You're the one built from my fantasies. You're the answer to our prayers. Something in your beautiful, breathtaking head will help us defeat Niles, I know it. The Well spent thousands of years crafting a world for you, making it a place you'll fight to protect, building a mate who deserved to be with you." He took a shuddering breath, laughing quietly to himself. "You got it wrong. It's not you who is the prize, it's me. I only exist to serve, protect, and love you. And, Nova..." His voice deepened dangerously. "I'm not running from that."

"You have a silver tongue, *Hoja*. You're the only person I can't fight for long." Her hands slid up his chest, curled behind his neck. He made sense. But it hurt. She didn't want to feel like this anymore, but there was no denying they were drawn to each other and linked by fate. Maybe it was time to lean into it. "Kiss me. Make the pain go away."

Hard lips crashed down onto hers. His tongue stole into her mouth, demanding every inch with hot, passionate sweeps. And dear God, she gave it to him. She grabbed those stupid elf ears and arched into him when he groaned openly against her mouth. He snarled softly and bit her bottom lip until she whimpered for more.

"No more fighting," he agreed raggedly, his fingers trembling on her face.

"I will never stop speaking my mind." Her hands snuck beneath his shirt and found his defined abdomen. *Hot. Smooth. Addictive.* She buried her hands lower, hunting for the laces keeping his trousers on. "I am not that kind of woman."

"Good." His lips curved with mischief. He tweaked her nipple until another whimper shot out of her lips. She melted, clinging to his hips and presenting her neck. He licked along her vein, shooting fire into her loins. Then he captured her mouth again, using slow, torturous strokes.

Needing to breathe, she broke apart from him. Wild blue eyes landed on her throbbing lip. He swiped his thumb along the seam and stared at the blood on his finger. Shame entered his eyes.

Don't you dare think about stopping. She lurched forward and kissed him again.

A strangled grunt of need rattled through his chest. He slipped his hand through the slit in her dress, stroked her thigh, and cupped her bottom. She hooked her leg around his waist, using it to tug him closer. They kissed so hard that they fell back through the curtain and into the staircase. He stopped them from falling and slammed her spine against the hollow's inner wall, pinning her in place with his hips.

The desire he stoked in her blood was impossible to quench. But somehow, his kisses slowed and eventually stopped until he breathed heavily through his nose, forehead pressed to hers.

"No," she begged, feeling her throat close up again. "Please don't stop."

"Nova." His voice roughened to gravel.

"Don't leave me to feel like this," she whispered. "I don't want to feel lost anymore."

He pulled back with disbelief. "I'm never letting you go."

"Then fuck me." She rocked her hips into his erection, teasing him. But he ignored the bait, and her world was ending. "Please, *Papi*. Make me feel good."

"I refuse to let our first time be a quick fuck inside the hollow of a tree during a wake." Determination hardened his jaw. "And certainly not while you're upset and confused."

Tears brimmed in her eyes. The battle left her, and she nodded. Her leg dropped from around his waist. Her feet hit the floor, and she tried to step past him, but he pulled her back into his arms. He crushed her face to his chest and tightened his embrace.

"Leaf." Her voice was muffled against his shirt, but the harder she resisted, the tighter he held. *"Let me go."*

"No."

She kicked and bucked and tried to throw him off. She tossed insults at his chest, but he refused to budge. And with each passing second, her sanity unraveled. She turned her face so she could breathe, but her ear stuck over his heart, and everything he said returned to her.

I'm not him. His memories are gone. Too much. He sacrificed them... for her. Always for her.

Tears started to fall, and she was powerless to stop them.

"It's okay," he murmured, stroking her hair.

"You don't know that." Her voice tightened.

"I do. And you need to grieve."

"Such arrogance for someone with such a strong heart."

It beat steadily beneath her ear. He believed it would be okay. Somehow, with his arms around her like this... she believed it too.

"I'm going to take care of you, Nova," he promised. "I'm going to love you and keep you."

Blue light fizzed up from the ground and spiraled around them. Energy tingled against Nova's skin. Panic gripped her heart. She clenched Leaf's shirt and whispered, "What's happening?"

He wasn't worried. Somehow, she felt his calm and... his self-disparaging amusement radiate into her.

"Leaf?" The blue was everywhere, sparking like fireworks and shooting from their bodies to light up the hollow.

His chest vibrated, and he shook his head, chuckling.

"What's so funny?" she gasped. "What's happening?

His warm, calloused hands cupped her face. The blue light reflected in his eyes like water on a summer's day. "The fucking Well is blessing us."

She scowled, pouting. "I don't want help from that damned—"

He captured her mouth with his own, kissing her deeply until she thought of nothing but his salty, heady taste, and his need to be with her.

When he eased off, the blue light had dimmed, and he stared at her lips with a hot look in his eyes. She felt his desire surge as though it were her own. Then his gaze skipped up to her cheeks and widened in shock. He brushed his thumb across the cheekbone, and that shock became trepidation.

"How can I feel your emotions?" Her arm was covered in blue, swirling patterns glittering like the Guardian drop beneath his eye. "Leaf... what is this?"

"It's the mating mark," he mumbled, still distracted by her cheeks, studying them like a scientist. He held his palm before her face so she could see the blue light glancing off his skin. "It bonds us forever, uniting our emotions. I can sense your location now, no matter where you are."

"Is my face blue?" she gasped.

He studied her cheeks with the perfect combination of awe and reverence. She wanted him never to stop looking at her this way. But not if her face was blue.

"Leaf?"

"It's not your entire face," he answered. "Just the smattering of glowing freckles that remind me of a constellation." His eyes narrowed on one particular spot. "This little one up north is the brightest."

Mi estrella del norte. Jace had called her that when they'd reunited before the world ended.

They'd just finished making love. She'd straddled him and looked down through the curtain of her hair.

"My North Star," he mumbled, gazing upon her with adoration.

She rocked her hips against his, chasing the warmth of their comple-

tion, wanting it to last forever. She moaned, biting her lip, hardly paying his words any attention. "What do you mean?"

"We may have been apart, and I may have lost my way, but you never did. Your convictions never wavered. Whenever I felt adrift, I looked you up and flicked through any news I could find of you. I needed to remind myself there were good people left in the world."

"You stalked me online?"

"Always." He smiled sheepishly. "Whenever I had a difficult decision, I imagined what you would do."

She swatted him playfully. "You could have called me and asked."

Darkness ghosted his features so briefly, Nova thought she imagined it.

"I was too afraid to... I thought he would... doesn't matter now. But I learned more Spanish, hoping that one day I could say this... Eres mi brillante estrella del norte. Dondequiera que vayas te sigo."

You are my North Star. Wherever you go, I follow you.

CHAPTER TWENTY-SIX

Leaf convinced Nova to return to the wake and watch the final performance. With her hand in his, their souls connected, he felt more whole than ever. She watched two wingless females dance on the parquetry to sultry music, moving and twirling as though in love. He meant what he said to her and that everything would be okay. Together, they could work on finding the answers they sought.

The Prime sat alone at the edge of the dance floor. She watched the performance with all the emotion of a stone statue. He couldn't tell if she was hiding her feelings or was truly empty inside. Would he detach or feel something else if he knew his death was on the horizon?

The Order would be left without a leader when they desperately needed one. With how the Prime had abandoned them lately, he wondered if it was her deliberate way of preparing them to sink or swim. But why hadn't she come to him for help?

He might not have the mind of her oldest friend, but he'd always given her the benefit of the doubt. Trepidation swirled in his chest. What if this death was the final part of the prophecy she wouldn't reveal? What if it had nothing to do with him at all? Casting his mind back over their conversations, his demands, and her replies, he looked deeper between the lines but still found nothing concrete.

The dance changed tempo, and a wingless male came into the mix. Dark hair, tanned skin, and... was that a baby?

Nova's gasp sent a cocktail of emotions surging through their bond. Leaf had trouble sorting them out. Shock, maybe. Dread?

"Nova?" He ducked his head to whisper. "What is it?"

Her mouth opened and closed. Something wasn't right, so Leaf guided her backward to the vine curtain by the stairs where they had privacy.

"This dance..." Nova said quietly. "Is it the personal history of your Prime?"

"The owl shifters value wisdom and memory. I believe that's what tonight is about—an artistic ode to the beauty and suffering of one's life. So we can all experience her memories..."

A way to experience Jackson Crimson's memories.

The Prime had always told Leaf that to find the last part of the prophecy, he would experience Crimson's memories. She never said how he would witness them. Right now, he was experiencing Aleksandra's memories through the dance. *Fuck.* This made Leaf's stubborn journey to find the journals seem so stupid.

"I think this is their life before the Fallout," he explained.

"I *knew* I recognized her." Sharp, bitter distrust seethed through their bond. "I didn't see it at first because she's changed, and she insisted she didn't recognize me. But, considering mine are fresher, I'm more inclined to trust my memories than hers."

"Are you saying you knew the Prime?"

"When Niles left my house that final day, I was so angry I chased him outside to... I don't know, shout some more stupid things at him. But when I got to the door, I watched a young girl run out of the car to meet him. I remember this so vividly because I couldn't exactly yell horrible things about him in front of his daughter. Two women were in the car. Your Prime was one of them, I'm sure of it."

"Could you see the face of the other woman?"

"No, but she had a similar complexion. I saw her hand."

"It might have been Maebh." Leaf's mind reeled with the implications. If Maebh and Aleksandra had known Niles all this time, they perhaps shared a child with him. Crimson wrote about those females' great loss and how it drove a divide between them, how it felt worse than his loss sometimes. Everyone felt pain in their own way, but Leaf could see how the loss of a child would feel so much worse.

When Willow was kidnapped, the Prime approved Order resources for a rescue mission. She rarely operated like this, and it was Clarke who nixed the rescue mission based on intel she'd received from the Six's Seer.

"We should say something," Nova said, eyes darting back to the dance.

"Wait." He stopped her from walking across the floor. "I want to see how this dance plays out. In Crimson's journals, he said they suffered from a great loss. What if it was a child?"

Nova's hand fluttered to her throat. "You think Niles would kill his own child?"

"He killed his parents. I wouldn't put it past him. But it's also possible he brought this child here to this time."

Leaf's gut said the Prime had no idea their child was another game piece for Nero... just as Nova was manipulated into believing her parents' deaths were natural.

Snow blasted into the room in gusts. The baby used in the dance was now a pre-teen and was being ripped from the arms of both mothers. The teen tossed herself from the bough where snow and darkness swallowed her whole.

The act ended with thunderous applause. As the music and lights lifted, Leaf glanced at Aleksandra. She stared impassively into the night, but a glimmering tear ran down her cheek.

"She didn't know," he whispered. "She believes her daughter is dead."

Maybe she was. But there was only one way to find out. He took Nova's hand and strode through the crowd blocking the dance floor. He shoved past grumbling shifters, pushing their impossible wings from his way. He lost his temper and started shoving hard, trying to carve a path through when the flute music stopped and shouts of offense rose.

The hairs on the back of Leaf's neck lifted. Turning around, he glimpsed a bruised Storm approaching him from between the gaps of wings. Upon seeing the mating marks glowing along Leaf and Nova's arms, the guard hesitated. Leaf continued toward the Prime, shoving the last few spectators out of the way, and stumbled onto the open dance floor.

The Prime wasn't in her seat but looking outside from the edge of the bough. Her robes and wings billowed from the icy wind, but the snow had stopped. The night was clear. Dancers with wild eyes whispered amongst each other with alarm, darting looks of confusion to the Prime. This mustn't be part of the next act.

"Aleksandra," Leaf called.

She faced him with resignation in her eyes.

"Don't come closer." She held out her hand. "We always knew it would end like this."

An ache tightened his chest. End like what? The *we* she referred to must be Crimson.

A fond smile tipped her ageless lips, and she gestured at his mating marks, silent tears now running down her face. Her voice was thick. "It wasn't too late after all. I'm so glad you chose the right path."

Warning bells rang in his mind. Anticipation. Soon. Whatever was supposed to happen, it was almost time.

"Stop," Leaf barked. "Listen—" He scoured the spectators for the dark-haired male dancer and found him two steps away. He pulled the frightened male onto the dance floor.

"Niles is Nova's twin brother," he said gravely, hoping the Prime remembered his original name. He couldn't come out and say Nero without risking chaos.

Recognition flashed in the Prime's sad eyes. She cocked her head, eyes darting between Nova and the dancer. "You're confused."

"We need to talk." Leaf lowered his tone and slowly approached. "Nova has much to share about her twin... remember? It's better if we return to the Order."

He implored her with his eyes.

More confusion and denial flashed over her face. More shaking of her head, white ringlets bouncing. Leaf's heart pounded with premonition. That ache in his chest grew tighter by the second. Something dangerous was approaching. The night looked clear. The owl shifters were relatively harmless. Only Storm seemed capable of attempting damage, but Leaf had bested him with a few punches. Nothing here should make him feel like danger was coming.

Nothing except the agony growing in his chest. He rubbed at the most acute spot, thinking he'd somehow been stabbed, but nothing was there.

An ear-piercing screech rent the night. One moment, the Prime stood on the edge of the bough, facing them. The next, tentacles wrapped around her body, face, and wings and sucked her into the night... just like the dancers had performed with her daughter.

Leaf ran forward, skidding at the edge. A receding blob of white faded into the darkness, high above their heads.

He yelled, "She might be alive!"

But whether the Prime heard him was a mystery. Whether she survived what Maebh had planned was another.

CHAPTER
TWENTY-SEVEN

Nova tucked her feet beneath her bottom and curled into a plush armchair by Leaf's bedroom window. They'd arrived in the night by a portal. Leaf quickly introduced the other residents, then spirited her away to his room while he gathered the council at the temple. He asked if she wanted to come, but she wanted to prepare herself before they revealed the truth about Niles, so she feigned exhaustion and asked to stay.

It was early morning now. The sun shone through the leaves outside, creating a dappled shadow on the windowsill. She could hear them talking in the hallway, wondering if they should come in and check on her. Eventually, they went away.

As team leader for the Guardian Cadre of Twelve, Leaf's quarters were the biggest. His suite included a bathroom, a walk-in closet, a drawing room, and a bedroom with a king-sized bed covered in dreamy pillows and soft furs. She liked the smell of his rooms—something like leather, steel, sunshine, cut lawn, and a hint of salty ocean. It all came together in a blend of Jace and Leaf, two lives as one.

She glanced down at the leather-bound journal in her hands. Before he left, Leaf had piled a collection of them on the bedside table so she could read Jace's private words. He wanted to give her time alone, said he'd skipped most of the passages about her because it hadn't appealed to him, and that he was glad he did.

He realized he didn't want someone else's memories of her clouding his mind. He wanted to make new ones, to learn about her through first-hand experience.

Nova stopped reading after the first entry. Jace's heartache was too much to bear. But after staring outside for hours, she'd eventually tried to skip ahead to read entries further into the future. But then she found his tone had changed. He wrote about her as if she was some goddess—had turned her into a perfect fantasy without flaws.

Somehow, that made it more difficult to read.

The dancing leaves outside were much prettier to watch. It reminded her of when she'd been lying beneath a tree, staring up at the leaves while Jace and Niles were on either side of her. They might have been in middle grade—because Jace grumbled about his parents wanting to send him to boarding school now that their business had been doing so well. Niles said it would be better than the dump they lived in. Nova told them both to shut up and watch the leaves.

"Nova."

She groaned. "I'm sleeping."

"I'm going to carry you to the bed."

Her eyes popped open. Leaf's handsome, concerned face hovered before hers. She smiled and touched his jaw but noticed the sun had set outside.

"I slept all day?" she moaned.

"I checked on you a few times, but yes." His brows lowered as he straightened to his full towering height, leaving her seated now she was awake. He looked delectable in his leather uniform and brooding expression. He jerked his chin toward the bed. "You should have slept there."

"I'm fine." She stretched her arms, popping her chest, and yawned.

A flash of desire caused heat to curl through her lower belly. It took her a moment to realize the emotion wasn't her own. She turned her glowing, marked hand to inspect the pattern. It was so strange—the markings were like a living tattoo inside her skin. And through that sparkling bond, she'd felt Leaf's emotional flare. When he'd left, Nova had reached for something that smelled like him. She wore the shirt she'd stolen from his closet. It was loose, white, and stopped at her thighs.

He strode to the bedside table and lit a candle, grumbling about not trusting tainted manabeeze in jars. Nova swiveled in the armchair, rested her elbow on the backrest, and enjoyed staring at him. Maybe it was the remnants of sleep or the warm and fuzzy feeling his shirt gave her, but she felt safe and content when he was with her. She felt like she was in the right place with the right person, even with all the confusion surrounding them.

Sensing her mood, he gave her a sideways glance, grumbled

some more, and stormed to the other side of the bed. His leather uniform creaked with jerky movements as he lit the next candle. A lock of long blond hair dangled as he bent forward, so he tucked it behind his ear.

"Are you going to watch me light all the candles?" he intoned without removing his eyes from the match as he struck. It flared too hot, and he almost burned himself. Cursing, he dropped the stick and stomped on it.

"Maybe." Her lips curved.

A wave of concern and frustration hit her through their connection. He tried to hide it, maybe even clamped down on whatever invisible tube allowed them to share, but she felt it. His lack of patience with the matches was another clue to something being wrong.

"How did the meeting go?" she asked.

"They want to talk with you."

"Okay."

"I said they had to wait." His scowl deepened as he took the matches to the drawing room.

"I don't mind. The sleep has done me good. Once we eat, I will be ready to take on the world."

He scoffed softly, lighting another match. It wouldn't strike. "Food isn't capable of miracles."

Right. Snarky, rude Leaf came out when he was bothered. She slid off the chair and walked to the drawing room. She took the matches from him and raised her brows. "Do you need help, *Papi?*"

He gestured at them. "The stupidest invention Trix has come up with."

"Trix?"

"She's from your time and likes to tinker with things," he mumbled. "Fae use mana to light candles, but I don't want the house to burn with the taint ruining things. These matches are what humans used in your time."

"I'm well aware of that." She smirked, pulled another stick from the book, and struck the end on the sandpaper. It fizzed and sparked, lighting with flame. "They're easy when you understand the right pressure and angle."

She gave him the lit match and leaned on the drawing room's doorframe, amused as he reluctantly lit the remaining two candles on the table for four. Beside it, near the window, were two upholstered settees of the same fabric as the armchair in his room. A framed picture of the ocean hung on the wall. A chandelier dangled from exposed wooden beams, but the glass canisters were empty. They might have held manabeeze once.

Seeing Leaf in this domestic setting reminded her of family meals at her kitchen table. She suddenly smelled her mother's spicy cooking and saw his younger self laughing and helping himself to more rice. She saw Niles argue with their father. She saw the crooked poem typewritten on yellowed paper on the frame on their wall.

"We used to have a poem near our kitchen table," she mused. "My mother loved it. My father hated it. My brother thought it was dumb. But Jace... he read it every time he came for dinner." She frowned as she tried to recall the words, but they flittered from her memory like one of the falling leaves outside. "Something about the world beginning and ending at the kitchen table."

Leaf joined her at the door. His gaze sharpened on her, and she sensed he was also listening to her emotions. She indulged in the details of his face. The brackets around his lips were from years of smiling, and like the fine lines outside his eyes, she realized they were from the sun—from the years he spent in the ocean, letting that heat bake down on his skin. When he became fae, he stopped aging, but it didn't reverse. Some of the fae Nova had met had skin so smooth sun damage was never a factor. Leaf's humanity never disappeared... even when he left Jackson Crimson behind.

Somehow, that thought made her smile.

"Did you read the journals?" His soft voice broke into her thoughts.

She hugged herself. "A page or two. But I couldn't read much."

"Do you need more time?" he offered. "I'll tell everyone to mind their own fucking business if they keep pestering me to meet you."

"They don't know you're... him?"

"I didn't presume you wanted them to know. It makes no difference to me."

She rested her head on the doorframe. "I think I know how you feel."

His fingers flexed once, then fisted as though he held back something. Candlelight flickered in his eyes, warming the blue. His sudden torrential release of emotions through their bond was a complicated mix of longing, need, concern, and fear. Her breath hitched at the intensity. His gaze darted to her lips, but he remained at a respectable distance.

The desire to reach out and drag him closer was impossible to deny. She wanted to finish what they started in the tree's hollow. She needed that comfort, so she pushed off the doorframe and closed the gap between them. She slid her palms up his leather jacket, bumping over the ribbing and piping until she locked her hands around his neck.

Tears stung her eyes as she remembered the first journal entry —Jace's agony when he woke from that illness at the Bellagio and found her gone and the world frozen around him. That illness was Jace's transformation into an elf. If she'd known all she had to do was wait it out with him, she'd never have left. She might have frozen anyway. His mutation might have raised his body temperature or made it possible for him to survive the temperature. She would never know.

"I flicked through the journals," she admitted, "but the more I read, the more I realized how much he missed me. How much he blamed himself for losing me. But then his accounts of me became unreal after a while. He wrote about me as if I was this perfect fantasy—he made me his religion. I was without flaws or mistakes, but..."

Guilt crushed her soul, growing bigger with each beat of her heart. She strode to the window near the drawing-room table. Like the one by the bed, the view was of a luscious tree at sunset. Folding her arms, she tried to stifle her temper. It was her instincts fighting to keep her afloat, to save herself from more misery by blaming Jace.

"What?" Leaf came to stand behind her. He swiped her hair to one side of her shoulders and lowered his lips to her bare neck. Their gazes clashed in the window's reflection. He had the face of the man she failed, the man she caused great suffering, and the man she didn't fight hard enough for... but she'd lost her chance to apologize for any of it.

"Leaf," she said to his reflection, "it took the world ending for us to reunite. Jace blamed himself for the distance that grew between us, but I could have fought harder. My brother caused all this pain, and I let him. I saw the signs and did nothing. I'm not this saint he made me out to be."

He rested his chin on her shoulder and his hands on her hips. "He remembered you the way lovers do."

"But I cry. I cuss. I shit just like anyone else. I'm not perfect, and... for him to wait so long for me like that... I'm..." She choked up, almost not wanting to voice the rest, but it came out anyway. "I'm glad he gave up. I'm glad he chose to wipe all that suffering away and start again. I loved him, but I wasn't perfect. If he met me now, with all those memories, he'd be disappointed in the reality."

Leaf sighed, and his mind went somewhere else for a while. Somewhere caught between the tree outside and the doubt swirling in his heart.

"So I won't read the journals," she announced. "I don't want to pollute my memory of Jace with the madness you said he eventually suffered. He had private thoughts I'm not sure were meant for me. He deserves to be remembered as the best version of himself."

"He wasn't mad," Leaf said quietly. "He was on his way but not insane yet."

"Can we... talk about something else? I want to move on with my life. Here. With you. With these people. I'm okay to meet them. And I'm ready to tell them about Niles."

"You don't have to do anything you don't want to," he mumbled, distracted.

Desire curled through their bond, heating her lower abdomen. In the reflection, Leaf stared with hot eyes as he traced idle patterns over her hips, bunching the shirt to reveal her thighs. He didn't realize she was watching him until she felt a bolt of lust and eagerness. He looked up. Their gazes clashed. He stepped back and cleared his throat.

"You are wearing my shirt," he noted.

She frowned. Why did he change the subject so swiftly? She faced him. "Your scent comforts me."

"But you're thinking of him."

She reached up and tugged his collar. "Does it matter?"

Despite his body language saying he wasn't interested, his desire flared when her fingers brushed his skin. And not just through their bond. She traced down the center of his jacket, popping studs to access his linen undershirt. The path of her fingers mesmerized them both.

Pop—she revealed a little more shirt.

Pop—their breathing shallowed.

Pop—she unlaced his shirt and glimpsed a defined, flat abdomen.

Pop—Leaf's steel grip wrapped around her wrists.

A warning flashed in his eyes.

"Has something changed?" she asked softly. "I thought you wanted this. We're mated now and..."

"You should take time to adjust," he said, voice far too husky to refute the desire scorching through their bond.

"No puedo creer mi suerte. Que tengo una pareja tan terco y tan estúpido que no puedes ver lo que está enfrente de tí. No sabes todo, Hoja."

His brow knitted adorably in concentration. He cocked his head, blue eyes darting between hers. "Did you just say that you can't believe your luck to have a... stupid mate who can't see what's right before you?" He blinked as more understanding came to him. "And then you said, 'You don't know everything, Leaf.'"

"*¡Ay Dios!* Can you understand me? Have you remembered?"

"No, I haven't remembered. But I somehow understood." His surprise darkened to anger. "Is this the sort of thing you've been lecturing me with all these times?"

Heat crept up her cheeks. "Well, in my defense, you do act arrogantly and stupidly. I can't help it if I need to get this frustration off my chest."

He let go of her wrists. His gaze dipped to her freckled cheeks. "Maybe our bond is deeper than emotion. There have always been rumors Well-blessed mates can share thoughts, but I've never seen it."

"So you know, then, Leaf of the Guardians. You know I do not want more time alone. I want to be with you. And if it is not me holding us back, then it is you. So spill. Why do you deny me now? Are you afraid I will think he was a better lover than you?" She folded her arms and raised her brows.

Pure, male ego shaped his expression into something Nova shouldn't be attracted to, but it made every nerve in her body tingle. His body had been hewn over numerous lifetimes from swinging a sword and hunting monsters. But if she told him how much hotter he was now, his ego would grow so big it would burst.

She folded her arms and raised her brow in question.

"It's not going to be the same," he warned. "You need to understand that."

She lifted to her toes and planted her lips on his. He froze. Tension flared and skipped over his skin like flames dancing across a log. A long second of doubt passed, then he released the hold on his emotions with a shuddering groan. He splayed his hands on her back and kissed her with deep, angry tongue swipes. She bowed backward under his brute force. A riot of lust and violence coursed through their bond. She whimpered as his passion drowned her. It was heady, dizzying, and ground-quaking.

He continued to kiss as he walked her to the bed, then pushed her down onto the mattress. She landed on her elbows while he looked down at her like a Greek god. Nothing but lust existed in his volcanic eyes.

"Take my shirt off," he ordered roughly, finally removing his jacket with harsh, hasty tugs.

She slipped the shirt over her head and was left naked except for her panties. His gaze blazed a path down her body, soaking in every inch. He froze, his shirt hanging off his arms. Nova's indulgent gaze lowered to his defined and tanned abdomen. Then down to the bulge tenting the leather at his groin.

The memory of him waking beside her, fisting his cock, came to mind. His smug grin as he caught her drooling over him. She bit her lip and crawled to him, tugging at his breeches, desperate to help him undress.

Shirt off, he dipped to capture her lips, demanding her attention. She whimpered and scrambled for his laces, still trying to have the best of both worlds. Finally, she gained access to his thick, hard cock and groaned with satisfaction.

Leaf flexed into her fist, gripped her hair, and pulled her head so she looked up to him. His next kiss was a mix of sharp stings in her head, teeth clashing, and insatiable desire unfurling.

"I want to taste you." She tried to dip her head.

He growled and pulled her hair, lifting her mouth back. Whimpering, she felt her need spiral out of control. He barely let her breathe, but when she did, she gasped, "I want to feel you in my mouth."

"No," he grunted and pushed her backward.

She bounced on the mattress, snarled at his denial, and tried to crawl back to take what she wanted. But he stood firm, holding her back with a lofty, calm expression that belied the tension in his body. Skin tight over muscle and sinew. Veins bulging and wreathing along his muscled forearms, at his temple and neck, and down at his taut abdomen. She licked her lips. His cock was so hard it jutted upward.

Breathing like a bull about to charge, he crossed to the window and closed the curtains. Turning back to her, he said, "Now we can fuck."

Her lips twitched. "Who's going to sit in a tree and watch us?"

"This is no one's fucking business but ours." He prowled back to her and roughly tugged her panties over her hips. He kissed her stomach and licked in circles, heading down to the junction between her thighs.

She fought him off with a smirk, then tried again to put his cock in her mouth. He stepped back, frustrated, and loomed over the bed with defiant eyes. His leather breeches were haphazard on his hips, and his hair was wild and loose, but he looked like a god to her—an angry god.

She loved knowing which buttons to push to make him lose control. It electrified her. It made her need more.

He shook her jaw gently. "I'd like to keep this pretty mouth in one piece. So don't tempt me."

"God," she moaned, "you say the hottest things to me."

His jaw set with frustration. "You're not understanding. If your mouth is the first part of you I fuck, I'll—"

"Oh, I know exactly what you mean, *Papi*." She licked her lips, sighing with feigned disappointment. "It's a shame you can't remember us back then because you'd see I took whatever he gave. He couldn't keep up with me. Maybe—"

"Fine. Have it your way." Leaf's eyes turned black, and he let go of her jaw. "Hands behind your back. Open your mouth."

CHAPTER
TWENTY-EIGHT

Nova sat back and opened her plump lips, and Leaf trembled. His vision darkened, and he stroked himself, trying to alleviate the agony of denying himself. But thousands of years of pining for her seemed to live beneath his skin. What other explanation was there for the intense need hammering his reason?

The moment their bond had triggered, he'd battled this desire. Logically, he knew he'd just met her. But every time he closed his eyes, he couldn't stop imagining this moment. Even as he found her sleeping, he'd fantasized about waking her by feasting between her thighs, licking up her slit and tonguing her clit until she grew wet.

Every time the urges hit, his eyes widened in horror, and he'd fled the room before making a fool of himself. This wild, burning desire to unleash was not him—he was civil and restrained. But Nova made an animal out of him. She sat so patiently, so eagerly, begging him to use her mouth. He sensed this obedience would be brief, and he liked that too. He liked that she wouldn't bend for him or anyone else. He liked that her soul was unbreakable, despite the tears.

"Such a needy little mouth," he murmured, swiping his thumb along her bottom lip, opening her wider. He dipped into her mouth to wet his thumb. "Show me."

Her pink tongue darted out, licked him, and then sucked him in deep. His cock jerked as her eyes met his. She made little, impatient whimpering sounds and shuffled forward on her knees.

"Nova..." he pleaded. His tone said to wait, but his hand guided the blunt tip of his erection over her wet lips. "You keep saying you're not perfect. But you are."

As he eased into her mouth, she closed her lips, and they groaned simultaneously. He shuddered from the agonizing pleasure pooling heat in his groin, begging him to thrust. She looked up at him, her eyes sharpened with sass, and her obedient streak was over. She gripped his buttocks and held firm as she licked and sucked and took him deep.

His restraint broke, and he thrust hard until his tip hit the back of her tight, slippery throat. One tiny point of contact and his eyes widened as he felt the first signs of orgasm heating. *Too soon.* He pulled out with a gasp and pushed her down on the bed. Before she could stop him, he climbed over her and claimed her lips. He reached between her thighs, and slid his fingers through her wet slit until she quivered with need. Breaking the kiss, she moaned, "You don't play fair."

"I won't until my mate has come at least twice." He nipped her lip, pinned her down with his body, and watched bliss enter her gaze as he coaxed out her first climax with his fingers. Deep satisfaction filled his soul when she melted for him. Sweeter than honey.

A sheen of sweat on her gorgeous skin, she panted while he slid down her body. His trail of kisses warned her of his intention as he nipped down her neck, forcing more gasps from her lips. Then he took her nipple into his mouth, swirled and sucked that little bud until her fingers threaded in his hair.

Then he continued south, spread her legs to accommodate his shoulders and did what he'd fantasized about all day. He licked straight down her drenched and quivering pussy, then feasted like a starved man.

"No... no more, *Papi*," she whined, writhing against his lips.

He grinned and looked up her body, caught her feverish gaze, and sensed her desire through their connection. "You say one thing, Estrella. Your body wants another."

"Too soon." She chased his lips with her pussy.

"Greedy little cunt." He kissed it. "Wants more, yes?"

She nodded, gripped his hair, and pressing his mouth to her clit. He slid his finger in, felt her tightness, and knew he wasn't done. She had to be ready to fit him, because he wasn't holding back once he filled her. He added a second finger.

"Oh fuck." Her breath hitched. "You're so... *mmm*." She bit the blanket as he fit a third finger, stretching her inner walls. More muffled words filled him as he tasted her desire and laved and sucked her with relentless rhythmic flicks. She broke apart on his tongue, her inner walls clenching around his fingers, as she gave a throaty cry, cursing the ceiling.

Finally, when she was too languid and spent to move, he kissed her inner thigh and reared back on his knees. Her flushed cheeks brightened her freckles. Sweat plastered some of her wild hair to her face. She breathed heavily, jutting her breasts. But her eyes—those saucy, tempestuous eyes promised a reckoning for his demanding behavior. His lips curved, inviting her wrath, welcoming it... needing it.

She pushed onto her elbows, and looked down her body at him, then held up two angry fingers. "That's how many you owe me in a row—" Her temper died. "Baby, why are you smiling like the wolf who ate the pig?"

"Because," he said, tugging her hips down to him. "Now I know you'll forgive me for this next bit."

He thrust in to the hilt, then stole her gasp with a plundering kiss. He pinned her wrists beside her head and snarled, "I'm so sorry, love." The restraint on his impossible hunger broke. He took her with ravaging, fast, and deep thrusts. He lost all sense of decorum or time and gave into his body's desperation to be inside her, feeling her, being surrounded by her, holding her. His orgasm ripped from somewhere deep with an intensity that shredded his nerves.

Lungs heaving with ragged, savage breaths, he looked into her eyes. He prayed she would understand and forgive him because he'd barely touched the sides of his need.

He wasn't deaf to others' opinions of him. He *was* arrogant. He *was* bossy. As it turned out, he had a right to be—he was Jackson fucking Crimson. The name every fae cursed or prayed to like a god. But he couldn't remember what he'd done to make him give up and walk into the lake.

Leaf needed Nova to stay with him. To work with him, even

when he made mistakes because he wasn't a god, and he would eventually fuck up.

"I didn't mean to be so..." he started, his voice rough. "I want... *Well-dammit,* I can't even say it right."

She cupped his face and looked deeply into his eyes. "I understand."

"You do?"

"Yes." She rocked her hips into his, pointing out that he was hard again. "You owe me one more."

She planted her hand on his chest and rolled them so she was on top. Her cocky eyebrow lifted, and she undulated her hips until his breath caught with desire. He reveled in her vibrant spirit. She gazed down at him through a curtain of long, wavy hair. Her heady mix of triumph and lust snuck through their bond. His lips parted, but she slapped her palm over his mouth and gave him a warning look.

No more talking. Message received. So he banded his arms around her, pinning her in place, and proved that it didn't matter if she was on top. He would always find a way to dominate... and she would always find a way to humble him.

Hours later, with her head on his chest, she traced circles on his abdomen and listened to his heartbeat. She admitted that since he'd shown her the trick with the horse, hugging and hearing hearts was her next favorite thing.

He finally found the right words. "You ground me, Nova."

"Hmm?" she murmured dreamily.

"That's what I wanted to say before and—" He frowned, already flustered again. "And I need that to never fade from our relationship."

She lifted her head to meet his gaze. "You mean you need me to keep your big head from floating away."

He chuckled. "If you have to put it like that, fine."

She dropped back down with a sigh. "I need you to always fight for me... even when... even when you're threatened. I would rather die than be pushed aside."

His heart clenched. "Why would you say that?"

"Because I think that's what Niles did to keep Jace away. I don't know if we will ever be in the same situation, but if we are—if we find ourselves back there by some chance of fate—you have to know I won't accept it this time. You, and your big head, are everything I need. I'd rather die than have a *gilipollas* like my brother come between us again."

"Nero won't be a problem," he murmured, kissing her temple.

Staring at the ceiling, he swiped her shoulder with his thumb, back and forth. He waited until her breathing evened out and she fell asleep before he started making plans in his mind. Then he closed his eyes and sank into his subconscious. He dropped to where the Well bubbled with power and whispered promises and lies—to where it had waited hundreds of years for his return.

"I'm here," he announced. "Whatever you need me to do, I'll do it. Whatever you want, I'll give. Just tell me how to fix this taint. I can't keep her safe unless it's gone. Tell me how to unmake Maebh."

CHAPTER TWENTY-NINE

Nova woke to blinding light shining through the window and Leaf's head buried between her naked thighs. His tongue worked lazy magic on her clit, stroking her nerves to life, spreading heat throughout her body. She moaned as he slid his finger in, curling to increase her pleasure.

"Hoja." Her fingers speared into his hair and fisted. "What a way to wake me."

Ocean-blue eyes clashed with hers, and he lifted his head to say, "Opening the curtains didn't work."

Then he returned his undivided attention to her pussy, bringing her to climax as though they had all the time in the world. He notched his cock to her entrance, ready to thrust in, but a pounding at the door stopped him.

"I heard you the first time," Leaf barked.

The first time? How long had someone been standing out there? Nova's eyes widened, and she whispered, "Who is that?"

"An imbecile with furry ears."

"I heard that!" A deep male voice returned. "And I can also hear *and* smell you're both awake, so get the fuck out here so Clarke will stop pestering me." A woman shouted from somewhere else in the house. The deep voice outside grumbled, "Now I'm in trouble. Get out here in five minutes, or I'm clawing my way inside."

Angry stomps receded down the hallway.

Leaf slid off the bed with a regretful glance between her open legs. He scrubbed his hand through his long hair and muttered something about the Well.

Nova dragged a sheet to cover her naked body. "What time is it?"

"Noon."

"What?" She jackknifed up. "But I wanted to make everyone dinner. I have to decide on the menu, find food, and determine how many people will come."

A crease formed between his brows as he tugged on his leather breeches. "Why?"

"I just wanted to make meeting them special."

"Again, why?"

She tossed the sheet and stormed over to poke him in the chest. The warm, slightly sweaty muscle distracted her momentarily, but she quickly rallied and scowled at him. "If you can't understand the concept of making a good first impression, then I'm afraid there's no hope for you, Mister High and Mighty *Hoja de los Guardianes.*"

His lip twitched, and his eyes danced with amusement, but then he frowned and touched her cheek. "You're afraid they'll hate you like they do your twin."

Her jaw dropped. A wash of embarrassment and shame heated her cheeks, but then Leaf's assurance hit her through their bond.

She tried to pull away, but he tugged her back, cupped her face, and kissed her lips tenderly.

"If I can love you, so will they."

"Seriously? Is that meant to be a compliment?"

Now it was his turn to feel embarrassed. She rewound her thoughts to what he'd said, then realized his confession.

"You love me?" she murmured.

"I probably shouldn't," he grumbled.

She smacked him on the shoulder. "Probably shouldn't?!"

He laughed, as if he'd intended to push her buttons, then sobered and said, "We're both so new at this, but—"

"But our hearts have known each other forever." She slid her palm over his smooth chest, feeling his beat beneath the bone. It was sad to think that Jace would never again be the driving force behind Leaf's words. There was much to learn about Leaf. But the heart mattered most, and hers told her that this elf was her one and only. She smirked at the apprehension on his face as he waited for her response. "I guess I love you, too."

"You guess?" he growled, his elven ears twitching.

"Your ears moved." She giggled and tried to touch them.

"They do that sometimes." He ducked to avoid her swiping fingers. "Not human anymore, remember?"

Tension crept into his shoulders, and he tried to brush her off again. With a huff, he turned to find his shirt, but she stood before him with a smile.

"*¡Ay, qué menso!* Of course, I love you." She continued in Spanish, laughing about how the big warrior with muscles as thick as her thighs and an ego as big as the tree outside was hurt by her little joke.

Eventually, he captured her hand, held it prisoner against his chest, and said, "Good."

"Ooh, good, he says," she mocked, rolling her eyes.

He dropped his lips to her ear and said hotly, "Remember that tonight when these 'big warrior muscles' finish what I started in bed."

At her shock, a self-satisfied smile tugged his lips, and he left to dress in his walk-in closet.

"You understood my words," she pouted. "I liked it better when you couldn't understand my insults!"

He returned in his Guardian uniform and tossed her a dress. "I borrowed that from one of the girls."

She slipped it over her head and tied the waistband. The skirt flared and dropped to her ankles, but the bodice was tight enough.

"It's nice," she said. "I'll have to thank whoever lent it."

"Clarke," he grumbled, scowling at Nova's chest. "I should have asked for something more tailored."

She tugged at the neckline. It was a little loose, and her girls were flowing free. She finished washing her face and tied back her hair, making sure to put on the hoop earrings Leaf gifted. When she went to apply the lip stain left from the wake, her glowing freckles halted her. Unease started to unfurl in her stomach, but before it spread too far, she finished painting her lips, rubbed some floral perfume on her neck, and joined Leaf in the main room.

"Don't be nervous," he said. "You'll meet just a few now. The rest are either sleeping, out on a mission, living in a fucking palace, or dealing with Maebh's war. You'll meet them at some point later."

"At dinner," she insisted. "Not just because I want them to like me, but because coming together over a regular meal is important for the survival of a family. Even though you don't say it, I think these people are your family. So they'll be mine, yes? The moment my family dinners failed, my family fell apart."

His brow arched. "I think you're overestimating your brother's capacity to be human."

She blinked. His words sparked something in her memory—something Niles said on that day he'd left. Sensing her worry increase, Leaf's eyes flashed with defense, and he gently touched her cheek.

"What's wrong?"

"I... you reminded me that Niles said he overestimated me as a threat. He'd come to dinner to 'tie up loose ends'—whatever that meant—but then... gosh, what did he say?" She tapped her forehead, trying to remember. It had something to do with... "Oh. He said, in hindsight, I was clueless about being the only person alive who knew everything, and he wasted his time coming."

"Tying up loose ends means he was going to kill you." His eyes darkened.

She wanted to say that Niles would never have done that, but it was a lie. She sat down on the bed, her throat closing up. "I almost didn't make it to Vegas. I almost never saw Jace again—or met you."

"Don't overthink it. The Well brought you here to me." Leaf kneeled before her and touched her knees. "I spent a decade avoiding my fate—I'm sure Clarke will tell you all about how stubborn I've been running from it. But I found you anyway, and you'd only thawed months before. The Well wants what it wants, Nova."

"You make this Well sound all-powerful, but if it is, then why is my brother winning?"

Emotion shuttered in his eyes, and he stood. Nova thought he wouldn't answer for a moment, but he stared out the window and said, "Crimson heard whispers from the Well. Some of these whispers became prophecies. The Well can control certain things like whether to preserve a human from the old world and when to let them thaw. But the Well can't control certain events, like free choice, or love and hate. That's where we come in. It's given us what our heart desires, and even if we fight it at first, inevitably, we all find our lives enriched by this relationship. It's only right that in return, we fight for what it needs to survive."

Her eyes watered. "You think I enrich your life?"

"Not just me. Everyone's life."

He lifted her from the bed and pulled her into his embrace. "The Well is just like all of us. It wants a happy ending."

CHAPTER THIRTY

Aleksandra lay in agony on the cold slate floor of Maebh's private chambers. Steel rods pierced and enveloped her wrists like manacles, cutting off her connection to the Well. But that wasn't what hurt the most; it was Maebh's betrayal. After all they'd shared, how could she do this?

She glanced around the royal apartments. Books were in tattered pieces and lying in ash or crumpled paper piles. Dried blood from rampaging, murderous feeds painted the walls. The demogorgon prowled, clicking deep in its throat, pacing alongside Aleksandra as though just waiting for permission to pounce.

Maebh wandered into the room, covered from head to toe in black, and blinked at Aleksandra with bloodshot eyes. Sometimes she rambled, sometimes she spat obscenities and threats, but most of all, she promised retribution.

Aleksandra wished she could muster empathy, but from the

moment Leaf had shouted those words as she was stolen in the air, her heart had only one thought: *She might be alive.*

For centuries she had known this day would come, that her fate was sealed when Leaf found his mate. She'd planned her exit from this world with meticulous care, right down to her wake. She'd packed and tidied as much of her house as she could without making it obvious that she was leaving and never returning. The Well would assign a new Prime, so naming a successor was unnecessary. As each dawn arrived, Aleksandra's heart hardened into stone.

The wake had crumbled and cracked that stone, giving her a taste of what it felt like to be human again. And then... she couldn't risk it. She couldn't risk facing the possibility that the daughter they thought dead in the Fallout was alive. And the man who fathered her was the enemy waiting at their gates. If only her memory stretched far enough to gather the details, to arm herself with ammunition and fight back.

She watched through the swollen slits of her eyes as Maebh paced by the doors and gave directions to her generals.

"The time has come," Maebh said, voice a hissed rasp. "We have the Prime."

"And the battleground?" a rough, high-pitched male voice.

Maebh paused, then glanced at Aleksandra through the archway. Although her face was hidden behind a veil, Aleksandra sensed her ex-partner's wicked smile as she said, "Send that rabid wolf king an invitation to meet us at the Cornucopia when the moon is highest during Samhain."

"But... I thought you said it was somewhere else?"

"It is, fool." There was a hissing snap from behind Maebh's veils.

"He will go there, and we will go to the Order. We will send decoys. Even if the portals don't work, we will have time before they realize their mistake. We will take the Order, raze it to the ground, and then while his people are in Cornucopia or racing to the aid of the Order, we'll move onto the Seelie Kingdoms. They'll be chasing our tails."

"We tried to attack the Order and... suffered casualties."

"We learned their weaknesses. And now, with the taint, most of their new power is null," corrected another male voice. This one sounded more seasoned. "What's more pressing, as I've mentioned to Our Illustrious Queen, is how a Guardian massacred an entire troop of our soldiers in one fell swoop. Do we risk the answer being the taint or wait to do our due diligence?"

Maebh took deep, raspy breaths. "I have the Prime. I have the demogorgon. And very soon, I'll have Wild Hunt at my command. Nothing else matters."

CHAPTER THIRTY-ONE

Leaf kept a protective hand on Nova's back as they walked down the creaking stairs and into the living room. Clarke and Rush waited on the sofa by a window that revealed the Twelve's training lawn. Thorne sat on an armchair with Laurel in his lap, his legs sprawled out and his face tipped to the ceiling in boredom.

On the other sofa, Forrest's auburn hair was notable next to Melody's pale blond curls. Leaf had spoken with Cloud, Shade, and other Councilors last night at the temple. Clarke and Rush were also there. They seemed to think they were honorary council members these days, but no one complained. The two worked hard at keeping things running here at the Order.

Part of their lengthy discussions revolved around whether they should rescue the Prime, but Preceptress Dawn warned against it. Not because she'd seen something with her second sight, but because she said Aleksandra knew this day would come. She left a sealed letter for Leaf. He'd not read it. She obviously knew he was Crimson, so she treated him differently than the other Guardians, grooming him to take back leadership of the Order.

But the Prime was still alive. The Well hadn't chosen him yet. He would deal with that problem if or when it arose.

This meeting served as an official introduction for Nova, and an opportunity for anyone to gain answers to questions that might be bothering them. There would be more meetings, he was sure. Given the circumstances, Rush pounding down his door was unnecessary. He was about to tell him so when Nova's anxiety surged. Coupled with the cautious hope on her face, he bit back his retort.

He didn't want to ruin this for her with his temper. So he clenched his jaw and made the introductions.

"Everyone, this is Nova—my mate. I believe a few of you saw us arrive last night."

"About time," growled Thorne. He looked ready to say more, but Laurel must have pinched him because he yipped like a dog and scowled at her. But she only glared back before giving Nova a friendly smile.

"Nice to meet you," she said. "I'm Laurel, and this bonehead is Thorne."

Thorne nipped her neck, making her giggle, and then he stared at Nova with unassuming eyes. "Welcome."

Excitement enlivened Clarke's face. She tried to launch off the sofa, but Rush yanked her back by the skirt, grumbling, "Don't frighten her away, princess."

"Sorry," she said, a bashful blush coloring her freckled cheeks. "I'm just sooo excited to meet you finally. And to ask a few things, but... okay, okay, I'll chill." She placated Rush with a pat on the thigh. "I'm Clarke, and this bossy-boots is Rush. He's also Thorne's father."

Nova frowned as her gaze darted between the two wolf shifters. She opened her mouth but then closed it. Leaf sensed her confusion and leaned in to remind her, "We don't age after hitting maturity. Neither will you now."

"Oh, that's right. Of course, how silly."

Forrest cleared his throat, waiting for them to look at him, and waved, "I'm Forrest, and this is Melody."

"*¡Ay me asustaste!*" Nova jolted and touched her heart as Melody waved. "Forgive me, but I thought he said Melody. As in Melody—"

"Yes, ma'am, that's me," Melody said, smiling. "Same boat as you, I'm afraid. Frozen and now here in the flesh. Although, I guess not exactly like these ladies and you. I was in Crystal City for a few years before this handsome elf barbarian snack swept me off my feet." She pouted and kissed Forrest daintily on the lips.

His cheeks turned beet red, and he laughed nervously, darting his gaze around as he mumbled to Melody, "I thought you weren't going to call me that in public?"

"This ain't public, sugar." She smirked.

"Great," Leaf grumbled. "Now introductions are over, we can—"

"Uh, *Hoja de los Guardianes*, introductions are not over. I have more to say, if you don't mind."

Leaf's eyes widened. Everyone watched him like a hawk, but there was nowhere to hide. He smiled and replied, "The floor's yours."

"Well, as I live and breathe," Melody gushed, her grin broadening on Nova. "You certainly are this male's perfect match. Ain't she, darlin'?"

Forrest grunted in agreement but refrained from comment. As did the rest of the males. Nova blushed and picked at the tie on her dress. Her nerves still vibrated enough for Leaf to feel them.

"I'm Nova Morales," she said, a slight tremble in her voice. "I don't think Leaf has explained who my twin brother is to you, but I firmly believe in laying your cards on the table as early as possible."

Leaf slid his hand beneath Nova's hair to cup her nape, letting her know he stood by her, no matter what she chose to say next. She sent him a grateful sideways glance and returned to the others in the room. "My twin's name is Niles Morales, but you probably know him as Nero."

"What!" Forrest bolted to his feet, his eyes ablaze with fury. Melody tugged him down, but concern never left her eyes. Leaf moved his hand to Nova's shoulder and pulled her beneath his arm.

"You said what?" Laurel spluttered.

A deep, animalistic snarl rumbled in Rush's chest, followed by Thorne's, like a pack of wolves sighting their next meal. From the pale look on Clarke's face, she'd not seen this development in her psychic visions. Leaf sensed Nova's panic rising. He'd overestimated their tolerance, but as his own violence rose in retaliation, so did the presence of the Well rolling like a wave in his mind. He relaxed his fist and exhaled. There was another way to go about this than with tempers.

"I'm Jackson Crimson," he announced.

All eyes snapped to him.

"What?" Clarke screeched.

"What!" someone bellowed from upstairs, likely Indigo or one of the vampires who should be sleeping but was instead listening in. Thudding footsteps down the stairs grew louder, and River burst

into the room. Disheveled blue-black hair, ruffled wings, and a tattooed shirtless torso. He wore his Guardian breeches, so had probably been avoiding the meeting rather than sleeping. Trust the crow to insert himself at the first sign of gossip.

"Let's sit down," Leaf grumbled, planting himself in the only free armchair and pulling Nova onto his lap.

River pointed at his face, stalking into the room. "Wait just a Well-damned minute. Did I hear what I thought I heard?"

"I think you did!" came a muffled shout upstairs—definitely Indigo.

"Let's not get too excited," Leaf said. "I don't remember a thing."

River folded his arms and stroked his jaw, eying Leaf with suspicion. "This makes so much sense." He spotted Nova, and suddenly his entire demeanor changed. He flashed a flirtatious grin and reached out to her. "Hi. I'm River."

She took his hand and shook it. "Hello. I'm Nova."

Leaf bit off his warning as the crow smirked at him with mischief, then skirted the armchair to stand behind Forrest and Melody... who still looked stunned. River's gaze narrowed as he surveyed the room. He tapped his chin and said, "I could be wrong, but I'm sensing a little hostility in the air."

"Shut up," Thorne snapped, his unwavering gaze on Nova.

Leaf's mate tensed, her breathing shallowed, and fear prickled through their bond.

"Listen up." Leaf's tone sharpened. He tugged his mate closer so he could glare at everyone over her shoulder. "Nova is not her brother. Do not lower the tone by treating her as a criminal without due cause. You're all better than that. Now, I'm sure you all have questions, and we will get to them over tonight's house dinner."

Nova's gaze snapped to his, but he held command of the room and continued. "I want to see everyone at that table, or I'll personally track you down and drag you back like children. We should be beyond this sort of reprehensible behavior by now."

Silence answered him. Nova said a few quiet words in Spanish about not needing him to fight her battles, but thank you very much for inflating his ego to clear the room of doubt. He replied, "You're welcome," to which she continued to voice her opinion about whether next time they should talk about how to reveal secrets that were obviously a big deal despite him acting on the contrary.

She tried to hide the feisty flare in her eyes from the room as she lectured him, but with each word spoken, he felt her tension ease. He would happily submit to eons of lectures if it helped her feel comfortable.

Laurel blurted. "You realize she spoke in Spanish, right?"

He shrugged. "Of course."

"But you don't remember anything about being Jackson Crimson. How did you learn Spanish? I haven't heard anyone speak it in Elphyne."

He stilled, realizing his faux pas. "I don't know."

He hadn't wanted to delve into detail about Nova's gift today, but he supposed her freckles were obvious. Someone was bound to ask soon.

Nova pointed to her face. "These are new. We don't know exactly what they're for, but sometimes Leaf can pick up memories. Or understand some things like the Spanish. That's weird, right?"

"Weird, but cool." Laurel leaned forward to inspect Nova's face from across the room. "They look pretty awesome, babe. I'm just saying if the Well had to give a girl a mark—cute glowing freckles are the way to go."

"I wish mine glowed." Clarke pouted, touching her freckle-laden face. Rush grumbled something in her ear, and she softened against him.

"I wish mine glowed," River mocked in a high-pitched voice.

"Shut up!" Clarke threw a cushion at his head.

He snatched it out of the air and smirked. Rush just shook his head, as if this tit-for-tat between the two was a common occurrence.

"Hun, we didn't mean to be rude," Melody told Nova. Forrest's glare remained hard, so she squeezed his thigh in warning. "Sugar, Leaf is right. Nova isn't her brother. And I, for one, would like to hear her story tonight over dinner. Who's cooking, by the way? Because I think y'all know I'm not a good chef."

"I'm cooking." Nova raised her voice. "It would be my pleasure."

Leaf grunted. "She's very good."

"Better not poison us," River grumbled as he strolled from the room.

"Don't mind him," Clarke said. "He's just feeling the pressure now he knows the crows are next in line to find their mates."

"Ah, yes," Nova said. "Leaf mentioned you were psychic."

"I had a little talent in our time, too. Unfortunately, your brother tortured Laurel so I would give him the nuclear codes." She melted back into the sofa. "It's hard not to blame myself for everything that followed."

Nova gasped. Leaf's gaze hardened at everyone in case they needed reminding about giving her a chance.

"I'm so sorry," Nova said to Clarke. "I know he's done horrible, unmentionable things. He..." She took a deep breath for courage. "He murdered our parents. He broke Jace and me up, and... I guess I'm not saying this as an excuse, but... I just... You have to know I will do everything possible to stop him."

After hearing her pain, they had the grace to look ashamed of their initial reactions.

"I believe you," Clarke said. "I wish I had seen more of you in my visions, but for some reason, you're a little like Nero—I call him the Void because he's managed to evade my attention. You're like a bright star, blinding me. I don't understand it."

Nova's thoughts turned inward, and Leaf said, "We'll discuss this later. Tell any of the Twelve you can find about dinner." To Clarke, he asked, "Where's Cloud?"

She shrugged, but something flickered in her gaze before asking, "Can we help with dinner?"

Nova slid off Leaf's lap. "Yes, actually. I have a few ideas but need help with... I guess everything else. Where do we find ingredients? And the kitchen?"

The women all stood and invited Nova to go with them. She kissed his cheek before going and whispered loudly, "Don't worry, *Papi*. I'm sure you'll be fine without me."

"Hmm, yes," Laurel added, smirking at him. "I'm sure they won't be angry that you've been hiding a very big secret."

Leaf's lips parted, but they left, chatting like old friends. He'd have marveled at how easily the women adjusted if he weren't dealing with a pack of angry Guardians. A flash of concern remained for his mate, and he vowed to keep an eye on her through their bond. If she felt threatened for one second, he would find her.

"So, what the fuck?" Thorne growled, his brows lifting.

Rush stared at Leaf, his dark brows lowering.

Forrest said, "How long have you known?"

"Only days," he replied.

"You expect us to believe you had *no clue* before then?" Sarcasm dripped from Cloud's voice as he emerged from the shadows of the unused dining room.

His unimpressed gaze swept up and down Leaf's body. He wore the same battle leathers as the previous night. Leaf could tell by the splash of dried blood on his cheek and arm.

"Good," he said, standing. "You're here. Tell your taloned friends to be at dinner tonight."

"That's it?" Thorne tossed his hands in the air. "You're just going to pretend this is nothing?"

"Why wouldn't he?" Cloud cocked his head. "Seems all he does these days is nothing."

Leaf sighed and pinched the bridge of his nose. "I have zero recollection of being that person, and I likely never will. Anything I glean is from the journals or Nova's memories. Now, if you're ready to pull your heads from your rear ends, I have the answer to how we unmake Maebh."

He crossed to the front door but found Ash quietly watching. The crow shifter's dark eyes didn't blink. Dark hair lifted from his shoulders as though a gust of wind had passed through the room. But no windows were open.

"Not much time between last night and now," Ash pointed out dryly. "Considering the entire house heard how busy you were, I'm not sure how you had time to find this answer... or were you keeping the secret all along?"

Danger fizzed through the air, lifting the hairs on Leaf's arms. He stared the crow shifter down and said, "If you're accusing me of something, spit it out."

"You could have mentioned this at the Council meeting," Cloud said. "But you didn't. What else are you keeping from us?"

Leaf glanced over his shoulder and saw River had returned. In his leathers now, ready to intimidate. This little confrontation must have been pre-meditated. Considering the others weren't defending Leaf, they also distrusted him. He was surprised Shade hadn't found a way to join in this ambush. Taking Leaf down a notch was his favorite pastime.

"Fine," Leaf said, returning to Cloud because he'd rather face a stab in his back. The crow was far from Maebh or Crimson's age, but his obsessive tendencies started showing. Leaf wanted to tell him what fate awaited him if he didn't change his priorities, but he knew the crow wouldn't listen. Only his two-winged friends might stand a chance at swaying his mind. But that was a problem for tomorrow.

"Maebh is mad," he said.

"Tell us something we don't know," River muttered.

"Aleksandra's heart has become stone," Leaf continued. "It seems Crimson was on the same path as Maebh. His journals increasingly grew fixated on finding his lost love and an artifact he believed would protect the Well, once and for all."

"Was this the missing prophecy you hunted for?" Rush narrowed his eyes.

"No," Leaf admitted. "This was all in the journals if anyone bothered to read them. I don't think the missing prophecy had anything to do with us but pertained to Aleksandra's death. She knew it was coming and planned for it. She told me I would find a way to relive Crimson's memories once I brought my mate to her... I took that as being about the prophecy, but as you saw with Nova's freckles, I can experience some of her memories, including the ones with Crimson."

"I'm still waiting to hear something new." Cloud's scarred eyebrow raised. "Like why we should trust your mate to be in the same room as us."

A small snort of disbelief puffed out of Leaf. He shook his head and raised his brows. Now he knew why the crows had avoided meeting Nova.

"That's ironic, coming from you," Leaf said. "Nova is why we have information that could help us save the Well. She's also revealed something that sheds doubt on your previous truths about Aurora."

"Bullshit." Cloud's eyes sparked with lightning.

Leaf turned his gaze to the others in the room, all watching with wary eyes. He asked, "Did anyone know Maebh and Aleksandra had a child *before* the Fallout?"

"I knew they had a relationship but nothing else," Rush replied. "What has this got to do with anything?"

"The Prime herself said there had been nothing between her and the Unseelie High Queen for centuries," Forrest added.

"Get to the point, Leaf," Thorne grumbled.

"Nova is Nero's twin—Crimson was their friend. Nero betrayed both of them. He murdered Nova's parents, and he destroyed the world so he could rebuild it. A man like that is very good at making plans." Leaf scrubbed his hand through his hair. "Not long before the Fallout, Nero went to see his sister one last time to gloat. He ate dinner with her at their family table, told her she'd lost some race she didn't know they competed in, and then walked outside to a family waiting for him in the car."

"Maebh and the Prime?" Ash's head tilted.

"And their daughter," Leaf confirmed, then looked at Cloud. "Their teenage daughter."

"Why are you looking at me?" he snapped.

"You told us Rory was Maebh's granddaughter." Leaf waited for the cogs to turn in Cloud's mind, and when they did, the response wasn't what Leaf expected.

"What the fuck does it matter?"

"Because if Maebh believes her daughter is still alive, I think there's a greater chance she'll voluntarily return every last drop of mana in her body to the Well. If she does this, she will become human again, thus unmaking herself."

"I'm with Cloud," River said. "If Maebh won't stop this bullshit for her granddaughter, then why would she do it for her daughter?"

"Obsession starts with a single point of origin," he explained. "Maybe a thought or person that won't leave your mind—every decision made circles back to that trigger. Even if the choices seem unconnected, they're not. Maebh's second child with Mithras could have been an attempt to replace her first. Then she sent her child away to be a changeling in Crystal City. Or so we've been told. Perhaps she did. But Mithras had something over her. Something happened, and he used it to blackmail Maebh into giving him half of Elphyne. She might have believed Cloud's claim for a while, but maybe she knew Rory was never her granddaughter."

Rush's gaze narrowed. He rubbed his beard and said, "It's

always struck me as odd that she never attempted to rescue her child. Ever."

A rumble of agreement passed over the seated Guardians.

Leaf nodded. "But if we can convince Maebh that saving Rory is—"

Cloud's words came from a dark, hidden place in his soul. "Saving that fucked-up bitch is not on the cards. Get that through your thick heads."

"You're willing to lose the Well and all you are because of a personal vendetta?"

The scowling fool pushed off the doorframe and came toe to toe with Leaf. "Mark my words, elf. I've waited a long time for her reckoning, and if you get in my way, I'll gladly call it a Vendetta. Every crow shifter I know will rally to hunt her down until she's murdered." He casually dusted imaginary lint from Leaf's collar before drawling, "And if you get in my way, I'll gladly add your feisty little whore's name to the list."

He shoved past and palmed the front door. It slammed open on its hinges. A cold breeze blustered in. Two breaths later, Cloud's wings beat, and he was gone.

"He doesn't mean it," River nervously laughed, glancing at Ash.

A tendon in Ash's jaw flexed, but he said nothing. He knew Cloud's threat wasn't in jest. Official Vendettas in their community weren't satisfied until their quarrel was dead. Too many innocent lives ended up ruined from the obsessive need for vengeance. As far as Leaf knew, no one had called one in decades for this reason. Courting madness was a fool's errand. But as they'd all just witnessed, Cloud was already halfway there.

As his closest friends, Ash and River would be honor-bound to participate if Cloud summoned them... no questions asked.

"For fuck's sake." River pointed at Leaf. "You'd better be one hundred percent certain about that claim, or you'll live to regret it."

He started for the stairs, but Ash's words stopped him dead in his tracks.

"Where did you learn how to unmake Maebh, Leaf?" His eyes narrowed. "Because the winds are telling me interesting things... like... I'm not the only one they whisper secrets to anymore."

Curious.

Leaf stared at Ash. "That's not the winds, D'arn Ash. It's the Well."

CHAPTER THIRTY-TWO

In the space of a few hours, and with the help of the women, Nova sourced enough ingredients for what she hoped would be the most delicious feast this ragtag family had ever tasted. It was hard to keep the eagerness from her eyes as they finished preparing in the kitchen. She hated looking desperate, but this cobblestone kitchen was gorgeous. The instant she stepped inside, she felt a kinship with the room.

Clarke tried unsuccessfully to cut salad ingredients as she sat on a stool at the butcher-block counter. Laurel worked on cocktails. Melody hummed a tune as she stirred a pot of chili. Every now and then, she put her finger in and then licked it. Nova took it as a good sign if Melody couldn't stop testing.

What Nova loved the most was these women's friendly acceptance with other fae who often dropped into the house from around the campus. Many sought out Clarke's advice. Apparently, she had a knack for sensing the truth or seeing through fae glamour.

Two house brownies usually managed the meals and upkeep of the home. They met Nova with obvious distrust, especially since she was taking over their kitchen—their territory. It seemed no one else enjoyed cooking much. Nova had invited them to stay, but they'd declined. Clarke said not to take it personally. The brownies were like that with everyone.

"Here." Nova grabbed Clarke's cutting board. "I will finish the salad for you."

Clarke groaned. "I'm so sorry. I'm the shittiest cook."

Nova laughed. "I enjoy it. My mama and I would treat our kitchen like a haven from the grumbling men. Of course, Jace never really got the memo. He would always insist he lend a hand. His help usually arrived in the form of taste testing."

Melody's finger paused in her mouth. Her eyes widened.

"I swear it was just once," she said, making them all laugh. "Hand on my heart, I swear. Okay fine. It was a few times, but honestly, Nova, this is the best goddamned tasting chili I've ever had."

"Must be the rich soil," she replied wistfully. "I used to... never mind."

"Tell us."

"You'll think I was one of those annoying activist people who chained themselves to trees."

"Okay, now I'm intrigued." Laurel poured her concoction into four awaiting glasses.

"I flunked high school," Nova said, focusing on slicing a vegetable similar to a tomato, but without seeds. "Niles was the star, and... anyway, after Jace moved away and took over his father's company, I decided there was nothing I wanted more than to fight to keep this planet on the right track. I spent many months overseas, clearing up trash from the oceans and trying to build better systems for all our waste. But eventually, I ran out of money and had to return home. I guess my point is that seeing how delicious this food tastes now can only mean the earth is unpolluted. It's being cared for. That's all I ever dreamed of."

"I love hearing that. I can see why the Well likes you." Laurel handed Nova a cocktail glass, then divided the rest. "Let's make a toast to—" She closed her mouth and glanced nervously at Nova.

Distrust simmered in the air. She had the sense it was aimed at her. Because of her brother, or who her mate was? Or something else altogether? Rather than stretch the awkwardness, Nova quickly lifted her glass and said, "We should toast to happier times. If the Well has brought so many strong women together like this, our future will be bright."

They studied Nova as if assessing her authenticity. Paranoia started to build. Why weren't they saying anything?

"To a brighter future," Clarke suddenly said and raised her glass. They all clinked their glasses together, but Nova couldn't shake the feeling of being on the outside.

"This tastes amazing," she said after her first sip.

"I'm getting pretty good at them." Laurel blushed. "It takes time to get used to being here. The food can be different. The customs. But it's worth it."

Clarke reached across the counter to squeeze Nova's hand. "Leaf has a good heart, Nova. He's always tried to do the right thing. Sometimes, he's a bit of an alpha, but it comes from a good place."

"He said the same thing about you all," Nova replied, tears

prickling her eyes. "I mean that you are good people. Not the alpha thing. That would be weird. Okay, what's an alpha?"

"Oh." Clarke frowned at herself. "It's a wolf shifter thing. Just another thing to get used to here. Each fae race has different customs."

Nova sniffed and forced a smile as she took the spoon from Melody. "Okay, time to round up your mates and get yourselves ready. We will dish up in about half an hour."

"You sure?" Melody hesitated, looking at the chili. "I could take over the salad."

"Go, please," she replied. "I like the solitude of a kitchen. It's like meditating."

Laurel's brow rose. "I'd rather go for a run, but whatever floats your boat, babe."

"The boys can do the dishes," Melody offered.

The girls were still laughing amongst themselves as they walked out. Once Nova was alone, she let her smile drop. She supposed fitting in would take time. It was hard to convince them she was honest, especially when she had no answer about what her magical talents were, or no solid answers about how she could help defeat her brother. To be honest, she would be suspicious of herself, too.

They'd asked a few questions about Leaf being Jackson Crimson but stayed away from anything too personal. Nova had returned plenty of questions about this place, and they'd been happy to answer. But it was all surface stuff. Hopefully having a weekly meal with them would help close the gap.

She stirred the pot and cast her eyes around the room. The stove was a stone and ceramic appliance that heated with wood fire and mana stones. Herbs hung in bouquets from the archway overhead. Cupboards with plenty of space filled the rest of the room, along with some stools around the butcher block. A dry goods storeroom and a cold room were built into a wall. The kitchen had a nice atmosphere. But it needed a poem in a picture frame.

And to be honest, she would love the brownies to accept her. Or at least let Nova join them with their usual cooking routine sometimes. This room was therapy for her, and she missed having it. She missed her mother most here.

Nova finished preparing the salad and was giving the chili one last check when she felt hands slide around her stomach. Startling, she almost threw the pot at her assailant.

"It's just me," Leaf's comforting voice rumbled near her ear.

She exhaled as he dropped his chin on her shoulder.

"You surprised me," she said.

"You couldn't feel me approaching through the bond?"

"I don't know."

"I need to train you. I've neglected my duty as Team Leader." Annoyance sharpened his tone. He shifted her hair to one side and then dropped a kiss on her neck. She shivered and melted into him, smiling as he added, "We don't even know what your elemental affinities are or if your gift will manifest."

"Maybe I'll just have the pretty freckles," she mumbled.

"Or maybe it's a lack of training or the taint holding you back." His warm palm grazed down her glowing arm. "You're connected to the Well. This is proof."

"I don't feel like..." She sighed.

"Like what?"

"Sometimes I don't feel like I'm meant to be here. I'm trying to find things to be excited about, but I've landed in the middle of a conflict that I feel like I've caused."

Nova's apprehension wasn't the only source shared through their bond. Leaf felt it too. He turned her to face him. As he swiped a lock of hair from her forehead, he looked deeply into her eyes and said, "You have as much right as anyone else to be here. The Well brought you back."

"What if... what if it was only because Jace asked for it? I know we had this argument already, but I can't stop thinking about it. A few thousand years of service has to get you a reward from the Well, right?"

"You are not a prize." His gaze darkened, and tension crept along his shoulders. "We don't know why the Well does what it does, but I know with one hundred percent certainty that it chooses good people to bless. That means you."

He kissed the tip of her nose, and Nova softened to his embrace.

"Keep romancing me, *Papi*."

"Don't tell anyone."

She chuckled, hugged him hard, and returned to the chili. It was done.

"How did the conversation go with your friends?" she asked.

"They're not my friends," he answered automatically. Then he shook his head in self-disparagement. "I suppose they are. At least, they're the closest things I have to friends."

"Seems like they're more like family. Family isn't always easy." She frowned, unsure if she believed her next words. "Usually, they're worth it."

Leaf's eyes filled with compassion, and he stroked her cheek. "Having a twin like that wouldn't have been easy. I feel your pain and guilt whenever you talk about him. You tried for so long to love him, but he couldn't feel love. You did more than humanly possible."

She sniffed. "I should have done less. Maybe if we'd cut him out of our lives earlier, my parents would still be alive, and the world wouldn't be a wasteland."

"Or maybe there would be nothing left. Have you ever thought about that? You could have delayed his descent or given him something else to focus on. But let's not talk about that before your dinner. Did the women behave?"

She sighed and looked for a way to turn off the oven. "They were nice to me. Very polite, and I think they—how do you turn this thing off?"

"I... have no idea."

She rounded on him. "*Hoja de los Guardianes*, don't tell me that in all your time living here, you've never once turned on the stove?"

"I won't tell you then." His lips curved, and he ducked to inspect the oven. He shot her a disarming smile from his knees, then reached around the side and turned a crank. The heat emanating from the stovetop died.

Nova opened the glass oven door, placed the pot inside to keep it warm, and said, "We only have a few minutes to get cleaned up before dishing up."

His brow arched. "How many?"

"Not enough." She waggled her finger at him. "And don't think I didn't notice you avoided my question about your meeting."

Heat flared in his eyes as he stood and tugged her close. "Don't think I've forgotten we were interrupted this morning."

A flood of endorphins filled her with warmth, and she lifted on her toes to press her lips to his.

"I love it when you look at me like that," she murmured against his lips. She slid her hands around his body and then down his spine to mold over his muscular buttocks. "But we have to go. Plenty of time for hot looks later. Wait—what's this?"

She pulled a crumpled letter from his back pocket.

He groaned. "It's from the Prime. I don't want to read it."

"*Hoja*, you probably should." Her tone of reproach was not met well.

"Later." He took it back and allowed her to drag him to his room. Another challenge was getting him to change into something other than a leather battle uniform. He kept trying to seduce her, especially after she walked out of the bathroom in a new dress Laurel had loaned. But, by some grace of God, he was finally dressed in casual trousers and a loose shirt, and they both made it down to the dining room to dish up meals as their guests started arriving.

CHAPTER THIRTY-THREE

Leaf didn't realize he was hungry until he placed the first mouthful of Nova's cooking into his mouth. It took every ounce of restraint to stop eating before everyone else was seated. If he ruined this night for Nova, he wouldn't forgive himself. Someone had to show these ingrates manners.

She stood at the dining room entrance, resplendent in a dress he thought was far too revealing for a meal at their own home... especially when three unmated Guardians still lived within these walls. But everything about her embodied a wild, free spirit—from her untamed long hair to her unorthodox freckles to the bountiful bosom no tailoring seemed to contain. Who was Leaf to tell her how to dress?

From his seat at the head of the long mahogany table, Leaf looked down at the bowl of chili. Nova doubted fitting in here, but he sensed that she would nurture this crew into a family, and they'd all end up loving her for it. With a frown, he realized that's all he'd ever wanted to do. Teach these rudderless souls how to be the best versions of themselves. There might not be many nights like this for a while.

Nova's laugh snapped his gaze up.

River stood at the doorway, flashing his roguish grin at her. Still in a dirty uniform, though, Leaf noted with disdain. He'd have a word with the shifter later about appropriate dress for mealtime. Nova gave a good-natured roll of her eyes at something he said and then gestured for him to join Leaf at the dining table. River sidled past Nova, obviously brushing his unique wings against her bare arms. Lucky for that crow, Leaf felt nothing but the same hopeful excitement Nova had projected through their bond since they arrived.

He caught a mouthful of feathers and fluff as River sat beside him. Annoyed, he pushed the wings out of his face and growled, "That's Nova's seat."

"Don't see her name here." River dragged Nova's bowl toward his face and inhaled. When he exhaled, steam puffed from his nostrils and he gave a full-body shiver that rippled his feathers. "Oh, yeah. She's a keeper."

Leaf glared as the crow shoveled food into his mouth and pinched his forefinger and thumb near River's face. "I'm this close to—"

"She's scowling at you, boss," River mumbled smugly through a mouthful.

Leaf's gaze slid to his mate, who was, indeed, giving him the warning look. *Behave.* So he smiled pleasantly and relaxed. River, the floater, gave her a finger wave and kissed the air. Leaf punched his thigh under the table, but when River laughed, he realized he needed a bigger lesson in respect.

"You have a death wish, don't you crow?" Rush grumbled as he took the other seat beside Leaf.

"Ever heard of table manners, crow?" Thorne grumbled, sitting beside Rush and glaring at River. "You're not supposed to start until we're all seated."

Thank fuck some of the Twelve weren't complete reprobates.

"I have no regrets," River muttered, leaning back and patting his stomach. He planted his boot on the wooden seat beside him and shoved it from the table. Ash walked in with a reluctant expression. Also in his Guardian leathers.

"New rule," Leaf ground out quietly as Ash sat. "No battle leathers at the dining table."

The women gathered at the room's entrance, chatting with a sudden high-pitched, bubbly tone. Leaf flinched and scowled suspiciously at them. But then Violet arrived with Peaches and her daughter, Jasmine. The pre-teen was a little older now than Willow had been when Leaf last saw her. But where Willow had been a visible presence at the house, Peaches and Haze's halfling daughter often slept during the day. It seemed her vampire side became more prevalent as she aged. She was already as tall as her five-foot mother. Not long ago, Haze told Leaf in confidence that he wouldn't be surprised if Jasmine shifted to have wings soon.

"Clarke!" Laurel shrieked, panic in her voice.

Every male jumped to their feet so violently that dishes and glasses were knocked over. Laurel held Clarke as she seized while gripping Nova's arm.

Rush shoved Thorne out of the way and ran to his mate. Leaf did the same, jogging down the other side of the table. Rush took over holding his mate, preventing her from falling.

"Are you hurt?" Leaf asked Nova. She shook her head, but fear glistened in her eyes.

"She just touched me and then—this. She won't let go."

"It's okay," he said, eyes darting over Clarke's slack face. He peeled her eyelids open and saw only white. "She's having a vision."

"Why won't she let go?" Nova breathed, wincing. Indents in her flesh beneath Clarke's grip looked like they might bruise tomorrow. But forcibly removing Clarke's arm while in the throes of a psychic spell could be dangerous.

Leaf searched the concerned faces around him, but no one seemed to have an answer to Nova's question. Not even her mate.

He didn't want to tell her that Clarke could spend days in a fugue state, trapped in a vision. Hopefully, this would be brief, because if Clarke was ripped from her vision too soon, her mind could stay in that faraway place.

"Should we send for Preceptress Dawn?" Peaches suggested from the doorway.

"Not yet," Rush answered gruffly. "But it might be a good idea to remain in the living room for safety."

"Safety?" Nova squeaked.

Leaf put his hand on her back and held her steady.

"It will be fine," he repeated. "Don't worry. Are you sure you're not hurting?"

"It's a little sore." Her bottom lip disappeared between her teeth. Her anxiety wound up, coiling tighter and tighter by the second. Everyone looked at her with suspicious eyes, probably wondering what she'd done to Clarke. It made Leaf furious to see how quickly their goodwill toward her had changed. Nova's gaze darted to the abandoned meal with regret.

Indigo and Haze arrived. The giant, hulking vampire took in the scenario, and his upper lip curled, flashing fangs at Nova as though she was a threat.

"Everyone calm the fuck down," Leaf growled.

Clarke gasped, breathing suddenly. Her eyes opened and returned to blue. She let go of Nova and immediately sought out her mate, twisting to face him and clutch at his shirt.

"I saw..." she spluttered. "Oh my God, I saw..."

"Saw what?" Leaf drew Nova into the shelter of his arms. As she curled into his body, he sensed her desperation to remain in control of her panic.

"A battle. A betrayal. A rain of blood." Her eyes watered and slid to Rush, and she whispered, "Willow."

The temperature dropped. It was as though death arrived with her words. Rush's face paled, and he shook his head. "No. She can't die. It must be the taint confusing you. It's wrong."

"She wasn't dead, but...so many others were." Clarke's eyes widened and darted about the room as she replayed the vision in her mind. "And we were there. And Jasper... and you—" She looked dead straight at Nova. "You were vital to everything. The key to victory, despite the snake I saw slithering in the grass. She's coming."

"She?" Leaf stifled his frustration. "Coming where?"

"*Maebh* is coming... no..." She squeezed her eyes shut and rubbed between her brows with a finger. "I saw a banner with Roses, thorns, and antlers on one side of the field. The other side was—" Her eyes flew open. "Jasper and Aeron. Nero was there. The Six. Everyone was *there*."

Fuck. Leaf closed his eyes to take a moment. They weren't ready for this. Instead of being here, preparing the Order for battle, Leaf had spent the past decade hunting down a prophecy that meant nothing in the end. They thought Maebh's interest in them was done after they'd embarrassed her last attempt at attacking them. But of course, she'd kidnapped Aleksandra. She wasn't done.

His thoughts turned to the unopened letter she'd left him. Perhaps it was time to read it. He opened his eyes and asked Clarke grimly, "When?"

"The night of Samhain."

The entrance door sounded like it opened, banging. Leaf's spine stiffened as he turned toward the living room. Caraway's deep voice boomed from somewhere, "She's declared war on Jasper!"

"We're in here!" Leaf yelled.

Heavy footsteps approached. The big muskox shifter appeared wrapped in a cape, his face burned from the wind. The last Leaf had heard, he'd been stationed in Crescent Hollow with Anise. His gaze searched the gathering, and he raised his brows. "What happened?"

"I had a vision," Clarke said.

"About the battle at Cornucopia?" he asked slowly. "Damn. I rode all night to tell you the news. My horse wasn't too happy about it."

"Wait." Clarke's brows drew together. "You sure it's not here?"

Caraway pulled a crumpled message from his pocket. It was an open letter with Maebh's broken seal on it, addressed to Jasper. "Apparently Aeron received the same challenge. A final battle to decide the fate of Elphyne."

"Perhaps your vision is wrong," Leaf suggested. "The taint is worsening, remember?"

"No." Clarke looked at Nova intently. "When I touched her, the flow of my mana was clean and fast. Or at least... I don't know how or why, but she's some kind of conduit filtering out the ink. She improved my targeting and focus." Her eyes darted about as she put her thoughts together. Leaf had inklings of his own, but he held his tongue to hear her ideas. "I've been training with Dawn to notice early warning signs for when a vision hits me. In case I need to get to safety or fall and knock my head. When I touched Nova and felt a sudden shift inside my body, it struck me as odd because usually at this point, my connection to the Well opens. I feel more of the taint. But this time, the flow of mana was clean. It all happened so fast. Come to think of it, maybe it wasn't like a sieve filtering out the taint. Maybe it was turning one tiny drop of clean mana into thousands."

Leaf tensed, thinking of his raw explosion at the Unseelie army camp. Perhaps Nova was connected to the Well back then, after all.

"There's something you should all know," he said, rubbing Nova's trembling arm to comfort her. "Our escape from the Unseelie war camp wasn't bloodless. My plan was to create portals as we fled. I figured at the very least, they'd cut holes in the enemy. But everyone within range was hit with a raw blast of power. Let's just say there was nothing identifiable left. The portals I created afterward were created with more intent, and they targeted true, and..." He glanced down at his mate. "I touched her every single time."

Ash folded his arms. "If she's an amplifier, she'll be the most valuable weapon in our arsenal."

Everyone stared at Nova. Some were suspicious, some hopeful, but none were thinking with their heads.

"Wait just a Well-damned minute," Leaf growled. "We need to test and train Nova before tossing her into a battlefield. We don't know enough about her gift."

"But if I can help," Nova said, her confidence building, "shouldn't I be where people need me most?"

"No."

Nova's indignation flared. "Why not?"

Leaf's eye twitched. He knew she wanted to help, but it was too risky. The thought of having her in danger meant he'd be distracted. He forced a smile and took his mate gently by the shoulder. He tried to keep his tone calm and his emotions in check. "You couldn't survive a camp with a few hundred Unseelie soldiers. Being on a battlefield is ten times worse. Most of these Well-blessed women have been here for over a decade. They have a little more training."

"Don't patronize me. All I'll need to do is stand there," Nova pointed out.

"Estrella, be reasonable."

"And don't you Estrella me. I want to help. Let me help."

He snapped, "We don't know what this does to you yet! You came down with the fever disease at Frostwing *after* I'd successfully used mana with minimal taint to make the portal. What if I drained you to the point you were human again?"

"I was fine after the war camp."

He took her shoulder and guided her back to the table, trying to lower his voice even though he knew it was redundant. "Freckles, for all we know, every other attempt to use your power will create an unreliable bomb like the one in the Unseelie camp."

"Are you a psychic now too?"

"I forbid you to be on the battlefield. There's simply not enough time. Until we know more, you're a liability."

The males widened their eyes as if Leaf had said something offensive, which was ridiculous. He was keeping his mate safe. Couldn't they see that?

Nova's expression deadpanned. She stared at Leaf for so long that heat crept up his neck. At least when she was angry, he knew where he stood. She always fought him when he was too forceful. But this... this was nothing. She walked away without another word. Before he could chase after her, the Six's Hive voice slid into his mind: *We are outside.*

"Fuck!" Leaf threw a bowl of chili against the wall. It smashed, leaving a dark chunky spatter that dripped down like gore, reminding him far too much of the devastation he'd left in that forest.

J.C. — ENTRY 540 ANF

If true love is paradise, then time spent alone is hell.

I'm not ready. I haven't found her. I can't give up. I beg the Whispering Well for more time... to stave the inevitable madness for a little longer.

I seem to dream of her more often these days. It's almost like my mind is trying to keep her alive, despite the fear in my soul she's never coming back. I also dream of him —the friend who betrayed me, who threatened her life if I remained by her side.

I replay that conversation in my head, wishing I was as strong back then as I am now. I would have crushed him, would have reached into his heart and ripped it out for daring to speak her name. But time is not reversible. It moves forward, regardless of my intention.

The Well tells me it's like being caught in a rip in the

ocean. What do you do when the current tries to take you under?

"That's easy," I reply every damn time. "You stop struggling. You go with the flow. Eventually, the current will take you back to shore."

But it's hard to believe that when the water is full of monsters.

CHAPTER
THIRTY-FOUR

Without waiting to see if the other Guardians followed, Leaf walked onto the porch of the Twelve's house and inhaled the crisp, fresh air. The night was clear of clouds. The moon shone brightly, but it wasn't quite full. It would be in a few nights' time—during Samhain.

If Maebh wanted a power boost for her war, she'd picked the night where the veil between the living and the dead was thinnest.

He scrutinized the night. Leaf had never seen the Sluagh training on this lawn, but all six stood in a line at the center. He'd never witnessed them in battle, but each moved with the confidence of apex predators.

Until recently, they often glamoured away more frightening aspects of their appearances. Two had horns protruding from their heads—one set was small, the other long and like a satyr. They also had tails lashing irritably at their rear ends. But the taint had made honest fae out of all of them it seemed.

Under the bright moon, their pale skin almost glowed. Even the Sluagh with his darker coloring, seemed paler tonight, almost like they were afraid of something. The talons of their tattered wings rested on their shoulders, and the rest draped behind them like a cape. Each somehow blurred or vibrated sporadically, as though they were unsettled and violently twitched.

Footsteps shuffled behind Leaf and then stopped as each of the Guardians joined him.

"Do you hear that?" Rush's deep voice was low.

"Buzzing," Thorne replied. "Like swarming bees."

"The souls they keep must be restless," River murmured.

Leaf couldn't care less. He jogged down the steps and strode across the dewy grass toward Legion, the leader of the Six, with his long dark hair moving about his face like a silken shadow. Six sets of wholly black eyes tracked Leaf as he approached.

A few decades ago, he wouldn't have been caught dead meeting these predators at night—their prime hunting time. But after the Well-blessed women arrived at the Order, these Sluagh were lured from hiding by the temptation of unique and tasty human souls. Fortunately, that never happened, and Leaf had never known why.

"I'm assuming you've already rifled through my mind and figured out that I know how to unmake Maebh," Leaf said, trying to anticipate their reasons for being here. "And if you've been spying on the events inside, you'll have learned about news that the coming battle is here, not Cornucopia." His jaw firmed and he tensed, sure to put enough warning into his glare for his next words. "You'll know what we suspect Nova's unique gift does, but the answer is no. You cannot now, nor ever, lay a hand on my mate —I don't care if it's to..."

Legion canted his head, and his skull flickered beneath his flesh. Energy rippled over Leaf's skin like a hot gust from an open oven. The wind somehow transferred *inside* his clothing, rippled along his arms to lift the hairs, then tightened like ghostly fingers around his throat.

We do not need your mate's gift, Legion said into Leaf's mind. *We are beings of the ink, not the light.*

Leaf tried to exhale, but the ghostly fingers squeezed tighter.

Understood, Leaf sent back to Legion.

The pressure around Leaf's neck evaporated. Legion's skull flickered beneath his skin once more, signaling his wraith form had returned to his body.

"Yes," Legion said aloud. "We are aware of the coming battle, but it is not for the reason you state." His dark eyes shifted over Leaf's shoulder to where the others prowled the lawn, slowly circling into a position around the Six.

Leaf rubbed his throat. At least they weren't standing on the porch like cowards while he was being choked. Probably his own fault, though. The more he fell in love with Nova, the more protective and irrational he became. And he had no boundary when she wasn't there to draw a line in the sand.

Laurel and Violet remained on the porch, both with weapons in their hands. But Clarke walked toward Rush on the lawn with no sense of the danger she headed into.

He had a sudden flash of the argument he'd overhead on the night he'd left the Order. What was it he'd overheard Clarke shout?

Unlike the hostile looks the Six had given Leaf, they watched Clarke and Rush approach with open curiosity.

"Maebh summons the Wild Hunt." Legion's tone was strained. "As Samhain draws near, we lose control over the souls we keep."

"I thought you weren't beholden to Maebh anymore," Clarke pointed out.

Bodin bared his fangs. "*We* are not, but the Horde is."

Legion's head tilted toward his second. Something passed between them. Each of the Six bristled as though displeased with the Hive's private conversation. With a flash of respect, Leaf sensed Legion was pulling them into order. Managing a team wasn't easy.

Eventually, the buzzing quietened, and tension fled the atmosphere.

"What are you saying?" Clarke asked them, frowning. "She can use the Wild Hunt in battle against us, despite you all being on our side?"

Legion hesitated. That ripple of discontent vibrated again through the Six. Dread dropped like a stone in Leaf's gut as he read between the lines.

"Or is it that she can control you while they're trapped inside you?" Leaf slowly ventured. "She can blackmail you?"

Each of the Six replied as one. "Yes. But the instant she frees them from our bodies, her death is imminent."

"Don't you need a queen?"

Legion's lips curved enigmatically, but he gave no reply.

"Okay." Leaf rubbed his temples. "Let me get this straight. You're warning us that Maebh has one shot to use the Hunt against us. But you'll have time to attack her if that happens?"

All six sets of black eyes blinked.

"Fuck me," Rush growled.

Leaf scrubbed his face as a realization hit. "You've all remained hidden for this reason?"

"Correct. She knows the moment she relieves us of the Hunt, we will have nothing holding us back. Her death is imminent."

"You said that already," Leaf snapped, pacing alongside the line of Sluagh. Why couldn't they speak plainly? They watched him with narrowed eyes, but he was beyond feeling unsettled by their rapt attention. His mind had already shifted to damage control.

If the Wild Hunt got loose, they were in trouble. So the only solution would be to either kill the Six—

That will release the Hunt, Legion explained.

Okay. So that option is out, Leaf thought. Not that they knew how to kill the Six apart from using Violet's ultraviolet summoning power. Even with Nova's help to avoid the taint, Violet must kill all Six to survive. It was risky. Too many ways it could go wrong.

If they couldn't kill the Six, they had to kill Maebh—or rather, unmake her. He stopped pacing at a worrisome thought.

"Does Maebh know you plan to kill her when she releases the Wild Hunt?"

"Yes," they replied.

"So this battle is a suicide mission." Leaf's blood drained from his face. "She's not planning on surviving. This means she doesn't care about anything left in the world. The Prime probably hasn't told her about their daughter being alive."

She was either too emotionless to care or didn't believe Leaf.

"We must hasten our plans to unmake Maebh sooner rather than later. We need to get a message to her, and likely to Rory—maybe to find a way to entice her to our side, or at least for Maebh to believe she will join us." He rolled his eyes to the moon, shaking his head at the ludicrous plan. "If Willow is still loyal to us, then perhaps she has already persuaded Rory, but if she's not..."

He failed to see how a child growing up behind enemy lines would owe anything to their fae enemies. Nero had successfully brainwashed and convinced many people that his cause was just.

"What do you mean, if she's not?" Rush growled.

"You haven't spoken to her in years," Leaf pointed out. "What if she's under Nero's control? Or what if she's grown up and hates her parents for abandoning her?"

"She's there because it's safest." Clarke's anger riled. "She knows this."

"Safest?" Leaf balked and glanced around. The Order of the Well was gated and protected by lethal soldiers who wielded magic. "*This* is the safest place for her. You said you left her in Crystal City because she refused to come with Forrest." He slid his gaze to the Six, who had grown quiet and watchful, almost as if they didn't want to say something they shouldn't. Suspicion drilled into Leaf's mind. He turned to Varen, their Seer. "You said that if Clarke continued interfering with Willow's fate, she would make it worse. What aren't you telling us?"

Clarke and Legion stared at each other for a lingering moment, clearly having a private conversation the rest weren't privy to.

"Enough," Leaf snapped. "We are about to enter a battle for the very survival of the Well. That includes the existence of each and every one of you. It's obvious you've been colluding on something, and quite frankly, I don't give a shit unless it affects our chances of surviving this battle or clearing the taint from the Well."

He raised a brow and waited for their answer, but neither were forthcoming.

Rush stepped between Clarke and Legion, folding his arms. He didn't seem happy with whatever it was. Leaf had the sense the seasoned Guardian would tell Legion if he thought it would hurt the Order, so he left it. For now.

Rush said, "We should focus on delivering a message to Maebh and Rory."

"Rory is easy," Leaf said. "We'll use your familial blood tie and a communication spell to contact Willow. With Nova's help, it will work."

"Absolutely not," Clarke snapped, furious. "We refuse to include our daughter in this war. I saw her covered in blood in my vision—my untainted vision, need I remind you. I won't invite that fate by calling on her when she's with a megalomaniac. The longer they stay behind Crystal City walls, the better."

"No one said she had to come with Rory." But he would have thought they'd jump at the chance of having their daughter here in Elphyne.

"She calls Rory Aunty. Of course, she'd come with her. Plus... the last we spoke, it seemed there were things she couldn't tell us about. She said he joined her too often in the garden. Do you know how risky it is to contact her out of the blue? Willow calls us, not the other way around."

"Silver's smuggling contacts have dried up," Leaf pointed out. "Even Sid's been in Elphyne for years now. There's no way to get a message to Rory other than through Willow. At least not with this urgent time frame."

As if voicing the name of his vengeance summoned him, Cloud dropped from the night sky like a falling shadow made flesh. He landed roughly in his haste and strode toward them, all fury and indignation at being left out of the conversation.

He took in their faces. "Start again."

There was no point telling him to piss off. He was on the Council. If Leaf had allowed Clarke to remain in this conversation, he had to do the same with Cloud. With a sigh, he prepared to rehash what they'd learned, but Cloud said, "I'll go."

It took Leaf a moment to realize Legion had caught Cloud up mind-to-mind.

"Go where?" Leaf asked, eyes narrowing to slits.

"To Crystal City to deliver the message."

Leaf's lips flattened, and he glanced at Legion. "You told him? You realize she'll die immediately after he delivers the message, right?"

"Which was why we did not ask him," Legion replied curtly, ignoring Cloud's increasing vexation. "*We* will do it."

Cloud's mocking eyebrow raised with scorn. "And you think Maebh will relinquish her power on your word that her daughter is alive? She needs to see the truth in the flesh."

Leaf could see his point, but he didn't trust the manic look in Cloud's eyes. It was worse than before. Something had happened since this morning. He looked ragged and travel weary.

"Where have you been?" Leaf asked.

"None of your fucking business." Cloud shifted his gaze to Clarke. "And I suppose this new intel about the battle is from her?"

"What's that tone supposed to mean?" she returned.

Cloud switched his attention to his fellow Guardians. "You should all know better than to trust humans."

A low snarl rumbled from the base of Rush's throat. Leaf really didn't want to break up in-house fighting tonight. He leveled his glare on Cloud. "She's been helping more than you."

"Yeah. I wonder why."

For fuck's sake. Maybe ignoring him was a better strategy. Leaf continued speaking with the rest of the group. "If getting a message to Rory risks Willow, we may have to work on getting a message to Maebh first."

Cloud grew still, almost with defeat. "You're all going to do whatever you want, regardless of my input." Paranoia flittered over his expression as he looked past Leaf to where the other Guardians were... to where River and Ash stood watching at the base of the porch steps. "Even you two—you're a bunch of pussies."

Before they could deter him with explanations, he took a running leap into the sky. River flew after him, but Ash remained, those quiet eyes watching Leaf and the rest. For all he knew, this was a part of Cloud's ruse. Make them think he was insane and his friends were no longer loyal. It would be the perfect way to trick secrets out of them.

If Leaf actually had any secrets. He met Ash's hard gaze, hoping that if the shifter heard the whispers from the Well, he had more sense than the rest of his trio.

He turned back to Legion. "You can't go to Maebh. You said it yourself, she'll use the Wild Hunt."

"Not until the battle. She won't want to die before then. But she is already on the move with her army, likely hiding and traveling here instead of Cornucopia. We are the only ones who can find her. We always know where our queen is."

Could they risk it? Leaf asked, "How soon can you get there?"

"By dawn."

"And then back to us?"

"Tomorrow night."

That was plenty of time before Samhain. He rubbed his jaw, thinking about it. Even if the Six failed in convincing Maebh, hopefully, they would still be able to return, knowing whether Aleksandra was alive and their location. Leaf could portal there and take the battle to them. No one would expect it with the taint running rampant.

"Go," he said. "If I don't see you by midnight tomorrow, I'll know something is wrong. We will move on to Plan B."

"One more thing," Legion said, his unnerving eyes locking on Leaf. "About your mate."

He tensed. "What?"

"You must keep her in the shadows if she's to remain alive."

"What does that mean?" His eye twitched.

"The Well doesn't bless Nero. He ages like any human. He steals mana and violates it to his will," Legion returned.

It was hard for Leaf to keep his patience right now. "We know this already. It's why he's mad—he ingests the memories of the creatures he steals from."

"Nero believes stealing the mana from his daughter staves off madness. But that supply is almost dried up."

Dread sank in Leaf's stomach as he recalled something Nova had told him. When her twin gloated about winning a race she knew nothing about, he said he overestimated her usefulness to him. That was the same day Nova had seen his daughter in the car outside her home. It solidified their theory that Rory was the same girl, and Nero had somehow manipulated their way into being frozen and then thawed in this era. He'd sired her to act as a personal mana supply for when his dwindled. And if both of them were out, discovering Nova existed would put her at risk.

"Clarke witnessed Nero drink stolen mana," Leaf said. "He's already mad. How can he believe that ingesting his daughter's will keep him sane?"

"What is more dangerous than a madman?" Fox asked, a twinkle in his eyes.

"Enlighten me."

"One who believes he is not."

CHAPTER
THIRTY-FIVE

Nova stepped out of the sixth elemental pool in the Order temple and onto a towel. Clarke spoke with two other fae introduced as Preceptress Dawn and Preceptress Colt. Both were intimidating, and Nova preferred to sit back and let them hash out the details of her elemental affinity results.

A rise in hushed conversation turned Nova's head to them as they discussed whether her results would be trusted because of the taint or if, on the flip side, her results were the only correct readings since the taint began. None of it made sense to Nova. But she was determined to wrap her head around it. She figured the more she learned, the more she could do to help, despite what her *menso* mate said.

It had been two days since her failed attempt at a dinner party. Two days since she'd given these people an ounce of hope with her mystery gift. But this was the first time anyone had a moment spare to test and train her. She had done her best to be useful while the

Order panicked about the impending battle. But there wasn't much she could do, and the house brownies had seen her attempts to take over cooking as an invasion of their territory. She'd been chased out with a broom earlier this morning.

Everyone ran on fumes and stress. Tempers flared more often than not. If it wasn't angry fights, it was the nihilistic and promiscuous behavior amongst the Mages and Guardians living on campus. Last night, Nova heard Leaf's unmistakable bellow at someone he'd caught "wasting time worrying about his cock when he should be worrying about his head."

She looked past the open temple columns to the sprawling campus far below and listened to water dripping from eaves and rain chains. Tiny culverts of flowing water surrounded the terrace. Behind them, on the opposite side of the main campus, steps led down to a private courtyard.

The sun left an idyllic golden haze on every object as it drifted across the sky. The air smelled fresh and sweet, and the temperature was warm enough that she didn't need a coat. Glass tiles glimmered on the academy's dome rooftops in the distance. Despite her brother's destruction, this world had still found a second chance at flourishing. And here at the Order of the Well, the world had found its champions. Jace—Leaf—had been its first.

This was the perfect place for Nova to be. This community was everything she'd ever dreamed of back in her time. She shouldn't be impatient while trying to fit in.

But she felt untethered again, floating in a sea of doubt and inadequacy. Leaf had been brutally honest about her being a liability. He was right. Did she have a right to be upset over it? So much was happening. He was busy trying to wrangle an enormous organization falling apart without a leader. He'd barely slept each night because every waking hour was spent preparing for a battle.

"Right," Clarke said, coming over. "We think we have a handle on your elemental split. It matches our theory about you being an amplifier. You have zero chaos affinity. This could be why you somehow led me to a single pure drop of mana amongst the taint and then magnified it. The Six also didn't want to use you. They're almost entirely chaos and draw from the inky side."

"That's good, right?" Nova bit her lip and glanced at Colt, who was rubbing her hand over Dawn's back as though consoling her.

Clarke squeezed Nova's shoulder. "Don't worry about them. That has nothing to do with you, so don't take it on your shoulders. Come on, I'll walk you to the academy, and Violet will give you a rundown of the theory behind your gift. Colt would do it, but Dawn isn't in a good place without the Prime. They were close."

"I didn't realize the Prime was respected around here. From what Leaf said, she'd hurt many people."

"She did," Clarke answered truthfully with a sigh. "But she's been alive longer than any of us. She's loved and lost. And lost. And lost. Then she put all her effort into the Order. Maybe if she kept her heart alive somehow, whether with Maebh or someone else, she'd have someone to ground her. Rush is the first person to tell me if I go off the rails. I don't know what I'd do without him. I certainly wouldn't have gotten through the past ten years away from our daughter without his level head to steer me in the right direction."

"How do you do it?" Nova asked. "Get through it, I mean. Sorry if that's too personal."

A small smile touched Clarke's lips. "It's okay. I don't mind. At first, it was insanely hard. This isn't the first child Rush was separated from during their youth. I was absolutely furious on his behalf. I wanted to protect him from that pain. But when we tried to rescue Willow against the advice of Varen"—she glanced over her shoulder at Colt and Dawn, still talking amongst themselves, then at Nova with serious eyes—"I learned something about Willow's fate that I wasn't willing to accept. Her being in the human city is only the beginning of it. You can't imagine how hard it is to make these decisions for your child, to know that she'll be hurt no matter our choice. We just want her to grow up and to be happy."

"That's all any good parent wants." Nova's hand fluttered to her throat. "Are you saying she won't?"

Clarke's gaze turned inward, and she frowned. "She will now. I might not have liked leaving her in Crystal City, but I know she's alive because of it."

"Parden me for saying so, but didn't you envision her covered in blood?"

"I did. But she was alive. It's likely someone else's blood. At the very least, Rory has trained her in self-defense and perhaps more. Come on, we can walk and talk if you have more questions."

Nova slipped on her sandals and followed Clarke to the edge of the temple.

"Actually, wait here. I'll be a moment," Nova said to Clarke and then went to the two women quietly talking amongst themselves. "I just wanted to express my gratitude that you took the time out of your busy day to help me."

Colt blinked at Nova. Dawn fiddled with a butterfly pin holding the hair between her curved horns.

Colt smiled and touched Nova on the arm. "We look forward to spending more time with you, dear. Please know that it's not always this tense around here."

Nova gave the women a nod and then started toward Clarke.

Dawn grabbed her wrist. "Was she happy?"

"Pardon?" Nova frowned, confused.

"Aleksandra," Dawn explained, her voice hoarse from grief. "You were the last to see her. Was she happy?"

Nova thought about it. "I didn't get to spend much time alone with her. She helped me when I was sick. That was very kind of her. And I'm sure I saw her shed a tear and smile when the dancers performed scenes from her old life. But there were moments when she looked empty and flat... or maybe accepting of her fate. I'm not sure I can help much more than that."

Dawn let go. "You have. We always knew this was coming. I'm sure D'arn Leaf has told you what was in her letter to him by now, but—"

"He hasn't read it."

Dawn's eyes widened. "Why not?"

Nova shrugged. She hadn't spoken much to Leaf since his outburst. It still infuriated her.

"I haven't read the letter," Dawn mumbled, almost to herself. "It was sealed. But I've been safeguarding it since Leaf first emerged from the lake. I had no idea he was Crimson. Maybe losing his memories saved him from being targeted. The soul is what drives the ripples in the Well. Please get him to read it."

"I'll see what I can do," Nova assured. At least that was something she could help with. She hoped.

"It will be okay, Dawn," Clarke said with confidence.

"How can you know?" Dawn's voice broke. "Nothing we predict turns out the way we think. It's all a mess."

"I just know," Clarke replied. "It's not my gift. It's not a truth-telling or anything like that. But having Nova gifted to us in these final hours of hopelessness has to mean the Well isn't done looking after us. Trust that she's the miracle we've been waiting for."

Nova's eyes teared up. She tried to blink them away but couldn't. Clarke caught her and said, "I don't mean for you to feel any pressure. And don't go getting a big head. We have enough of those around here—oh look, speaking of big heads..."

Leaf crested the vast temple steps with a basket in his hand. His cheeks were red from the walk up, and his blond hair was windblown, but he was still somehow so sexy with that leather battle uniform hugging his muscular physique. Blue eyes clashed with Nova's, and she scowled at him.

"I'd like time alone with my mate," he decreed gruffly to the others.

"No can do, compadre," Clarke said, taking Nova's hand. "We have work to do—work, need I remind you, that *you* ordered? She must learn the basics of her gift, we have to establish a baseline of health, and then we need to test her limits as Mages draw on mana while touching her."

Colt and Dawn sent Leaf an irritated look, but then smiled at Nova before they left. Clarke folded her arms and stood her ground as Leaf's expression became a mix of exhaustion, anger, and bewilderment.

"I'm serious," Clarke said, her eyebrows raising. "We all want alone time with our mates, believe me, but we need to suck it up and work out how to survive this battle. Egos can check themselves at the door."

"I'll take care of her training," he replied curtly.

"You have Guardians to wrangle and the Prime's position to fill."

"She's not dead yet," he snapped. "Filling the Prime's role isn't part of my job."

Clarke's jaw dropped. "Then what have you been doing all this time?"

Nova watched the exchange and felt her blood boil with every word out of Leaf's mouth. How could he say the nicest things sometimes and then this? It was true. He needed someone to pop that balloon head of his. He'd been alone for far too long. Pushing up her metaphorical sleeves, she decided she had plenty of work to do. No time to hold grudges.

"You haven't asked if I want you to train me," she said. "You just waltz in here like you own the place and assume you can boss me around. So excuse us if we think you will step in and provide these people some much-needed stability in the absence of their leader. So which one are you? The boss or not?"

"Um..." He gave Clarke a helpless look, but her expression said he was on his own. Her foot tapped, waiting for his response.

But when none came, she finished for him. "Demanding I drop everything at your whim is not nice. Forbidding me to help is *not nice*. My feelings matter."

That last sentence caught in her throat. She hadn't meant to refer to his demands last night, but there it was. Leaf's eyes widened briefly. Clarke scrunched up her freckled nose and glanced away.

"You need to eat, Nova." Leaf's tone dropped an octave. "Don't think I haven't noticed you've avoided the kitchen. You've left plates in our room half full."

"The brownies don't want me in the kitchen."

"I'll have a word—"

"That's not what I asked, and you know it." She shook her head, exasperated. "I'll see you tonight."

"Wait." Leaf took a deep breath and exhaled. He looked at Clarke and said, "You're right about the testing. I did ask for it to be done. If it's okay with you, I can test Nova's capabilities and return her to you at the academy by nightfall. If she agrees."

Clarke folded her arms and stared at him. It seemed she would fight Leaf on the subject, but she also dropped her shoulders and exhaled. "We're all very tense right now. I get it. If you want to take over the testing, I don't see a problem as long as Nova agrees."

When his hopeful gaze met hers, she knew she had to hear him out.

"Fine," she said through clenched teeth.

"She has no chaos whatsoever," Clarke explained to Leaf. "That's likely why she can amplify a single drop of pure mana. Do your testing and then..." Another sigh. "Like I said, we're all a little stressed. Who knows what tomorrow will bring? Maybe we should all enjoy the evening with our loved ones." To Nova, she added, "Don't feel pressured about what I said earlier. Just be yourself."

CHAPTER THIRTY-SIX

As Clarke walked down the long steps, Nova turned to Leaf. His emotions jumbled through their bond, but she could read his face. He still held so many of Jace's natural characteristics and quirks. She'd seen this look on him many times, like before a track race at school or... after Niles had said that one thing that sent him away.

It peeked through his stoic mask and was in the tension line across his broad shoulders. His hair was swept off his forehead like he'd run his fingers through it too many times. His jaw ticked. He breathed quietly, as though uncertain of himself.

One emotion started to overpower the rest through their bond. Nova focused on his feelings and realized she'd been wrong. She hadn't quite hit the nail on the head when reading his expression all these years. She thought he'd been annoyed, angry, or uncertain.

"You're afraid," she blurted.

Blue eyes snapped to hers. "Yes."

"Why?"

"Take your pick." A sharp laugh huffed from his twisted lips. He ran his fingers through his hair again, inhaled, and then let it all out on the exhale. "I'm afraid because of this battle. I'm afraid I cannot control my fate. I'm afraid I'll lose you before I show you I'm not this insensitive elf all the time. I'm afraid I won't be able to protect you." He frowned, looked at the floor, and murmured, "I'm afraid I'll fail you."

She stared at him, long and hard. There were so many things she could say to that. She was afraid, too. Fear wasn't an excuse for being a *pendejo*. She failed him in their old life just as much as he thought he failed her.

"Why?" she asked.

Confusion crossed over his features. "Why?"

"Yes, *Papi*. Why are you afraid you'll fail? Why is it something you fear?"

"I..." His brows knitted together. "I don't like it."

"Why?"

"Because it doesn't feel good," he snapped, growing irritated.

"Why?"

"Are you a precocious child now?"

She smirked, stepped up to him, and stroked his collar. "Sometimes repeating that one word is the only way to get to the root of your troubles. So, my love, why doesn't it feel good?"

His temper flared. The basket creaked under his grip. She sensed he considered ignoring her but finally answered, "It doesn't feel good because it never has, and I don't know why. Not knowing why drives me insane."

"I can tell you why," she replied softly, taking his hand. "I'm going to remember a few things about Jace. Will you let me share those memories?"

He tried to tug his hand away, but she held on tighter.

"You say you don't want to know anything about your old life, but you must. Or you'll never understand why you do the things you do."

"What are you going to show me?"

"Nothing traumatic."

"I don't see how this will help."

She closed her eyes and conjured memories from her childhood. The first was that day he'd moved in. She'd watched his family unload the car for hours, trying to pluck up the courage to go and speak with him. But she witnessed Jace's father growling at him multiple times. It was always about something not done quite right. Whether the boxing tape was ripped off, him being too rough with a delicate box, or unpacking from the wrong section. Then she shifted her memories to the future when he'd run track at school and how he had to be first because his father used to be the school champion. Then she remembered his father berating Jace for his hairstyle and surfing hobby, calling him a bum. Then it was an argument about Jace's grades and a lecture about him needing to be better if he wanted to take over the company—an oil company that made more money every quarter. Finally, she remembered the day Jace told her he was being sent to a boarding school.

"Why?" she'd asked back then.

"Because it's my duty," he'd replied. "I can't learn to be the best at a public school... or in this neighborhood, apparently. They're moving, too."

Nova let go of Leaf's hand and opened her eyes. He blinked, and his frown deepened. She wasn't sure what response she wanted, but he didn't give it. He collected her furled cape from the stone bench and gestured for her to follow him. "Let's eat."

Sighing, she followed him down a narrow stairwell inside the temple. She didn't realize this access was here because the temple stood on a small, solid hill with steps outside. It reminded her of a monastery temple in Tibet when she'd first arrived. But it was like a pyramid with a labyrinth of secrets. It became darker as they descended the musty stairwell until only bioluminescent moss lit the way. Water dripped and smelled like sulfur. Every so often, the stairwell broke into an offshoot corridor leading to a room full of ancient artifacts.

She wanted to explore, but Leaf continued ahead without pausing. Natural light grew brighter near the ground level, revealing a mosaic mural on the walls. She paused to run her fingers along the bumpy surface.

"This is you," she murmured, surprised.

Leaf's gaze dipped to the wall, and he frowned. "I never stopped to study it before, but I suppose it is. There's something similar at the academy."

Nova stood back and swept her gaze from start to finish. "No, the one in the academy is different. Look—that panel has you with human ears."

Leaf walked to where Nova had pointed. "It's my life... all of it."

"If it's down here, then maybe it's not meant for everyone's eyes."

"Hmm. No one comes this way." He ran his fingers over the bumpy tiles as he walked. "It starts with snow falling in a desert—the start of the Nuclear Winter. Then here... with a woman by a fountain." He glanced at Nova and then back to the mural. "It's you."

Nova's eyes widened, and she hurried to his side. It was a scene depicting their reunion in Vegas. Well, not the intimate parts. But a representation of their love. She smiled as tears gathered in her eyes.

Her throat closed when she saw the next scene. Jackson—Jace—had grown sick. He crawled alone through the snow under the light of a shining star. But on closer inspection, he was joined to the star like a balloon. When the sun shone again, he stood tall but with pointed ears. He met Maebh and Aleksandra. He heard the Well whispering and went into the lake despite them trying to hold him back. He did all this still with that star attached to his hand by a piece of string.

When he emerged, he had the blue Guardian mark and held a set of scales. They were evenly weighted with one dark drop and a light drop. It was the logo on every Guardian and Mage uniform. They followed the story as Jackson helped found the Order of the Well. But as he did, Aleksandra moved closer to him and further from Maebh. Maebh eventually left and took many others with her.

They reached the end of the corridor and the last mosaic panel, where he cut the string to his star and entered the lake alone. Watching from a dark obsidian palace on the opposite wall was Maebh under the moonlight. Nova's gaze darted between the two murals, between day and night.

Leaf stared hard at the panel with Aleksandra facing the lake, holding the book, and with her back to Maebh. He crouched and touched her white feathers and blue dress. In the rest of the panels, she'd worn cream.

"It's my fault," he said softly. "I left, and Aleksandra became the Prime. She probably didn't even choose it."

Her gaze skipped along the mosaic—half in the light at this end, the other half enshrouded in shadow and glimmering under the bioluminescent vines. "I still review events to see if I could have paid more attention to Nile's red flags. But there's only so much I could do. We all think, in hindsight, we can change the past, but we wouldn't be who we are today without it. I would never have fought so hard to clean up the environment... You would never have followed your star to the Order of the Well."

Nova pointed at the star Jackson had kept close. "Look at how far you traveled, how hard you pushed to honor me. And then, finally, you accepted that you had to let me go."

Leaf straightened. His eyes narrowed on hers. "I *failed* you. I couldn't find you. I didn't let you go."

"Perhaps you should stop making up your own version of history, *Hoja de los Guardianes*. Read the damned letter."

Amusement twinkled in his eyes before that lofty arrogance took control.

"I'll read the letter," he ground out. "But only because you asked so nicely."

She loved how his steel will bent for her. Even when he said hurtful things, she needed to remind herself that it was only a matter of time before he saw sense and apologized. From how his possessive eyes filled with heat as he looked her over, the apology wouldn't be far off. Maybe it would involve more of that insistence to pleasure her until she screamed—multiple times.

Nova's body reacted, her skin tightening with arousal. Seizing the opportunity, Leaf used his hard body to flatten her against the wall. More amusement flickered in his gaze.

"Does the thought of me reading a letter get you hot?"

"Umm." She dug her hands into his belt and glanced at him through her lashes. "It's when you look at me like that."

"Like what?" His voice was low as he nipped her chin. A shiver skated through her body.

"Like you'll keep me in line."

He pulled back, and that frown had returned. "But when I said you won't be at the battle, you didn't like it."

"Of course not. You decided *without* consulting me. In life, we are equals. But in the bedroom..." She smirked wickedly. "I like it when you get all bossy Team Leader with me. I like feeling safe enough to let go of needing to protect myself."

Her brows puckered at the self-realization. She'd always left her defenses on her entire life, or Niles would get the better of her. Even when she'd left the States to work in poor countries, she'd had to be careful with her trust. And Jace, bless his soul, hadn't protected her from Niles.

Leaf's frown deepened as he said, "But I want you to feel safe in life, too."

"Oh, *Papi*." She brushed her thumb along his jaw. "I do feel safe. With you, I've felt safer than I've ever felt. But being included in decisions that affect my life also makes me feel safe. And I understand you don't want me in the thick of battle. That makes sense. But acting like I don't have a say or treating me like one of your subordinates, especially in front of them, hurts my feelings. Do you understand?"

"Maybe," he grumbled, then nodded to the garden through the exit. "Let's eat."

Maybe meant yes. Nova smiled as she followed him into a private, sunken courtyard and gasped. It was beautiful. Unlike the steps at the front, which had tiny culverts bordering them, these steps were filled with cascading water that joined a small, churning pool. Around the pool, ferns and flourishing plants grew. It smelled so fresh. A soft green lawn with tiny purple flowers carpeted a curved area behind the water. A tall tree provided shelter but let in enough sunlight that it wasn't too cold.

Leaf strode to the lawn and spread Nova's cape for them to sit on. He lowered himself and opened the basket, then lifted his gaze expectantly. Seeing the big, muscular elf in leather battle gear trying to set up a picnic was adorable. She kicked off her sandals and crossed the grass on bare feet.

"Oh, God," she moaned, taking that first step. She wiggled her toes and massaged more tingling grass into the soles of her feet. "This feels so good."

Leaf's brows lifted, and he sprawled back on his elbows, watching her with a slight curve to his lips. "This entire grotto is a source of power," he said. "Everywhere you touch, you'll feel your connection to the Well strengthen. It's why the Order was set up here."

"I thought it was because of the ceremonial lake nearby."

"That, too, but..." His gaze flicked to a cluster of reeds with white flowers bursting from their stems. "They look rather like stars, don't you think?"

CHAPTER THIRTY-SEVEN

Leaf watched Nova's cheeks flush as she went to touch the starry flowers. She held one to her nose and inhaled. She glanced at him, and her emotions soared with love and melancholy.

"Come here." He patted the cape beside him.

She nodded and padded over, sinking into a pool of her dress skirt. He tugged her down the rest of the way until she pressed against him, lying on her side. He brushed hair from her face and couldn't believe how beautiful her eyes were under the sky.

"Why so sad?" he asked.

"You spent eons loving me. I only had a few short years, and now..." She glanced up at the blue sky. "Now I think I'm afraid of losing you, too."

"I won't let that happen." A protective surge locked his muscles, and his grip on her jaw hardened. "Look at me."

She lifted her warm brown gaze to his. "I won't either. I mean it. I want to protect you, too. If you try to stop me, I'll find a way."

"I know." He forced his fingers to relax.

"So you'll test my gift? You'll make sure I'm ready for the battle?"

"One can never truly be ready for battle. It's..." He shut his eyes against an onslaught of images from his past. All the blood he'd spilled in the name of the Order. "But we can prepare."

"Start now." She pushed him onto his back, hitched her dress, and straddled his hips. The sun caught strands of curly hair around her head, making them glow like a halo. But she was no angel. A deviousness flickered in her eyes, and she raised her brows haughtily. "I'm ready for your lessons."

His own brows lifted. "Lessons?"

"Whatever this testing business is, yes?" She tilted her head to the sky and shimmied her shoulders like she was about to take a hit in the heart. "Lay it on me."

Leaf wanted to laugh at her ignorance, but he was mesmerized by how her body moved. Her dress hugged her breasts, showing him where her nipples were as she jiggled. The long line of her graceful neck always made his mouth water with the need to kiss her there. Her pose felt more like surrendering to him rather than to the testing.

His gaze darted back to her nipples, hardening but not quite stiff. He wondered how long it would take to get them to that point if he took them in his mouth. Nova opened one eye and glanced down at him with a knowing smirk. She knew exactly what he was thinking.

Clarke's voice came back loud and clear: *Who knows what tomorrow will bring?*

Tomorrow, the battle would be at their doorstep. He needed her ready to face the blood, violence, and tears. Tomorrow, he might never see her again. His fear of failing, of being anything less than perfect, wound its way into his bones and paralyzed him.

He was surrounded by beauty, and all he could think of was never seeing it again. The mosaic played games in his mind, Crimson's journey and the centuries he spent tethered to that star. All those journal entries where he pined over his lost love. The heartache. The agony.

To hurt was to know love. He couldn't regret a single minute of it when she was here with him, and his heart felt like it would burst from his chest.

"Come on, Mister I-want-to-spend-time-with-my-mate. Test me." A wicked gleam entered her gaze. "Use your magic and draw from mine. See what it does to me."

"Nova," he said, voice soft as his gaze flicked to the hallway with the mosaics. "Let's just spend this time together."

Nova's lips pursed, and her jaw did a little side-to-side jig as she gathered her temper. "You won't test my gift?"

He opened the basket. "I think we should enjoy being together. While we can."

A slice of hot, peppery defiance cut him through their bond. She reached into the basket, grabbed whatever her hand landed on, and mashed it onto Leaf's lips. She pushed until juice burst and dripped down his chin.

"Enjoy that," she said, eyes flashing.

Leaf darted his tongue out and licked the juice from his lips. Berries.

"You want me to test you?" he ground out. "Fine. I'll test you."

He gripped her hips and flipped their positions, pushing her against the ground. Her eyes widened at the impact. The jolt was just enough to knock some sense into her. Or so he thought.

Nova reached blindly for another berry. Something red and big, but she didn't use it. Not yet. She held it out threateningly, challenging him. Pinning her shoulder with one hand, he freed his other and flicked his fingers toward the pool, instructing his mana where to go. Water responded to his call, but he wasn't fast enough. The next berry slammed into his jaw.

"Tickles," he teased as the juice ran down his neck. She'd have to do better than berries if she wanted to tempt him into losing control.

Her smile of triumph died as he sent a bubble of water about the size of a bucket through the air and hovered it over her head.

She gasped. "You wouldn't."

Oh, yes, he would. His eyebrow arched. He let the bubble rotate and catch the sunlight. The sparkles it left on her face rivaled the stars on her cheeks. His gaze dipped to her soft, sassy lips.

"I have a better idea," he said, voice rough with lust.

He pinned her wrists over her head, reaching beyond her cape to rest on the lawn.

"What are you doing?" She tried to look up, arching and twisting to catch a glimpse.

"Testing your gift." He smirked, sending the water to bind her wrists with the lawn before turning it to ice.

Nova gasped at the temperature. Ice manacles bound her to

each blade of grass, making it difficult for her to move. Difficult, but not impossible. She could break free if she truly wanted to, but he knew this was exactly the kind of bedroom treatment she had been talking about. Anticipation skipped through their connection, silently begging him for more.

Leaf held her gaze, undid the studs on his Guardian jacket, then tossed it to the side. His shirt came next. A breeze tickled the wetness the berry juice left behind, so he knew exactly where the stain was without glancing down. He planted his elbows beside her head and presented his sticky neck.

"Clean me with your tongue," he ordered.

She pretended to fight him, thrashed a little, and then her freckles flared as Spanish words spilled from her pretty little mouth. He somehow understood every filthy syllable uttered, and his lips curved. He lowered his lips to her ear and said, "Calling me a jackass will only make this... *test*... last longer."

"Yes, please," she begged.

A bolt of heat hit his groin. His erection jerked against his leather pants, and he groaned, "Lick it off, Freckles."

Nova poked out her tongue like a petulant teen. He lowered his jaw, and she licked him from chin to ear. It started off reluctant, but soon, her tongue lingered on his skin. Every lave sent shockwaves of arousal skipping through his body. He trembled and almost collapsed his arms. But he made her lap every last drop of juice that had run down from his jaw to his throat. When she circled his ear, he almost snarled with his need to take her.

"Mmm," she murmured, twirling her slick tongue around his lobe. "I like this test. What's next?"

It felt as though that single point of contact was all of him. With ragged breaths, he straightened and stared down at her, his hair spilling around her face. She was so fucking beautiful. From the bee-stung lips, to the smooth skin, to the curve of her bosom pressing against her dress. He hooked a finger into the neckline and tugged, exposing one of her breasts until her nipple popped out, and she whimpered. Watching arousal capture her face, he circled a finger around her areola, feeling the bud tighten to a stiff peak. Didn't take long, after all, he mused.

Her eyes glazed. Her cheeks flushed. He pinched until her gaze sharpened again. She arched into him, already panting.

"What's next, *Papi*?" she prompted.

"Next?" he muttered, letting his gaze travel south. "I'll have to think of something creative, won't I?"

Her dress was buttoned down the center, all the way to the skirt's hem. He glanced at the bubble still hovering nearby, then back at her, devising a plan to use the water to wring pleasure from her body. He could bring her to orgasm without lifting a finger.

CHAPTER THIRTY-EIGHT

One look into Leaf's eyes made Nova feel safe and cherished. One look said he would burn the world down to be with her. But she felt other emotions through their bond—confusing ones, like determination.

"What are you thinking?" she asked huskily.

He answered in a deep, ponderous tone. "I'm thinking you said you were afraid to lose me, and I'm thinking that's because you've never seen the full extent of my power. I'm thinking you need a demonstration to set your mind at ease."

Had she not seen the full extent of his power? "Obliterating an army wasn't enough?"

"That was instinct. It was messy." Self-disparagement ghosted over his face. Then he locked it away and crooked a finger toward the bubble. A thin ribbon of water separated and floated down toward Nova. "It was lucky," he said, aloof eyes watching the stream slither closer through the air. Her pulse spiked. What was he going to do with it? "And it was undisciplined."

The ribbon brushed her cheek, leaving a cold, wet path that sent a shiver down her spine. It curled along her jaw, lovingly caressing down her neck where it wove along the dip of her décolletage. She gasped as it burrowed under her neckline, its head hardening to ice.

Now watching intently, he murmured, "I have skill—" Movement beneath the fabric tickled, and then *Pop!* Her button was released from the buttonhole from beneath. "Finesse." She gasped as it continued south. *Pop!* "And power." *Pop! Pop! Pop!*

Nova's body was a bag of sensations. Icy slides, cool air, hot breath, and scorching tingles. He straddled her hips, grasping her thighs.

"I know you have those things, Leaf. You don't need to prove it to me." *Yes, please. Show me more.*

He shuffled backward, widened her legs to kneel between them, then separated her unbuttoned dress. His gaze heated as the ribbon of icy water trailed circles around her belly button. Every inch of skin covered caused a seismic reaction in her blood. She whimpered, needing more, but he retained that bored look.

No, not bored. This display of magic was child's play for him. He'd probably seen something like it a million times. Being as old as he was in body, if not in mind, the Well had likely granted him much power. She recalled how he'd confidently moved when fighting Grung by that river. Worry had rarely entered his mind. Adrenaline was his disciple.

Was he holding back?

A curl of lust shot through her.

She licked her lips and taunted him. "I know you want to show me all the clever things you've learned as a big boy, so do it."

"Big boy?" Heat flashed in that lazy blue-eyed stare. "I don't need to boast, Estrella. But I do need to know you'll trust me when this battle comes."

Her gaze softened. "Of course I will."

His grunt was noncommittal, perhaps unimpressed with her answer, but then he steered his gaze between her open thighs. "Wet already?"

"You don't need to be a rocket scientist to see that," she teased him again.

When he didn't answer, she tried to wrap her legs around his waist, but he quickly snapped his hands over her ankles, pinning her down with a *No-No* glance.

As she sensed his need to command rise, so did the wind through the grotto. Reeds undulated. Foliage whipped. Heat baked down on her, but the sun was still in the same low position. Her breathing grew ragged. Sweat prickled her scalp. The icy water ribbon soothed her parched skin. Steam curled in its wake, arousing her to the point of insanity.

"Leaf," she begged, twisting and writhing. "I need you."

"Yes, you do."

She yanked on her icy restraints and kicked against his hands.

"Not yet," he teased.

"When?" she whined out.

His lips curved. "First, tell me how you need me. Rough? Slow? Passionate?"

Looming over her, with the sun haloing his hair and baking his muscular torso, she glimpsed a flash of Jace. She frowned, urging her thoughts out of the way, and said, "Anything but soft."

Because gentle and loving was Jace. Gentle and loving would hurt her too much.

"I want to feel your power," she continued. "I want to feel your muscles roll under my hands."

He gave another unreadable grunt, almost like a CEO who'd taken a suggestion on board but committed to nothing because he would do whatever the fuck he wanted.

"Hurry," she begged.

The water ribbon stopped circling her belly button and moved down her hot skin. She groaned at the tingling relief. The cool, slick sensation slid through her folds, stroking her like a finger—or a tongue. *Oh, God, that felt good.* Nova's eyes rolled back as the leisurely pace became ripples and hard pulses. She cried out and met his satisfied gaze.

"Like that?" he murmured.

Unable to form words, she couldn't answer. At his command, the pulsing vibrated faster and then slowed and teased.

"Oh my God," she breathed. "Fine. I admit it. You're—fuck. Oh, my God. Like that. Don't stop!"

Before she threw her head back and gave herself to his sweet assault, his lazy look became volcanic. Pleasure coiled through her body, lighting up every nerve ending.

She vaguely felt her lips move and her voice box tremble. Maybe she teased him or cursed him, but whatever it was, her voice triggered his loss of control. He snapped and let the ribbon go. Water and tiny shards of ice splashed down her thighs.

"I was almost there," she complained—well, she'd intended to complain, but Leaf buried his face between her thighs. He proved he was just as talented with that cocky mouth as he was with his magic. His kisses became ferocious as he growled against her sensitive flesh. He gripped her bottom and pulled her pussy to his lips. He feasted until she was back at that impossible place, begging, twisting, and squirming with the need to finish.

"Leaf," she begged. "I—"

"Come for me," he demanded.

Stars exploded behind her eyelids. Pleasure cascaded through her loins and curled her toes. Leaf lapped at her orgasm with as much desire as he'd started, touching and feasting with insatiable craving. Nova struggled to catch her breath. Her body felt flayed. Her nerves were raw.

He lovingly kissed his way up her stomach, crooning platitudes and praise to her flesh. The ice around her wrists melted, and he pulled them to his mouth. The rough pad of his tongue lapped the last vestiges of water from her skin, and then he inspected her for damage. A pleasant, energizing feeling rolled through her veins, healing the tiniest cramp with his magic.

"Are you healing me, *Papi*?"

"Need to make sure you're in fighting shape."

Once satisfied every ache was gone, he turned his attention to her hair. He combed it around her face and buttoned up her dress.

"Now you must eat," he said matter-of-factly.

That was the best orgasm of her life, but he carried the look and feel of someone frustrated.

"What is it?" She took his face between his hands and drew his reluctant gaze to hers.

His nostrils flared. She thought he'd hold whatever bothered him inside, but he confessed, "I was meant to demonstrate how much discipline I have, but I couldn't even last a few minutes without tasting you." He laughed at himself in an adorable, awkward way that seemed too youthful for his face. "Your taste makes my mouth water in the most delicious... ugh."

His frustration took over again.

But Nova wasn't so upset. She felt proud. Exalted. Here was a god undone by the sight of her. A god who'd loved her when he was just a man and still fell to pieces from needing her. He was that young teenager claiming her virginity again, so horny and passionate. She moaned and tugged the laces at his breeches. "You're making me hot again, *Papi*."

His uncertainty rocked through the bond, followed swiftly by pure primal hunger as she found his stiff shaft and squeezed.

"Fuck," he bit out, thrusting into her hand.

"You're exactly what I need," she praised and stroked. "What I want. What I love."

She smiled as his eyelashes fluttered and his brows joined in the middle. Nova shifted onto her hands and knees, then lowered her mouth over the tip of his cock. Her tongue swirled around the broad head and then up and down his slit. Every time she did that, he shuddered.

With each passing second, his composure broke a little more. She loved how his breath hitched and caught, as though he tried to stop himself from feeling too much too soon. She loved how his fingers flexed in her hair, as though he wanted to push down and impale her mouth on his shaft. She loved how his smooth skin was tight over defined muscle. His emotions tumbled through their connection. He was helpless, falling, and desperate. Needy and ravenous.

"Do it," she murmured. "Make a mess of my mouth."

Finally, he pushed her scalp while he thrusted deep into her throat. She relaxed and let him take over, let him fuck her mouth as he'd once warned. He used her to the point she couldn't breathe, but she loved it. When black dots swam before her vision from lack of air, his fingers curled on her head, pulling hair and stinging like needles. He yanked her off with a hard growl.

She gulped for air and felt water leak from her eyes. Then she grinned and looked up at him.

"You're too good for me," he groaned, cleaning her chin with his thumb. His cock bobbed angrily, just out of reach of her swollen lips. She chased the tip, but he flexed it out of her way with a flash of teeth through his smile.

Leaf's grin devastated her dignity.

"Finish," she begged and opened her mouth, but this time, he used those strong warrior's hands to move her about like a rag doll. With a few quick touches on her hips and shoulders, she suddenly found herself on her back again. He climbed over her and braced a forearm beside her head.

"There you go," he crooned, swiping his fingers along her slit, pushing gently into her tight pussy. "This is how I want you right now."

"Tease."

He replied by gliding his velvety shaft along her sensitive entrance. Impatiently, she pushed against him. "No more playing, *Hoja*."

So he reached between them, fit himself to her opening, and entered at a leisurely pace.

"Oh, God. You fill me so good."

He slid out, then eased back with a hoarse rasp, "And you take me so good."

Nova moaned as her body gave way to his, begging as he refused to move faster. Eventually, the intensity of his thrusts picked up. He started slowly but ended hard, slapping his hips against hers and jolting pleasure through her.

"Fuck," she bit out as he slammed into her again. "I hope to God no one is in that temple looking down at us."

Because her whimpers were becoming loud cries of abandon.

"They're all screwing anyway," he growled. "Why the fuck not us?"

Her grin widened. She'd intended to say something about how proud she was, how he finally looked after his own needs before duty, but he caught her looking at him. He took her mouth in a blistering kiss that stole her breath.

His intense emotions spiraled Nova into the past. She relived that last night with Jace. He'd made love to her with trembling hands, long kisses, and slow, indulgent thrusts.

Maybe Leaf plucked the memory from her mind because he started to mimic the movements, almost as if they were second nature. He treated her like his world. Like she would float away if he stopped touching her, like she would float away if he let go.

"Never," he said.

CHAPTER
THIRTY-NINE

From the stone bench inside the secret garden, Willow stared at the dry fountain. President Nero—or Uncle Nero, as he preferred her to call him—encouraged her to spend time in the garden. He wanted her connected to the Well so she would be powerful enough to summon an army of the dead.

Besides him, Willow was the only one allowed down here now. The garden was in ruin. Weeds and invasive vines covered much of the stony architecture. Most animals had fled when Uncle Forrest cut the barbed netting during his escape a decade ago. They fixed the net but never replenished the animals.

In these lonely moments, when not even the voices in Willow's head answered, she sometimes wished she'd left with Uncle Forrest that day. She'd stopped enjoying herself long ago but was not allowed to return to Elphyne.

"It's to keep you safe," her mother had once said during an earlier communication through the water. Willow remembered the bright

red of her mother's hair shining through the blue. She also remembered the pain in her father's golden eyes when she begged to come home.

We can't, he said, deep voice breaking. "You'll understand one day."

"But I want to come home!"

"We promise you'll be home when you become an adult. Then we'll make up for lost time," he'd replied. "Now, have you been practicing setting traps like I showed you?"

"But what's so dangerous out there?" she'd asked, ignoring his comment. "It's worse in here."

"You're alive. You're safe. That's all that matters. Now, back to the hunting. Don't forget the prayer of gratitude to the Well if you take your prey's manabeeze."

They never explained what was so dangerous out there, but even the voices in her head said she had to remain here until the right time. They kept her company with tales of dragons, and conquering demon knights and their queen. Her parents distracted her with education about Elphyne, saying she'd want to fit in when they reunited. Her father made her learn all the monsters' names, their strengths, and their weaknesses. Her mother taught her to thieve, pickpocket, and use her wits to—how did she put it? Oh, yes. It was to "pull the wool over someone's eyes." But she also lectured about responsible use of power and more boring stuff about consequences.

Her father could shift into a wolf and catch his prey. Willow could only shift partly into a wolf—her ears became pointed, her canines elongated, and claws distended from her fingertips. She could smell, hear, and see a thousand times better. Her father said she was likely faster in this form, so she might even be able to catch prey with her hands. But any animal left after the net had broken was now dead from her practice sessions with Nero. For a while, she thought he'd stop if there were no test subjects, but then he'd brought in people.

She shuddered and blocked out the memory.

She'd tried to convince Aunty Rory to take her to Elphyne to practice combat skills, but she barely left this Tower. Willow desperately needed to speak with her parents again. The instant she hit puberty, changes in her biology became difficult to suppress. Not only was it embarrassing around humans, but she worried her safety here wasn't as ironclad as her parents thought.

Willow touched her pointed fae ears, and her lower stomach tingled with desire. No human was like this—she'd asked once after drinking too much wine at a dinner party. They'd thought she was joking and laughed it off. Sensitive ears were only the beginning of her problems.

She turned eighteen in a few months. Plans were already underway to present her to Tower Society as a debutante. Some girls were given betrothal belts at earlier ages, but Willow's marriage was political. All the men wanted to get closer to Nero by marrying his "niece." Rory had never been available.

Once, Willow had asked her aunty why. Rory said her father had other plans for her. But when Willow pressed, Rory's mind turned to mush. Nero had manipulated her mind so much that she forgot who she was.

Some days were good. Some were bad.

Those earlier days in the garden, training with Rory, were some of her happiest here. Her aunt was vibrant and full of life, even a little grumpy. Now, she was a ghost of herself. The sinking feeling that Willow had failed her aunt weighed her down... but she couldn't remember why. It was as though that cloud in Rory's head had leaked into Willow's.

Nero manipulated her. She used to somehow fight off the effects after a stay in the garden, but sometimes it didn't work. A frequent sense of déjà vu drove her nuts. A tear leaked from her eye, and she dashed it away. *There's no use thinking about it now.* For her own sanity, she had to turn her mind to the immediate problems. The upcoming debutante ball and the list of suitors presenting a belt to her.

Her friend Alfie had turned eighteen last year and had just been promoted to an aeronautics captaincy. He did everything Nero asked and was the favorite.

She liked Alfie. She truly did. They'd been friends since she arrived in Crystal City. But Alfie didn't make her stomach tingle like when her ears were touched. With a sigh, she stretched her neck and slid off the bench seat to practice her martial arts moves. But her attention span was short and with no one to push her, she plucked weeds from around the broken fountain until she heard a heavy metal door opening.

Willow lifted her nose and sniffed. *Copper, jasmine, and lanolin oil.*

Aunty Rory. She grinned and ran through the garden to the door, excited. It had been over a year since Rory had come down here. Willow's jog slowed as she approached the door and saw Rory hadn't entered the garden. She stood in the shadows of the doorway, her arms folded.

Fine lines had appeared at the corners of Rory's dull eyes. Her caramel skin looked sallow and her usually beautiful lips were thin and downturned. Gray streaks had appeared in her dark hair. She used to spend hours wrangling her hair into braids clamped with copper beads. She also used to shave one side over her ear. But lately, she wore her hair scraped back into a bun at her nape. Little fuzzy bits escaped. The copper epaulets on her military uniform were tarnished, and a button was mismatched on the front.

She looked like she hadn't slept for a week. Worry churned in Willow's gut.

"What's happened?" she asked.

Her aunt shielded her eyes from the light in the garden.

"We've had word that the fae are heading into battle," she explained. "This is the moment we've been waiting for. It's time to prepare."

Her voice was soulless. Willow narrowed her eyes and tried to take a closer look at her aunty, but the woman turned away.

"What happened to you, I meant," Willow said. "You look tired. Why don't you come into the garden and spend time in the sun? Five minutes will make you feel better."

"I can't." Rory retreated further into the shadows.

"Okay," she said, shoulders slumping. "I haven't spent my allocated time here yet. I have at least another hour."

"You can return tonight," Rory replied. "But for now, Nero needs you in the war room."

CHAPTER
FORTY

Leaf woke to a pitch-black room, his heart pounding and his senses racing. He lay there for a minute, taking stock of everything around him. No sound—just Nova's steady breathing in the bed beside him. The wind whistled gently through the gaps in the window. He searched the darkest corners but found no threat.

Samhain had arrived today but without the usual fanfare. The women had briefly spoken about their pumpkin tradition but ultimately opted for some much-needed rest.

It had been three days since Clarke had the psychic vision about the battle. Despite braving their house and pounding on the doors, he'd not heard a peep from the Sluagh. No one was home. The scouts Leaf had sent to locate Maebh's army had returned empty-handed. It didn't make sense. She should be here... or near Cornucopia.

The moon was still low, so he'd not slept long.

He placed his palm over his sternum, felt his beating heart, and tried to recall if he'd had a nightmare but came up empty. He glanced at his sleeping mate, reached for her, but snatched his hand back with a frown. She'd had a few long days training with the other women, cramming as much as possible in this short time they had to prepare. He wished he had been the one to teach her. But she insisted he go where he was needed more.

Duty once again pulled him from what he desired most—time with Nova.

Leaf scrubbed his face and swung his legs over the edge of the bed. His gaze landed on the unopened letter on his bedside table, the Prime's wax seal unbroken.

He promised Nova he'd read it, but time kept passing. He feared his avoidance had something to do with intuition, something Crimson knew. But if he kept avoiding the truth, he would be back where he started—ignoring fate and making mistakes. So he snatched the letter and cracked the wax seal.

IN THE EVENT OF MY DEATH

Jackson, if you're reading this, the fate you predicted has come true. You finally found the woman who makes you whole.

I wish I could be happy about it, but I am miserable. You left me. You left us. Now that you're gone, who will keep us from tearing each other apart? Who will be the voice of reason?

If sighs could be translated into words, many would be on this page. I sigh because it is wrong to be angry at you. This is what we both agreed to.

I have nothing left while you were promised everything, but only my selfishness caused my fate. You listened to the Well. Maebh bargained. I ignored.

We never gave what it asked—unwavering trust. You did. Over the centuries, our friendship kept me from sinking.

Now that you're gone, I will do as you did and trust. I will follow in the footsteps of someone I admired but have lost.

Your final words before entering the lake were this: My death will come after your heart returns, but so will my prayers be answered.

I spent centuries alone after that. I thought you were talking about yourself, but yesterday, you emerged from the lake. Your arrogance had multiplied. I laugh now, thinking about it. But then, your first words were that you were a Guardian.

You had no idea of your past. Too shocked to do anything but follow protocol, I asked what your new name would be. What would symbolize leaving your old life behind and embracing servitude to the Well? You looked up at the rustling trees for such a long time that I thought you might have lost more than your memories.

But then you answered, "Leaf. For what else has perfected the art of rebirth?"

You were not dead as I feared, but starting anew. I realized your last words spoken as Jackson Crimson were a reflection, and the voice had been mine.

If you're reading this, then I am right. For once. Ha!

If you're reading this, then finally, after thousands of years, you're thinking about your own heart first. You found your mate. You never gave up on your Estrella or the artifact she will lead you to.

What I mistook for weakness, you proved was strength. You saw our minds crumbling under the weight of time, so you asked the Well for more. You continued fighting to reunite with your love, even if that meant losing your cherished memories of her.

I have loved you as a brother. I have fought with you as such. What I should have done was listen to your advice. I should have kept fighting for those I love against all odds. I should have remembered I still had breath in my body, and blood in my veins.

I failed because unlike you I wasn't willing to give up my cherished memories. But it seems time has taken most anyway. All I have left are remnants of feelings. So, until we meet again, I will turn my last years of sanity to holding the fort. You said you would return and bring a new generation who will bear the torch for us. I didn't believe you. But if you're back, then it's highly likely the rest of your prophecy will come true. New Well-blessed souls are awakening in Elphyne. I imagine there is much to do.

If you're reading this, then our jobs are done. Go live your happily ever after before it slips through your fingers again. Leave the rest to the next generation. It's their time now.

Yours,

Aleksandra.

P.S. If you're still reading this, you haven't heard a word I've said. Stop overthinking it. Stop feeling guilty about it. Just... go live. Then I'll know at least one of us did something right.

CHAPTER
FORTY-ONE

Leaf folded the letter and placed it down on the bedside table. He stared at the tree's moving shadows outside, trying to process the words of a ghost. The Aleksandra today was never so emotional.

It felt good to know he never gave up searching for Nova. Instead, he'd asked for more time. But that was the only part he liked about the letter. Aleksandra became the Prime because he'd abandoned her. She said not to feel guilty or overthink it, but how could he let that go? She'd suffered because of him. She made her choices, yes. And she was likely on the same cold path anyway, but...

He scrubbed his eyes and exhaled. He let go of his tension and accepted his fate.

His job wasn't done. Not until Nero was eliminated. But he wouldn't do it alone.

Nova's hands slid around his bare torso, and she kissed his shoulder.

"What's wrong?" she asked.

Need swiftly built in his body, and the urge to be with her outshone everything else. She always had this effect—this way of pulling him back from the brink and grounding him. He understood why Crimson spent so long hunting her down, why he'd tethered her light to his wrist.

Leaf guided Nova's hands south, bumping her fingers over his taut abdomen to where his erection strained against his leg. She made an appreciative sound and adjusted to kneel on her haunches behind him. Her thighs widened, and she pressed her body against the length of his back. Then she wet her palm with saliva and started stroking him.

"You haven't answered me," she murmured, amused as she pumped him hard. "But I'll allow it. For now."

A grateful smile touched his lips, and he rested his head on her shoulder. He let himself exist in the moment. He listened to her breathing grow shallow. When she started rocking her hips into him, he twisted, tossed her down on the bed, and drove his cock into her tight, slick core.

They made love with needy hands, mouths, and hearts. No memories invaded his mind this time. It was just the two of them in the moment, enjoying each other.

When it was over, and they lounged on the bed, he decided to show her the letter. Her eyes teared up when she read why he'd chosen his new name.

"I said that to you once," she whispered, voice tight. "The bit about new life. You keep saying you're not him, but a part of you remembered me."

He opened his mouth to reply, but the haunting blare of a war horn outside cut him off. He jackknifed up, eyes wide.

"What's that?" Nova asked.

"An alarm." He grabbed the leather breeches he'd left nearby on the floor and tugged them on as he stood up.

"Is it time?" Nova scrambled to the edge of the bed. "The battle?"

He slipped on a loose undershirt, rushed to the window, and searched the grounds below. People had started to gather on the lawn. "Shit."

Nova wrapped a sheet around her body and arrived at the window as he put on boots. She peered into the darkness and squinted, seeing what he had. All Guardians were dressed for battle. Others were rushing onto the field from either the barracks or the house.

She glanced at Leaf, stuck out her chin, and said, "I'm coming with you, so don't try to stop me."

He fitted his baldric over his jacket and glanced at the Prime's letter. Alone was not a place he ever wanted to return to. He finished buckling, sheathed *Reckoning* between his shoulder blades, and kissed her hard.

It lasted ten dizzying seconds, and then he rested his forehead against hers and admitted, "I'm not letting anything separate us. That means you're sticking to me like glue."

She pulled back in disbelief, raising her brow. "Even if you have to fight?"

"Especially then." He pulled back and frowned at the sheet. "Did Violet drop off a spare set of battle leathers?"

"Yes."

"Good. Get dressed, then meet me on the lawn as soon as possible. I think we won't see our beds for a while."

CHAPTER
FORTY-TWO

Leaf left his room and jogged down the staircase as Forrest crashed into the balustrade. His messy auburn hair dangled as he leaned over.

"What is it?" he asked.

"Likely what we've been waiting for. Get in your gear and prepare for the worst." Leaf paused, then glanced up. "Find Melody something suitable for battle."

Forrest gave a curt nod, and Leaf hurried down. Exiting the house and entering the brisk night, he sensed panic amongst the gathering. Shade, Haze, and Indigo were at the center of the furor, trying to calm down those who'd arrived, but voices shouted atop each other. Other fae had arrived—some in robes, some in night-clothes, others in day clothes.

Leaf counted the Guardians present. None of the Six were there. It didn't bode well, considering they couldn't deliver a message to Rory through Crystal City. If Maebh's army was truly here, it would attack without question.

Sid, a rookie Guardian and ex-Reaper from Crystal City, calmly strode toward Leaf. He had the same long blond hair as Leaf but tied his back. Sid was human and recently mated to a pixie princess. He'd proven himself worthy of the Well and was making amends for his past as a fae killer under Nero's command.

He had little mana, but the Well gave him the power to share his ability to hold forbidden items and channel mana with his mate. They'd successfully beaten out raiders from a forest, saving it from joining the wastelands. Sid was the first human to pass the Guardian initiation at the Ceremonial Lake. He'd pave the way for many others if he continued proving himself.

"Is it time?" Sid asked.

"Not sure." Leaf was about to push through the rabble when Haze's booming voice roared across the din.

"ENOUGH!"

Jolts of surprise rippled across the crowd. Leaf shouldered through to the inner circle. The vampires were arguing with Rush, River, and Cloud.

"Who blew the horn?" Leaf asked.

"He did." Shade pointed at Indigo.

"For good reason," he replied grimly.

Leaf's jaw clenched. To Haze, he said, "Let's get the evacuation underway. Get everyone here and organized into orderly lines."

If they'd evacuated earlier, Maebh's spies would have noticed. Leaf wanted the Seelie army's arrival to be a surprise.

Being a head taller than most others, Haze gave a shrill whistle and barked orders. Forrest and Sid helped usher the crowd away, telling them to collect belongings integral to survival. When most had left the area, Leaf gave Indigo the order to debrief.

But before he could talk, Cloud asked him, "Are you abso-fucking-lutely sure she's on her way here and not Cornucopia?"

"Let the vampire speak." Leaf's ire was wasted on the crow, who looked gaunt and sleep-deprived. He might have to force Cloud to take time off after this. He clearly needed a break. Leaf returned his gaze to Indigo. "Please, continue."

"I saw her army, the demogorgon, a fucking manticore, and white feathers in a lumpy sack hanging from her pet's talons. I think it's the Prime."

Blood rushed in Leaf's ears. He heard his own heart pound.

"How long until she's here?" he asked, folding his arms.

"One turn of the hourglass, maybe two." He rubbed his fist in a circle over his heart. "I thought I'd find them further out, but they managed to get closer without me seeing. This is my fault we don't have enough warning."

"No use pointing fingers," Leaf said. "You did good."

"One portal won't be enough for both an evacuation and reinforcements," River muttered, scrubbing his hair.

"Then open two," Nova's voice had Leaf turning.

She arrived with the other Well-blessed women. He was happy to see they all wore protective gear, even Clarke.

"If you think you can take it," he said to his mate.

"I can take whatever you throw at me." She smirked.

"Then we'll portal to Helianthus. Jasper's on standby. I'll open the portals. Everyone else, find your stations. Wait for orders."

They scattered. The last to leave was Cloud. He looked far too bitter for Leaf's liking. Almost like he'd hoped Clarke had lied about her vision, and the battle was still at Cornucopia.

Leaf took Nova's hand and asked, "You ready?"

She nodded. "Let's do this."

Even though she hadn't caught the fever disease again, and she'd had her gift used repeatedly over the past three days, he still worried he would drain her. All Well-blessed women had reported physical consequences when their mates borrowed too much, too fast. But the time for doubt was over. Their lives depended on getting Jasper and Aeron's army here.

The smell of ozone blasted into the air as he conjured the first portal. It targeted true and opened on the beachside sandy shore, just outside the Helianthus citadel's glimmering outer walls.

"We'll cross," he told Haze, who'd returned and directed the evacuees into a line. "I'll hold the portal open from there and deliver the message to Jasper's guards. When I signal, get started sending people through. In about five minutes, I'll create a second portal right there—" He pointed to the area beside the current portal. "Ensure no one stands there, or they'll end up dead."

Shouts from guards through the portal revealed Leaf had been noticed. Keeping hold of Nova's hand, he armed himself with a shielding spell in case they attacked first and asked questions later. They stepped through, and the guards lowered their bows and arrows.

The smell of seaweed, brine, and bird shit assaulted his nose. The ocean crashed somewhere behind them.

"D'arn Leaf." One of the guards pushed forward. "What's the news?"

"Tell your High King that Maebh is at the Order as predicted. He must rally his troops and join us immediately."

The guard nodded, then sent another off to find the king. Leaf stepped to the side and opened a second portal with ease. Then he shouted through the first, "All clear, Haze."

The first civilians walked through the portal, and the Helianthus guards directed them to the beach, far from where the soldiers would arrive. Everything went smoothly until two riders on horseback approached at a breakneck speed. Evacuees leaving the Order stopped. It caused the flow to bottleneck. Haze's loud shout on the other side caused the problematic evacuees to return and wait.

As the first rider drew close, Leaf recognized Jasper's black-tipped brown hair whipping around his face. His glass crown was absent, but he wore intricately embossed leather armor fit for a king. Aeron galloped behind him on a mare, his long brown hair in a single braid. His armor looked like carved wood—maybe it was. As the Spring Court King, Aeron had access to the best wood weavers in Elphyne. Both kings wore a steel sword between their shoulder blades, still taking full advantage of their Guardian gifts.

Jasper reined in his stallion and pulled to a stop before Leaf. He glanced at Nova, frowned in confusion, then back at Leaf. "So it's true?"

Leaf's brow arched in question. "That Maebh is attacking the Order? Yes. The second portal is for your armies, per the missive we sent."

Aeron hand-signed to Jasper with sharp movements, his face growing impatient.

Just as irritated, Jasper hand-signed something back. "Yes, I'm getting to it."

It seemed the two kings had spent time learning the old-world gesture language Aeron needed to communicate without his sense of hearing.

"Getting to what?" Leaf snapped.

Jasper's expression turned grim. "You may recall a stone sarcophagus in the Summer Court palace gardens left from Mithras's reign. We never checked inside until recently."

Leaf's gaze narrowed. Agitated voices from the other side of the evacuee portal drew his attention.

"Hold that thought," he said, then shouted for Haze to send people through again. He was beginning to feel his mana stores drop from the expenditure. It wasn't much, but he was aware of movement. He returned to Jasper, who had an indignant look on his face. Clearly, the *king* was unhappy about Leaf's interruption. He'd have to wait a little longer because Leaf hadn't introduced Nova yet.

"This is my mate," he said, holding up the hand linked with hers. "Nova Morales, this is Jasper, and that's Aeron."

Nerves flittered through their bond, but she smiled graciously at the two kings. Jasper sniffed in her direction. His fur-tipped pointed ears lowered briefly before perking up. Contrition washed over his expression, and he inclined his head to Nova.

"I should have realized who you were. Congratulations on your blessed mating." He screwed his nose at Leaf. "I think."

If Leaf had less control of his decorum, he'd have flipped up his middle finger at the wolf shifter. Nova touched her fingers to her lips and pushed them down and toward the king.

"Nova's gift amplifies clean mana," Leaf explained. "So we can have two portals being used concurrently."

"Great." Jasper returned to Leaf. "But you need to know we

discovered a corpse inside the sarcophagus with an inscription proving she was Mithras and Maebh's changeling daughter." He paused. "She was too young to have borne a child. So your plan to use this woman in Crystal City to appeal to Maebh will not work."

"I'll stop you right there," Leaf said gruffly. "We don't think Rory is her granddaughter. She's her daughter from the old world. Nero is Nova's twin. That's how we found out."

"You didn't tell us?"

"We wanted first to get a message to Crystal City or Maebh. We failed. The battle is on at this point, so her identity likely makes no difference unless Maebh agrees to a parley."

Jasper wanted to say more, but Leaf didn't give him the opportunity. The first unit of Helianthus soldiers arrived, and he directed them through the second portal.

"I'll wait here for ten minutes," Leaf said to Jasper. "Then I'm holding the portal from the other side. If we're attacked, I must close the portals and join the fight."

"Fuck." Jasper turned his horse and galloped away, riding along the marching army and barking orders for them not to dally. Some soldiers were airborne, but most were on horse or foot.

The Seelie had fewer winged shifters than the Unseelie, but if this battle raged for days or weeks, then the Seelie would have an advantage. Leaf glanced up at the moon. Midnight wasn't far off. That Maebh made her play now—when the night was half over—likely meant she expected an easy massacre, and the battle would be done before dawn.

Leaf didn't like the unease in his gut. Surely, Maebh wouldn't be such a fool to believe they'd go down that easily.

Aeron stared at Leaf for a long, hard moment, then at Nova.

Thoughts raced in his silent gaze. He would have questions. Jasper didn't respond to hearing Nova's relation to Nero. He'd probably not paid attention, focusing on the fact they had little time to move an army instead. But Aeron was more astute. Leaf prayed they would remain alive long enough for him to answer Aeron's questions. The moment the king galloped away, a youthful voice spoke up.

"So it's true?" A gangly figure walked out from behind the closest portal. Tall, with blond shaggy hair, golden eyes, and a sense of entitlement.

"Prince Aspen," Leaf greeted. The boy was a toddler the last Leaf had seen him. He was perhaps thirteen or so now. His ears were fur-tipped, so he likely took after his father and could shift into a wolf. He wore a defiant expression like armor. "Do your parents know you're here? It's not safe."

Nova squeezed Leaf's hand and raised her brows.

"He's Jasper and Ada's son," Leaf explained.

"I asked if it's true," Aspen repeated, glancing at the portal with a look that made Leaf uncomfortable. "Is Maebh at the Order?"

"She's on her way, yes. Why doesn't anyone believe us here?"

"Dad received messages that the battle was still at Cornucopia." His eyes widened as he looked at the portal. "If it's true, then I should go and help."

Leaf blocked the teen's way and grabbed him by the scruff of his embroidered collar. He pulled him toward the glowing citadel walls.

"You must remain here," Leaf said.

"Yes, *mijo*," Nova added with much more compassion. "You're much safer here. Your mother will be worried if she can't find you."

But Aspen thrashed and twisted, trying to escape Leaf's hold. "Is Jasmine coming here?"

"Haze's daughter is none of my concern," Leaf replied, his tone hardening. He let go of the boy and gestured for him to go. "And we don't have time for this. Go before I make you."

"You can't make me do anything."

"Aspen? I'm Nova. I saw Jasmine only moments ago with her mother at the house. She'll probably come through the evacuee portal." Nova pointed to the closest one, where the steady line of people continued. "Your best bet is to find a place to see the line and wait for her."

The prince's gaze narrowed on Nova, then at her glowing Well-blessed markings.

"You're like my mother," he said with a note of pride in his tone.

"Yes," she answered.

"And your mana can stabilize the taint?"

Leaf's stomach dropped. Had he been spying on the conversation with his father?

"Yes," Nova replied slowly.

Alarm prickled. Too late, Leaf reached for the teen, but Aspen touched Nova's arm with a recalcitrant wink and then disappeared into thin air.

"Little shit," he muttered.

"Where did he go?" Nova's panic bled into him. "I didn't do anything."

"Wasn't you, Freckles." Leaf's tone softened. "The kid can portal like his father. He's probably at the Order now, looking for his friend."

"Oh." Her shoulders slumped.

"Hey," he said, touching her cheek. "None of that. Tonight is going to be rough. Being alert is important. Shit is going to happen. Try not to dwell on it, and keep going."

She looked at him with a mix of awe and bewilderment. "You really have changed."

"Aspen!" Ada's shrill voice pierced the rumbling din of troops and horses.

"Here!" Leaf called, lifting his free hand.

The blond queen ran around the soldiers and scrambled down the small embankment onto the shore. Trix wasn't far behind. Both women were out of royal garments and in something less conspicu- ous. But neither were prepared for battle, Leaf noted. Which meant the two weren't planning on coming through. He frowned. They needed all the help they could get, and Ada's healing skills were second to none.

"He portaled to the Order," Leaf explained. "Didn't like that we tried to make him stay when he couldn't find Jasmine."

Ada made a frustrated sound. "Goddammit. That kid will be the death of me."

Leaf grunted.

"Hi," Ada said to Nova, touching her hips and catching her breath. "You must be Nova."

Nova gave a nervous smile and wave. Trix bumbled down the embankment onto the sandy shore and almost tripped into Leaf.

"My bad," she said, grinning from ear to ear. Her curly dark hair looked like a nest suitable for birds. Her cheeks were flushed and bright, and she held a few of her invented handheld glass devices. "I ran all the way here after Aeron told me about your—hi—I'm Trix. I'm... *bloody hell*, what's on your face?" She widened her eyes and then apologized. "I mean, they look lovely. I've just never seen blue, Well-blessed freckles before."

"Trix," Leaf warned gently. "We have five minutes, and then we're heading back through the portal."

She startled. "Right! You'll need these, then. Also—hi, Nova. I said hi, right?"

Nova's nerves melted at Trix's genuine appeal. "You did."

"Cool." She shoved the devices at Leaf. "If Nova can amplify, it's worth testing the blood communication spells. These can help get the word out to everyone if she's nearby. Give one each to Thorne, Rush, and Forrest. Aeron has one already."

"Good thinking." Leaf nodded.

Trix stood back and raised her brows. "Did you just compliment me?"

Ada's brow lifted wryly. "I think he did."

Leaf's gaze darkened in a scowl, and he grumbled, "Tell your mates to hurry the fuck up."

Nova whispered in Spanish to watch his temper. The other women gawped at him. Both were clever—Trix was a genius in her time. Her finger waggled between Nova and Leaf, her lips parting to speak, but he tugged Nova toward the portal before any questions could pop out.

He would answer them later. Hopefully.

CHAPTER FORTY-THREE

Nova's anger at Leaf's brash reaction evaporated when she stepped on the lawn outside the Twelve's house. Reality sank in and she realized such worries now were silly. Soldiers were everywhere, from all sorts of kingdoms in all sorts of armor. People were shouting. Panic, fear, and excitement thickened the atmosphere. But Nova felt dread.

"What's wrong?" Leaf asked, his voice intimate as they took a position between the portals.

"I just—" She swallowed a lump. "It just hit me. This is war."

He studied her. "Yes."

She faced him, wide-eyed. "It didn't register before now. We could die. People *will* die. I—" Bloody visions from her beginnings here in Elphyne flashed before her eyes. The panic, the nausea, the helplessness. Her chest felt like something sat on it. She couldn't breathe.

Leaf's hand cupped her face. "And what happened last time?"

He forced her gaze to meet his.

"You saved me," she replied.

"That's right." His sword-calloused thumb rubbed her cheek. "This might be new to you, but it's not to me, as sad as that sounds. I want you to do something for me. Whenever you feel panic and dread rising, listen through our bond and concentrate on how I feel. Inhale, then exhale. Good." His eyes searched hers. "I protect what's mine, Nova. To my dying breath and then some."

Tears stung her eyes. The gravity of his words settled like a warm blanket around her shoulders. He'd lived through an apocalypse, through mutation, through the beginnings of madness, and then, in a way, death... all to be with her. If there was anyone in the world she felt safe around, it was him. And if this was the way she went out, then at least they went together. She smiled through trembling lips and said, "Let's hope it doesn't come to that."

He held her gaze a moment longer, then turned his attention to the sky, perhaps looking for signs of attack. Nova took a moment to admire the love of her life. As he'd said, when she focused on their bond, she only felt his resolute determination. The portals bloomed in the night, causing a stark contrast of light and shadow on his austere face. Every feature looked sharper as he scoured the surroundings. Long blond hair hung down his back where his sword waited to be used.

She glanced between that sword and his face—particularly the Guardian teardrop, almost invisible with the bright lights on his face. He kept insisting they would remain together, but he was a warrior. He would need to fight with his hands as much as his magic. At some point, she might have to be the one who told him it was okay for him to leave her.

Her gaze landed on the breadth of his shoulders, his biceps straining the seams of his jacket. She'd experienced his strength so many times already. It was comforting to remind herself how easily he'd maneuvered her in the bedroom.

Leaf gave her a sideways look. "Now, if you keep sending me images like that, I'm going to lose concentration."

A blush heated her cheeks. "I didn't realize."

He chuckled, eyes softening, then his brows together, and he glanced up.

"How long?" he barked at the night sky.

An ear-piercing screech stole the answer of whoever flew above. Leaf's hand clenched around Nova's, and then a cool, calm detachment washed over him. In the silence that followed, he bellowed, "They're here!"

A bomb landed from the sky, blowing up dirt and lawn before Nova. She flinched, shielding her eyes. It wasn't a bomb, but a vampire—the big one, Haze.

His calm eyes met Leaf's, and he held up three fingers. "Aerial units from the east. Two from the west. Another on foot through the forest. Indi spotted a manticore's tail whipping about. We've also had reports of trembling underground—probably a wyrm. She had a few captive at the Winter Court. That screech you heard was the demogorgon landing on the field before the Order."

"With Maebh?"

Haze's jaw clenched. "And the Prime."

"She's alive?"

He gave a nod. "She doesn't look good. She was carried in a sack by the beast, and she looks... aged."

Nova's eyes widened. Did that mean someone had been stealing her mana?

"The Six?" Leaf asked.

"Nowhere in sight," Haze replied.

"Fuckers." Leaf scrubbed his face, then glanced at the portals where a steady stream of soldiers still arrived. "Make sure they're headed in the right direction. Where's Jasper?"

"Near the portcullis, ready upon your word."

"Aeron?"

"With his foot squadron near the west point. The crows are with the aerial units, ready to go over the wall."

"Cloud too?"

Haze hesitated, then said, "I didn't see him. That doesn't mean he's not there."

"He's up to something." Leaf's brows lowered. "Wait. You said the crows are ready. As in, they're going over anyway?"

Haze's big shoulders bunched in a shrug. He looked exasperated.

"Tell Shade to manage them," Leaf suggested. "If he can't keep them in line, then—fuck it. Let them kill themselves."

"Fine."

"Who's keeping an eye on the north? Assuming the poison forest will keep Maebh out is foolish."

"I'll send someone."

"Good." Leaf picked up one of Trix's communicators from the ground and handed it to Haze. "Take that to Forrest and tell him Aeron has one. Then... find Jasper's little shit of a kid and tell him to come here. Give this second set to his father. With any luck, I can communicate with them and keep this portal open a little longer."

"Aspen's a kid," Haze grumbled. "Leave him out of this."

"He's old enough to sneak in here looking for your daughter," Leaf pointed out. "And he's older than half the Guardians were when they got initiated."

A tension-filled silence extended.

"Maebh's been calling for you," Haze said, eyes stark as he looked at the communicator.

"Me?" Leaf tensed.

Haze paused, glanced at Nova, then said, "The other you."

"*For Crimson's sake,*" Leaf cursed, then caught himself in the awkward reference. He said to Haze, "Go. I'll remain here as long as I can. Knowing Maebh, she won't attack immediately if I don't come out. She'll pick at our flanks enough to annoy us. It will give us time to get more soldiers in. When it looks like she's about to blow, get a message to me and I'll come."

"You could leave Nova with Shade or—"

"She goes where I go," Leaf growled.

Haze's deep voice lowered. "She's valuable to more than one person, Leaf."

"*D'arn* Leaf," he corrected. "I'm your team leader. If you want to stay in the loop, send your daughter here. Considering she and Aspen are inseparable, she can be your blood link. If I can communicate with you and Jasper, we can coordinate our efforts."

Haze's fangs bared in a snarl. Nova wasn't sure how Leaf remained untouched by the menacing giant.

"My daughter is too young. She's staying with Peaches, out of sight in the house."

"She's the same age as Aspen."

As if his name was a spell conjuring him, the prince emerged from the shadows. His eyes were wide and bright with excitement. He immediately went to Haze without fear. "Jasmine wants to help!"

Dismayed, Haze's gaze darted about. "Jaz! Get your pup-ass out here."

Jasmine stepped out of the shadows with a guilty look, twisting her long braid in her fingers. Haze's dark-haired daughter was as tall as Aspen. At this pubescent age, her delicate features and tall size clashed awkwardly, but Nova imagined when she finished growing, she'd be a force to reckon with—both in beauty and strength.

Haze exhaled impatiently through his nose. He opened his mouth to speak, but his daughter beat him to it.

"Don't worry," she said. "Mom knows where I am. We promise to get to the basement if anything goes wrong. If Leaf leaves, we'll stay here." Haze's brows snapped together. He tried to speak again, but Jasmine grinned and wrapped her arm around Aspen's shoulder. "And we'll stick together."

Haze's jaw clicked shut. He gave Nova a pleading look. "Say something."

She shrugged. "In my experience, the more you try to stop kids, the more they do it behind your back."

"Fine," Haze grumbled, then pointed his big, blunt finger at Aspen's face and leaned close until the blond flinched. "If she gets hurt, I'm blaming you."

"Dad!"

Haze unfurled his grand leathery wings, ready to take off.

Leaf said, "If you need your shadow tonight, find us."

When Haze was gone, Leaf looked at Nova. "Are you well? I'm

not overtaxing you?"

She smiled gently. "I feel fine."

"Good." The night turned his blue eyes as dark as the ocean. The glowing portals gave them stars. But nothing hid the tumultuous thoughts within. "We might have to leave this sanctuary sooner than later. Will you work with the kids to establish a communication spell so I can focus on other things?"

"I guess. I haven't done one of those spells before."

"They'll know how. Anyone with a biological blood link knows. I just need you to keep an eye on them."

"Got it." Adrenaline kept her alert. She held Leaf's hand but faced the two teens fidgeting with excitement. Leaf stepped closer to one of the portals and started talking with a close soldier.

"So," Nova said to the teens. "You're both much braver than I am."

Jasmine blushed, but Aspen puffed his chest out and spoke in a forced, deep tone. "Tell my dad that."

"Doesn't he know you're here?" Nova asked.

His gaze widened, and he looked at his feet. "Mom doesn't either."

"Oh dear." Nova tapped her lip. "I did see her on the other side, worried. I told her you were here, but perhaps you should contact her first. Oh wait, does she need one of those glass things?"

"She just needs to be near water," Jasmine replied and shook her communicator. Trapped water sloshed between the two panes of glass. Her eyes filled with hope. "Is it true if we touch you, we can use mana like they used to?"

It occurred to Nova that they'd lived most of their lives affected by the taint. She smiled back at them in a way she hoped was full of assurance and said, "Yes. And hopefully, after tonight, you will all be able to do the same. Okay, who can tell me how to work this thing?"

"Pull the stopper," Aspen explained, his voice deep again. Nova tried not to smile. "Then we drop some of our blood into the water and focus on the family member we want to contact."

"Alright, you'd better go first," Nova said. "But hold my hand when you do it."

Aspen's brows knit together when he realized he couldn't do everything at once. He could have let go of the device but was frozen with nerves. Jasmine tucked her device under her arm and then took Aspen's. She popped the cork and returned it. Another frustrated look came over the teen when he tried to pierce his finger one-handed with a dagger.

"Should I let go of your hand?" he asked Nova.

"It depends on when you need to activate the spell."

Again, Jasmine came to the rescue and bared her razor-sharp fangs with a grin.

With a blush, Aspen pricked his finger on her fang. Jasmine helped squeeze a drop of his blood through the cork and into the water. She put the stopper on as Aspen concentrated on the device. Blue light glimmered from within the glass. High Queen Ada's distraught face appeared moments later. Nova gave a quick wave to let Ada know she was there, then looked away while the two spoke.

They helped Aspen contact Jasper next, and while Leaf communicated with him, Nova assisted Jasmine in doing the same to Haze. By the time both spells ran, she felt suitably useful. Leaf's inner calm remained. All things considered, this war wasn't that bad.

But then the ground trembled beneath their feet.

CHAPTER

FORTY-FOUR

The ground quaked beneath Leaf's boots seconds before a wyrm burst through the lawn. The twenty-foot monster was three yards wide, with a slimy, segmented body. It shot upward until gravity pulled it down, slamming its body on any poor fool in the way.

"What was that!" Jasper's voice warbled through the dropped communicator.

The wyrm's multi-fanged mouth opened, poisonous spittle sizzled where it landed, and the beast came right for Leaf. He shoved the teens behind the portal, knowing it would shield them so long as he held it open. As fangs descended, he weighed his options.

Use *Reckoning*—let go of Nova. But the portals might close. The kids would be sitting ducks.

Okay, magic then.

He widened the release valve on his mana. The portals flared brightly until he split the flow and directed half through his arm. Conjured water cascaded from his hand straight down the beast's open throat. The wyrm choked on the torrent. With a twist of Leaf's free hand, he turned the stream into ice, expanding the substance and shooting shards into its flesh from the inside. The wyrm convulsed, bloated, then exploded from the pressure. Monster bile and blubber sprayed into the night.

Screams and shouts joined the splats.

Someone cried out. Leaf checked over his shoulder, but it wasn't the teens who were still safe behind the portal, or his mate who was shielded by his body, clinging to his hand. He met her wide-eyed gaze. "You hurt?"

She shook her head.

His jaw set and he let go of her hand. After making sure nothing else came through the wyrm's hole in the ground, he sent the teens through the portals to Helianthus City and then closed them. Most of the soldiers were through now. When the buzzing ozone subsided, he said to Nova, "I guess that was Maebh's last straw."

"It's time to meet her, isn't it?"

He gave a grim nod, tugging her close, unable to staunch the helplessness swimming to the surface of his control. He'd promised Nova he would remain calm, but Maebh calling him out like this wasn't good, for that was surely what had happened. The wyrm came straight for him.

Her war was about vengeance. She somehow managed to inspire loyalty—or it was just terror that kept her people fighting for her.

And who had controlled the wyrm? He frowned at the thought. The taint affected everyone, even Maebh. She was either lucky, or she'd found a way to harness mana. Or perhaps she'd spent this past decade training the beast the old way—by scent and pain. Maybe a little of all because the army managed to remain hidden.

Everyone on this campus could be dead by dawn.

Jasper would leave his son and mate. Haze, the same. Clarke and Rush still hoped to reunite with their daughter in Crystal City. The stark reality of Leaf's failings had come to a head—here, tonight. But he couldn't go there. Couldn't wrap his mind around that dark place filled with what-ifs and maybes. All he could do was trust that the Well had a purpose, and he was part of it.

Aleksandra's letter reminded him to keep the faith. It didn't fail him before. It wouldn't now.

So it all came down to Maebh unmaking herself.

Leaf bent his head and pressed his lips against Nova's. Behind his closed eyelids, one of her memories played out. She kissed him, but not him. It was Jackson Crimson, sick and puffy eared in a luxurious bed. His fingers gripped hers, unwilling to let go as she pulled away. His words "I'll find you" echoed in her mind as she walked down a carpeted hallway, choking on her emotions.

Leaf opened his eyes and pulled back. If she was thinking of the day she lost him, then she was more than afraid. Or she was preparing herself to fight? During an apocalypse her brother created, she had walked into unknown danger to find Crimson medicine. His chest constricted against his slowing heart, making the beating pained.

She'd better not be thinking about doing something silly now.

Her glowing freckles flickered, and a tear broke free from her eyes. He smudged his thumb across her cheekbone, clearing the path for them to shine again.

"Freckles," he murmured and swiped his thumb again. An idea struck him. "You can push memories into my mind."

Confusion tightened her brows. "What are you getting at, *Papi*?"

"What if you can push that memory into Maebh's mind?" he asked. "She might not have believed it if Aleksandra told her about their daughter, but if she saw the memory for herself, perhaps she'd believe."

If Maebh wasn't too insane to care. But as he'd explained before, obsession had a single point of origin. Losing her child was the reason for the Unseelie Queen's insanity. Depending on how far she stood from the Order gates, Nova could reach her from the battlements. This could all be over before anyone else got hurt.

"I could try. You might need to help me." Nova's brows lifted in the middle. "But she'll only believe if she sees me in the flesh, too. Then she'll recognize me as the woman in the memory."

"You're right." *Well-dammit.* That meant he had to bring Nova with him into danger. Worse, they had to get close enough for Maebh to lay eyes on Nova's face.

Unlike Aleksandra, who seemed to have lost memories that meant so much to her, Maebh held onto them like a vice. This move was a long shot, but the only one they had.

"We have to try." He squeezed Nova's hand. "But I won't force you into danger."

Her jaw set, and her eyes hardened. "I won't sweep my brother's mistakes under the rug. I ignored them for too long. And this child is my family, right? I can't abandon her to this fate."

"She's definitely not a child anymore. Cloud thinks she's as cruel and demented as her father."

"And you?"

"I don't know. Right now, all that matters is that Maebh believes she's alive."

"Okay then. V*amanos*. Before I lose my nerve."

Leaf held her hand with his left, and *Reckoning* with his right as they jogged toward the front gates. When they arrived, Jasper and his soldiers tried to stop Leaf from opening the gates.

"You can't go out there!" Jasper looked at him like he was mad. "It's what she wants. Obviously, it's a trap."

"I have a plan," he returned.

"Of course you fucking do." Jasper's expression darkened. "You always have a plan. If you shared it once in a while, we wouldn't be in this mess. I want to say fine, to leave you to your death. It's the same respect you showed me when Mithras had me caged."

Leaf winced at the truth. Before Nova, he was the biggest supporter of keeping out of fae politics, and Mithras killing every bastard he'd sired had nothing to do with the Order. Technically, Maebh's vendetta with Aleksandra had nothing to do with the Order either.

But now Leaf knew there was no such thing as remaining impartial. Every action affected the people he cared about or the integrity of the Well.

Leaf had supported the Prime's directive to not search for Jasper when he went missing. But it turned out, Jasper was fated to become the Seelie High King and ended up mated in a Well-blessed union. Thorne saving him had been just as important to the survival of the Well as this battle was. Aleksandra had moved her chess pieces around to help this prophecy come to light, but sometimes Leaf wondered if she did it on purpose, or if it was like Leaf ignoring his responsibility. Fate found Jasper anyway. One way was easier, the other more painful.

He opened his mouth to apologize, but Jasper gave him a placating look and lifted the still-active communicator, the watery surface showing his son's blurry face. "Aspen told me you saved his life. He disobeyed me and portaled to the Order. You could have ignored him, but you found a use for him and Jasmine. You kept them distracted so they stayed out of trouble, and then you pushed them to safety and closed the portals." His shrewd gaze turned to Nova, then back to Leaf. "The Crimson who founded the Order wouldn't have done that. He was like that woman out there—" He pointed to the gates. "Obsessed with one thing, even if he wasn't insane yet. So, if you think your plan is our best bet, I trust you. Tell us what to do."

Leaf could do him one better. "I'll share the plan instead."

Jasper's brows lifted. Screeches beyond the gates sent Leaf's pulse skyrocketing. They didn't have much time before Maebh picked at their seams again. Dawn approached at lightning speed. It made strategic sense for the Seelie to wait for the sun when they faced an army of nocturnal fae. But even though the sun weakened their opponents, it also made them desperate. And a desperate foe was not someone Leaf wanted to face.

CHAPTER FORTY-FIVE

Morning birds chirped in the poisonous trees outside the Order walls. They had maybe two turns of the hourglass before the sun rose. Leaf quickly outlined to Jasper what he intended to do, including why.

"And if it turns to shit?" Jasper asked.

"Then we do our best to stop her any way we can." Leaf shrugged. "If it comes to that, it's best if I get a shot of raw power out before your soldiers join the fray—unless they want to join the casualties."

Jasper folded his arms, looking at Leaf intently. "I heard about the army in the woods. They said flesh was flayed from bone."

"It's true," Leaf admitted, but would not divulge that he hadn't intended it. No need to worry the king. "A wave of raw power should buy me time to bring Nova back here to the wall, and then we can coordinate which Guardians or Well-blessed women to use first."

"Who's leading the Guardians while you're gone?"

His words hung suspended in the air. In other words, he meant who will lead if Leaf dies. He frowned and glanced at the Guardians manning the walls and hovering in the air, their wings beating as they aimed metal arrows knocked in bows. He scanned the line. Shade and one of the crows further down were together, heads close in conversation. It wasn't Cloud.

On the wall, Rush and Thorne prowled behind the guards. The silhouette of Caraway's big body and unmistakable horns walked along another wall. Leaf returned his gaze to Jasper and said, "Shade is the only reliable Guardian in the Council left."

Jasper nodded, then motioned for his soldiers to make a path. Keeping his spine straight and his will like steel, Leaf took the only woman he'd ever loved with him into possible death.

The grand wooden gates of the Order opened with a creak, and they stepped through. The Guardians on battlement curtain trained their arrows ahead of Leaf and Nova—warning anyone who attacked that they'd be killed. High above the walls, winged Guardians prepared to do the same.

To the right, left, and rear of the Order, a poisonous forest sheltered the campus from intruders. But the field ahead was vast, open, and the perfect battleground for war.

It wasn't hard to spot Maebh in the line of soldiers waiting a few hundred feet away. She stood resplendent on a ten-foot-wide litter resting upon the shoulders of muscular orcs. Other queens might remain at a safe distance. Not Maebh. She was high, in the open, and a target.

That was all Leaf needed to know about her mental state—she thought she'd already won. She thought she was invincible. She was out of touch with reality. Leaf's blast of power might not kill the demogorgon prowling below the litter, but it would kill Maebh and a good portion of her army. That might mean something, if not for the hundreds—possibly thousands—of soldiers hiding in the shadows behind that first line.

The demogorgon used to be Nero's right-hand man, Bones. Its tentacled wings thrashed about in agitation. The wind whipped Maebh's dark embroidered dress into a frenzy. No veil, he noticed, as he guided Nova forward. Reports from the Winter Court said Maebh was so aged and decrepit that she had to cover her appearance. But the closer he and Nova approached across the field, the more he realized those reports were exaggerated, or she'd found a way to turn back time... just like Nero had.

Leaf's gaze slid to the wilted owl shifter at Maebh's feet. Indigo had been right, she had aged. Aleksandra glanced up, her gaze clashing with Leaf's and filling with emotion. Her relief surprised him. He'd all but left the Prime to her fate. Just moments ago, he'd been reminded by Jasper that he'd not exactly been an example of compassion before he'd met Nova. It seemed he had a long way to go before he learned more.

The demogorgon stilled as Leaf and Nova hit the halfway mark, their boots crushing grass, thistle, and dandelion. Soon, the miasmatic stench of beasts, blood, and sweat would violate the beautiful bouquet he associated with his home. Even long after the killing was done and the last manabee shed, war had a way of erasing everything good about a place.

"Finally, he comes to face his doom," Maebh snarled, her voice a husky rasp. Red war paint covered her face from nose to forehead. Red ribbons twisted her afro hair into severe rolls scraped from her face. They entwined on the top like a crown, then rolled down her back in dreadlocks. No vampire wings were out tonight, but that wasn't unusual. She was rarely seen with them anyway. Behind her, the line of shadows rippled. Soldiers upon soldiers. All kinds, from Redcap goblins to orcs, trolls, elves, and vampires. Too many fae had rallied under her banner to distinguish.

An earth-quaking roar lifted the hairs on Leaf's arms. A shadow blocked the moon. Knowing the demogorgon was on the ground, Leaf's pulse quickened, and he glanced up. A leonine beast with draconic wings and a scorpion's tail circled above Maebh.

The creature was an elusive, mana-warped monster. It rarely bothered the public, and its habitat was a mystery to most. Those cages at the Unseelie war camp along the river made sense now. They'd been hunting monsters—this one in particular. The manticore's venomous tail wasn't its most terrifying part; it was the cleverness inside that swiveling, humanlike head.

Nova's breath hitched, and fear trickled through their bond. He forced himself to remain calm and squeezed her hand. He kept scanning the sky and relaxed a little.

Maebh had a manticore but no Sluagh. Not yet, anyway. This meant the monsters were the first priority if Leaf succeeded in killing the queen with his raw power and her army continued to attack. Forrest's gift was mind-to-mind animal control. If Leaf couldn't get Maebh to stop this war and failed to make a devastating hit, he'd call the elf to the wall. Perhaps with Nova's amplification, Forrest could control one of Maebh's beasts before too much damage was done.

If that failed, Melody's voice was next. More tactics entered Leaf's mind. Satisfied he had enough contingencies, he let them go and focused on the immediate threat. The demogorgon snarled as Leaf and Nova approached the twenty-foot mark and stopped.

"Let's talk about this," Leaf shouted to Maebh. "We used to be friends. Surely there's a solution that avoids shedding fae blood."

Maebh cackled. "You must think I'm a fool. I was friends with Crimson, not you. You're just a shell of that elf and a puppet of hers. I called you out here because the three of us started this. It's only fitting we are together at the end."

As she planted a boot on Aleksandra's head and kicked, spilling white ringlets and battered wings, a ripple of discontent traveled over her soldiers. It wasn't from the treatment of the Prime, but their queen's suicidal declaration. It seemed she might have promised them something else, like glory and riches. Not to be part of some kind of death pact. One of her generals gave a side-eye from a few feet away. Maybe the army would stand down if Leaf killed the queen.

His heart tugged at his leader hunching to protect her frail body as Maebh kicked her again.

"We don't need to fight," Leaf yelled, trying again. "It's what Nero wants. You might better know him as Niles Morales."

Maebh's gaze snapped to him. Confusion flitted in the madness. Only for a moment, then it was gone. The sound of buzzing was coming from somewhere.

"You're mistaken," she seethed. "This isn't a fight. This is an annihilation."

Ghostly faces manifested behind the queen. One, two, three... six beautiful males with tattered wings, each with a blue glimmering teardrop beneath their left eye. Legion's cold, midnight eyes met Leaf's.

This better be part of your plan. Leaf sent his thought to Legion.

No answer. Each of the Six looked down at Leaf with a blank expression. Did Maebh control them again? Or were they switching sides? Were they ever on the side of the Order?

Behind Leaf, someone at the Order shouted, "Traitors!"

Maebh's black-stained lips curved, and suddenly, the soldier who shouted choked as though invisible fingers clenched around his throat. Leaf's heart leaped into his throat. Emrys's skull was illuminated beneath his skin, turning his pale complexion vibrant in places. His wraith form must be attacking that soldier as Legion's had once attacked Leaf.

Moments after Leaf realized what had happened, chaos erupted. Maebh raised her hand and sliced forward. Battle cries tore through the night on both sides. The ground trembled as soldiers stampeded across the field. Leaf pinned Nova to his chest and raised *Reckoning*. Filling himself with mana, he prepared to unleash a wave of raw power, but the Hive voice burst into his mind: *WAIT.*

All six Sluagh turned their demonic gazes on Leaf as he hesitated. His hand trembled with the effort of restraining his power. He clenched his jaw and sent back, *You have seconds to explain.*

Seconds, and then Leaf's opportunity was gone. If she couldn't be reasoned with, the queen had to die.

We misjudged, they admitted. *She controls us through the Wild Hunt. Share the memory now, and we will help direct it into her mind.*

Nova twisted to look at Leaf with wide eyes. "They want me to share my memory."

"I heard too." Those precious seconds evaporated. Soldiers leaped from the shadows, faces fierce as they attacked. Leaf staked *Reckoning* into the ground and released power. An invisible wave radiated outward, scorching the earth and flaying skin from flesh and bone.

A groove forged ahead of him, where his power carved a channel toward Maebh's litter. Her shocked face glimmered from her soldiers' manabeeze floating into the sky, already on their way to the Cosmic Well.

Leaf had targeted a good chunk of soldiers with his magic—maybe a hundred or so. But he'd held back, only killing those within his immediate range. It was a warning. A demonstration to Maebh that they were not powerless. They would not go down gently.

Pulling *Reckoning* from the ground, and keeping Nova pinned to his front by his forearm, he stepped over corpses and advanced on Maebh.

CHAPTER FORTY-SIX

Nova was scared shitless, but she was proud of herself for not showing it. At least, not outwardly. Bright balls of light blinded her as they escaped the corpses Leaf had wrought. Beyond the light, sounds of battle raged on. Fae tore each other apart on either side of her and Leaf. The steady heat of his hard body pushed her forward, and she had to trust him. She had to focus on his confidence emanating through their bond. *Trust him. Trust him,* she kept telling herself. He would keep her safe. All she had to do was what she was told, like a good little mate.

She almost laughed hysterically at the reminder of his words so long ago. She'd hated him for it then, but no truer words had been spoken for this moment.

Leaf stomped and then shoved his sword forward. A gale-force wind from his hand blew manabeeze from their path, helping them avoid the intoxicating balls of energy. When the dust cleared, a nightmarish creature with split mandibles waited for them a few feet away. Its flesh had pulled apart from Leaf's blast but now knitted back together. It drooled and pawed at the ground.

"Oh God." Nova's heart rattled in her chest. It didn't look so frightening from a distance. "What is that?"

"The demogorgon. Used to be human," Leaf grunted near her ear. "Your twin's right-hand man before Maebh got her hands on him."

A shadow rushed from the right. Leaf blocked with his sword, steel clashing with a serrated bone sword. Leaf lunged forward, driving his sword into something—Nova was yanked along with him. She couldn't see anything beyond the immediate, but could hear the blade squishing into flesh and meeting bone. Next came a wet crunch, the gushing of blood, and a male grunt of bewilderment.

Leaf corrected their balance and pulled Nova to the foot of the litter. High above on the rickety platform, the fae queen and her six pretty monsters stared down at them. Leaf's recent power blast had left their hair sticking up, their faces blotched as though windburned. But no other damage. Blood and viscera spattered the carved wooden litter and the orcs holding it up. With horror, Nova realized some were missing flesh. Bone and strips of tendon dangled from gaping holes in jaws. The litter rocked, unbalanced, as one orc collapsed dead on the ground.

Their spines suddenly snapped stiff, filling them with unnatural vigor until the litter righted. Maebh was too busy trying to hold herself in balance. What a powerful queen she must have become.

"Too busy to use magic," Leaf mumbled, almost to himself. "Must have placed a compulsion geas on them a while back. Otherwise, they'd have fallen with that damage."

"What are you all doing?" Maebh shrieked at her army. "Attack!"

The sounds of battle fired up again. Now steady on her feet, Maebh's gaze landed on Nova's face and did a double take.

Do it now, voices screamed in Nova's mind. *Share the memory or we kill her.*

"Wh-what?" she muttered, wondering who said that, but then remembered the Six standing behind the queen. They stared at her with wide, inky eyes. "They want me to share the memory," Nova repeated to Leaf, hardly able to hear herself over the screams of the dying.

Leaf's breath was hot at her ear. "If they're giving you an option, they must be still with us. Otherwise, they'd simply rip the memory from your mind." He swung his fist, and two yards away, a trio of soldiers about to attack jerked with unseen magic. They continued to walk forward, straining against the power, but then Leaf shot a blast of water from his hand like a firehose. "Do it," he rasped behind the cover of mist. "While you can still concentrate."

Rallying her courage, Nova focused on the queen. She conjured the memory. Gripping Leaf's forearm across her sternum, she closed her eyes and trusted her mate to keep her safe.

Then she relived the worst day of her life.

"I DID what I always said I would do." Nile's emotionless eyes were at odds with his words. "I beat you. I'll always beat you."

"I didn't realize we were competing," Nova replied.

"We've competed since we were born." His lip curled. "In the womb, for our parents' love, at school, at friendship. You always seemed to win. But I've been playing the long game, Nova."

Who was this man?

"You know..." He sighed as though this conversation bored him. "I came here to tie up loose ends. You're the only one alive who knows everything. I thought you were my greatest chess opponent, but I see now that I've been playing with a pigeon. In hindsight, I overestimated you. Using you would have been easier than creating another biological energy source, but..." Another sigh. "Let's just say things turned out for the better."

He left the kitchen.

"Come back here and explain yourself," she shouted. "Niles!"

But he strolled to the front door, passing the family pictures in the hall without stopping. He opened the front door, stepped into the rain, and looked at the coming storm as though the sun shone on his face.

"I always thought that name sounded weak," he said, disgust oozing from his tone. "They gave you a beautiful, powerful name. Nova. Like a bursting star. I used to obsess over it. Why? Why would they stack the odds against me? Then I realized... the other side of a supernova is the black hole it creates in its wake—the Void."

He slid his dark gaze to Nova and stared until she shuddered, as though a film of evil had lowered itself on her heart. She narrowed her eyes at him, at the feeling bouncing between them. They'd always had a twin connection, always had a sense of what the other was feeling or where they were. But this evil—this was new.

No... not new. Just unhidden.

There was no joke in his eyes. No humor. This was the real Niles, and he was right. She may have been a pigeon knocking over his chess pieces, not even understanding the game they'd played. But she'd always had the sense he was up to no good. She should have trusted her instincts. Should have been brave enough to call him out.

She lifted her chin and said, "Mama and Papa would be ashamed of this man you have become."

"Lucky then, isn't it?" His gaze turned cruel. "Lucky they both died at the same time."

The screen door clanged as he walked away, and his expensive loafers slapped through puddles on the stone porch. With her heart in her throat, she chased after him. Furious.

She had no idea what to say, but it wasn't her logic driving her. Emotion and fury pushed her forward, her hand on the door, her feet outside, and into the rain.

A young girl's voice stopped Nova in her tracks.

"Dad!"

Shock barreled through her as her twin brother approached a parked car in their driveway. The rear door opened and a young girl burst out, running toward Niles. Perhaps in her early teens, her complexion was similar to Niles and Nova, but her hair... her hair had a texture that kinked in places and was straight in others. It seemed to match her effervescent personality.

Flinging her arms wide, she launched into Nile's arms. Nova gripped the slippery porch railing. Rain pelted her face.

"You're making me wet, Aurora," Niles growled. "Get back in the car."

The girl whined, but when he plucked her from his body and shoved her into the car, Nova glimpsed two women inside. Both African American, they enveloped the young girl, showering her with love. One woman glared at Niles as he slid into the driver's seat. The other wiped a tear from their daughter's eye as it mixed with the rain.

"Did you have to be so cruel?" Her sharp voice carried through the open window. "She missed you. That's all."

The other added with reproach, "What's gotten into you these days?"

Niles sent Nova a smug look as he turned the key in the ignition. It was pure, evil triumph. The car reversed out of the driveway, but before they drove away, the first woman turned and gave Nova a quizzical look. It was as though she had no idea Nova existed either, but recognized they were family... the child connecting them.

An agonized scream rose above the din of battle. Nova's eyes opened and locked onto Maebh as she staggered to her knees, her mouth a wide *O* shape. She looked about to vomit, and gripped one of the Sluagh's tattered wings, perhaps sending a silent command. But when it failed to respond, she reached for the Prime with her other hand. Aleksandra's gnarled, shaky hand met hers and clasped in acknowledgment of her pain... perhaps forgiveness. Maebh turned bleary, red-rimmed eyes to Nova and cried hoarsely, "Why did you show me that?"

"Because I'm the woman on the steps," Nova replied, proud that her voice remained steady. "You must recognize me from the porch that day. Niles is my twin. He's now known as Nero—the president of Crystal City and the man who destroyed the old world. That young girl in the car—they tell me she's alive in Crystal City. I can show you more memories. Leaf can share his from when he saw her—"

"No!" Maebh clutched her head, tears running down her cheeks. "I don't want these lies."

"She's alive!" Leaf confirmed, his voice as steady as Nova's. "Niles lied to you both. He used you both. He preyed on your desire to have a child and then stole her because a biological daughter meant he could feed off her mana without going mad. Surely you remember Crimson telling you about a friend who'd betrayed him. A neighbor—the twin of his greatest love. This is her, Crimson's—*my* Estrella."

"You lie!" Maebh cried, shaking her head. "Aurora died!"

Leaf stepped back as the demogorgon pounced, protecting its queen. Nova's scream caught as Leaf yanked her behind him and raised his sword.

Her ears popped as the air pressure changed. Her throat tingled. Everything itched, and oxygen evaporated from her lungs. So it wasn't her shriek that came out. It was the demogorgon's as it clashed with a wall of solid air—or *something*—Leaf conjured around them like an invisible shield. She glanced at her mate and found his face reddening from the strain of holding the barrier. Veins protruded on his forehead. Tendons popped along his neck.

God, she wished she could do something other than stand there and be used for her magic. The beast clawed at the invisible shield, its tentacles slapping over them like a Kraken gripping the hull of a see-through ship. Its muscles churned and undulated like oil beneath scaly skin. It snapped its mandibles.

Nova stared into those furious eyes and saw nothing human

left. Nothing but hunger and thirst and triumph as its claws started to breach the barrier.

"*Well-dammit,* Maebh. She's alive!" Leaf bellowed. "Your changeling daughter died. Mithras buried her in his backyard." He paused at Maebh's pained expression. His tone softened. "She was still a child. So Rory can't be your granddaughter. Don't you see? Killing fae is not the way to bring her back. It's handing your daughter's legacy to your enemy on a silver platter. Use the Sluagh to look into your pet's mind. He knew Niles—Nero! He knew your daughter."

Maebh shook her head. "My Sluagh pillaged his mind before we changed him. There was nothing there proving your claim."

Unless they wanted it that way.

Legion said something to Maebh, too quiet for them to hear from the ground below. Maebh's gaze settled on her pet as it tried to push its claws further through the invisible shield. The demogorgon suddenly seized as though electrocuted. It went limp, sliding down the barrier to the ground, and writhed in agony. A clicking sound in its throat deepened, and it slinked away, tentacles between its legs. It disappeared into the darkness beneath the litter like a wounded dog.

Nova thought the Unseelie High Queen was dangerous before, but the expression on her face now was murderous. Nova pressed back into Leaf as the shield dropped.

"He's right, Maebh." The Prime rose on shaky legs but stumbled on her robe—the same cream robe from the wake. Maebh caught her elbows, supporting her. White lashes lifted as the Prime met her gaze. "He played us for fools. Chess with pigeons, Maebh. Isn't that what he always used to say? That this world was full of pigeons. Oh, how we should have realized he spoke about us."

Nova's memory must have gone to the Prime as well.

"You wanted to leave a legacy for her," Leaf reminded her. "So give fae-kind back their power. Unmake yourself. Restore the balance you disrupted. Give your daughter a chance to escape him —give her a sanctuary to run to. Stop the fighting so we can talk about this."

Nova lifted her chin and added, "I may have only arrived in Elphyne a few months ago, but that means my memories of my brother are fresh. I know how his mind works; believe me, he's still scheming. You think he's in that city hiding, but he's always got a plan. He's a patient man who loves playing games, and he—"

Chess with pigeons.

The words sliced a path deep into Nova's memories, returning her to when her parents organized a family game night. They must have been twelve or thirteen, and Niles and Nova's competitive nature emerged. Eventually, he mastered every game they'd played or destroyed those he couldn't in a tantrum. But there was one puzzle their mother found that Nova and Niles worked together to solve. The cryptix was a cylinder invented by Davinci. Niles loved the sinister notion that whatever was inside was destroyed if they got it wrong. Nova just loved that he saw her as a partner... until they solved it.

"You could hold nuclear codes in here," he'd mumbled, awed as they pulled a scrap of paper from inside. "Or a map to secret treasure."

Before Nova could voice her revelation to Leaf, he blocked another attack. The sudden movement jerked her back to reality.

Maebh stared down at Nova, her eyes wide and furious. "I should kill you for what he did to us."

"He hates me more than anyone," she yelled back, no longer hiding the fear from her voice. "Killing me won't do anything. But I know him—you're playing into his plan. Don't give him the satisfaction."

She gestured at the battle. Floating manabeeze coalesced, making it seem like the sun had risen early.

Two of the Six hissed, glancing up and beyond Nova's head—somewhere in the sky behind them. Another gasped. A ripple of disquiet washed over them, and that buzzing sound grew louder than the cacophony of battle. Nova thought she'd seen every kind of nightmare since waking in this time, but the terror those fae devils instilled was the worst. Their black eyes seemed to echo the darkness of her soul, her greatest fear and shame all rolled into one.

And they were hunting for something. Desperate.

Legion snarled at Maebh, his fangs flashing. "Unmake yourself, Queen, or the moment you release the Hunt, you're dead."

"Shit," Leaf muttered, his shrewd gaze on the Six. A sheen of perspiration covered each of their faces, giving their flesh a pearlescent glow. They flickered, almost like a picture television trying to pick up the signal in a storm. They winced as though their very atoms were being ripped apart. Her mate murmured low near her ear, "The souls they keep are barely restrained. Maebh is the Hive's queen, the only one who can stop the Wild Hunt from killing everything in sight." Then, almost to himself, he added, "I thought they were on our side. Why would they want that?"

Six united voices replied in Nova's mind, *Because there can be only one queen.*

CHAPTER
FORTY-SEVEN

The ice-cold wind lashed Nero's face as he looked through the spyglass to the battle a thousand feet below. His mechanical breathing apparatus kept the thin air from suffocating him but made annoying wheezing sounds. His goggles—one of the Tinker's better inventions before she betrayed humanity—had a night vision function. He couldn't see colors in the shadows, but he could see well enough. Except for the manabeeze in the way as they rose from dead bodies and were captured in their airship's net.

A sudden gust of wind cleared the balls of light just enough for him to see. And then the supply started slowing.

"No," Nero muttered, moving along the starboard railing to try and see from a better angle. They should be gushing up here like a torrent.

"We're too high!" Rory shouted from his side, her voice muffled by her breathing apparatus.

"I know that," he snapped.

"She's not well. We have to lower altitude," she returned, insistent. "It's different this time. Maybe too many times too quickly."

Nero glanced at his silver-haired protégé slumped against the gunwale, sickly and clammy from her loss of connection to the Well. They'd spent far too long hovering over the decrepit fae city of Cornucopia, hoping for a sign of the warring fae to turn up. Their fuel sources were almost depleted. All had seemed lost until a bird swooped the deck and dropped a message.

He didn't care why or who it was, only that the intelligence proved true when they'd arrived here. The fae had changed their battle plans but were still moving ahead. Everything went according to plan until the manabeeze stopped filling the night sky. By his count, there should be plenty more to come.

Irritated, Nero lifted his goggles and winced at the wind burning his eyes. He fitted the eyepiece to his socket and adjusted the telescopic lens. The sun was coming up soon, so he might not need the night vision. Bright balls drifted like stars until darkness arrived again. He zoomed to the ground where the hordes of Tainted had gathered, pigeons about to be squashed beneath his boot.

But something was wrong. The battle had stopped. Why? They should be killing each other—ripping each other's throats out. And he should be harvesting more manabeeze they could use to fuel portals. This was supposed to be his moment. Then his spyglass landed on a blond Guardian standing before some dais or platform. The leaders must be parleying. The fae queen was dressed extravagantly. Dark afro hair, brown skin. Another had white hair and wings. The Guardian held a woman at his chest—his heart skipped a beat as he focused on her features, but they were too far away, and it was still too dark. Blood rushed in his ears as familiarity triggered confusion.

The spyglass darted between the blond Guardian, the queen, and—

"Father!"

Nero jolted as Rory growled near his ear.

He ignored her and went back to spying but lost his place. He cared little for the comfort of these people or the fae ward. The timing had to be right before humanity played its hand. Soon, he would give the order to swoop in and take advantage of the injured and weak. The girl would return to her magic source, so they should just shut the fuck up and wait like the rest of the soldiers.

"Sir." The young captain joined him at the railing. "With respect, sir. I agree with your daughter. My betrothed's health is in jeopardy. We must lower the ship. We've avoided detection this far. Surely we can—"

Anger turned Nero's vision red. He should never have allowed the captain betrothal status last night. Clenching his jaw, Nero faced him. Above the breathing apparatus, the boy's goggle-free eyes squinted so his inflated arrogance was clear. Nero struck his freckled temple with the back of his hand. The captain's head whipped to the side, dislodging his breathing apparatus and allowing thin air to filter in. Wheezing and blinking, the young ginger-haired man clutched his smarting temple in shock. Aviators and soldiers froze, awkwardly looking on.

"Don't you *dare* presume to dictate my plans," Nero snarled at him, his voice hollow through the mechanism. "I say when, I say how high, I say who. Understood?"

"Yes, Mr. President." The young captain straightened his spine and fixed his mouthpiece, breathing easily again. "I'll wait for your orders."

Nero glanced over the gunwale, grimly taking in the scene below. Something didn't feel right. Why did those fae look familiar? Why did he have this feeling churning in his gut?

Their nets weren't nearly full enough to call this expedition a success. The green pins would still sit in the bowls, waiting to join the others on his war map. Whatever the case, one thing was for sure. The fighting had stopped. This could be his only opportunity to use the card he'd been holding up his sleeve for the past decade.

"Lower altitude," he bellowed.

The captain repeated his directive and walked down the deck, ensuring the aviation crew had heard. They scurried about the decks, moving into positions and adjusting the balloon's engines and hot air. Nero's gaze landed on his daughter, his only companion from the old world. She was the shark he turned into a pigeon. She appeared older than him now, more aged. Since his last session extracting her mana, wrinkles gathered around her eyes. White, wiry strands streaked her dark hair, knotted at her nape. She looked like a sad old matron.

There was a time he thought he cared enough to keep her pain at a minimum for these extractions and trips in and out of the garden, adjusting her connection to the Well. But then she'd stopped feeling pain like his silver-haired halfling ward. And he'd stopped caring.

For a while, he trained her and taught her how to have a mind as sharp as his. He thought if there were two of him against the world, he could achieve greatness in half the time. But then she'd beat him at a game of chess, and it reminded him so much of his twin. She'd turned *him* into a pigeon and laughed like his twin sister used to. Like beating him was somehow hilarious.

So Nero took everything from her.

His breathing mask hid the slow smile spreading across his lips as Aurora kneeled to check on the halfling. She was so caught up with this little mutant's health she didn't even realize their time was almost up.

The airship lowered, Nero's ears popped, and the air became warmer and breathable. He pulled his apparatus off and then inhaled the fresh predawn air. *Almost time.* He checked his wrist, where a new portal device was attached. The engineer who replaced the Tinker had built on her designs, and Nero couldn't say he was disappointed. He'd even wondered if the Tinker was holding back her best ideas.

No matter what happened next, Nero would escape to safety. A few hand-picked others across their airship fleet had the device, too. But not his daughter and not the halfling.

He looked over the gunwale at the approaching ground. *This is it.* He never thought he could still feel excitement, but his bones vibrated with anticipation. He'd spent the better part of the past decade teaching the halfling how to use her gift and manipulate the dead. He'd been locked up in that insufferable tower for so long, but soon he would be the leader of everything.

Then, the real fun would start.

The halfling gasped from the deck, breathing in great gulps. The whites of her eyes showed. Her skin blushed as it filled with color again. She looked like a junkie who'd just taken a hit.

He was no fool. He knew she remained loyal to her kind, but

there was a reason he'd allowed her talks with her parents to continue, just as he'd allowed her friendships while in Crystal City and given her the luxury of a caretaker in Aurora.

"Ready the pilot ladder," he barked.

The captain stepped forward, his breathing apparatus gone. "Sir? I thought we weren't sending them down. It's too dangerous with that many soldiers still alive."

Nero counted to three in his mind and willed his patience to return.

"The closer she is to the corpses," he explained through gritted teeth, "the more power she holds over them." Nero straightened the young man's collar and adjusted the gold military epaulets declaring his high rank. "You'll be going with her. Along with a team of Reapers, of course."

The captain's confused gaze darted to his halfling betrothed and then back to Nero. He wasn't battle-ready, and he knew it. But he couldn't very well say no to Nero. It made him look unworthy of being her betrothed.

"Don't worry," Nero said with a smile. "We'll leave the ladder down."

His smile died when he returned to the spyglass. The sun had lightened the sky enough for him to see why the fighting had stopped. He was close enough to see the face of the Unseelie Queen, and when she looked up at the sound of the airship engines, ice trickled into his veins.

The surrogate... but how? And the woman at her feet was the second mother... but with wings and white hair. They were meant to be expendable—faces he dealt with for a decade while pretending to be the father and donor they needed. Of course, they knew nothing about his real life with the Cartel, and he was frequently away on business trips. It had been so long since Nero had seen their faces.

Nero slid the spyglass to others on the ground and choked. The blond Guardian looked like... *Jace.* And then the woman in his arms was Nova, Nero's twin. Blue, glowing marks on their arms matched. Seething bitterness punched Nero's gut. They'd found a way to join forces against him, and their magic source had blessed them.

The horizon shifted, and he had to clutch the gunwale to stop from tumbling over. He stepped away from the view of the ground. He didn't think they'd seen him, but what kind of madness was this? First, Clarke had awoken in this time, and now them? And... the mothers appeared aged. But they were definitely fae. How?

His mind raced with explanations, trying to defuse his paranoia. Could it be they'd all been alive since the Fallout? It was possible. He and Aurora had manufactured their frozen sleep through the predictions of one of his psychics. That woman was dead now. She made too many demands, so Nero killed her after he'd learned Clarke had arisen. A mistake. How narrow-minded of him to think Clarke had been given to him by fate...

His gaze slid to the halfling, who'd strangely started panting like a wolf. She snarled at something unseen over the bow. It was as though she expected the air to jump up and attack her.

Willow was Clarke's daughter, so perhaps fate had given Nero a gift after all. Maybe seeing these faces from his past wouldn't be so bad. Maybe this could still be salvaged.

Willow's yellow-eyed gaze snapped to Nero. Something dark and twisted lurked behind her eyes as the wind lifted her long, silver hair, revealing her pointed fae ears flattened with aggression. Her lip curled, flashing her dainty wolfish canines.

This feral side of her was such a shame. The girl had grown into a powerful, exotic beauty. He'd even considered taking her as his wife. But then Nero's physician reported she'd gone into heat, like a bitch. *Disgusting.* If she refused to do his bidding, he had enough mana trapped in his body to compel her. If that failed, he planned to put her down anyway.

The three Reapers he'd put on standby stood two yards away, their mechanical rifles ready.

"Time to raise our army, my dear," he said, voice steady. "Kill them all. But bring the woman with glowing blue freckles to me. Alive."

Nero wanted to laugh. For all his talk about fate forgetting him, here was another example of a gift. He'd emptied one biological mana source in his daughter, but another had walked in. Nova was Well-blessed. She would keep him young and powerful for eons to come.

"Fuck you," Willow spat, her eyes flashing.

Her betrothed captain gasped like a schoolboy. "Willow!"

"I'm not killing them," she said to him, her voice softer, proving she had feelings for him. Good. Feelings were easily manipulated.

Nero nodded to the Reapers waiting for his command.

A masked, tall one fisted Willow's hair and shoved her toward the gangplank, where the rope ladder unfurled and dropped below. Nero gestured to the other Reapers, who trained their guns on Aurora.

"Why are you pointing your guns at me?" she asked, cocking her head. To his daughter's credit, despite the fog in her mind from his copious treatments over the years, she looked as sharp as a tack now. And deadly. Unlike these fools, she'd had decades, if not centuries, to hone her craft as a Reaper. The taint had made it difficult to maintain the level of compulsion he needed for her to stop asking questions over the past decade. She'd been remembering things she shouldn't, and it was precisely why she'd outlived her usefulness to him.

"Because if the halfling doesn't do as she's told," Nero explained, "you're dead."

"You wouldn't." Aurora's gaze narrowed on him. She was dressed in all-black military fatigues and was missing the copper epaulets stating her rank. Copper was a precious resource. He'd thought ahead to ensure she left them behind. But the captain's participation was newly improvised. Nero ripped off the gold decorating his shoulders. No use in it going to waste.

"Ensure she does her job, and I'll return these."

It was remarkable how lies flowed off his tongue these days.

"Don't worry about me," Aurora told Willow as the Reaper shoved them toward the ladder.

The captain was already over the edge and dangling a few rungs down. Willow was next, but her wide eyes sought Aurora's as she resisted the Reaper.

"For fuck's sake," Nero muttered. He had to do everything himself.

He grabbed the knot at his daughter's nape and pushed her to the gangplank. She gripped Nero's wrists to stop him from scalping her.

Cruel pride swelled in his chest. His daughter was a magnificent specimen of his DNA, even aging as she was. She still had all the strength and fortitude he possessed, and he took a moment to appraise her. That fire in her eyes was finally back. He pulled so hard on her hair that strands plucked from her scalp, yet one wouldn't know she was in pain if not for her pupils contracting.

This kind of resilience was a talent. Most people crumbled.

She couldn't complain he'd never given her anything.

For a moment, something in her honey-colored gaze gave him pause. It caused the tiny hairs on his neck to stand upright. The prickling sensation crawled along his skin, down his spine, and along his arms. *Danger*, his instincts screamed.

Unlike him, she'd awoken from their frozen sleep with a natural capacity for magical energy. But he'd known that would happen. He'd planned for it. He'd built a cult around it—the same ones who quarantined themselves in the Crystal City bunkers. They'd been there ready and waiting when it was time for Nero and Aurora to thaw, arms wide in welcome.

"Do as you're told," he said to her, bleeding compulsion into his voice. The air between them vibrated, and the emptiness returned in her eyes.

She let go of his wrists and then went over the ladder's edge after Willow. Three Reapers descended after them. While they dangled on the long rope, the airship continued to a lower altitude.

As they neared the ground, Nero sucked in a breath. A tremor in his body remained. He couldn't get that look in his daughter's eyes out of his mind. That unnamed *thing* he'd seen when she held his stare. Frowning, he pointed at the Reapers remaining. Each had a sniper rifle ready, their bodies all flattened on the deck, aiming through the scuppers.

He rubbed his wrists to ease the burn from where she'd gripped him. Surprise sliced through him as his fingers slid over his left wrist—his *bare* left wrist. The portal device was gone. He rushed to the gunwale as the ladder reached a patch of dirt in the center of the battlefield. War-weary soldiers had retreated to their sides but watched their leaders over the field of littered corpses. No one had noticed the lowering airship yet.

A warning shout carried across the field.

Well, now they'd noticed.

Nero's lips curved as Alfred and Willow jumped off the rope. The three Reapers were next. Before she joined them, Aurora lifted her face and sought Nero out. When their eyes met, he found the compulsion had regrettably worn off. He finally recognized that unnamed *thing* lurking in her eyes—payback.

CHAPTER FORTY-EIGHT

More airships appeared above the first, blobs of shadow against the purple sky. They'd been up there all this time, collecting mana like vultures picking at carrion. Silver had warned this would happen, as did Trix. And the Order had been prepared, but no one reported airships, and now Leaf knew why. They'd flown to an altitude the Well couldn't reach.

Clever.

And possibly fae-kind's doom.

As a rope ladder unfurled from the lowest airship, Leaf pleaded with Maebh. She'd already approved a suspension of hostilities. Both sides of the war glared at each other from across the field, warily waiting for instructions. Some stared at the ships with curiosity, not fear. Most of these fae couldn't fathom the destructive power of human war machines.

And without clean mana to use, they would be slaughtered. Unless... Leaf searched the airships and was relieved that there was no heavy artillery. Maybe a cannon or two. Perhaps the rest had been sacrificed for the harvesting nets. But then, why were they sending down people on the ladder?

"Unmake yourself, Maebh," he implored. "We cannot fight them like this."

But Maebh's wide-eyed gaze was somewhere behind Leaf. Already unhinged, learning about her daughter seemed to both tip her over the edge and keep her from falling. But this look in her eyes was something else. Her fangs bared, and her ink-stained fingers fashioned into claws.

"No!" one of the Six bellowed, but Leaf couldn't tell who. They were all distressed. The rising sun caused them discomfort. Unlike vampires who wouldn't die, the Sluagh burned in ultraviolet rays. Legion had admitted as much to Violet and Indigo.

Leaf pulled Nova back to his chest. Whispers of warnings flooded his mind. The Well spoke to him, urging him to hurry. Danger, chaos, and death were coming. But as he scanned the frozen battlefield and glanced up, he wasn't sure where the threat was worse.

"Your brother," he said quietly for Nova's ears only. "He's on one of those ships."

She squeezed his forearm and whispered, "Whatever you need from me, take it."

Bodin snarled, holding Maebh back with a taloned hand on her shoulder. Her face hardened into violence, cracking the red war paint on her face. Her gaze was still locked on the airship—more precisely, on those descending the ladder. From this distance, Leaf couldn't make out anything special until he found the female with long, billowing silver hair as she clung to the swinging rope.

The haunting sound of a wolf howling rose above all else. Another joined it. Up on the Order battlement, two great white wolves tipped their noses to the sky, their maws gaping as they heralded their kin's return.

"Shit," Leaf mumbled, taking in all the ways this could go wrong. It was lucky Rush and Thorne had shifted to wolf without the taint warping their transformation. But he doubted it would be so smooth returning to human form.

Something was severely wrong with Maebh... more than usual. She lashed against Bodin like a maniac, trying to get onto the battlefield.

The airship hovered, and rifles pointed through holes in the hull. He returned his gaze to the ladder. The instant Willow's feet landed on Elphyne soil, a silent, invisible force exploded outward from her. Horror filled Leaf as the blast wave approached, kicking up dust and dirt. Leaf planted his feet and shielded Nova with his body, weathering the blast. It was just air and stinging grains of sand. The turbulence rocked the wounded orcs holding Maebh's litter. The platform tilted. The Sluagh's wings lifted from their shoulders, vibrating in a blur to hold them above until the orcs rebalanced.

Leaf's ears inner ears hurt, and his face tingled.

"You good?" he asked Nova.

She nodded but clung to him in fright. No one seemed injured. What in the Well's name was that blast? Everyone had the same bewildered look except for Maebh and the Six. Leaf tracked her blood-thirsty gaze through the shadows to where Willow's silver hair shone like the moon itself.

"Get ahold of yourself, Maebh," Aleksandra's comforting voice rose from the chaos. She stepped before the Unseelie High Queen and forced her to meet her eyes. "Our daughter is out there too—*look!*"

Maebh's gaze flickered with doubt. It was enough to pierce the berserker haze. Her rage melted. She gripped the Prime's shoulders, and tears formed in her eyes.

"I see her," she rasped, then sucked in a pained breath. "My God, she's beautiful. Oh, how she's grown. Our little butterfly."

But as Leaf's relief formed, the ground trembled.

"Another wrym?" he asked. "For Crimson's sake, Maebh. Enough is enough!"

"It's not me."

With Maebh contained, each dark-eyed Sluagh stared at the battlefield with rapt, almost maniacal attention. No, not just the battlefield—they stared at the humans. And Willow.

Then the stampede started. Fae from both sides of the war fled the human interlopers in a wave, not unlike the speed of the blast. Leaf could hardly distinguish the reason. There weren't *that* many humans on the ground—no gunfire from the airships.

But as terrified retreating soldiers arrived, Leaf had no time to ponder. Heart leaping into his throat, he blocked anyone passing too closely with his sword. Nova's scream made him work harder to keep her safe. The stampeding soldiers thinned as he was about to throw up another protective shield.

Dust bloomed on the battlefield, hiding everything from view. The sun needed to rise already. He needed more light. Shielding his eyes, he squinted into the murky haze and willed his lungs to take shallow breaths.

He scoured the shadows with every sense, listening and

searching for danger. A blood-curdling scream. Another howl. A predator's yellow eyes blinked where he'd last seen Willow.

Leaf sent a sliver of wind toward her. The dust cleared in whorls. When Willow appeared, her face was consumed with the same berserker rage as Maebh. Crouched to the ground, Willow's fist was already buried in the dirt.

"*Shit*," he muttered. Fae burrowed beneath the earth when they wanted a deeper connection to the Well... for more power and range.

Willow's rage focused on Maebh.

Danger... Wrong. Flee. Hurry. Fix... Clean. Last chance. The Well whispered too fast.

Someone shouted from the battlements, but he couldn't understand what was happening—the sounds of fighting renewed with terrified screams. More dust and dirt rose, blocking Leaf's vision. Manabeeze drifted into the air.

Nearby, a wounded Unseelie soldier stumbled from a dirt cloud. Blood covered his face. His arm hung loosely, as if dislocated. His throat was torn out, revealing tendons and vertebrae. He shouldn't be alive.

The soldier locked eyes on Nova, sniffed, then snarled at Leaf as though he was the obstacle.

"Fuck off," Leaf warned. "Get to a healer."

But the soldier attacked. Leaf twisted, both protecting Nova with his body and stabbing the soldier in the torso. Confused, the soldier glanced down at *Reckoning* and then mindlessly skewered himself on the blade, reaching for Nova. The stench of rotten breath bloomed as he snapped his teeth inches from Leaf's face.

"He's sick," Leaf grunted. "Maybe the taint has infected his mind."

He planted his boot on the soldier's hip and then yanked his sword out. Leaf let go of Nova, pivoted, and used the full force of his weight to decapitate. His body fell and twitched on the ground while his head rolled into the dusty shadows where another wounded fae appeared, charging at Leaf. And another. And more. They were everywhere. He cut and chopped, stabbed and blocked, but all were relentless in their attack, all frenzied and mindless to get to Nova. Not just her. They leaped onto the litter, desperate to kill the Unseelie High Queen.

Tainted mana was used on the battlefield as others protected themselves from the infected. Colored light bloomed in the dust between the white glow of manabeeze. The taint created nonsense and warped things—a rainbow, then snow, and silk ribbons cascading from someone's hand.

With each passing second, more manabeeze floated, and fewer cries were heard from wounded soldiers. More frenzied, mindless, and feral mortally wounded emerged from the dust cloud. Some had Seelie uniforms, others wore Guardian leathers.

Leaf dispatched each attack with *Reckoning*. He shouted for the Six to help, but they ignored him. When he had a moment to look, Fox's face held a devious grin as he stared in Willow's direction.

This is madness.

The headless soldier on the ground moaned—or rather, the sound came from the head half-buried in the dirt. The body clambered to its feet.

"Zombies," Nova shrieked. "They're goddamn zombies."

The word wasn't familiar, but her terror was. When he questioned her with his eyes, she added, "They're dead. Undead."

His mind filled with pictures of stumbling, rotten corpses groaning about brains. She must have sent him the memory.

"You had these monsters in your time?" he asked.

She shook her head wildly. "Only in stories. On TV. Never in real life. I think you have to shoot their brains. And if they bite you, you become infected and become them."

Leaf sliced his sword across the scalp of a goblin, cutting the top off like a lid. Nova vomited behind him as gray brain matter spilled out. But within seconds, the corpse twitched, and the goblin tried to rise again.

"Not these ones," Leaf confirmed, cutting down the middle of the decapitated body as it fumbled toward him. "They can't be killed."

Willow's berserker gaze flashed in his mind. She must have betrayed them despite what her parents believed. That was the only logic he could muster. Somehow, Willow had sent an army of undead, frenzied warriors to kill them.

"I'm going to have to kill her," Leaf said, glancing at the Prime.

Pain sliced through his body before another word escaped his lips, locking his muscles. Cold fingers wrapped around Leaf's throat as a head with dark brows, short white hair, and a skull flashing beneath the porcelain skin appeared inches away. Black tattoos on Emrys' body writhed under his skin with ancient promises as black as his eyes.

The Sluagh trailed his nose along Leaf's jaw, inhaling the scent of fear like a drug. His exhale sounded aroused, eager. "Try. I dare you."

Sharp talons pricked Leaf's neck. Behind Emrys, Maebh lifted her fist and swung her arm away. Emrys hurtled off Leaf as though pulled by an invisible string. His draconic wings flared wide, gracefully balancing him. His grin bared sharp fangs, and his wholly black eyes narrowed on Leaf, intensifying. Leaf was still frozen in place by Emrys's invisible wraith form.

He tried to step forward, to free himself of the metaphysical shackles. Maebh's pet burst from the shadows and attacked the Sluagh. Emrys smirked at Leaf, then flickered out of the way. Each time the demogorgon attacked, his smile stretched into something more wicked. He toyed with the monster, like a cat with a mouse.

Until more undead clambered over corpses. The hold on Leaf released in time for him to ward off the attack.

"We don't have time to fight amongst ourselves," Leaf growled, flicking blood off his sword.

Maebh gave him a flat but agreeable look. The madness seemed less in her eyes now. She sent her pet away from Emrys and into the unending army of corpses—ordering it to keep them away. Then she yanked on Emrys' puppet strings, somehow jerking around the souls inside him until they buzzed with a deafening roar.

"Do not attack him again," Maebh ordered.

But the Sluagh was not pacified. He paced like a tiger in a cage. All Six were just as agitated, their gazes intent on their future queen, sweat dappling their skin as though the small shafts of sunlight were as hot as an oven.

Nova launched into his arms, trembling.

"I'm fine," he whispered, stroking her hair.

The leader of the Six ignored Leaf with implacable stoicism. Leaf's jaw clenched. He collected *Reckoning* and again had a moment of hopelessness. "What the fuck is going on with you and the Sluagh?"

Maebh's lips parted, and she squeezed her eyes shut, convulsing slightly as though stopping herself from vomiting. When her eyes opened again, she answered Leaf. "They're protecting their new queen."

Leaf's gaze whipped to the battlefield. "Willow?"

"I read about this in the ancient lore. Her wave of power was the challenge, an instinctive call to arms. Every ounce of being in my body wanted to rip her apart. If it weren't for my daughter standing by her side, she'd be *dead* by now."

The vehemence in her voice sent shivers skating down Leaf's spine.

Our wolf queen is mighty. Bodin's lips curved wickedly, and Leaf swore pride washed over his handsome features.

Leaf's gaze slid to Varen, the Six's seer, and everything made sense. These mysterious, private Guardians had either meddled with missions or offered help at the strangest of times. They never explained their motives and rarely came when the Prime called.

Varen said, "The moment of her conception caused a stir within the Well. She was both blessed and cursed at once. A gift of both worlds, a true queen of the between and of all."

"The prophecy," the Prime gasped, understanding coming over her haggard features. "It's not about Clarke, but her daughter. Rush was cursed at the time—they're the ones who told me how to do it."

A mournful smile touched Legion's lips. "We have waited eons for one who sees in the dark, just as us. One who is neither a dream nor a nightmare. She is our skin."

Maebh's eyes darted back and forth. "How long have you planned my ruin?"

"By murdering our Seventh," Legion replied, "you sealed your doom. You bargained with the Well for us, but we bargained for her. Everything afterward, including this"—he gestured at the glowing blue drop beneath his eye—"was for her."

Fox chuckled, his tail lashing. "There cannot be two in one place. We knew you'd have the will to rein in the compulsion to kill her—with the right ammunition." His smile died. "But you'd have destroyed her as a child, so we sent her away."

"To grow fierce," grumbled Spike from the shadows.

"And strong," added Legion.

"To wait until you withered," Emrys drawled.

"Or to be unmade," Bodin smirked.

Even as the dawn weakened them, they smiled triumphantly at their old queen. Leaf had the sense they were toying with her, just as Emrys had played with the demogorgon. And he feared this game wasn't over.

Betrayal flashed across Maebh's features, followed swiftly by dismay and fear. She knew she was weakened... the Sluagh had orchestrated events for this precise moment—the blood they'd fed Shade and Indigo, the way Maebh turned Bones into the demogorgon afterward, inevitably creating the taint and her lack of mana. She had to steal from the Prime, but that wouldn't last. Stolen mana was finite and would not replenish from the Cosmic Well.

The Six had orchestrated everything. *Fuck.*

How many fae would die, all so they could claim their new queen?

CHAPTER FORTY-NINE

Leaf fought off more undead breaking past the demogorgon's barrier.

The Sluagh cared nothing about fae lives, nothing about humans. They only wanted a queen who didn't control them like Maebh did—a true mate.

More of the frenzied surged. No one stood by idly. No more talking. Aleksandra, Maebh, and any Unseelie brave enough left to stand by their queen. Even the Six plucked the frenzied from their bodies like pests.

When the horde grew thick, Leaf released a blast of raw power from his dwindling resources. At this point, he didn't care. He wanted them gone. He needed this to be over. He was tired of fighting. Tired of this never-ending cycle of death and life.

With a deep dig into his reserves, he pulled enough mana to throw up another shield. Undead hit the invisible wall and shook their heads, dazed. Then they continued to batter the air. Now and then, the demogorgon emerged from the darkness and plucked one off the shield, dragging it back into the fray.

"I just need a moment," Leaf rasped, lungs heaving. Every muscle in his body ached. "I just need... a moment."

Nova made a pained sound.

"What's wrong?" he asked, tightening his grip on her hand.

Her face paled. "I feel... sluggish."

"I'm almost out of mana," he confessed. "Perhaps you're linked to my levels. I don't know."

This wasn't good.

Despair trickled into Leaf's soul and those damned Sluagh looked at him with hungry eyes.

Scanning the battlefield over the writhing undead and brave soldiers left fighting, he glimpsed white and bloodied fur carving a way toward Willow, but still too far. Glinting flashes of metal, both in the sky and on the ground, revealed more of the Twelve were out there, fighting as best they could. He even spotted Cloud, his tattoos a clear marker of his identity. But with each enemy felled, more rose. Willow somehow turned the newly deceased into puppets, much like how Maebh had controlled the Sluagh—the ghostly warriors who existed between death and life. And this was Samhain, after all. The night the veil was thinnest. Except the night was done.

Gunfire peppered the air. A woman's broken and agonized scream cut through the air like a knife. Leaf felt the anguish down to his bone. The Six tried to go to Willow, but Maebh held them back through the souls they kept.

They became feral, frenzied, desperate. Leaf had never seen them so wild.

Maebh's panicked gaze snapped to the Prime. Her expression hardened, and she promised, "I won't let her die, not like this. Not before she claims her inheritance." Tears welled in her eyes, spilling over her cracked war paint. "I built this for her!"

"I know," the Prime replied hoarsely. "But we don't know who screamed. It might not be her. They wouldn't be so wild if it was."

The Six snarled, thrashing against Maebh's restraint, and promised death in their eyes. But so long as the souls were trapped inside them, they couldn't move against Maebh. The rising sun weakened them. The sky had become a canvas of pink, orange, and blue hues.

The agonized scream rose in pitch, a fatal plea for help. It was no sound a parent, or mate, could resist.

"Aleksandra is right," Leaf rasped, trying to calm them down. Panic was a land of mistakes. He couldn't forget his goal. "It's too hard to see."

"I don't care." Desperation filled Maebh's bloodshot eyes with madness. "If it's the last thing I do, I'll keep her safe."

"Maebh, stop!" he roared.

But the buzzing inside the Sluagh intensified. Their wings vibrated. Alarm sliced through Leaf. He blocked his ears and pulled Nova close, but how could he save her when he had no idea what was happening?

The Six straightened like pins, bodies stiff and spines bowed. An empty silence stretched. Time stopped. Then darkness erupted from their hearts. Swarms of black buzzing and flying things spilled from their chests.

Fuck.

Leaf dropped to the ground and took Nova with him, remembering to lower his shield. It had been cast over all of them, and he didn't want to be trapped inside with the swarm. But that opened the path for the undead.

Dawn reversed into night as the droning darkness coalesced above their heads, blocking out the sky as it grew in size. And grew. And grew.

"The Wild Hunt," he whispered.

Every imprisoned ghost, soul, and spirit moaned and shrieked gleefully. Dark gaping jaws emerged from the bubbling, misty swarm. Just as quickly, it melted back into the mist. Another limb pulsed out, revealing scaled hindquarters and claws. As it returned, draconic and tattered wings spread wide, beating and disturbing the dark mist in whorls.

The shadowed cloud was the length of the Twelve's training field. The pulsing and buzzing stopped. Leaf held his breath, prepared to portal them out of there.

A beat of time passed.

The world held its breath.

And then a white-skulled dragon burst from the shadows, roaring in triumph. Horrified and grisly faces pressed against oily scales—trapped inside. They were the horde of the unforgiven dead, the souls the Six had eaten and kept as punishment for their perceived evildoings.

A shiver ran down Leaf's spine. For the Sluagh to judge these souls evil, they must be the worst kind. Clicking from the battlefield warned them before the demogorgon emerged, prowling like a loyal foot soldier back to his queen, ready to protect her with his life. Covered in gore, the beast tracked the Wild Hunt above as it flew over Maebh's head.

The Six were on bended knee, their wings spilling like knightly capes behind them. But they weren't bowing. They panted and wheezed.

Another agonized scream reached them. This time, it sounded mournful. Bereft. The Sluagh lifted their heavy heads, crestfallen and heartsick. Maebh glared across the battlefield and took a breath —the kind one took before striking. A silken shadow clashed with white before her, knocking her backward. Leaf blinked, and the silken shadow took the shape of Legion with his fist buried inside Aleksandra's chest. The Prime had stepped in the way, shielding her ex-lover and torturer. Blood bubbled from her mouth.

"No!" Maebh shrieked, dropping to her knees as the Prime collapsed, desperately trying to hold her upright through thick feathered wings. "Sandy! What have you done?"

With her attention diverted, the Wild Hunt released a roar that rattled the sky. Like an unwatched naughty child, it flew into the battle, swooping and snapping up anything in its path.

Legion yanked his bloody fist from Aleksandra's chest, then all Six Sluagh flickered away. One moment they were there, the next gone.

Shrieks and cries echoed around him. Ringing in his ears intensified.

He didn't know what to do.

He *always* knew what to do.

But why?

Why bother?

Why keep fighting?

Crimson's despairing journal entries circled Leaf's mind like water down a drain.

Life on this planet seems doomed to repeat until there is nothing left.

"*Papi.*" Nova shook him by the collar.

But his mind was trapped in the past, in the cold hopelessness of time.

We are born. Our flaws pass from generation to generation. We ignore warnings from the planet that feeds us. We refuse to change our destructive and selfish ways. We become extinct.

"What's the fucking point?" he mumbled, dazed. He had almost nothing in his reserves. No mana to stop this madness from spreading. He'd spent too much time running from his fate and hiding beneath duty that he'd ruined everything. It was too late.

"*Hoja de los Guardianes. Escúchame bien.*" Nova slapped him across the jaw. *Hard*. Blinking, he looked down at her and found her gaze fierce, alive. She gripped his collar and shook him. "Don't think like that!"

He blinked rapidly against the burn. But this felt like another failure—the worst.

"It's true," he confessed. "Your brother won. Even the Sluagh—" He frowned, unsure what to think of them. Were they any worse than the Prime, Maebh, or... him? What lengths would he go to if his happy ending was threatened?

CHAPTER FIFTY

The ringing in Leaf's ears grew louder in the unfolding destruction.

The Wild Hunt fed on anything and everything. From frenzied to fae to humans plucked from decks. One by one, the airships started to retreat. At least the chaos gave them that.

Over the battlefield, Rory tugged Willow up the dangling rope ladder, desperately trying to save her from the clawing undead. The airship above rocked and swayed as they tried to recover from the Hunt's latest pass. But the Six were nowhere in sight.

"I don't know what to do," Leaf mumbled, disorientated.

"Start with her." Nova dragged him to where Maebh shrieked over Aleksandra's bleeding body. "You healed me in the garden, right? What about her?"

Dawn's first rays had breached the horizon, brightening the red-stained feathers. Leaf scrubbed his face and glanced around to check if they were under immediate threat, but it seemed the demogorgon still worked to keep the worst from their perimeter. The ringing in his ears stopped.

He nodded.

"Good," she said, tone gentling. "This is the point, *mi alma*. This is what separates us from them. This is why we keep fighting."

Mi alma—my soul. That he understood her meant everything.

He crouched and lifted Maebh's sticky hands from Aleksandra's chest to inspect the wound and gasped. Unconscious, the owl shifter didn't even blink when her shredded heart was exposed. It pumped once.

Barely alive.

But not ruined. When he realized his hand was on the wrong heart, Legion must have pulled his punch.

Maebh cried, "Why did she do it? Why, after everything I've done to her... to all of you?"

He recalled her letter.

"She wants to do something right," he answered, throat tight. "She's fixing a mistake."

"Mistake?"

"She regrets not fighting for those she loved against all odds." Leaf sent his awareness down into his personal well, to where only puddles remained. Should he heal her or use the last of his mana to keep Nova alive for as long as he could?

"While I have breath in my body," Maebh sobbed, holding Aleksandra's wilted, frail, and graying face. "And blood in my veins."

How could he deny them this? Aleksandra was here because of him. Exhaling, he tapped into Nova's gift and repaired his friend's gaping chest wound, knitting the lacerations over an empty heart that somehow still managed to pump blood through her veins.

He leaned down to study his work, to weave the intricate currents of mana through the abused flesh. Maebh's tears fell onto the Prime's exposed organs. Another drop fell—this one from Nova as she wept for a woman she barely knew, but who was a victim of her brother, just like her.

Leaf's Guardian teardrop reflected against the tear-glossed organs. The reflections multiplied as the tears fell, and more surfaces shined. Like in a room of shattered glass, one drop became hundreds.

He suddenly realized why each Guardian and Mage had a single teardrop representing their dedication to the Well. Alone, a single drop of water was nothing. Together, they filled a well, powered a wave, or carried a ship.

This was the point.

The people. Their connections. Their family. Not just one single obsession. All of them.

The Prime's white lashes fluttered.

"Sandy?" Maebh's fingers tightened on white feathers. "Can you hear me? I'm sorry. I'm sorry for what I've done. It's unforgivable. I deserve everything—"

Aleksandra's gnarled hand latched onto Maebh's. She licked her lips, glancing around with clouded eyes that sharpened upon seeing Leaf. Something like recognition flickered and then she said to Maebh, "We'll go together."

"Wh-what?" Maebh blustered, turning her bleary gaze in the direction the airship flew. "But Aurora... our—"

"You apologized to me. You owe me a debt. Aurora needs something to inherit. She needs to see we have atoned for our sins." Her knuckles paled on her skin. "We must *show* her the right path home.

We must be worthy of forgiveness, otherwise no matter what we do... she is lost."

The Wild Hunt swooped, snapping its fangs. They ducked, throwing up their hands for protection. But the mindless beast continued back to the battlefield. Any soldiers or Guardians left fighting were tiring. The sun was up. Nocturnal fae retreated. A wolf's haunting and melancholy howl prickled Leaf's skin.

"They're not staying dead," he muttered, studying the corpses twitching, trying to rise despite missing limbs. "They don't even release manabeeze."

"No, they don't," the Prime agreed. "It's almost like they have no souls."

Leaf's gaze clashed with hers. That was it, the reason why they couldn't kill the undead.

He said to Maebh, "The Wild Hunt."

"Can send its souls into the undead," the Prime finished.

Understanding dawned in Maebh's eyes. "Of course. To understand death, a soul must release."

Maebh shielded her eyes against the new sun's glare and gave a penetrating look in the direction the Six had fled. She seemed to consider something they weren't privy to, but then nodded and stood. She wiped her dusty hands down her battered dress. A breeze brought a whiff of death and dirt. She steeled her spine, then hesitated, glancing at the Prime.

Aleksandra nodded, encouraging her.

Maebh's skin crackled with energy. Her eyes became as fathomless as the Sluagh's, echoing the cries of the unforgiven dead, claiming them as her own.

The demonic dragon suddenly turned mid-air, banking its

wings. It circled above the battlefield, once, twice, resisting her demand. Maebh grunted with effort, stumbling under the strain of power. Leaf feared it was too late. The leash had slackened too much.

Nova gripped Maebh's arm, gifting her mana. Maebh's power amplified. Electricity skipped over Leaf's skin, crackling and snapping. The hairs on his body lifted with static charge.

"Go," Maebh snarled to the souls within the beast. "No queen holds you now. You're free."

The dragon's roar abruptly cut off as its body burst into a swarm again, darkness spilling in all directions. Within the rolling storm, little stars twinkled like lightning.

"Find a body and make it your home," Maebh ordered. "Live again. Be free of this unending torture."

Stars fell, whistling and whining, shooting off in all directions. A ribbon of shadow trailed behind each, and then they clashed with the undead. Life returned to their eyes. First, it was the excitement, the thrill of being alive again. But then came the wickedness, the cruel intent. These souls were the worst in existence.

The distraction was enough for Rory and Willow to finally escape the horde. With the ladder freed, the airship lifted them clear from the ground. Maebh squeezed the Prime's hand and whispered, bleary-eyed, "We saved her."

"Yes," the Prime returned, her soft gaze turning hard on the evil souls, now understanding they'd been given a second chance. "But now the work begins."

"Now we kill them." Leaf rotated *Reckoning*. Steel glinted in the sun. "For good."

"Go," Nova urged, gesturing to the battlefield. "Tell your friends what to do. I'll stay here and—"

"Watch over us," the Prime finished. "Your mate will watch over us as we return balance to the Well."

Nova walked around the fallen litter to ransack the dead orcs for a weapon.

Leaf didn't want to leave her.

Aleksandra and Maebh clutched each other's elbows tightly as though their embrace held salvation. Perhaps it did. *Life on Earth moves in cycles.* White wings on one side, black on the other. Slowly, they started to shift. Feathers and fangs melted away. White lashes and hair turned black.

Devastation shone through Maebh's war-painted face. Grief on Aleksandra's. This was their fae sides returning to the Well—becoming human again.

The demogorgon's screech grew louder as it slinked over from the battlefield, low and appearing wounded. Tentacled wings dragged on the dirt and slid over bodies. Liquid eyes begged Leaf for help, but he stood back. It had to be unmade, too. It started shifting, skin rolling and muscles pulsating. Animalistic hands reached for their maker. Claws morphed into fingers. Maebh gasped and sobbed, clutching Aleksandra tighter, steeling her resolve against her pet's whimpers of pain.

Leaf felt a shift in the atmosphere—ripples in the Well.

Nova picked up an orc's fallen bone sword with a scrunched nose and noticed he hadn't left.

"Go help your friends," she said to him, bravely trying to hide her frayed nerves. "I survived months in a war camp alone. I can survive this."

He believed her. Most of the danger was elsewhere by now. Violent love spilled from his heart. He rushed to her in two quick strides, gripped her hair, and tilted her face to his. His mouth opened to say something, anything to let her know how much he needed her.

"I know, *Papi*," she whispered, her gaze softening.

His lips clashed with hers. His tongue drove into her mouth, demanding entrance and laying claim to everything she was. As he deepened their kiss, bending her back with his passion, he made promises in his mind—to hold her, to kiss her, to always miss her. To trust her, to listen to her, and to stay up all night making love to her. Breathlessly, he pulled away and brushed her glowing freckles with his thumb.

"I love you," he said, looking deeply into her eyes.

"I love you, too."

"Now, be a good girl, and don't die while I show these imbeciles what to do."

A sharp laugh burst from her lips. She wiped her wet eyes. "You love them too. Admit it."

"Only when they do as they're told," he joked, then ran headlong into the horde.

CHAPTER
FIFTY-ONE

Pain squeezed Willow's lungs. No, this was worse than pain. When she reached deep inside, she felt the dry and crumbling cavity where her well used to flourish.

Shadows swarmed around her. Flashes of movement in the sunlight. Someone shouted a warning, but she got hit—rocked to the side—as they fought. The sudden movement jolted tears from her eyes.

Gone.

Empty.

Dry.

She had no idea what had happened. Her last sane thought was when she followed Alfie down the ladder. She wanted to help her friends forge a way to safety—toward her family howling in the distance like a beacon of hope. But then her feet hit the ground, and her keen shifter nose scented competition—a rival.

Across the battlefield, a queen wanted Willow dead.

The hand of fate reached into her soul and pulled out an insatiable urge to dominate. Her wolfish fangs elongated. Ears flattened. Hackles raised. Her fist plunged into soil soaked with blood. She clawed at the essence of creation and then did what Nero trained her to do, what she vowed never to do.

She violated nature.

And it felt good.

Freeing. Cathartic. A rite of passage. What she was born to do.

Willow became a slave to her instincts. She pumped the world's veins with her almighty, churning soul.

Rise.

Wake.

Like the birds she'd summoned from the other side of death, fae corpses twitched with life, rising stiffly with jilted movements.

Kill the queen, she decreed.

Each dead thing on the ground, even those buried beneath, awaited her bidding. They hunted. They ripped and shredded. But then her rival queen fought back... or someone by her side. A new power answered Willow's. It carved a path from her enemy, digging a groove in the ground. Bright and clean, it made hers feel murky and wrong. Her gaze found the source through dust—a male elf with hard blue eyes and long blond hair.

Familiar. Perhaps...

Willow's gaze tugged to the right, to the queen she must destroy. She snarled again. The need was in every fiber of her being, ripping apart her will. The murderous compulsion teased her parched bones, making her thirst for something she didn't understand.

But then her gaze pulled again, toward a group of hauntingly beautiful men. Her need shifted in tempo and became hot, pulsing, demanding. It felt like those times when she had to numb her "*beastly needs*" with iced water at the Tower, hiding in the bathroom. She locked eyes with one of them and fell into the fathomless night. The impact of his presence stole her breath. Dark, sculpted brows. High cheekbones. A sharp, masculine jaw but soft, sensuous lips. Porcelain skin. Long, silken black hair cascading from a widow's peak. He was a being made for seduction, but there was sadness in his eyes. He tried to hide it behind a hotter, darker emotion.

Others beside him stole her attention: fallen angels, each as hauntingly beautiful as the first but different in their own way. Unique. Precious. Caught in the between, like her. Belonging to neither place but forged from both.

Not enough, her dark friends whispered in her mind, urging her onward. *She must die for you to live.*

"Not enough," she replied, agreeing.

And so she reached into that other place beneath the first, the midnight behind the ink. The place she feared to touch. But somehow, with them so near, she felt safe. Home.

More, they whispered in her mind. *Close the gap between life and death. Tear a hole in the veil.*

The gap.

Buzzing. Humming. Souls swarming and begging, waiting in the wings.

The gap.

The space between. This dragon, these six beautiful nightmares, they were just like her. Different, never quite fitting in. Even Willow's parents sometimes looked at her strangely. Oh, how they'd loved her. But they'd misunderstood her. Even as a small child, she'd felt different. So when Rory stole her away, and the voices told her it was okay, she believed them.

But as she grew, so did the taunts.

Halfing freak. Tainted One. Ugly. Weird. Beastly. Bitch. Nothing. *You don't belong here. They don't want you.*

At first, Nero had made her hide her fae side. She was happy pretending for a while. Eventually, they started asking questions about her gold eyes, her strange biology, and her purpose for being there. Willow learned Nero brainwashed them all using stolen mana from his daughter. But when the taint worsened, he conserved his resources. Forced to find alternatives to control his people, he turned her into a halfling savior so they had a distraction.

"She is the best of us from both worlds," he'd said. "The tainted lied! She can live here and still possess magic. She can heal from sickness and be powerful. We don't need to turn into animals like her. Her mother was human. Don't you all want to be powerful and immortal like her?"

The problem was that having a foot in both worlds meant she belonged to none.

She felt a thicker kinship with these beautiful monsters than with her family. She saw understanding, acceptance, need, and desire—beings trapped in the dark who wanted a slice of the light.

Yes, little wolf. It is not night when we see your face. Tear a hole in the veil. Close the gap. Be our skin.

The whispers were so familiar. They'd comforted her in lonely times. They'd dreamt alongside her. They'd wiped her tears. And now, they needed her to save them.

Defiance burned through Willow. She submitted to her

instincts. The world fell away. Sound dimmed beneath the roar of buzzing wings until her heart pounded like a drum, and her power shot into the stars.

There, she found what she needed. She latched on, clawing into it. Then she tugged it back to the earth. Brought it closer, closing the gap.

Wake.

Rise.

There is no between, only life—one existence for all.

Willow lost all sense of reality. There was nothing after that but blood, buzzing swarms, screams, and the sense something wasn't going according to plan. The taint in the Well changed her intention and mixed everything up. Pain, agony, and the horrifying realization that her power leaked from her body like blood from a gaping wound.

Worse than leaked—something sucked it out like a vampire, and it wasn't the queen across the battlefield. It was someone far, far away, and hungry. Ancient. Greedy. Righteous.

Willow fought, scrambled, lashed, and tried to hold on. But it was as futile as catching air. She wasn't experienced enough. This ancient entity was borne of stardust, and Willow had woken it from slumber along with everything else.

An ear-piercing scream ripped from her throat. A tether snapped inside of her. And then there was nothing but the dry, crumbling hole inside her body.

Sweating, panting, numb, she looked around, dazed. The world seemed so dull now. A familiar voice shouted two inches from Willow's face.

"What?" Willow mumbled, touching her ears. Blood oozed out,

but they were still pointed, still fae. So then, why did she feel so barren inside?

"We have to go!" Rory barked, eyes flashing.

Burning seared Willow's jaw and shoulder, knocking her to the side. Crying out, she clutched her arm and felt a warm, sticky wetness on her dirty flesh. A man's face appeared before hers. His nose was gone, and she could see bone. The clothes hanging from his body were threadbare. He reached for her with fingers worn to the bone, like he'd torn through something. Dirt, she realized. He'd dug himself out of a grave. Rory yanked Willow out of the way and slammed her boot into the noseless man's face.

A screech in the dawn sky lifted their gazes. A demonic dragon flew over the battlefield, its jaw gaping as it swooped and stole souls for supper. Each time it fed, its body shimmered like an oil slick. Its white exposed skull and horns glimmered on the outside of its head, but its jaw was covered in black scales. Dark, fathomless eyes looked right at her as it passed. An acknowledgment.

"Up!" Rory growled, taking Willow's numb hands and placing them on the ladder's rungs. "Climb!"

"What—what happened?" She let go, turning back to the battle.

Rory screamed in frustration and used her weight to shoulder another undead out of the way. "Snap out of it if you want to live. Climb."

Willow's understanding of events returned with sudden clarity. This devastation was because of her. She'd called the army of undead like Nero had wanted. Or something else had wanted. But she lost control of them. They attacked heedlessly, turning on their master because... Willow's power was gone.

Broken teeth snapped at her. Darting back, she tripped and fell.

She landed hard, jarring her spine. She fought back as the undead fell on top of her, desperately trying to recall Rory's lessons.

Block. Calm yourself. Your body is a weapon.

But Willow's claws had slipped beneath her fingertips. She kicked and shoved, lashing the undead away. Each time she scraped spongy skin, it tore off their face like paper. The rank smell of death smothered her. She averted her face as the creature gnashed, spraying spittle.

I'm going to die, she thought, squeezing her eyes shut.

The weight lifted. Cold air whooshed in. Willow opened her eyes, gulping in fresh air, and glimpsed a handsome face flashing with the imprint of a skull beneath his skin. Then he was gone. Darkness shrouded her. She tried to lever off the corpse to stand, but her arms trembled, and she slipped on bloody flesh.

Featherlight pressure surrounded her limbs. Her stomach dropped as ghostly hands lifted her. For a horrifying moment in time, she was weightless, powerless. And then her feet touched the ground. Confused, she looked around as six sets of dark wings swooped, their owners twisting to kneel before her in a circle. The fallen angels bowed like knights before a queen, their wings like veils spilling behind them to cover the gore and death.

Oddly, beyond their circle, the undead were held back by an invisible force. But nothing penetrated that ring.

Rory grabbed Willow's scruff and pulled her to the ladder. "Climb, *goddammit,* girl."

Fear trembled in her voice. Rory was rarely afraid. Willow turned back at the six beautiful monsters, and that fear infected her. Willow gripped the rope and lifted herself onto a rung.

The dragon shrieked. She glanced back and saw both a miraculous sight and something frightening. It became a shadow again, sparkling with stars. Willow's dark protectors struggled to stand, exhausted. Undead broke through the invisible barrier. But one with long black hair locked his fingers around her ankle. Those sad eyes beseeched. *Don't leave,* he seemed to say. A jolt of connection rippled through her body, and his expression morphed into confusion.

"We worked for so long to have you, but you're not our queen?" he rasped, dismayed. "You're nothing."

I'm nothing? Rejection slammed into her chest. Her dry insides crumbled. She tugged her foot back, planted her boot on his face, and shouted hoarsely, "Then you're *monsters!*"

He fell back into the fray, swallowed by undulating undead. His sad eyes still looked at her as stars fell from the sky.

"Willow!" Rory's voice sliced through the air above. "Now, while they're distracted."

Jolting, she glanced up and climbed.

"What about Alfie?" she choked out, not wanting to look back. Was he alive?

Rory paused.

"He's not coming," she said and resumed climbing.

CHAPTER FIFTY-TWO

With Rory's help, Willow climbed onto the wooden deck. She rolled to her back, gasping to catch her breath. She was safe. Alive. But her world was still ending. Her family would never forgive her for what she'd done, and she had no explanation. No excuses. The white balloon pumped with gas and shimmering harvested manabeeze wouldn't hold the answers.

"Willow." Rory's warning tone drew her gaze.

Four aviators aimed their guns at them. To the side, Nero stood with a murderous expression on his face. But he was still clean, still without a speck of blood on his brown leather jacket or face.

Willow's face and shoulder burned from the undead's nails. Rory limped and panted heavily, her tight hairstyle frizzy and lopsided. Blood dripped from a cut over her eye.

Slowly rolling to her feet, Willow searched their surroundings. Just beyond this airship, another sailed away—its propellers whirring at full speed, its sails unfurled and catching the wind. Another harvesting airship coasted a few hundred yards behind them, almost as if it waited for Nero's instructions.

His fingers stroked his bare left wrist as his gaze ping-ponged between Willow and Rory. Finally, he settled on Willow and barked, "What the fuck was that dragon?"

She flinched.

"I don't know," she admitted. "I didn't do it. I think it was the Wild Hunt."

He blinked, recognition hitting his expression. Tales of the Wild Hunt were sung about in the dining hall as part of his propaganda. It kept people afraid of leaving the Crystal City walls.

"You're lucky it didn't eat us all," he returned, furious. That's when Willow noticed the dead bodies slumped in the corners of the deck, piled as though about to be tossed overboard.

The whirring of engines and propellers increased in pitch as the airship rotated, changing direction to return to Crystal City. The air felt thinner, even though they hadn't lifted altitude.

Willow shouldn't be here. The only reason Nero wanted her was for her power. But that was gone. She wasn't even sure she could return to her family. Not like this—not after what she'd done.

"What's with the third degree?" Rory ground out, her hand hovering over her sheathed dagger—the only weapon she had left. Her gaze darted over the crew.

A man with windburned cheeks and a long nose narrowed his gaze. "You should have stayed down there with your tainted freak."

"Excuse me?" Her brows lifted, incredulous at his rancor. "You left the ladder down."

"A mistake," Nero smirked coldly. "We were too busy fighting off that dragon and turning the ship around. We didn't have time to cut the rope."

Pain and betrayal flashed in Rory's eyes as Nero gestured for his men to advance.

"Why?" she croaked.

"You're traitors," he declared. "Sending one of your beasts to kill us."

Willow gaped. She'd just told him that she didn't do it. For the first time since Willow had known her, Rory looked lost. Until now, Willow hadn't realized the full extent of Rory's brain damage from her father's so-called treatments. She kept forgetting all the bad things he'd done to her, making excuses for his behavior.

After failing to be the savior he touted, the only recourse was to change the narrative and paint Willow as a betrayer. But his own daughter? He'd used her. They didn't owe him anything.

Use it, Rory had taught her. *Channel all that emotion into your fight.*

Willow's gaze hardened. "You sicken me. Nothing is ever enough for you." She turned to the others. "He's been manipulating you for decades, using stolen mana to make you forget the truth. He stole his daughter's mana to do it. Talk about being a traitor." She laughed. "He's been using 'tainted' fae magic on you all for centuries. He changed your memories and made you believe he's just recently taken over the presidency. But he's been here for over a century. Why else do you think he traps people in the Tower? It's easier for him to persuade smaller groups of indoctrinated people. You're all part of his cult! But he's—"

"Enough lies," Nero barked.

"You won't shoot us," Rory scoffed, lowering her hand from her belt. "A stray bullet in the blimp's canvas will rip a hole and release manabeeze."

"Return the device you stole," Nero growled, nodding to her wrist. "And we'll let you disembark here. That's the best offer you'll get."

Her furrowed gaze dropped to her wrist—to a band with a sparkling portal device wrapped around it. It was almost like she'd not known it was there. Blinking rapidly, a sharper light returned to her eyes. Her jaw set with determination, she caught Willow's wrist and hit a button on the device.

Electricity fired through their bodies. The next time Willow opened her eyes, she was on the deck of the third airship hundreds of yards away, sailing full speed toward Crystal City. The gray blimp above their heads had fins directing the wind. It always reminded Willow of a shark.

A wave of nausea rose, and she retched. An aviator on the deck glanced over, gasping at their sudden arrival. As if immune to the disorientation of portaling, Rory pushed to her feet. That's all Willow glimpsed before another wave of sickness claimed her.

Boots scuffled. The aviator's cry grew shrill and then distant, falling away. When Willow could breathe again, she glanced up as Rory dropped her shoulder and tackled a second crew member, taking him to the ground. As they grappled, she shouted at Willow, "Get to the wheel! Head east."

East. Not west. Not to Crystal City. Willow ran to the quarterdeck and latched onto the wheel's smooth wooden poles. She pushed a nearby lever that cranked the propeller's engines like she'd seen Alfie do before.

Alfie. Her heart clenched, and a new wave of grief threatened to overcome her.

Use it. Use your hate and pain and grief. *Use it to fuel your strength.*

Willow's muscles screamed as she pulled the wheel to one side, changing the rudder's direction and peeling skin from her fingers. Crew from below deck spilled out from the hatch, shouting in surprise. None looked like soldiers or, worse, Reapers. Willow wasn't even sure they'd been told about their apparent betrayal. Nero must have decided right then and there that he would get rid of them. Rory overpowered the aviator, stole his goggles, then used Nero's lie against him.

"They were traitors," she announced. "Get back to work!"

The crew jumped at her orders, most returning below deck. A few with guilty looks stayed above to check the rigging and other jobs they'd likely ignored without a proper captain on board.

Rory limped up to the quarterdeck with wide eyes and checked they were at full speed. She gave the goggles to Willow.

"Won't you need them?" Willow asked, squinting against the wind.

"Put them on." Rory's voice was low. Her hair had untied, and the long, kinky strands blew in the wind. Without the copper beads, she looked like a different person. Normal. Covered in blood and wounded, but normal. Perhaps it was the relief Willow detected on her face. She finally knew what was wrong with her mind, and this was them making a break for it.

Rory winced and checked her arm, where an open gash oozed blood.

"Keep this altitude," she ordered briskly. "They're too afraid of fae catching up. It's safer here."

She limped to the lower deck, resting against a rail to check her injuries.

Willow did as instructed, put the goggles on, and faced the bow. But she couldn't get the bloody splashes of battle out of her mind. Her body was still raw. Her soul was so empty. She pushed the lever, cranking the engines faster. She didn't want to slow down because then she'd have to face what she'd done. They were almost out of sight from the battlefield when one of the crew pointed behind them.

"Wait," he shouted. "Look!"

She glanced over her shoulder. More manabeeze lifted into the sky from the battlefield. Thinking of her family, Willow's heart clenched. She had been so close to reuniting with them. Those manabeeze might be theirs.

"We should go back," the aviator said, looking through his spyglass. "Our harvesting net has more room."

Maybe those manabeeze were a good sign. Maybe it meant the fae had overpowered the undead. But the moment she thought it, she knew it was wrong. The undead were as empty as she was.

"Keep going," Rory shouted breathlessly from the railing, barely standing upright from her exhaustion.

The aviator frowned as his spyglass moved to the airship gaining on them. Willow could tell the exact moment he realized Rory had lied to them. Tension crept over his shoulders. His knuckles whitened on the brass cylinder. When he lowered it, his eyes darted about, and he licked his lips.

He bellowed a warning shout to the crew below deck. Willow

stole his spyglass and used it to knock him out. Their pursuers' bowsprit rammed into their hull, splintering wood. Their airship teetered and jerked as the balloon filled with manabeeze jostled. Bodies and cargo slid across the tilting deck. The wheel spun as the rudder changed direction. The rigging creaked as it stretched.

Holding the wheel for dear life, Willow feared they'd capsize. A crew member slid past her, hit the quarterdeck railing, and ricocheted overboard. The wind swallowed his cry.

Manabeeze swarming inside the balloon somehow balanced the ship. Shouts of chaos came from both crews. Clambering to her feet, ignoring the blisters on her skin, Willow checked the other airship and found them scrambling to patch a hole in their canvas. A slow trickle of glowing balls popped out of the tear. Nero paced the deck, barking orders. They must have damaged their own when they rammed. Grinning, she returned to the wheel, thinking she could steer them away, but instead locked eyes with the real reason for that tear—an angry tattooed crow shifter, half covered in blood.

CHAPTER FIFTY-THREE

Air whipped the shifter's mop of black hair into angry blue eyes. His well-used leather armor was streaked with gore and dirt. He must have come straight from the battle. Unlike Rory, who had a single dagger left, he retained a full arsenal across his muscular body.

Heart leaping into her throat, Willow looked for a weapon, maybe a splintered piece of wood. The spyglass had rolled away. Nothing. There was nothing. Taking a chance, she glanced over the taffrail to the landscape below. Water glistened under the morning sun. And bioluminescent trees. Lots of them. They were over the ceremonial lake, not far from the Order. It had been years since Willow was here, but she remembered the lake was deep and large. Maybe she could jump.

The intruder's brow arched mockingly as if daring her to try. Inky tattoos on his neck glimmered, reminding her of the dragon's scales. A blue sparkling teardrop winked beneath his left eye.

Although he seemed deadly, he put his tattooed finger to his lips and quietly stalked past her.

A Guardian.

She exhaled and wracked her brain, trying to remember which one. Did he know her father, Rush? An image flashed in her mind. On the day she'd been kidnapped, this brooding Guardian was there. He'd looked at Rory like he knew her, like he wanted to murder her.

Oh no.

Willow had been wrong to call the six beautiful monsters fallen angels. Now that she had a comparison, she could see the difference. This Guardian had smile lines at the edges of his eyes—as though he'd been happy once, long ago. A true fallen angel, someone who'd lost his way. The others were devils born into the darkness... souls that had never seen the light.

It is not night when we see your face.

Dashing their words away, she watched warily as the Guardian crept up on Rory. She was hunched over one of the crew, blocking his windpipe with her forearm. The fallen angel's fists flexed at his side as though he restrained himself from the impulse to strangle.

He glanced toward the airship still working to fix their leak. The angle revealed his face again. Willow had seen that same look on Nero after the first time she'd accused him of stealing his daughter's mana. She'd only been eleven or twelve. They'd been playing chess in the garden, and Nero had left momentarily. When he returned, his old man's gray hair was gone. Her aunty returned with more.

"And what are you going to do about it?" Nero taunted Willow.

"I'll tell her what you've done!" she sobbed out.

Nero sat back, glanced at the chessboard, and moved his pawn, taking the queen. Then he tipped over the king.

"Checkmate," he'd said, a slow smile curving his lips.

Victory—that was the look on the Guardian's face.

His boot scuffed the deck as he drew closer. Whether Rory heard above the wind and engines or sensed a shift in the atmosphere, she tensed without looking up. She let the unconscious crew member fall and straightened to her full height, stepping to the side.

When she faced the Guardian, a look of tired resignation met him.

An aviator jumped out from behind a crate. He took two brave steps, then lightning struck him. He burst like a balloon, spattering innards and blood over their faces. Through the mess, the Guardian's smile didn't reach his eyes.

Rory hadn't flinched. She didn't even wipe the blood from her face. Despite her father's actions, she was fearless, unbreakable, and never cowed. Willow wished she could be that brave.

"How did you do that?" Rory's gaze narrowed on the Guardian as he circled her. "You're a little too high to be connected to the Well, right?"

"We both know I can fly higher than most." Cocky ego flashed in his eyes.

Rory's brows raised, confused. He stalked to the carved taffrail and glanced over, checking the other airship. Satisfied they were still busy, he leaned a casual hip against the wood.

They stared at each other for a long, hard minute. Willow swore she felt the air crackle against her skin. The smell of lightning burned her nostrils. Tension increased until it felt like something would snap. Maybe Willow imagined it. Maybe they were friends.

But then Rory showed her palms and nodded to Willow. "I came here to return her to her family. I won't stop you."

His lashes lowered, wary.

"It's true," Willow yelled, running down from the quarterdeck. Why was her heart skipping a million miles an hour? Why did her instincts beg her to find a weapon?

Rory pursed her lips at his lack of response. "You'd better take her now before he boards this airship." She peeled off the portal device on her wrist and tossed it. "He's coming for this."

His gaze flicked to Nero's airship, then shrugged. "I'm not afraid of him. He's next."

She laughed. "Look, whoever you are, underestimating my father is not a smart thing to do."

Blue fire seethed in the Guardian's eyes. "*Whoever I am*?"

"Yes," she replied, exasperated. "If you're not here to take Willow down, let me get her to safety and then..." Her words trailed off as she stared at his face, then his feathers. Brows furrowing, she shook her head and blinked. "Cielo?"

"Speak that name again, and I'll cut out your tongue," he barked, suddenly off the gunwale and in her face. "My name is Cloud!"

Rory murmured, "Willow doesn't deserve to die for my sins."

"Cloud," he bellowed, spittle hitting her face. "Say it. Say, 'You're nothing but a cloud in my head.' Remember?"

Rory shook her head, dismayed. He searched her face for something he'd never find.

"I know you care," Rory urged, pointing to Willow. "Or you'd have killed her by now. So fly her to shore before it's too late. They're almost done patching their balloon."

"Care..." He canted his head like the bird he shifted into... that curious look the crow gave before it pecked out your eyes. "You bled that out of me, too."

"You don't mean that. She's your kind—she's one of you."

"I'm loyal to no one." Something stark appeared in his eyes. "Who else do you think fed information about the war to your father?"

Willow gaped. He'd betrayed his own kind... her father and mother... all for what? For revenge against Rory?

"Don't look at me like that." His upper lip curled at Willow's expression. "As if you didn't just raise an army of the dead."

His wings suddenly disappeared, shifting through the leather slits of his jacket. A few tiny black feathers drifted behind. He started walking toward Rory, pulling daggers from his belt, dropping them.

Thud. Step. Thud. Step. Thud. Step.

It was a countdown, a ticking clock, a challenge—run or face your death.

I hope you run, his gleaming eyes said. *I want you to beg as I feel your life slipping through my bare hands.*

Willow couldn't allow this madness to continue. The only constant she had in her life at Crystal City was Rory. She lunged for one of his fallen daggers with a hopeless plan. But stormy eyes slid her way. An instant later, Willow was on her back, staring up at the bright balloon. Ringing in her ears drowned out the engines. Dazed, she blinked, confused. Pain in the back of her head throbbed. Reaching with trembling fingers, she was relieved to find she wasn't bleeding. He must have used magic, too fast for her to catch.

And now Willow was human. Lesser. She would be no match for

him. Stifling a groan, she sat up and fought a wave of dizziness. Rory launched at Cloud, throwing vicious jabs, holding nothing back. Angry words passed between them through clenched teeth, but Willow couldn't make them out. He was enraged. She was too —because he attacked Willow. But then Rory looked bewildered, tired, and on the back foot.

Use it. Her lessons were all Willow had left. *Use everything, anything, even each other.*

She picked up the fallen dagger, clutched the hilt until her bleeding palms wept, then charged at the dueling couple as they neared the port side. Cloud's fist wrapped around Rory's throat as Willow sliced toward his neck. He twisted and blocked, taking her blade on his leather gauntlet. The dagger glanced to the side, and so did Willow—right over the wooden taffrail.

Screaming as she fell overboard, Willow reached for help, for something to latch onto. Cloud's free hand lashed out, catching her hand. Gravity yanked her down, almost ripping her arm from her socket. Her legs kicked.

Cloud's panicked eyes filled with something like regret. His gaze darted between the two women he held—one like a noose, the other by the hand. Blood rushed to his head as he strained under their weight. A roar of defiance trembled. Black feathered wings exploded from his back, flapping manically as he propped his feet against the hull, trying to lever them both up.

"Let me go," Rory rasped, smacking his hand that gripped her throat. Capillaries burst in her eyes.

"No!" Willow's shriek turned into a wail. "Not her! Me!"

"You know it should be me," Rory hissed to Cloud. "Kill me."

His veins bulged in his temples. The strain was so much that he couldn't speak. One more breath might make him slip.

"Maybe we'll land in the water," Willow cried.

The hopeless look in Cloud's eyes said everything. There was something in the deep, something horrifying none of them wanted to face. Willow vaguely remembered stories from her Uncle Thorne. Warnings never to wander down there alone.

"If you hate me, then kill me!" Rory's voice was a hissed gurgle, breaking under his grip.

He roared in her face. It was so powerful, so full of deep-seated rage that it vibrated the air. But he didn't let go. His wings continued to flap. He continued to hold both of them, paralyzed by the decision.

The airship jerked to the side. Cloud's grip on them slipped. Willow screamed as she dropped an inch. Warning shouts somewhere behind him—the metallic click of guns.

Nero was here.

Cloud's mistake was looking over his shoulder. He should have been looking at the strong-willed woman he held by the throat. She gripped his forearms, stopped kicking, and hoisted herself up. Her weight pulled him down. His head lowered enough for her to whisper something in his ear. His eyes widened, lips parted, and then she plunged her dagger into his tattooed hand, forcing him to let go.

Agony crumpled his face as Rory fell. Her dark hair streamed like ribbons. But she didn't flail. She didn't scream. She held Cloud's gaze until the deep blue water swallowed her whole.

CHAPTER
FIFTY-FOUR

Crows had long memories. Their nightmares never left. River was not new to violence. Crow shifters rarely were. He'd seen things in battle, things that didn't make sense. Even with distance, sometimes clarity eluded him. At the worst times, random memories from battles sliced into his mind, haunting him in his sleep.

Blood. Gore. Broken wings. Teeth. Hair attached to membranes. Talons attached to dismembered fingers. Shadows. Strange sounds. Feelings of terror. Mystical lights.

The times he'd awoken in a confused, cold sweat were too many to count. He knew his mind tried to piece together the information he'd seen. It wanted to reassess the threat before it was too late.

The danger that sent him here—flying toward the ceremonial lake—was not from an enemy but a friend. While in the throes of battle, a shadow blotted out the rising sun. River had glanced up to see Willow and Rory escaping to their airship. Then he was struck by one of the undead. When he looked again, the airship was a speck in the distance while another tinier speck followed behind—a shadow with black feathered wings.

Suddenly, the taint in the Well oozed away. Energizing clarity washed over him. His wings found a little more power, his heart more strength. Cloud was his oldest, closest friend. They were brothers. River couldn't let him make the biggest mistake of his life by exacting vengeance on the woman he used to love, who tortured and tore his heart out. It wouldn't heal him. It would only make him worse.

This was exactly why River had never fallen in love. He'd seen firsthand how a gullible heart could be used, bruised, and abused. So he'd avoided it at all costs. The only time he'd ever regretted that decision were the nights he woke in terror, confused, and needing the comfort of a female's arms—or between her thighs.

A storm brewed in the distance. River's wings never beat so hard, something telling him to pick up speed. He dug deep into his reserves but knew he was almost spent, battle-weary, heavy, and sore. But this instinct buzzed across his skin. He didn't want to get caught in the rain and could already hear thunder roll and lightning crack.

Glowing bioluminescent trees appeared—their lights brighter beneath the dark clouds. River's gaze snagged on a silver head of hair on the shore of the Ceremonial Lake. He tucked his wings and dove.

Before he landed, he gave a quick survey of Willow's surroundings but found no immediate threat.

The teenager was alive.

She was safe.

But alone, hugging her knees and rocking.

Landing without grace, River's boots stumbled into a jog along the sandy beach. Lungs heaving, wheezing from their abuse, he pushed himself to get to her. Thunder cracked. He could taste rain and electricity in the air.

"Willow!"

Her head whipped toward him. Her red-rimmed eyes widened as she sobbed, and it occurred to River that she might think him the enemy. She'd been gone for so long from Elphyne, at such an integral part of her development. Who knew what happened behind the walls of Crystal City? And then there were the horrors they'd witnessed during the battle. That scream of anguish she'd released still sent shivers down River's spine.

Tears created tracks down her dirty and blood-stained cheeks. She sobbed so hard she couldn't breathe and gulped for air, trying to speak but unable. Her black military-style clothing was dirty and bloody. Torn in places. He forced his steps to slow, his aching wings to pin behind his back, and approached her as one would a caged animal.

"Willow, it's River." He kept his tone low and calm. He pointed to the Guardian teardrop beneath his left eye. "D'arn River. I'm a friend of your parents. I work with your father, Rush. Do you remember me?"

Whimpers shot from her cracked lips as she tried to gain control of her spasming diaphragm.

For Crimson's sake. She was traumatized. Her hands were torn, and she cradled her arm like it was broken. Another crack of thunder startled her, and she squeezed her eyes shut and resumed rocking.

"Hey, Willow." He crouched and tried to still his rabbiting heart. "Are you hurt?"

Her brows lifted in the middle, and she hugged her knees tighter and nodded.

"Your arm?"

She shook her head, but then nodded.

Crimson. There might be wounds too deep to comprehend.

"Is it broken?" he asked, pointing to it. "Can I see? I'm not a great healer like your Aunt Ada, but I know injuries. I can take a look. I'll be gentle, I promise."

Unable to meet his eyes, she gingerly twisted toward him. The wrist was bruised and purple. Her shoulder sank at an odd angle, the bone popping.

"Looks like your shoulder is dislocated," he said, indicating where the shape was wrong at her shoulder. "The wrist could be broken. Where does it hurt more?"

"Shoulder," she whispered.

"Right. I think it's dislocated. If I pop your arm back into the joint, it will alleviate that shoulder pain. But the wrist will have to wait until a healer sees you."

River got down on a knee, and tested her arm and shoulder. She cried out sharply, but he had to do this. He didn't know if anyone noticed him leave. Damn it. He should have said something before shooting off after Cloud.

"I'm going to sit behind you and then push the arm in. It's going to hurt like a motherfucker. But then it will feel better almost instantly."

She nodded. Fuck, she was brave. Or she just had no idea how much it would hurt. Oh well. Better get it done. He positioned himself, supported her, and popped her arm back in.

No sound came out of her mouth when she screamed. He held her tight and said, "Feels better now, right?"

She whimpered but nodded.

"Good. That's good." He reached for her other hand, intending to check it for injuries because her fist was clenched, but she opened her hand, and a black feather fell out. His blood turned to ice.

Was that Cloud's?

Was she trying to hide it, or was she clutching at it?

It started to rain. Big drops fell, hitting the sand with loud plops. Willow squeezed her eyes shut and shook her head, refusing to budge. River spread his wings to shield her from the rain and glanced up, but a drop splashed in his eye. Wincing, he wiped it off, and a familiar coppery scent bloomed. He forced his trembling, wet fingers before his face. *Blood.*

No.

He looked up and squinted against the falling blood rain. Amongst the storm, lightning arced behind an airship drifting idly, swaying in the breeze as if no one piloted the craft. Each time the airship tilted, blood sloshed from the deck, and showered down.

"Fuck me," he breathed as the realization dawned on him. It wasn't a storm. It was Cloud.

Movement in River's periphery. He withdrew his dagger and spun as a familiar wolpertinger in tiny form emerged from the forest and hopped toward Willow. Tinger froze upon seeing River's blade glint in the lightning. The little fur ball trembled, but River hardened his jaw and waved it closer. The wolpertinger had lost the ability to shift when Maebh stole most of his mana.

"Stay with Willow until her parents get here," he ordered, as if the animal could understand him. "Protect her."

It was only a tiny thing, but hopefully, it would comfort her until the cavalry arrived. Then he crouched, spread his wings, and took to the sky. He weaved through the blood rain, arming himself with mana, ready to put his life on the line to save his friend. But when he landed on the deck, he slipped in blood.

"Holy Well," he murmured as he scanned the destruction with wide eyes. Nothing moved beyond the hum of an engine, the flap of sails, and smoke and small fires from the lightning strikes.

The entire crew was dead. Perhaps even fae. It was impossible to identify the mess. River tracked the destruction across scorched wood and nonsensical gouge marks to where movement caught his eye on the upper deck.

Cloud was crouched and digging around somewhere near his feet. The wind caused his wet hair to whip his face, but he paid it no mind; such was the concentration on his face as he worked. River quickly took stock of the area, checking for any threats he might have missed. But the only living thing was the tattooed Guardian in his leather uniform, his wilted wings resting on the bloody deck behind him.

Alarm prickled River's skin. Something wasn't right. Cloud should have looked up by now, but he attacked his subject with single-minded tenacity until he finally tossed his dagger over his shoulder. It skidded down to the quarterdeck with a clang. He scrubbed his face, cleaning it. Then used three fingers to paint a stripe of blood from his temple to his clenched jaw, and the same for the other side.

River always asked Cloud why he left his face clean of power-enhancing tattoos when every other inch of him was covered. He was obsessed with gaining power, never to be vulnerable again—but it always seemed a missed opportunity. Was it vanity? Or refusal to mar the handsome features so many females drooled over?

But as Cloud stood, his blue eyes stark amongst the red, River finally understood why.

He had saved that canvas for this special moment—so no one mistook the V of blood on his face.

It felt like centuries ago when a featherless crow fell from the sky and landed broken and twitching at River's feet. Cloud—or Cielo, as he was called back then—had been missing from Elphyne for decades. They'd all thought he was dead.

River should have known someone who breathed through sheer willpower alone would survive decades of torture in Crystal City... from a human who said she loved him. River had scooped up the tiny, trembling body covered in scars. He refused to shift—or couldn't. So River did the only thing he could. He nursed the broken crow back to health, caring for him until his feathers grew thicker and more robust. He kept the secret about the love who'd betrayed him. He talked to Cloud as though nothing had changed. Eventually, Cloud learned to shift again. He learned to speak.

But Cloud never once called a Vendetta. He never once asked his friends and family to take arms against the enemy to repay the cruelty he'd suffered.

"Tell me," River had begged. "Tell me who did this. We'll call every crow we know—Nikan, Carmine, and Tommas. Your father. My family. We'll call them all and rain murder from the sky. On them and their

descendants. Just say the words, and we'll paint your enemy's blood on our faces."

"No," Cloud had croaked, his voice raw from misuse, his fists flexing at his side. "Her death belongs to me."

"Cloud," River said, trying to smooth the tremble in his voice. "What happened?"

Crows had long memories. They never forgot the faces of their enemies. And when one of their own painted a V of blood on their face, every crow knew it was a cry for help—a vow to inflict pain on their enemies tenfold until no more blood was left to spill. Only then was the Vendetta satisfied, and the crow community could return to their lives... if anything was left.

For this reason, Vendettas were rarely called. Too often, more lives were lost than saved.

But something was missing in Cloud's stark blue eyes as they met River's gaze.

"They killed her," he intoned, eyes glazed.

"Killed who?"

"Aurora."

"But... I thought that's what you wanted."

"She was *mine* to kill." Cloud beat his blood-stained heart with his fist. "*Mine* to reckon with, and they ruined that for me. They stole—" His voice cracked with emotion. Agony flashed across his face as he sucked in a breath. It was as though the very air cut his lungs like razor blades. "They distracted me."

Pain meant feeling. Pain meant being alive. So long as Cloud felt something, there was hope. But then his eyes dulled. His expression deadpanned. He beat his wings, and it sounded like a war drum in River's ears. Faster, and faster, Cloud beat them, gathering momentum and filling himself with raw power until energy crackled along every surface of his body, oil-slick tattoos igniting with fireworks. Lighting consumed his eyes, making them glow white.

River's instincts told him to run, but he stood his ground. If the object of Cloud's obsession was dead, then this wasn't going to end well. The storm above their heads grew, gray clouds rolling and blooming out to cover the lake. The sun disappeared altogether.

"Tell me who the Vendetta is against, and I'll join you," he shouted. "You're not alone!"

Lightning gathered in Cloud's hands. It was as though every atom, every spark, every breath in the world rushed to his bidding. Then he unleashed it at River's feet, splitting the airship in half.

CHAPTER

FIFTY-FIVE

Nova stood guard before the two women relinquishing everything that made them fae. She gripped her borrowed bone sword, one eye on the battlefield and one on the dying creature who once had tentacles. He appeared more human now, but misshapen and twisted, still whimpering and clawing at the ground to get to his maker, leaving tracks in the sand with his useless legs. But Maebh and Alexandra were locked together, on their knees, oblivious to his pleas as they committed to their promise. White strands in the queen's hair multiplied with each passing second.

A screech overhead drew Nova's gaze. She feared the dragon had returned, but nothing blocked her view of the sky. Whatever it was had left already, but her pulse wouldn't return to normal. Far beyond the battle, lightning flashed in a distant storm. God, she hoped it didn't come here. A battle was frightful enough during the night, but to add rain and storm clouds now, she wasn't sure her courage would last.

Leaf's confidence and position filtered through their bond. She knew exactly where he was and how he was doing. A small smile tilted her lips when she realized he was probably thinking the same thing. He'd be here in an instant if she freaked out too much.

Another screech. Her gaze darted to and fro, looking wherever the loudest sound came from. Most of the fighting was now closer to the center of the field. A cry. A scream. A gurgle. A snarl. She lifted her sword each time something breached the cluster closest to her on the battlefield. But a soldier always pulled the danger back into the fray. The more the Well rebalanced, the faster the tide of the battle turned. Unseelie soldiers loyal to Maebh continued to fight nearby but no longer fought against the Seelie. The fae pooled resources to eradicate the horde, regardless of which side of the war they were on.

After a time, the manabeeze slowed in their glittering ascent. Nova's sword dropped to her side, and she grinned, realizing what that meant.

"You did it!" Nova exclaimed to the women. But when she turned, neither responded. They drooped against each other, hunching. Heart pounding, Nova ran to them. "Hey! Hey, you did it. Look."

She fell to her knees and placed a palm on each woman's back, fearing the worst. But their ribcages expanded. They breathed. They wheezed. Maebh's hair was completely white, now matching the Prime's. Age spots covered their hands. Skin sagged. Lips sank into gummy mouths. It was almost as if two thousand years had caught up with them. Slowly, Maebh lifted her heavy-lidded gaze to Nova. She tried to speak, but nothing came out.

"You did it." Nova smiled, hoping it kept the alarm from her eyes.

Maebh whispered something. It sounded like a hiss. Panic gripped Nova's throat when she couldn't make out the words. They seemed important, urgent.

"I can't understand you," she said, holding back tears.

More ineligible whispers. Aleksandra squeezed Nova's hand and rasped, "Tell our daughter. What we did."

"Of course," she replied. "As soon as I see her, I will."

She nodded, tired. "Tell Crimson." She shook her head. "Leaf..."

Her whisper turned into an exhale and nothing else. Silence for so long, Nova thought it had been her last breath.

"Hey." Nova shook them awake. Please don't die. "Wake up."

Footsteps thudded behind her. Voices. She whipped around, scrambling for the fallen sword, but it was just two female fae—the ones from the temple. Colt and Dawn. A third was behind them. He had a long white beard and hair like a wizard. Nova had met him at the academy. He was another Councillor—Preceptor Barrow. Dawn cried out in dismay at seeing their Prime on her knees, so emaciated and withered.

Nova wiped her eyes and said, "They unmade themselves. I think they're human now."

Human, but ancient. It was impossible to be this old, yet they were still breathing.

Colt's pixie wings fluttered as she kneeled beside the women and placed her fingers on their necks. "They're alive. Barely."

Dawn's cloven feet arrived next to where Nova crouched. A

touch on her shoulder drew her attention to the Seer's white eyes. Her tone was calm and all-knowing as she said, "You're going to let us take them."

"I am?"

"You are."

Behind Dawn, Colt and Barrow helped the women stand on shaky feet. Nova didn't quite understand why they were worried until she saw Colt continuously checking over her shoulder to see if anyone would stop them.

"They'll kill the queen," Nova murmured. "For her crimes."

"They'll try," Dawn agreed. "But you won't let them."

"No," she answered, her confidence steeling her spine. "I won't."

While Nova believed in justice, she also believed these women had suffered enough. They wouldn't live for very long—maybe days or hours.

Nile's cruelty was like a stone dropped into a calm pond. The ripples he caused touched everything, but those closest to him drowned in the waves. Whatever time these women had left, they deserved to spend it together.

"Go," Nova said. "I can feel Leaf coming. He must have sensed my panic when you arrived. He'll bring others. And the Unseelie will try to stop you from taking their queen."

Already, Nova noticed those who'd been fighting nearby face them, frowning.

Barrow pulled a stone from his robe's pocket to open a portal behind the litter and dead orcs. After they all crossed to the other side, Aleksandra looked back at Nova and found the strength to finish her earlier message.

"Tell him not to let it slip through his fingers."

The portal closed, and Nova was left alone on the wrong side of the field. The whimpering, twisted human moaned. A screech rent the air as the manticore swooped down. It landed with a thud, folded its wings as it slowed to a trot, and sniffed the air where the portal had closed. Nova's eyes widened as it turned its freakishly humanlike head toward her.

Battle sounds behind her stopped. The sounds of Unseelie soldiers breathing grew louder, drowning out blood rushing in Nova's ears.

"Where's our queen?" a raspy voice said behind her.

She opened her mouth but didn't know what to tell them. The monster lifted his scorpion tail, venom dripped from the point, and he roared. When Nova thought she was dead, a brutish hand landed on her shoulder and shoved her aside. One of the big Unseelie soldiers took the scorpion tail on his arm. Nova fell to the ground, skidding back onto her hands. Glancing up, shocked, she saw it wasn't a soldier—just a giant shadow. An instant later, a portal opened where the manticore stood, slicing it in two.

Through the portal, Leaf stood next to Haze. His blue eyes landed on Nova and searched her for obvious injuries. Haze's shadow helped Nova stand, bringing her into Leaf's arms as he crossed to her side.

"Found you," he murmured against her hair, clutching her hard.

"I knew you would."

They embraced for a long minute, simply enjoying being in each other's arms. The sounds of voices increased as more people crossed through the portal. Still hugging Nova, Leaf barked orders and said other things she stopped listening to. All that mattered was the soldiers left them alone. All she cared about at that moment was the sound of his heart beating against her ear, the deep rumble of his voice muffled through his chest. Eventually, he pulled her away and asked, "What happened to them?"

"I let them go," she said, wincing. "They were human again and so old, *Hoja*. Like really old. Dawn, Colt, and Barrow took them. I know you'll all be angry with me because the queen had crimes to pay for and..." She inhaled. "I just couldn't. They've suffered enough."

"Okay." His thumb brushed her cheek.

"Okay?"

"Yes." His eyes crinkled briefly, then turned serious again as Laurel arrived with Thorne and Clarke through the open portal.

In her battle leathers, Laurel was a fierce example of female empowerment. Just as dirty and blood-stained as the males, she was who Nova wanted to be when she grew up. As Clarke and Thorne locked on Leaf and strode over, Laurel's sharp gaze landed on the writhing, demented man on the ground. Some bones appeared outside his body, but he jerked and moved alive. Nova had been too frightened to approach him, but Laurel split from the group and strode over.

"Leaf," Clarke said, a strain in her voice. "We found Willow. She's at the lake. Can you portal us there?"

He gave a curt nod. "Where's Rush?"

"He ran off the instant Clarke had the vision," Thorne answered. "Just in case we couldn't find you." His gaze became distracted, darting to where his mate crouched. "Laurel, what are you—what the fuck is that?"

He pulled his great battle ax from his holster and swung it in a big loop, preparing to chop, but Laurel put up her palm, stopping him. She curiously inspected the broken man's pained face, then faced Nova and asked, "Who is this?"

"That was the tentacle monster," Nova replied. "When the queen unmade herself, he became this."

"Bones." Laurel jumped to her feet and stepped back.

A snarl burst from Thorne's lips. He was at his mate's side instantly, glaring down at the man begging for mercy. Now that his queen was no longer there, he crawled toward Laurel.

"He's in pain," Laurel said.

"Good," Thorne replied darkly. "Leave him like that."

"No." Laurel straightened her spine and looked down her nose at him. "We're putting an end to that cycle of punishment. Mercy is the only way we'll all heal."

Flames erupted along her hand, licking around her fingers and crackling with eagerness. She glanced at her mate, briefly seeking his opinion with her eyes. He gently touched her lower back and said, "If it's what you want."

She nodded, then directed Thorne to move Bones onto the wooden litter where the other orcs rested. Once done, she set the agonized creature on fire. The pyre burned so hot they had to step back and shield their eyes. Within seconds, there was nothing left except a pile of smoldering ash.

"Leaf," Clarke urged, her eyes full of panic. "I need to see her."

"Of course. Let's go." He took Nova's hand, closed the old portal, then started another.

When it opened, they saw directly through to bright sandy shores, a lake glistening under the sun, and burning debris floating on the water.

CHAPTER
FIFTY-SIX

By sunset that evening, the armies had mostly dispersed from the Order grounds. The original members of the Cadre of Twelve, plus Caraway and his mate, gathered on the lawn before their house. Leaf had called the meeting after he'd returned from the lake with Willow and her family.

She was injured, traumatized, and sadly missing her mana after what happened on the battlefield. She wouldn't go into details, and Leaf hadn't pressed. All he knew right now was what he'd seen on the battlefield, and that Rory and Cloud had fought. Then somehow, the two women had been tossed overboard. Cloud had caught them, but unable to carry the weight of both, Rory chose for him. She sacrificed herself for Willow.

This would complicate things with the Unseelie. It didn't sit well in Leaf's gut that Maebh was still alive out there, even as old as Nova said she was. In his opinion, nothing ended until the last manabee exited one's body.

The rest of Willow's account was a little murky. She said blood had rained from the sky after Rory died and that River, who'd found her by the lake, had flown to the airship to investigate. He was on board when an explosion destroyed the vessel, releasing Nero's harvested manabeeze into the wild.

Leaf found River floating in the lake, burned, battered, and barely alive. Ada healed what he couldn't, but it would take time for the crows feathers and hair to grow back.

Cloud was the only one from the original Twelve missing tonight.

Leaf looked at each in turn and said, "The Well is whole, but Elphyne is not."

"Neither is the Order," Shade grumbled. "It's a mess."

"I don't disagree," he replied.

"River, what happened at the lake?" Trix's voice rose above the rest. She translated for Aeron, who signed his question. When the crow shifter ignored her, the elf king's impatience grew. He signed something to Jasper, who nodded grimly but didn't comment.

Leaf filled them in with what he'd learned, but Aeron wasn't satisfied River was telling the whole truth. More questions fired between the group: Where were Maebh and the Prime? Where are the Six now? Who's responsible for the airship explosion? Where is Cloud? Do we think the Unseelie will blame the Order for what happened to Maebh? Did Nero retreat? Did he get what he came for? What did he come for?

Some had answers others sought, at least parts of them, but not all were willing to depart with them.

"I'm sick of all this bullshit." Clarke pulled her long hair at the roots, her eyes wild as she paced the grass. "Fae keep saying they can't lie, but each of you keeps secrets that are just as harmful. How can we stop Nero from finishing the job he started if we can't trust each other?"

"Princess," Rush murmured, trying to placate her. His gaze landed on River. "Sometimes the truth can be painful."

Clarke stopped pacing. Her hands balled into fists, and she slowly turned with cold determination in her eyes. Alarm prickled through Leaf when he sensed a rise in energy.

"Clarke," Leaf warned. "Whatever you're thinking of doing, don't."

Blue eyes clashed with his. "It's the only way we can be sure we're all on the same page."

The atmosphere crackled, and Clarke's eyes turned white. Power rippled through the air, his lungs, and heart. A single invisible force seized each person in the circle. The urge to spill every last one of his secrets was on the tip of Leaf's tongue.

When did Clarke get so strong?

"Tell me the truth." She pushed compulsion into her voice. "If anyone holds secrets that can harm the other, spea—"

Her words cut off as Rush whispered something into her ear. Her face crumpled, and she nodded, then collapsed into his arms, sobbing uncontrollably. Suddenly released from her metaphysical attack, many in the circle armed themselves with power, preparing to defend or retaliate for Clarke's attempt to violate their will. Part of Leaf wanted to be angry at what she'd just tried, but the other part sympathized with her pain. And also knew how hard that was to let go.

This meeting would escalate poorly if someone didn't take control, but everyone was out for themselves. With no Prime to reign them in, no one wanted to assume responsibility, including Leaf.

"They lied to us," Clarke suddenly said, extricating herself from Rush's arms and gesturing at the Six's house. "They used our love for our daughter, our fear of Rush losing another child, and they kept her from us. For a decade!"

"They saved her life," Rush said reluctantly. "You saw what happened between Willow and Maebh. They hadn't lied about that part."

"Willow has no mana! She's Lesser because of them."

"I do not condone what they did, Clarke." His stern response was loud. "But I can't hate them for it. Better for her to have no magic than to be dead."

"I know. It still sucks." She wiped tears and looked at the Twelve's house where their daughter slept. "I'm not sure if Willow will agree."

"What happened between Willow and Maebh?" Ada asked gently. "If you don't mind sharing?"

Rush scrubbed his hand through his beard. "Willow was conceived while I was cursed."

Clarke squeezed his hand, adding, "It made her very special. I don't have the full story yet, but she wasn't psychic like we thought. I think the Six were feeding her stories from Varen about the future. I think they had good intentions—they wanted her alive and safe until she was old enough to face a battle with the queen."

Leaf's eyes narrowed as he remembered. "They said Maebh killed their Seventh. For that, they wanted her dead. The moment she released the souls inside their bodies, Legion tried to kill her. But Aleksandra got in the way." As he recalled the rest, he winced, but Clarke and Rush deserved to know. "They made it sound like they'd been waiting for your daughter's birth for eons. They called her their skin."

"And then they abandoned her after she lost her mana?" Clarke gaped.

Rush's anger was palpable. "If I ever see them again, I'll find a way to kill them."

"Just tell me when and where," Violet declared, despite the disconcerted look on Indigo's face.

"So, what was Willow's gift?" Laurel went to her friend. "I thought she raised the undead for Nero."

"I don't think she meant to," Clarke whispered, eyes haunted. "I think she intended to use this opportunity to find us. But it all went wrong when she arrived. Maybe her gift was necromancy, like Maebh's."

Leaf shook his head. "Maebh bargained for that ability. I don't think she was meant to have it, and it changed her."

Rush's brows joined in the middle. "Why would the Well give Maebh such an ability if it would lead to its undoing?"

"The Well isn't just made up of the light side. It's dark, too. Each half has its own agenda," Leaf replied. "But that's assuming it was the Well Maebh bargained with. Legion also said he bargained with the Well... perhaps that's how they became Guardians."

"What do you mean?"

"There's a lot about this world we still don't know. Before us, other fae existed and other magics. Maebh was fascinated with old-world folklore." Leaf swallowed, remembering some of Crimson's journal entries. She had suggested new names for this world based on the old tales. The ice queen had played with fire, something she didn't understand.

"Whatever Willow's gift was, it's gone now." Clarke took a deep breath and said, "I shouldn't have tried to force the truth out of everyone. In fact, I owe you all a debt of gratitude and another heartfelt apology. You're my family, too. I love you all. Please know that if anyone needs help, I'm here. No judgment. I want you to trust me enough to reveal secrets or fears you might have. If I hadn't been so... scared of the Six, maybe they would have told me what Willow would grow to mean to them."

A ripple of something unknown was felt in the air. It brushed over everyone's faces, and Leaf didn't think it was due to a debt owed. This was something else. Nova stepped toward Clarke with compassion in her eyes. "I agree with you about the secrets. Honesty is the only way forward if you want to build a better place."

"I ate the pie you left cooling on the windowsill." River gingerly raised his hand. "It was me."

Laughter burst from every mouth, sufficiently breaking the tension. But River didn't fool Leaf with his humor. Pain lurked behind his lashless eyes. Jokers often used humor to hide the saddest parts of themselves. Whatever happened on that airship involved Cloud and betrayal. Leaf sensed it in his bones.

The body felt pain for a reason—to sound the alarm when something was wrong. The Prime and Maebh had lost their daughter after the Fallout. They refused to deal with that loss, and in the end, both suffered because of it. No one knew where Cloud was now, but his mental health would be on Ash and River's minds.

"What now?" Shade asked, his expression grim.

Leaf folded his arms and wondered about the future of the Order, Elphyne, and the people in it.

"Nero's not done," he replied. "But before we can determine what's next, we need a new Prime. We need to find out what happened to the Six, and I guess even our stance on the Unseelie territory. With Maebh gone, who is to rule? Will the Order get involved or remain impartial as usual?" He gestured to Jasper and Aeron. "I don't want you to deal with that alone."

"I don't have an answer for you," Jasper replied. "But we're not alone. Even if the Order returns to that impartial place, I know each of you will come to our assistance if we need it. We've already proven we have each other's backs."

"So who's the Prime?" Shade asked. "I don't want the job."

Every set of eyes turned to Leaf. His pulse quickened, and his skin prickled with heat. The world seemed to close in on him. He shook his head. "No. No more."

"But you're Jackson Crimson," Indigo pointed out. "There's no one more suited to running the organization you started."

"No." Leaf was done. Too much of his life revolved around this. He turned to Nova for help, a plea in his voice. "I've given enough."

"I know," she whispered. "But I also know there is much work to do."

"How does one become the Prime?" Laurel asked, cocking her hip.

Thorne gaped, his eyes wide. "You want the position?"

"God, no." She shook her head vehemently. "No way."

"Not saying I want the job either, but back to what Laurel asked?" Haze rumbled, frowning at Leaf.

Shrugging, Leaf replied, "Perhaps it's the same as when the Well passes a tithe from one ruler to another. Isn't that what happened to Jasper when he killed Mithras and took the glass crown?"

"The Prime unmade herself, though," Shade returned. "There was no clear handover of power."

"Maybe someone needs to volunteer for the role," Leaf added.

They all looked around at each other, each as wary as the first.

"I don't think anyone here can claim they had the Well's best interest at heart these past few years." Forrest looked at Leaf. "Especially not you."

"There is one person," Leaf said, surprising himself. "One who stepped up, even when her gift was muted."

He looked at Clarke.

CHAPTER
FIFTY-SEVEN

Leaf shifted his gaze to Clarke, the only one who'd been selflessly directing each Guardian to find their Well-blessed mate. Even when she'd lost her gift, she still tried to keep Leaf on that track. And what he found most impressive was how much she continued to grow as a person.

Her lips parted. She glanced over her shoulder, thinking it was someone else. When she realized no one was behind her, she pointed to her chest and raised her brows. "Me?"

Shade scoffed. "She sent Forrest to Crystal City for selfish reasons."

"True, but she also knew he'd find his mate there," Leaf returned. "And when she found out her daughter's life was at risk if she continued, she stopped and apologized. She understood exactly what the Prime's manipulation did to you all. She turned her efforts to finding everyone's mates and defeating Nero. Even when the taint threatened to ruin everything, she educated us about the problem." His thoughts turned inward as he recalled the Prime's letter. "It's time for a new generation to take over. One that's seen what neglecting the Well can do. I think Clarke is the chosen one... always has been."

"Don't I get a say in this?" Clarke asked, glancing at Rush. "Doesn't he?"

Rush looked at his mate with apprehension, then glanced toward the Prime's house and said, "We're not living in her house. That's all I care about."

"But—"

"Clarke." Leaf drew her attention back to him. "Have you felt an increase in your power recently, specifically after Aleksandra unmade herself?"

She laughed nervously, eyes darting around. "Yeah, but that was because the taint cleared from the Well. We all felt a boost, right?"

Multiple sets of eyes widened in disbelief. One by one, each Guardian or their mate shook their head. The truth settled on the redhead like a blanket. Her shoulders sank.

"I can't be the new Prime. I'm a thief! I cheat. I steal, and I... literally just tried to manipulate you all moments ago. I mean, I didn't. And I said sorry, so I guess I owe you all..." Her voice trailed off as Rush's lips curved into a prideful smile at his mate. She whispered, "But I'm not qualified to lead."

"Seems like the Well has already chosen," Ash said, cocking his head and listening to the wind. Satisfied with what he heard, his gaze hardened. "Now that's settled, we must decide what to do about Nero."

Nova raised her hand. "I think I can help with that."

"But..." Helplessness bloomed in Clarke's eyes.

"Babe." Laurel hugged her. "You'll be the best boss lady this place has seen. And we're all here helping you."

Murmurs of agreement rippled around the circle. Each person present nodded their approval of Clarke taking over as the next Prime.

"Oh my God, I'm going to be sick." Clarke's face paled.

Rush yanked her into his arms and kissed the top of her head. "Now you'll be insufferable with your demands."

She punched him in the gut, but his grin widened. Clarke turned to Nova and said, "I didn't mean to interrupt. What were you going to say about helping?"

Nova cast a nervous glance around the group, then rubbed her hoop earrings. "It's a theory."

Leaf smoothed his hand over her shoulder. "A theory is better than anything we have right now."

She took a deep breath, then exhaled slowly through her mouth. He sent her courage through their bond until she smiled gratefully and started speaking.

"When we were young, my twin and I would play games against each other. He loved beating me at everything. And mostly, he did... but there was one puzzle that I always solved, no matter how hard he tried. We used to play together, then he would try to outsmart me. When he revealed his true self to me those days before the fallout, he admitted to overestimating me. It made me think of that puzzle—of how he'd claimed it was the best place to hide a map to treasure... or the codes to nuclear warheads."

"What puzzle?" Clarke asked.

"What does it look like?" Peaches added.

"It's called a cryptix." Nova held her hands apart, then gestured the shape of a small cylinder. "It's made from brass. It has little moving wheels on the barrel, and when aligned just right, they open the device like a lock on a safe. If you get it wrong and try to open it, a vial of ink breaks inside, destroying everything. I think Niles hid a map to where he stashed one last nuclear warhead. I know how his mind works. If he couldn't win the game, he threw a tantrum. That bomb will be his tantrum." Nova met Leaf's gaze, and a chill ran down his spine.

"He'll either come for you," Leaf said. "Or he'll come for his bomb."

"I don't think he'll bother with finding me." She shrugged. "I think he'll find that first, make sure it's where he left it two thousand years ago, then maybe if he's feeling benevolent try one more play at taking over Elphyne. Either way, we have to find it first."

"Why hasn't he retrieved it yet?" Rush asked.

"We might know," River replied, looking at Ash.

The two shared a moment, both having the same daunting realization. Leaf had never seen the crow shifter look afraid, but Ash's expression shut down, and he stepped back. "I'm not going back there."

"Where?" Leaf prompted.

"To the Collector's," River replied solemnly. "When we were young, we witnessed Cloud trading a device he stole from the human leader. It matches your description."

Leaf's brows lifted. He had heard tales of the Collector—a female more crow than human. She had a reputation for shrewd deals and harsh punishments for intruders. The location of her lair was shrouded in mystery.

"What did he trade it for?" he asked.

“That’s not important,” Ash snapped.

Leaf felt the tension rise at the evasion. Clarke, particularly, struggled to hold back her anger at the secret. But perhaps this was a secret not meant for them. Unlike their missing friend, the two crows were here, helping. He said to them, “Someone should go to the Collector’s and find it.”

“I’ll do it,” River offered grimly. “I know where she lives.”

“Don’t,” Ash warned, a plea in his eyes.

“Someone needs to,” he said casually, as if it didn’t bother him. But the crow was still wounded. Until his feathers grew back, he wouldn’t be able to fly himself there. Shifting regularly helped with the growth, but Leaf still wasn’t sure it should be River.

“You don’t have to go alone,” Clarke said. “I’m sure one of the other Guardians can go with you.”

“Is that an order?” Shade raised his brows.

Everyone grew silent. Leaf glared at Shade, wondering if he’d used that mocking tone on purpose, but when Rush failed to growl at his disrespect, Leaf caught the twitch in the vampire’s lips.

Huh.

There was a time Shade would have done anything to become the next Prime, but Leaf supposed his priorities shifted after mating with Silver. Just as Leaf’s had.

“Har har.” Clarke pointed at his face. “You can get down and give me twenty for being disrespectful.”

“Twenty of what?” Shade’s brow furrowed.

The old-world women laughed, which infuriated Shade until Silver pointed out it was just a stupid saying from their time—something about doing push-ups in the military.

"That's dumb," Shade said to Indigo, who tried to hide his smirk.

Shade's scowl deepened, and he took Silver's hand. Ribbons of shadow enveloped them both and then they were gone.

As if that was a cue to disperse, Clarke clapped her hands and said, "I guess that's it for now, guys. We can finish worrying about tomorrow, tomorrow. Right now, we need to go and check on our daughter."

She glanced at her mate and whispered, "That was leaderly, right?"

He dropped a kiss on her nose. "Perfect, Princess."

Jasper nodded to them. "We'll talk."

Aeron hand signed, and Trix translated. "He thinks we should create a new Council, but to include leaders from all over Elphyne."

"I like it." Clarke pointed at him. "I don't want to lose what we all have. Let's talk more about it later."

Leaf opened a portal for anyone who needed it, and secretly loved that he could without using up too much of his mana. But at the same time, he realized this gift of power—both his and Nova's—meant he couldn't turn his back on the Well or Elphyne. After everyone was gone, he put his arm around Nova's shoulders and walked with her behind Clarke and Rush as they returned to the house.

"Are you sure, Clarke?" he forced the question out. It wasn't as though he thought she could reverse her decision easily, but he didn't want her to feel cornered.

She plucked at the end of a lock of red hair. "It's already happened, right?"

He nodded. "But Aleksandra relinquished the right. I'm sure you can, too."

"Why, have you decided you want the job after all?"

Panic squeezed his insides. Nova's hand slid around Leaf's waist, but the only emotion he sensed from her was support. She'd never liked how much of his life Crimson had given to duty, but she was willing to stand by him if he had to step in as Prime. He loved her even more for it. Perhaps that gave him the courage to reply to Clarke, "Not in a million years."

Rush grunted in a way Leaf supposed was humor. Clarke smirked at her mate, but then stopped and took Leaf's hands in hers.

"I know we've not always seen eye to eye," she said, holding his gaze steady. "But I agree. You've given too much already. You deserve a little happiness with your mate."

"You deserve to be happy, too," he replied softly. "You both do."

"We'll have it," she assured him. "Don't worry."

Leaf's brow arched. "You've seen it?"

"No. But I feel it. And as Prime, I can continue the work I've already started. Everyone supports me, so that's good enough for me. Once the final three of the Twelve find their Well-blessed mates, something tells me we'll have our solution to defeating your twin, Nova."

"I hope so," she replied. Her somber expression brightened. "We should have a dinner to celebrate. Don't you think? Your daughter is home. You're going to make a magnificent leader. We survived! Wait. Too soon?"

She cast her gaze around warily.

Clarke let go of Leaf's hands. Probably because of the way Rush glared at the joining but also because she seemed at peace with her decision. Perhaps the Well already knew this when it afforded her Aleksandra's tithe of power. Perhaps it also knew something they didn't, and Clarke needed that boost for a reason.

Clarke smiled at Nova. Genuine warmth bounced between the two women. "I think a dinner is a perfect idea. Laurel said something about cocktails just now, but to be honest, adding food to the mix is better for everyone. The sooner we give Willow a positive, routine environment, the better."

As they passed the Six's empty house, Clarke stopped again. She tugged Rush to her side and pondered the darkness. "Something about what they did doesn't add up."

"What do you mean?" Rush's deep rumble contained a hint of threat as he faced the decrepit house.

"It's just, they went to such pains to keep Willow alive long enough for them to claim her as their queen."

Rush growled, disapproval rumbling off his tongue.

"Pipe down," Clarke sighed at him. "They're gone now. You can feel it. Even that house seems like... well, just a house now. And... I don't know. What if we move in there instead of the Prime's old house? Maybe Haze and Peaches can take Aleksandra's, then the Twelve will have their child-free house back."

"You want to move in there?" Rush's brows lifted.

"With a new paint job, it won't be so bad. Besides," she said. "If I'm in that house, I think I'll be able to connect with their vibes, you know? I want to know why they left a young woman they insisted was their true queen—one they said was so rare. Think of it this way, would you have left me if I lost my connection to the Well?"

"Fuck no."

"See?" Her pondering gaze returned to the dark house. "I don't think they meant to leave Willow after she lost her mana. There's more to the story. We owe it to Willow to find out what it is."

Leaf clapped the dismayed shifter on the back. "Good luck, Prime's mate."

"Fuck off," he grumbled.

Leaf laughed heartily and tugged his mate home. His laughter became a roar after he heard Clarke behind them say to Rush, "I like this new Leaf. He's funny."

The mood was somber when Leaf and Nova walked into the house. A few Guardians had gathered in the lounge room for some elixir or ale. Laurel had a cup shaped like an inverted triangle on a stick. He'd come to learn this was her cocktail glass. Leaf tried to sneak past with Nova, but Laurel noticed and invited them in. He winced and kept walking Nova toward the staircase.

"Hey," she snapped at him. "*Hoja de Los Guardianes.* Maybe I want to join them."

"Not unless you want me to fuck you in front of everyone," he whispered hoarsely in her ear. At her responding hitched breath, arousal squeezed his cock. "I need to feel you, Estrella."

He needed her smell, her arms around him, and to be buried balls deep inside her. He wanted all of it, and she came first. This battle had been harder on her than she wanted to admit. He wanted to give her time alone to recoup. Nothing was as important to him than her wellbeing. Not some stupid drinks with umbrellas in them, and not even spending time with this family.

"We can come back later," he promised quietly. "After I make you come at least once."

She all but purred as she slid her hands around his neck. "Will you do that thing with the water?"

"I can hear you!" Thorne's voice boomed from the living room.

"Yeah, lovebirds. Get a room!" Indigo chuckled.

Nova giggled and ran up the stairs. Leaf chased her, caught her, and trapped her in his room. His clothes were off in seconds. Hers were next. Then he claimed her with hard, vicious thrusts until he lost sight of his original goal to make her feel good first. She had a way of consuming his logic with all that shining beauty. After he finished, he apologized for his frenzy by doing all the things she wanted—with water, with heat, with his tongue, and then again with his cock. Afterward, while they lay panting and recovering in bed, contentment spilled through every limb in his body.

"What's that for," she mumbled sleepily, sensing his mood.

"I'm happy." He trailed his thumb absentmindedly over her shoulder. "I'm home. The taint is clean. I'm not the Prime. We have work to do, but"—he rolled on top of her and kissed each of her eyelids—"I think it's safe to say we have our happy ending."

She smiled at first, but then concern darkened her eyes and skated through her bond. He recognized her unique chaser of guilt that followed. She often felt the same duo of emotions when thinking of her brother. He might try to use her as a replacement for his daughter's mana supply.

Over Leaf's dead body, and so long as he remained connected to the Well, that wouldn't happen for a very long time.

Nova sensed his protective surge and squeezed his naked rear end with a saucy gleam in her eyes. She trusted him to keep her safe, and she loved him for it.

It struck Leaf that this part of her right here—her unbreakable spirit—was what frightened her twin the most. Nero had to plan and play games. He spent years practicing and plotting. Yet all Nova did was be herself, and she shone bright enough to change the world. He lowered his lips to claim hers, but she stopped him with three murmured words. "You're wrong, *Papi*."

"Oh really?" He arched back and cocked an eyebrow. "About what?"

"This isn't our happy ending." She grinned. "We're only just beginning."

EPILOGUE

Nero had held it together when that fucking carrion crow started attacking. He'd kept it together when half their harvest was ruined. He held it the fuck together all the way back to Crystal City, up the elevator, and into his conservatory.

Roaring with fury, Nero swiped pins from the map on his conservatory desk. Everything went flying, tearing, and crumpling as it fell to the ground.

"Mr. President?"

"Shut the fuck up!" he bellowed, eyes wide and puffing like a bull. The soldier behind him startled, clenched his jaw, but held his ground. With young Alfred's demise, a slot was open for the captain. Everyone wanted to be the president's next shit sniffer. It made him sick.

He'd been blissfully lost in his egotistical head before recognizing Nova, Jace, and Aurora's mothers. How long had she been here, infecting those Tainted fucks with her sickening optimism?

He glanced at the fallen pins and map, then cocked his head. A nearby lantern cast an unusual shadow on the map, reminding him of a chess piece—a bishop.

There was a move in chess called the Bishop's Opening. It was used to surprise and overwhelm the opponent. Nova's appearance was a surprise. It had thrown him off, but it wasn't sophisticated and planned. It was an accident. Nero could do better than an accident.

Thirty minutes later, he stood in the freezing bunker below the Sky Tower. This room was the reason this building had been constructed here. The six grave-like holes had been dug two thousand years ago and then filled with water. The three that housed himself, Aurora, and Bones were empty. But three more were still filled with water and frozen over, waiting for the right time to be melted.

Bones wreaked unmentionable havoc in Elphyne before the fae took him. That was one man. Imagine what three could do.

Feeling his spark return, Nero dropped to his knees at the first pod. He ignored the ice cutting his hands and scraped the worst from the surface, intending to check which of his crew was housed below.

Empty.

His pulse caught in his throat.

Impossible.

He rubbed the surface a little more, using his sleeve to polish the ice to a slick gleam. Bones's face had been an inch beneath the surface. But as far as he could see, there was nothing here but water.

Come to think of it, the surface was slightly lower than it should be. Almost as if a body had been pulled out... or sank further beneath the earth. How? No one knew about this room anymore. Nero had killed every member of his doomsday cult that kept it safe. Rushing to the next pod, he hastily scraped ice. Again, no face rested just below the surface. It was also lower in volume. As the bile rose in his gullet, he forced himself to check the third and almost wept with relief when the face belonging to his most favored mercenary was revealed.

He had no idea how the other two had disappeared. But these pods were just holes in the ground. The method wasn't foolproof. The old psychic had warned him that her prediction of their safe arrival only stretched so far. Whatever the case, all wasn't lost. Nero had one piece left on the board. It might not be his bishop, as he'd first hoped, but maybe it was better.

Dusting his icy hands on his trousers, he collected the pickax hanging on the hook behind the door. Then he slammed it down on the ice... right beside his queen's face.

THANK you for reading Leaf and Nova's book. It's not over for the Fae Guardians by a long shot. But before we get River's book, we'll finally learn about our morally gray Guardians – The Six.

Order *Castle of Nevers and Nightmares,* the first book in the Fae Devils Series.

Can't wait until then? Start reading short stories, serials, and NSFW art as they are released in Patreon. Become a VIP Guardian Angel at www.patreon.com/lanacreates.

ACKNOWLEDGMENTS

Wow. What a bumper book this turned out to be. It's officially the longest I've written. Lots of personal setbacks this year, but I don't think I'm alone. I hope this book gives you all a lovely slice of fantasy romance to escape to if you're having difficulties.

Thank you to Angelica Luevano, who, not only is an ARC Angel, but she helped me come up with some authentic Spanish words Nova speaks to Papi, I mean Leaf.

Thank you to Erika Robles, who helped with beta reading. She's also my awesome Portuguese translator for this series.

Thank you, Kelly Messenger, for putting up with me shifting the line for the proofing edits and fitting it in before your big trip overseas. I'm eternally grateful.

To the ARC Angels who are still with me, even though I fell off the face of a cliff this year. Lol. THANK YOU.

And all the Patreon Angels, who give me ongoing enthusiasm, ideas, and encouragement. You're all gems.

Until next time,

Lana

xx

TALK TO OTHER READERS

Join Lana's Angels Facebook Group for fun chats, giveaways, and exclusive content. https://www.facebook.com/groups/lanasangels

ALSO BY LANA PECHERCZYK

THE FAE GUARDIANS WORLD

Fae Guardians - Elphyne

(Fantasy/Paranormal Romance)

Season of the Wolf Trilogy

The Longing of Lone Wolves

The Solace of Sharp Claws

Of Kisses & Wishes Novella (free for subscribers)

The Dreams of Broken Kings

Season of the Vampire Trilogy

The Secrets in Shadow and Blood

A Labyrinth of Fangs and Thorns

A Symphony of Savage Hearts

Season of the Elf Trilogy

A Song of Sky and Sacrifice

A Crown of Cruel Lies

A War of Ruin and Reckoning

Fae Devils

(Fae Guardians Sluagh Spin-off)

Castle of Nevers and Nightmares

THE DEADLYVERSE

The Sinner Sisterhood

(Demon-hunting Paranormal Romance)

The Sinner and the Scholar

The Sinner and the Gunslinger

The Sinner and the Priest

The Deadly Seven

(Fated Mate Paranormal/Sci-Fi Romance)

The Deadly Seven Box Set Books 1-3

Sinner

Envy

Greed

Wrath

Sloth

Gluttony

Lust

Pride

Despair

ABOUT THE AUTHOR

OMG! How do you say my name?

Lana (straight forward enough - Lah-nah) **Pecherczyk** (this is where it gets tricky - Pe-her-chick).

I've been called Lana Price-Check, Lana Pera-Chickywack, Lana

Pressed-Chicken, Lana Pech...*that girl!* You name it, they said it. So if it's so hard to spell, why on earth would I use this name instead of an easy pen name?

To put it simply, it belonged to my mother. And she was my dream champion.

For most of my life, I've been good at one thing – art. The world around me saw my work, and said I should do more of it, so I did.

But, when at the age of eight, I said I wanted to write stories, and even though we were poor, my mother came home with a blank notebook and a pencil saying I should follow my dreams, no matter where they take me for they will make me happy. I wasn't very good at it, but it didn't matter because I had her support and I liked it.

She died when I was thirteen, and left her four daughters orphaned. Suddenly, I had lost my dream champion, I was split from my youngest two sisters and had no one to talk to about the challenge of life.

So, I wrote in secret. I poured my heart out daily to a diary and sometimes imagined that she would listen. At the end of the day, even if she couldn't hear, writing kept that dream alive.

Eventually, after having my own children (two firecrackers in the guise of little boys) and ignoring my inner voice for too long, I decided to lead by example. How could I teach my children to follow their dreams if I wasn't? I became my own dream champion and the rest is history, here I am.

When I'm not writing the next great action-packed romantic novel, or wrangling the rug rats, or rescuing GI Joe from the jaws of my Kelpie, I fight evil by moonlight, win love by daylight and never run from a real fight.

I live in Australia, but I'm up for a chat anytime online. Come and find me.

Subscribe & Follow

subscribe.lanapecherczyk.com

lp@lanapecherczyk.com

facebook.com/lanapecherczykauthor

instagram.com/lana_p_author

amazon.com/-/e/B00V2TP0HG

tiktok.com/@lanapauthor

goodreads.com/lana_p_author

patreon.com/lanacreates

Printed in the USA
CPSIA information can be obtained
at www.ICGtesting.com
LVHW040143101223
766037LV00038B/1777/J